COMING
ATTRACTIONS

COMING ATTRACTIONS

a wonderful novel

by
FANNIE FLAGG

WILLIAM MORROW AND COMPANY, INC.
New York   1981

Library of Congress Cataloging in Publication Data

Flagg, Fannie.
    Coming attractions.

    I. Title.
PS3556.L26C6   813'.54   80-29451
ISBN 0-688-00472-5

Printed in the United States of America

First Edition

1   2   3   4   5   6   7   8   9   10

For Marion, Bill and Patsy

WHAT YOU ARE ABOUT TO READ . . . REALLY
DID HAPPEN TO ME . . . OR MAYBE IT DIDN'T
. . . I'M NOT SURE . . . BUT IT DOESN'T MAT-
TER . . . BECAUSE IT'S TRUE . . .
                              —DAISY FAY HARPER

COMING
ATTRACTIONS

1952

April 1, 1952

Hello there . . . my name is Daisy Fay Harper and I was eleven years old yesterday. My Grandmother Pettibone won the jackpot at the VFW bingo game and bought me a typewriter for my birthday. She wants me to practice typing so when I grow up, I can be a secretary, but my cat, Felix, who is pregnant, threw up on it and ruined it, which is OK with me. I don't know what is the matter with Grandma. I have told her a hundred times I want to be a tree surgeon or a blacksmith.

I got a Red Ryder BB gun from Daddy and some Jantzen mix-and-match outfits Momma bought me at the Smart and Sassy Shop. Ugh! Grandma Harper sent me a pair of brown and white saddle shoes—Momma won't let me wear loafers, she says they will ruin my feet—and a blue cellophane windmill on a stick I am way too old for.

Momma took me downtown to see a movie called *His Kind of Woman* with Robert Mitchum and Jane Russell, billed as the hottest pair on the screen. I wanted to see *Pals of the Golden West* with Roy Rogers and Dale Evans, where Roy patrols the border for cattle-smuggling bandits. But Momma is mad at Daddy for giving me a BB gun so I didn't push it. I'm not doing much except sitting around waiting for the sixth grade. My friend Peggy Box who is thirteen won't play with me anymore. All she wants to do is listen to Johnnie Ray sing "The Little White Cloud That Cried."

I am an only child. Momma didn't even know she was going to have a baby. Daddy was in bed with the flu, and when the doctor came to see Daddy, Momma said all of a sudden a big lump came up on her right side. She said, "Doctor look at this!" He told Daddy to get out of bed and for Momma to get in it. He said that lump was a baby, maybe even twins. Boy, was Momma surprised. But it wasn't twins, it was only me. Momma was in labor for a long time and Daddy got mad about it and choked the doctor. When I was being born, I kicked Momma so hard that now she can't have any more children. I don't remember kicking her at all. It wasn't my fault I was so fat and if Daddy hadn't choked the doctor and made him nervous, I would have been born better. Whenever she tells anybody the story about having me, her labor gets longer and longer. Daddy says I would have to have been a three-year-old child with hair and teeth and everything, to hear Momma tell it.

I was born in Jackson, Mississippi, and as far as me being a girl it was just fine because my daddy wanted a little girl. He said he knew I'd be a girl and he wrote a poem about me that was published in the newspaper in the Letters to the Editor section before I ever got here.

> We are expecting a blessed event in just a week or two
> And if my wife's cravings are to be a clue
> Then our daughter is going to be a little pig . . . it's true
> Because all her mother craves night and day is barbecue

I'm glad Daddy wanted a girl. Most men want boys. Daddy never wanted any old stinky boy who might grow up to have a big neck and play football. He feels those kind of people are dangerous. Baseball is our game. Jim Piersall is our favorite player. He screams and hollers and causes trouble and has a true understanding of the game.

Daddy says that everybody in history has a twin and that he and Mr. Harry Truman could be equals in history. Daddy and Mr. Truman both wear glasses, have a daughter, and are Democrats. I think that's why when it looked as though Thomas Dewey would win the election, Daddy jumped in the Pearl River and tried to drown himself. It took four of his friends to pull him out, one a member of the Elks Club.

Momma said he just did it to show off, besides, he had had eighteen Pabst Blue Ribbon beers. Momma says he isn't anything like Harry Truman at all. Mr. Truman's little girl is named Margaret. I got stuck with Daisy Fay. . . . Most people call me little Fay because they call my Mother Big Fay, although I don't know why, she isn't all that big. Momma wanted to name me Mignon after her sister, but Daddy pitched a fit and said he didn't want his only daughter named after a steak. He was making such a commotion, and the woman with the birth certificate was tired of waiting, so Grandma Pettibone settled the whole thing by naming me Daisy, just because there happened to be a vase of daisies in the room. I sure would love to know who sent those rotten daisies anyway. Daddy and I hate that name because it sounds country and we are not country at all. Jackson is a big city and we live in an apartment. I prefer the name Dale or Olive, not after Olive Oyl but after the actress sister of Joan Fontaine, Olive de Havilland.

Momma and Daddy are fighting all the time now. An Army Air Force buddy of Daddy's named Jimmy Snow called and told him that if he could get $500 Daddy could buy a half interest in a malt shop in Shell Beach, Mississippi, and make a fortune. The malt shop is right on a beach that looks just like Florida.

Jimmy won a half interest in the malt shop in a poker game and needs $500 to get the other half. He's a crop duster, so Daddy could run the whole thing and he would be a silent partner. Daddy has been crazy trying to get the money. He made Momma mad because he wanted to sell her diamond rings. She said they were not worth $500 and how dare he try and take the rings off her fingers! Besides, she wasn't going anywhere with him, him drinking so much. So, he invented a practical joke he was sure he could sell for $500. A friend of his has a filling station with an outhouse where he tried out his invention. He put a speaker under the outhouse and connected it to a microphone in the filling station. He made the mistake of trying it out on Momma. He waited until she went in and had time to sit down, then he disguised his voice and said, "Could you move over, lady, we're working down here!" Momma, who's very modest and says Daddy has never seen her fully undressed, screamed and ran out the door and cried for five hours. She said it was the most disgusting thing that ever happened to her.

This joke on Momma caused her to leave him and go visit her sister in Virginia to think about a divorce, something she does all the time. I had to go with her. The child always goes with the mother. My aunt has so many children that it made Momma nervous at dinnertime, so we came home.

I hope Daddy gets the money soon. If we move to Shell Beach, I can have a pony and go swimming every day. Daddy is busy working on his new invention. He has an English red worm bed in the backyard and as soon as they grow, he is going to freeze them and sell them all over the country.

A lot of people think Daddy is peculiar, including the members of his immediate family, but not me. His name is William Harper, Jr. Momma says that he got this idea to get out of Jackson when he was in the Army and learned to like Yankees. He still hates hunters, though. Whenever he reads in the paper where one of them shoots another, he laughs and chalks one up for our side. He loves all animals, cats in particular. He swears all dictators hate cats because they can't dominate them. Hitler would foam at the mouth at the sight of one, and I guess my daddy knows because he fought him in the war.

He was drafted in the Army Air Corps when I was only two years old. He cost them a lot of money because he is so skinny they had to make him special uniforms and special goggles with his own prescription so he could see.

But as Daddy says, "When you're at war, they'll take anything." Daddy didn't get out of the United States, but he did break his toe when he hit the ground before his parachute opened in Louisiana. The plane had already landed in the swamp when he jumped, so he could have just stayed in the plane, but Daddy lost his glasses and didn't see it had landed. That's where he met Jimmy Snow. Jimmy was a pilot and was always yelling bail out over the headset as a joke.

After Daddy left Lousiana, he was stationed in California and got Margaret O'Brien to sign the back of one of my pictures. He said she has false teeth just like Grandma. He also said that Red Skelton was a wonderful guy and told the boys dirty jokes to cheer them up. All of my Hollywood true-life stories come as a result of Daddy having been there during the war. Clark Gable is the best-looking man Daddy has ever seen, even though his mustache is uneven. Also, did you know that Dorothy Lamour has such ugly feet that they gave her rubber feet to wear every time she played a native? Momma says that's a lie, but I've never seen a picture of her with her shoes off unless she is in a movie. I wish he had met Audie Murphy, but he didn't. Daddy tells me when I grow up I am going to look just like Celeste Holm.

Daddy believes that if Momma had moved to Hollywood, California, after the war just like he had wanted to, we would be rich and I would probably be a star by now. I would love to meet Bomba the Jungle Boy and Judy Canova. But Momma wouldn't leave Jackson for anything.

Daddy hated being a soldier and was busted six times. Whenever he got a furlough, he wouldn't go back until the MPs came for him. One time when I was in the bathroom, they were banging on the door hollering for Daddy. Momma wanted me to hurry up and finish so I could say good-bye, but all that knocking made me nervous and Momma believes that is the reason I have to have so many enemas now. Momma blames the Military Police for ruining what had been a very successful toilet training period.

While Daddy was in the war, Momma and I lived in a big white house with my Grandmother and Grandfather Pettibone. We lived on one side and they lived on the other. Grandpa was sure funny. He stayed up all night once and planted a Victory garden that had forty-seven whiskey bottles lined up in a row. He loved whiskey and could put his leg over his head and do cartwheels. Grandma met him when she was in college. She was in a receiving line and when Granddaddy stopped in front of her, she laughed in his face, so they got married and moved to Virginia. He was very rich, and Grandma brought all her sisters but one to Virginia and married them off to rich men. But then Grandpa got to drinking too much and his family disowned him, and they had to move back to Jackson. Boy, was Grandma furious having to leave her rich sisters.

Grandpa became a pest control exterminator and raised chickens on the side. He was crazy about poultry of any kind and he used to play checkers on the kitchen table with this old rooster he had. Grandma says they weren't really playing checkers, but I think they were.

I had a good time living with Grandma and Grandpa, all except for the ducks and chickens in the backyard that used to peck my toes. They thought my toes were corn. Stupid things. I wasn't too crazy about Grandma wringing those chickens' necks either . . . one time one of them without a head chased me all over the backyard. It scared me so bad that I ran right through the screen door and ruined it.

Grandpa liked me a lot. He was always sneaking over to Momma's side of the back porch and stealing me out of my baby bed and carrying me down to the Social Grill and sitting me up on the bar. Once he took me to see a friend of his that was in jail. It made Momma and Grandma mad. They said I was too young to be visiting jails.

When Daddy came home from the Army for good, he brought me a rabbit fur coat from Hollywood and some Chiclets chewing gum and twenty Hershey bars. By then he had been busted down to private again, but he had a Good Conduct Medal. Momma says he must have bought it.

We didn't live with Grandma and Granddaddy too long, though. They didn't like Daddy and thought he was a little worm. Anyway, that's what Grandma called him. When Grandpa would get drunk, he would put chickens in Daddy's room. He also sent Momma a telegram that said there was a big rat living on the other side of the house. Then one night he got his pest control equipment and shot rat poison through our door, so we had to move. Right after that Grandpa went off to the Social Grill to have a drink and never came back. Somebody said they saw him driving a cab in Tupelo, Mississippi, but we don't know where he is. He left his chickens and everything. I sure do miss him. I have to go now. Felix is having kittens in the back of the refrigerator and Momma is having a fit. . . .

April 2, 1952

Guess what? I saw the kittens being born . . . I'm never going to have children. No wonder Momma was mad at me for weighing nine pounds.

I've told you a lot about my daddy, but the thing that makes him really special is that he is a motion picture operator and so is his daddy. I come from a show business family; even my mother once was a movie cashier. She was working in the theater because it was the Depression and because her daddy didn't worry about her if he could see her sitting in her glass cage.

Daddy running the movies makes me special. Some people call it cocky, but Daddy admires that in a person and told me that I don't have to say "Yes, sir" and "Yes, ma'am." He doesn't want his daughter sounding like a servant. I never do say it either, unless I am trying to be real sincere . . . or Momma is around.

Right after the Army, Daddy worked at the Woodlawn Theater. I spent every Saturday and Sunday in the projection booth in the balcony where colored people used to sit before they got smart and opened up their own movie houses. After that, white people wouldn't sit up there, which suited me fine because I had the whole balcony to myself. The theater had red seats and big green lights that looked like lilies going up the sides of the wall. I could hang over the rail and drop things on people I didn't like.

Momma says sitting in that balcony, looking down on people, has given me a superiority complex. Maybe so, but Daddy didn't want me downstairs where some child molester might sit down by me and then Daddy would have to kill him. However, I have my own instructions as far as that nonsense is concerned; if anybody gets funny with me, I am supposed to stand up and scream out loud, "This is a molester. Arrest him." Daddy told me that if everybody did that, there would be very few molesters.

He also gave me other useful information to protect me in the real world. If anyone hits me, I'm not to hit them back.

I wait until their back is turned, then hit them in the head with a brick. I have a beautiful aristocratic nose and Daddy doesn't want it hurt. He himself has been saved from many a severe beating by bigger men by threatening to stab them in their sleep. The only bad time I ever had sitting in that balcony was while I was watching the movie *Mighty Joe Young* with Terry Moore. I was under the seat during the part of the picture where poor Mighty Joe Young was being hurt—I couldn't stand him being so unhappy. Some people see fit to stick their old gum under their seat. Daddy had to cut a lot of my hair off that night. I say that people should put their gum on the side of the pop-corn box or else in a candy wrapper. Momma says I shouldn't sit under any more seats.

The Woodlawn Theater showed a lot of cheap movies. As I have gotten older, I am surprised to find out that Patricia Medina is not the star I thought she was. However, I still say that Mr. Goodbars and Raisinets are your best buy. Zeros, Zagnuts and Butterfingers are good, but a Bit-O-Honey lasts longer. I got a JuJu stuck in my ear once, so I stay away from them. Momma blames my cavities on eating all that candy, but I can pop gum better than anybody.

The Woodlawn Theater ran weekly serials: Buster Crabbe, the Green Hornet and Jungle Jim. My favorite is Nyoka, the Jungle Girl, who I like even better than Jungle Jim. Who cares about Johnny Weissmuller without Boy and Jane? Some people have no business sense. Nyoka could swing through the jungle faster than Tarzan any day.

Daddy would show me next week's serial at night when the theater closed. I was always the first to know that Nyoka hadn't been killed. I swear I never told, not once.

Nyoka has a lot to do with how I look in person. Daddy spent a whole day making me a swing rope on a tree in the backyard, but unfortunately he made an error in dynamics, as he put it. I grabbed ahold of the rope and he ran me back as far as he could and let go and it swung me right into the tree and now my right front tooth is chipped. Daddy thinks it makes me look different. Momma thinks it is awful.

Momma has a theory that Daddy has tried to kill me on several occasions. Once when I fell asleep in the living room, Daddy cracked my head carrying me into the bedroom. He also knocked me off the pier into the Pearl River when I was three and didn't come after me for a long time because he felt that young children, like young animals, could swim if they were scared enough. But I wasn't scared enough. You should have seen the trash I saw on the bottom of that river when I was waiting for him to come and get me . . . tin cans, an old Roi • Tan cigar box and an old Firestone tire. The Pearl River attracts a lower class of people if you ask me.

Then there was the time when he picked up a two-by-four on the side of the road and put it in the front seat by me and stuck it out the window. He told me to hold it, which I did, but when the wind hit the board, it turned around and hit me in the head and knocked me out. Another time, when a friend of Daddy's bought a brand-new Buick, Daddy pressed the push-button window up on my neck. But that time I think it was just a matter of him not being familiar with the equipment.

The main thing Momma bases her theory on is once Daddy, who is very artistic, wanted to make a life mask of my face. He put plaster of paris on me but forgot the breathing holes. On top of that he also forgot to put Vaseline on my face. He had to crack the plaster off with a hammer. Momma didn't speak to him for a week on that one. I myself was sorry that it didn't turn out.

She also says he is going to ruin my nervous system because of the time he sneaked up on me when I was listening to *Inner Sanctum* on the radio. Just as the squeaking door opened, he grabbed me and yelled, "Got ya," real loud, which caused me to faint. She also didn't like him telling me Santa Claus had been killed in a bus accident and making me throw up.

The Pettibones have very delicate nervous systems. That's true. Momma is nervous all the time. She's worn a hole in the floor on the passenger's side of Daddy's car from putting on the brakes. Momma always looks like she is on the verge of a hissy fit, but that's mainly because when she was eighteen, she stuck her head in a gas oven looking at some biscuits and blew her eyebrows off. So she paints them on like little half-moons. People love to talk to her because she always looks interested, even if she isn't.

If Daddy is dangerous to my health, Momma's not much better. She nearly got us both killed in the street last winter. Momma had read the movie ad saying, "Every woman will want to see Joan Crawford as the woman who loves Johnny Guitar," and I guess she did. I wanted to see *Francis, the Talking Mule*, so I wasn't in a good mood anyway. When Momma takes me downtown, it is an all-day ordeal. She was crazy about mother-and-daughter dresses at the time and she made me wear some ratty dress I hated. Whenever we go downtown, she starts her window shopping. Look, look, look! It drives me crazy.

We always go to Morrison's Cafeteria to eat. That's OK because I can get three Jell-Os instead of vegetables. After the meal, Momma sits and smokes and drinks coffee. I have to watch her like a hawk. My job is getting up and pouring her more coffee. That goes on for hours. Then I have to pull her chair out and help her on with her coat. She is big on children having manners. This night I sat through eight cups of coffee and Joan Crawford, so to make me feel better she said I could pull the cord on the streetcar on the way home.

It wasn't my fault that there was a country woman on the streetcar that was crazy and talking into a paper sack. I was busy looking at her and missed our stop. Momma was mad because it was so cold and we had to walk two blocks back. She had on a big silver fox fur coat and she had her alligator purse, with the alligator head on it.

It was so dark we had to walk in the middle of the street. We'd gone about a block when she saw a car coming a mile away. She got hysterical and started running and screaming for me to get out of the street and jump up on the curb. I just stood there and watched her have a fit. She ran over to the side of the road and jumped up on the curb, but there wasn't even a curb on that side, just an embankment. She hit the side of it so hard that her high heels stuck in the mud and she bounced back out into the middle of the street. When she landed, her coat flew over her head and she skidded with her purse out in front of her.

By this time the car had come around the corner, and when

its lights hit the eyes on her alligator purse, the man in the car ran off the side of the road. I hadn't moved because it was so interesting to see Momma having a running fit like that, and the man didn't get out for a long time. All he saw was an alligator head on a fur body in the middle of the winter in Jackson, Mississippi.

Finally, I went over and told him that it was only a woman in a coat that had jumped on the side of a hill. We helped her up, and I got her high heels out of the mud. Boy, was she mad. She wasn't hurt much, just skinned her knees and ruined her stockings and lost an earring.

Walking behind her the rest of the way home, I started to laugh and almost choked myself to death trying not to because I knew for sure she would kill me. I tried to pretend I was coughing. My face turned beet red and tears were streaming down my face. It's funny how when your life is in danger, you can't stop laughing, but when Momma turned around to beat me to death or worse, I was saved. She started to laugh. Then we both laughed so hard we had to sit down in the street and I ruined my mother-daughter dress.

But I'm in a lot of trouble with her now for a play I wrote. I thought it was real good. We put it on at school. It was called *The Devil-May-Care Girls.* Two beautiful career girls live in New York and wear evening gowns all the time. When the maid tells them Harry Truman is coming to dinner, they invite all their friends and hire a band and everything. It turns out that Mr. Truman is an insurance man with the same name. Ha-ha, boy, were they surprised!

I was the star, and my best friend, Jennifer May, was the other girl. Sara Jane Brady was the maid. I only cast her because she was so tall. She almost ruined the play by reading all of her lines right out of a notebook. Other than that, it went very well. We did it for the whole school. Momma is mad because I had the girls drink twenty-seven gin martinis.

I try hard to please her, but I think she is disappointed in me. Every time she gets mad at me she says I'm just like my daddy. I made her cry last Easter. She had bought me a pretty Easter outfit with a pink straw hat, white patent pumps and purse to match, but I got a black eye the day before Easter when Bill Shasa called my daddy a drunk. I tried to hit him in the back of the head with a brick, but I missed. I hate a boy who will hit a girl, don't you? We spoiled his Easter, too, though. Daddy gave me some Ex-Lax in a candy wrapper and Bill ate the whole thing.

Momma had her heart set on me playing the harp after someone once said I looked like a little angel. There wasn't anybody in Jackson who could teach harp music, so she settled on tap dancing. The Neva Jean School of Tap and Ballet promised to have your child on their toes in thirty days. The school was on top of the Whatley Drugstore, where they make the best banana splits in the whole world. I was a petal in the recital called "Springtime in Greentime" with a special number by the Gainer Triplets, who played a three-leaf clover. Skooter Olgerson was cast as a weed, but his momma didn't want him playing a weed and she yanked him out of the show. I didn't do too good in the recital. I was not in step but once.

Momma let me quit when I ruined all her hardwood floors practicing my shuffleball chain. Besides, Neva Jean said I was holding the whole class back. The only fun I ever had in that dance class was the day when Buster Sessions showed up in tap shoes that were too big for him. He is a real sissy and when his momma came to see him in the class, he got to tapping so fast, showing off, that one of his shoes flew off and hit the piano player, Mrs. Vella Fussel, in the back. Buster's mother wasn't even looking. She was sitting there in a fold-up chair, chewing a whole pack of Juicy Fruit gum and reading *Screen Secrets.*

Daddy and I bought a record of Mario Lanza singing "Because of You," as a surprise, and I learned the whole thing for Momma's birthday. When she had some of her girlfriends over, Daddy put me in one of his jackets and a tie and painted a mustache on my face. He announced me and I came in the room and sang "Because of You" as loud as I could. Momma suggested maybe I should learn one of Patti Page's hits.

She was expecting a Mixmaster for her birthday, but Daddy got her a pair of expensive toenail clippers instead. I got her some Coty toilet water with sachet powder and two giant tubes of Colgate toothpaste and some Palmolive shaving cream for her legs. She tried to pretend she liked what I got her, but I know she didn't. I'm too young to buy a Mixmaster and I don't even know where they sell them.

What I can't figure out is, Felix is a calico cat and her kittens are black and white and real ugly.

April 12, 1952

Well, you are not going to believe what happened. Daddy froze five cartons of English red worms and when we thawed them out, they were all dead as door nails! Nobody is going to buy dead English red worms. Rats! The only other way Daddy could get that $500 is to ask his daddy to loan it to him, but Grandfather Harper won't do it because he is mad at Daddy and is never going to speak to him again as long as he lives.

My granddaddy, Blondie Harper, is pretty well known around Jackson. When they used to have stage shows here, he ran the spotlight at the Pantages Theater. He was mean and if he didn't like someone's act, he would holler at them and turn the spotlight off. People used to come to the theater just to hear what he would yell at the Yankee comedians.

When Granddaddy first started the stagehands' union in Mississippi, he put stink bombs in theaters where they didn't want the unions, and that is why he is president of the stagehands' union to this day.

He never liked my daddy from the beginning. He thought Daddy was too little and skinny, and worse, he wore glasses and did bird imitations. Grandpa thinks he is a sissy, which he isn't.

Grandpa bought me a blue suede cowgirl outfit with white

leather trim and boots to match, so he's all right in my book, but I feel sorry for Daddy. Grandpa calls Daddy a bad husband and father and all kinds of ugly things just because he happened to see him talking to a woman at Dr. Gus's Beer Joint. Daddy explained that he was simply talking union business. Grandpa said there weren't any women in the union. Daddy said that was exactly what he had been talking about at the time. If things weren't bad enough already, last week he had to go and put a whiz bomb in Grandpa's car.

I'll miss not seeing my Grandpa and Grandma Harper. I used to love to go see Momma Harper, because she and Aunt Helen would let me open their Miller High Life beers for them and have a sip.

My Aunt Helen is real pretty. As a little girl, she used to sleep with her arms folded like an angel, so if she died in the middle of the night, she would look beautiful. She doesn't like Daddy, either, because he put her boyfriend's picture on the back of the toilet seat once.

Momma still doesn't want to move to Shell Beach, but Daddy says that since nobody in her family or his family is speaking to him, we wouldn't be all that happy in Jackson anyway.

The only good thing that happened was that last night my dog, named Lassie, ate Momma's roast beef right off the table and we had to go out for supper so I got to see my Aunt Bess, who runs the Irondale Café across town. She's about sixty-five years old and has never been married. She told me that they may put "Miss" on her tombstone, but that she hasn't missed a thing.

She is Grandma Pettibone's sister. Her café is great. It is right by the railroad tracks and most of her customers are railroad men. The food is good, too. She has five colored ladies that work for her and they cook biscuits, turnip greens and pork chops. Aunt Bess even has possum listed on her menu. Momma said it was only a joke or she hoped it was.

When Aunt Bess was twenty, her daddy looked at her and knew she was never going to get married like her other sisters, so he gave her enough money to start a business. She opened a barbershop, but sold that. Then she and her friend Sue Lovells started the Irondale Café. It is very successful.

All of the Pettibones are Methodist and hit the church every time the doors open. They get upset with Aunt Bess because she won't go with them. She loves to fish and one time when my grandmother was having one of her bingo parties at home, Aunt Bess, who was drinking, drove up to her house with a string of dead trout hanging out the side of the car. George, the colored man that she takes with her, was sitting right beside her in the front seat.

Aunt Bess is getting rich because all the old railroad men die and leave her their money. Most of them are bachelors and love Aunt Bess. But she gives it all away.

The café has gunshot holes all over the floor and ceiling from when Aunt Bess plays poker with the railroad men after she closes. They get to drinking and pretty soon there's a fight. Aunt Bess watches until she thinks it has gone on long enough, then she shoots off her gun.

Aunt Bess likes Daddy—thank goodness! The other night she kept slipping him Wild Turkey whiskey in a paper cup and it made Momma mad. Momma is real proper and hates it when Daddy has a good time. She put me in Catholic school because she thought it would make up for having Daddy for a daddy. Everybody says he is a bad influence on me.

Daddy won't let me be baptized a Catholic, but those nuns are having a good time trying. I have a lot of holy cards and get lots of attention because they think I'm going to hell. I like the nuns very much, all except Sister Plasida.

I have two boyfriends, Dwane Crawford and Luther Willis. Luther wears bow ties. When we had our fifth-grade dance, Luther and I were dancing to "The Tennessee Waltz" and Sister Plasida came over and took me into the hall and tried to wipe the lipstick and rouge off of me, which I wasn't even wearing. Momma, who was there in the PTA group, came in and told her not to do that because when I got excited, I had natural coloring.

I don't like catechism too much either. Daddy was the one

that told me that the Epistles were the wives of the Apostles. That old priest went all funny when I asked him if Mary Magdalene was Jesus' girlfriend. He doesn't want you to ask questions at all.

I am a second-year Brownie. I got a first-aid badge that really comes in handy. One time after school, Jimmy Lee got hit by a car and was bleeding all over the place. I remembered what to do. I sat down and put my head between my knees to keep from fainting.

Once a colored man was in a wreck in front of my grandmother's house and had his ear cut off. When the ambulance came, they said to my grandmother, "We can't take him, you'll have to call a colored ambulance." Can you believe that they wouldn't help him with his ear? Boy, were we mad. Daddy said things were pretty bad when rednecks were in the medical profession.

I personally don't trust any of them as far as I can throw a gum wrapper, especially after the time Dr. Clyde told Momma that my tonsils would have to come out and that it would be a snap. He talked all about the ice cream I could eat and what fun it would be, and Momma took me to the Rexall and bought me a Sparkle Plenty doll.

When I got to the hospital, Dr. Clyde promised me my momma and daddy would be with me the whole time. Then they put me on this table and rolled me down the hall. I was OK until we got to these two big screen doors and my momma and daddy were told they would have to wait outside. I sat right up when I heard that. Momma and Daddy were looking scared, but those people at the hospital rolled me in the room alone and closed the doors.

Then some other people with masks started fooling around and even tried to take my Sparkle Plenty doll away. They asked if I was Catholic, which made me real nervous before an operation, and then they put this strainer on my face and tried to kill me with ether, one of the worst-smelling things I have ever smelled in my life.

When I heard a commotion outside the door, I tried to get up, but five against a little child is not fair. It was the worst experience of my life. I heard bells, sirens, and saw terrible things. I dreamed a story about a magician with a magic stick that scared me to death.

I found out later that as I was being rolled into the operating room Momma turned to say something to Daddy, but Daddy had run down to the end of the hall and shut himself into a telephone booth. Some doctors got him out and gave him a shot, he was so upset. I love him, but Daddy isn't much help in a real-life crisis.

Don't ever let them fool you with that ice cream stuff. I couldn't even taste it and didn't want it, to boot. After I got my strength back, I opened up the head of my Sparkle Plenty doll and pulled the eyes out.

Grandma Pettibone came over to the hospital and fanned me with a bingo card and I got to miss school, but other than that, the hospital was the pits.

May 2, 1952

Jimmy Snow called Daddy and asked if he had the $500 yet. I got to talk to him, and he sounds very nice. Daddy has decided to try and get on *I've Got a Secret* to win the money. Boy, you should hear some of the secrets he has come up with so far. When Momma told him the secrets have to be true, he put me in training for *Beat the Clock*. He thinks I can beat the clock because I am very well coordinated. Nobody has the heart to tell him they don't let children on the show.

Momma took me to the doctor again today, but I was just overheated because Daddy made me push the car a couple of blocks.

Life is not much fun. Momma is watching me like a hawk. She has taken me to the doctor four times this past month thinking I have polio. She won't let me go swimming or to the movies and she won't even let me eat a Popsicle because someone told her that the little colored boys take the wrappers off and lick them before they sell them.

Daddy sneaked me a grape Popsicle the other day, but it turned my lips purple and she found out. That's what you get when you have fair skin.

Grandmother Pettibone's neighbor's little boy got polio and is in an iron lung. His daddy had his head chopped off by the Japanese in the war. I can't do my imitation of the little crippled match girl anymore. I better not get polio. My momma would have a fit.

Daddy had to promise Momma he would stop drinking so much after he got drunk at work and put the movie on backwards. Now all Daddy drinks is Hadacol to build up his blood. He drinks it all day. I don't know how he can stand it. It tastes like swamp water. I hope Daddy gets his $500 soon, and we can move.

I hate Rose Mary Salvage. She stole my best friend, Jennifer May, by telling her she had a lot of information about the facts of life. I ask you just how much can you know in the fifth grade, even if you are an Italian?

As for me, Momma says for me not to listen to any facts of life and if I do hear some not to believe them. Besides, I am not interested after seeing those kittens born. I think I'd be better off not knowing.

I ran into my Granddaddy Harper downtown the other day. He was standing in front of the pawnshop, talking to some of his friends. When he saw me, he called me over and asked me how I was and gave me $5. When he saw Daddy come around the corner, he just looked at him and said, "Nuts to you, bub," and went on down the street.

I bought myself a Davy Crockett hat and a Gorgeous George paper doll book and a lot of jewelry from Woolworth's.

Momma says she is convinced I have Indian blood because I like colored beads so much, but I think I get it from my Grandmother Pettibone. She has tons of colored beads. I would give anything to have her yellow crystal beads and her multicolored stone earrings.

Grandma Harper has two green bottles shaped like women with black hair painted on their heads and a yellow glass colored captain's hat that she keeps her face powder in that I want, too, and a picture of a naked girl in a swing, swinging way up in the air over castles in a blue sky.

I don't know why I want those things. I just do.

May 6, 1952

Last night was the night of the biggest bingo game in town. The East Lake VFW was giving away $500 for the jackpot. Momma was a nervous wreck all day. Daddy was trying to figure out a way to cheat and was making fake bingo cards in the basement. She kept telling him there was no way to cheat at bingo and even if there was, she wouldn't do it, because she was the mother of a small child and had no intentions of going to jail in disgrace.

Finally, Momma sent him over to the Wagon Wheel to have a few beers. That was the first time she ever told him to go for a drink. He was out the door in jig time, then she grabbed me and braided my hair so tight I had a headache.

She wouldn't let me pull the cord on the streetcar, even though we were an hour early. She took me to the Rexall and bought me a June Allyson and Van Johnson coloring book, a Little Audrey comic book and a Casper the Friendly Ghost coloring book, so I would be plenty busy and leave her alone.

The East Lake VFW Bingo Hall has big blue neon VFW

letters out front and hundreds of yellow faded pictures of soldiers all over the wall, and lots of flags. They are very patriotic. Everybody was at the bingo game early, trying to get a good seat.

The Catholic women showed up and some people from the American Legion bingo parties came and they don't even like the VFW people. We got a seat and saved Grandma a bingo table. Everybody was carrying on about what they were going to do with that $500 if they won it.

Snookie, the most famous bingo caller in Jackson, was there in his Cootie uniform with his stupid hat with the tassels on and was walking all over the room shaking hands with everyone. People thought he called the numbers too fast, but they were all sweet to him, trying to butter him up.

Snookie's organization with the VFW is called the Cooties because their job in the war had been to travel in boxcars with mules and they caught cooties from the mules. I sure wouldn't have told anyone I was a Cootie.

When the bar opened up, all the poor husbands, drug there by their wives, rushed in to get their beer. Momma was dressed up in her aqua wool dress with the accordion sleeves. I thought it was a terrible outfit for playing bingo and I told her so.

She gave me fifty cents to go over and buy Mr. Bill a drink. Mr. Bill is great. Every week he's at the bar with a baseball cap on. He is a veteran of three wars: the Spanish-American, World War One and Two. He is real old and has no teeth and will tip his cap when you give him money. I like to see him eat potato chips. Boy, is that a mess. He was just getting ready to eat some when my Grandma Pettibone came in the door.

The whole VFW hall got quiet. They were scared of her because she was on a winning streak and could play seventeen cards at once. She was wearing her lucky blue and white polka-dotted dress and her multicolored jeweled earrings.

She must have gone over to Bootie's Beauty Shop that day because her hair was bright purple. Her two friends Ollie Meeks and Pearl Tatum were with her. They are the three most feared bingo players in the state of Mississippi and even play penny bingo in the daytime just to keep sharp. I know 'cause I've been there. One of the reasons my Grandpa Pettibone left was because he said those old women used to scare his chickens to death yelling, "Bingo."

When Momma saw Grandma, she said, "Mother, you know I hate your hair purple!"

Grandma said, "It is not purple, it is bluish gray and I have the box top to prove it, miss," and pulled it out from her purse and gave it to Momma.

Momma didn't say anything else. I love it when Grandma fusses at Momma, but Grandma's hair was purple. She had two round circles of powdered rouge on her cheeks and a little dot of lipstick on her lips. Her hair is so thin you can see right through it in the light. Sometimes she lets me play with the fat on her arms during the nickel games. I don't think she looked like a Shriner clown, no matter what Momma said.

Momma never could get anywhere with Grandma. Momma told me I was lucky to be her granddaughter and not her daughter.

When the official games were about to start, Grandma sent me up to look at the wooden bingo balls in the cage and tell her what numbers looked the best and for me to be real sweet to Snookie. Ugh!

He never took that smelly old cigar out of his mouth the whole time he was telling me how lucky I was to be the granddaughter of Leona Pettibone and would I be a sweet girl and draw the lucky number for the door prize later. I told Grandma that I 29 looked good to me and she got seventeen cards with I 29 on them.

Just then my Aunt Bess came in the door with some old railroad men friends of hers and hollered at Grandma, "Hey, Leona, what you gonna do with that five hundred dollars, girl?"

Grandma pretended she didn't know her. She doesn't like Aunt Bess to come around her friends.

One time three days before Christmas, Grandma was downtown when somebody she knew saw her and said, "Leona, come up to the toy department and look at this crazy drunk woman who's sitting on Santa's lap, getting her picture made." Grandma turned on her heels and marched right out of the ladies' lingerie department. She knew it was Bess because Bess gets drunk and has her picture made with Santa Claus every year.

Bess never comes to the bingo game much and I was glad to see her. Besides, she gave me a present, a little colored baby doll. She'd put mustard in its diaper as a joke. Momma thought it was sickening, but I like jokes.

Aunt Bess knew she couldn't have any fun with Momma and Grandma when they were in their bingo moods, so she went on over to the bar to have a good time with Mr. Bill and her friends. Momma wouldn't let me go with Aunt Bess. Instead, she told me to shut up and sit down and color my books, but I had to go to the bathroom. Momma made me promise not to sit on the seats because all the old ladies peed on them.

I tried and tried not to sit down, but my legs started to shake and wouldn't you know it, I sat right down on the seat by mistake and got the back of my dress wet.

There must have been twenty old ladies who came in and every one of them pinched my cheek and asked if I was having fun. When my dress dried off a little, I went back to Momma's table and sat down fast.

The games started. I colored my June Allyson and Van Johnson coloring book and read my Little Audrey comic book, but I couldn't concentrate. Those wooden balls rattling in that cage make a lot of noise. I tried to color Casper the Friendly Ghost, but how many colors can you color a ghost? Snookie told everyone to be ready because after the next game for $10, the big jackpot was coming up. Everyone started getting nervous, and I had to buy Momma and Grandma Coca-Colas and cheese crackers.

Almost nobody played that game. They all headed for the bathroom. Grandma's friend Pearl Tatum won the $10. She was mad about it because she said she used up her good luck for just $10. Grandma told her not to be upset. She might win again, but Pearl said, "Lightning doesn't strike twice," and asked Grandma if she would play her cards for her in the jackpot game.

That meant Grandma would have to play thirty-two cards at one time. Grandma thought about it and said she would, but if she did bingo on Pearl's card, Pearl would have to give her half. They set up all the cards on one table. Momma told her not to try it, but Grandma never listens to Momma. She told her to worry about her own cards.

Grandma had to stand up to play. The game started. Grandma was going great guns. You should have seen her. She was smoking her Camel cigarette, and Pearl Tatum was handing her those red bingo chips just like they were bobby pins at the beauty parlor. She was doing great, up until Snookie called the number I 29, that Grandma had on twenty-four of her cards.

When Snookie called the next number, B 3, Grandma hadn't finished covering all her I 29s and she and Pearl Tatum and Ollie Meeks started hollering at Snookie to slow down.

The other women sitting around them screamed at them to shut up because they couldn't hear the numbers being called. But Grandma, Pearl and Ollie kept screaming for Snookie to slow down. The other women got madder and madder, and pretty soon this Italian woman called Ollie Meeks an old bat.

Ollie ran over to her table and knocked all the bingo chips off the woman's card. Then the Italian woman's friend got mad and threw a handful of vanilla wafers at Grandma. Pearl Tatum knocked them away like they were Ping-Pong balls. It was great. All the Italian women started screaming, and Pearl Tatum got mad and threw down her bingo chips, took her Coca-Cola bottle and shook it up and spewed the whole table right down the line.

Meantime, people were pulling for their numbers all over the room, "I need N thirty-two," or whatever number they needed.

Grandma hadn't missed a beat. She still was going strong when one of those women hit her in the head with a piece of fruitcake. It was at that moment that someone in the room yelled, "Bingo!"

Everybody turned around and it was MY MOMMA! She bingoed on I 69 and hit the jackpot. Aunt Bess whooped and knocked Mr. Bill right off the barstool. It took seven of those VFW men to hold back the Italian women from killing Grandma and Ollie Meeks and Pearl Tatum. All I could think was: We are on our way to Shell Beach!

May 19, 1952

Momma almost didn't give Daddy the money after she had won. She was still scared to death to go off with Daddy even though he promised that if she would give him the money to put down on that shop, he would not drink on holidays and not look at any other women. It was just what he had been waiting for, a chance to be his own boss and quit running movies. He might even join the Lions Club. He promised her the moon.

I told her I would stop singing like Mario Lanza, which was hard because it was still my best imitation.

Daddy said for her not to think of how he had acted in the past, but to think of our new life just like Coming Attractions in the movies.

She finally said yes. We are leaving in three days. Boy, did I get Rose Mary Salvage and Jennifer May! I told them that I was moving to Russia to be a spy and for them not to write me. Imagine how surprised they will be when I come back to Jackson in my mink coat, the wealthy daughter of a very successful businessman.

Daddy and I had fun his last night as a motion picture operator. I stayed in the booth with him and we broke eighty-three intermission records over our heads. I ate five Mr. Goodbars and a Baby Ruth.

Momma, who was in the audience, was embarrassed. Nobody enjoyed the movie, *Johnny Belinda*, which had a lot of silent parts in it, because of the noise we made. When Daddy missed his changeover and the audience started clapping, she clapped right along with them. She didn't want anyone to know she was related to the operator. I myself remained loyal and leaned over the balcony and screamed, "Shut up." After all, it was only a four-minute wait. Some people have disgusting habits.

Felix, plus two of her kittens, and Lassie are going to Shell Beach with us.

We are driving down in our Crosley car. It is real little and

Momma hates it. She says she feels like she is riding in a washing machine.

I'm going to name my pony Trigger, or Helen if it is a girl.

May 29, 1952

I am in Shell Beach, Mississippi, almost 300 miles from Jackson. Wow! We have been here a week and a lot has happened. The trip down was great. I saw real cotton growing and cows and read Burma Shave signs and there were rednecks all along the side of the road. Momma says I have white trash blood on my father's side, but I don't believe it.

The trip took about nine hours. We had to keep stopping for Lassie and Felix and her kittens to go to the bathroom and Felix ran away in a field once. Momma cried all the way and wouldn't even eat her bacon, lettuce and tomato sandwich.

We met Jimmy Snow at a filling station ten miles from the beach and he gave Daddy the key to the malt shop and wished him good luck. He sure is funny-looking. He has snow white hair and snow white eyebrows and he isn't even old. He said he would be down and see us later.

At about four-thirty in the afternoon we reached Shell Beach and it is the most beautiful place I have ever seen. The beach has sand white as flour and the water is green and clear, not like the Pearl River at all. There is not a tree anywhere.

Daddy's place is located at the end of the road that goes straight to the beach. Even I can tell it is a prime location. It is across the street from a dance hall called the Little Casino. Daddy got the key out and opened the door.

The malt shop is terrific. It has six booths, made out of lime green plastic, and six tables and chairs to match, and you can see the Gulf of Mexico right out the window. It has a kitchen and a jukebox with pink and green lights and red buttons that I get to play free.

We couldn't tell much about the floor because the place was closed all winter and it had about two feet of sand in it. Daddy said we could clean that up in jig time. However, it took us four days. Sand can fool you. We are living in the back of the malt shop, which is one large room with a sun porch. Daddy is turning the sun porch into a bedroom for me. The malt shop is made of green asbestos and has a big picture window in the front.

Our very first visitors were the Romeos, who live up the road and have an Italian restaurant and about eight summer cottages. They have a son named Michael, who is visiting his cousins in Jackson and will be back home in about two weeks. Mrs. Romeo said the only other person down here my age is a girl named Kay Bob Benson.

The Romeos were very nice and helpful. They told us about the money prospects of Shell Beach. Mr. Romeo said there were only three months a year that you could make money: June, July and August. The rest of the year nobody ever comes down here. There are only about fifteen people who live in Shell Beach year round. Even in the summer there aren't that many people because everybody wants to go to Florida. The main highway to Florida bypasses Shell Beach by thirty miles.

Momma looked at Daddy like she could kill him when she heard that one.

Most of the people who come to Shell Beach are from Hattiesburg. Mr. Romeo said we would learn to hate people from Hattiesburg fast. If you own an eating establishment, they are the worst form of humanity alive because they come to the beach on Saturdays and Sundays by the carloads and bring their own lunches. If they rent a cottage, they bring their own groceries.

My daddy is not a man to let little things upset him. He looked upon this news as a challenge, but Momma is worried. She told Daddy he should have known all this before we moved.

Later we sat down and figured out a plan to turn our business into a profit-making organization. The first thing we did was to decide on a name for the place. We settled on Harper's Malt Shop and ordered a big pink neon sign with a big blue neon arrow pointing to the door.

One of the things Daddy told Momma in order to get her to marry him was that one day he would put her name up in lights. I don't think Harper's Malt Shop is what Momma had in mind. Daddy barely got Momma to marry him. She thought he was ugly, too little and skinny, but he wouldn't leave her alone. He wrote her poems and when she said she didn't want to marry him, he cried and carried on so, everybody felt sorry for him. He would spend all night hollering on her front porch.

Her mother said she better marry him because he wasn't going to leave. I'm sure glad she said yes. Look at all the free movies I've seen, not to mention getting to live on the beach.

Daddy and I have been working to get ready to open. We changed the names over the bathroom doors from "Men" and "Women" to "Buoys" and "Gulls." We also painted a lot of signs that say "Harper's Malt Shop and Delicatessen." He and Momma argued a lot about the word "delicatessen." She said it was a Yankee word and nobody in Mississippi knew what it meant, including her.

Daddy has some great ideas about merchandise. He feels that we shouldn't just limit ourselves to food, especially since most people bring their own. We took all the tables and chairs out of the middle of the room and left the booths. We built huge display shelves where we are going to have souvenirs, sunglasses, suntan lotion and everything you can think of.

We've ordered hats, beach balls, inner tubes, sand buckets and shovels for young children, cigars and cigarettes, Zippo see-through lighters that have fishing lures and dice right in them, and every kind of headache and stomachache remedy you can think of. We ordered magazines, and Kodak film, mosquito repellent, fishing equipment and candy. We even sell a joke. It is a jar that says "Old Indian Hemorrhoid Medicine." When you open it up, a rubber finger pops out!

Daddy let me pick out the water floats. I think our biggest seller will be a Moby Dick or the Howdy Doody inner tube, but the things that will really sell are the shells stuck in pink plaster of paris, with a pink plastic flamingo or a cross on them. They also have a light and can be used as a lamp or a centerpiece, and there's a gold decal on them that says "Shell Beach, Mississippi."

We also ordered a lot of little antebellum women made out of shells. We're going to get all the latest magazines and I can read them if I don't get them dirty. Our jukebox has "Wheel of Fortune" by Kay Starr and "Too Young" by Nat King Cole and my favorite, "Come ona My House" by Rosemary Clooney. Momma loves to play "Blue Tango." I wish I hadn't told Rose Mary Salvage I was going to Russia so she could hear I had my own jukebox. Momma is going to be the hostess and cashier. Daddy is going to be the cook. I am the buying consultant.

We met some more people yesterday, Mr. and Mrs. Dudley Dot. They live at the beach. I don't like him very much, but I like Mrs. Dot. She had on a big hat and never lets the sun hit her face. She said she would rather take poison than ruin her skin. She has a club that she wants me to join called the Jr. Debutantes' Club. It meets in the back of the live bait store every week. She feels it is her duty as a southern woman to help bring culture to the young ladies of Shell Beach. Momma said I have to go.

Mrs. Dot writes a column for the Magnolia Springs paper and she put us in it. The column is called "Dashes from Dot." It said: "Shell Beach has a new family, the William Harpers and their darling daughter, Daisy. They've moved from Jackson, Mississippi, and purchased the malt shop at the end of Highway 4. Mr. Harper was previously employed in the finest theaters in Jackson as a master projectionist. We wish them good luck!" Daddy said we would probably be in the paper a lot because there are only twenty people living here.

The closest town is Magnolia Springs, ten miles up the highway. Mrs. Dot said Shell Beach was ten miles to a loaf of bread and twenty-five miles to a spool of pink thread. I went to Magnolia Springs the other day and it has one street, and that's it. But it has a movie. I saw Lash La Rue in *Frontier Phantom*. It's funny to sit in the audience and not in the balcony.

The other morning I woke up about seven o'clock. I thought

a war had started. Guns were going off and we heard an army marching up and down the beach and some man shouting orders. Daddy ran out the door in his underwear.

And guess what? There was a whole group of women in boots and uniforms doing maneuvers right in our backyard, charging along the sand dunes. Daddy went over to the man giving the orders and found out his name was Mr. Curtis Honeywell. He owns the Stars and Stripes Insurance Company in Magnolia Springs. His army is all the secretaries and the receptionist that work there.

He was in a uniform with a big hat with a feather on it from Australia. Mr. Honeywell swears the Communists are coming to take over and are going to land right on our beach. He's getting his army ready to defend the Gulf Coast of Mississippi as his patriotic responsibility.

The girls are called the Mississippi Maidens for Freedom. If you are a secretary at his insurance company, you have to be in the army and train three times a week.

Daddy said he didn't think Communists were interested in Shell Beach.

Mr. Honeywell asked Daddy if he knew that in the Second World War they found three Japanese submarines with dead Japanese soldiers still in them right up the road, in the Mississippi Sound.

Daddy said, "No, I didn't know that and what in the world would the Japanese want in Mississippi?" and went back to bed.

I was dressed because I sleep in my swim trunks, so I stayed out there with the Mississippi Maidens shooting their guns. Halting and coming to attention is what they do best. Mr. Honeywell said I could be the mascot. I told him I had a BB gun and would be happy to shoot with them. The girls were real nice.

Daddy asked Mr. Romeo about Curtis Honeywell. He said that he always had an all-woman army and he owns almost all of Harwin County.

Momma said he must be crazy as a loon. I think it is great and I feel very safe. If I were a Communist, I wouldn't want to tangle with those girls.

The only bad thing is that I'm not getting to swim in the Gulf as much as I thought I was going to because Momma has to watch me. She is afraid the undertow will get me.

June 4, 1952

Jimmy Snow came down to see us the other day and said the place looked great. The reason he hasn't been here sooner was he was busy crop-dusting. After he left, Daddy said that Jimmy was a great guy and got drunk one time and dusted crops in downtown Tupelo. Momma didn't think that was funny. But I do.

I finally met Kay Bob Benson. I don't think she likes me much. I had to go to her house and look at the dumb collection of dolls that she has in a glass cage. She is real impressed because she has some Madame Alexander dolls. Big deal! What good are dolls in a glass cage?

She is president of the Jr. Debutantes' Club and gets to go to camp every summer. I don't understand why she would want to leave the beach. She told me that she was such a pretty little girl that they used her picture on Sunshine bread as Little Miss Sunshine. I don't believe it. Her mother is famous because she found a man's leg that washed up on the beach. They knew it was a man's leg because it had a golf shoe on it. Nobody knew who it belonged to. It could have come from Cuba even. Some people have all the luck.

Kay Bob Benson's name is in Mrs. Dot's column every week because her mother is Mrs. Dot's best friend. I wish Momma would get friendly with Mrs. Dot. Also, Kay Bob said I could never be a model because I have a chipped tooth. Who cares?

We don't open our store until next Saturday, but in the meantime, Daddy and I are exploring the territory and meeting people.

We drove six miles up the road to the Bon Secour River. It is surrounded by huge trees with Spanish moss hanging on them all the way to the ground. People call it the singing river because it is famous for a strange music that is heard coming from beneath the water. The Indians say the music is the ghost of dead Indians singing. Daddy likes to go there to fish and eat oysters. The Bon Secour is where the best oysters in the world come from and Daddy knows a man that sells him a croker sack full for a quarter. Daddy eats them raw. Ugh! I don't know why he does it. He never finds any pearls. I row the boat while Daddy fishes. Momma says it looks bad for a little girl to be rowing a grown man up and down the river, but I'm a very good rower. The man who rents us our boat, Mr. Charles Wentzel, holds the record for catching a speckled trout that was one yard long.

Mr. Wentzel lives across the street from some people called the Caldwells. The Caldwells are what Daddy calls Bible thumpers, crazy over religion. We Harpers are not at all religious, a fact my daddy is proud of and brags about. He claims that he lost his faith behind the Rahoma Baptist Church when he was eleven. As far as Momma goes, she believes in God, but church is such a sore spot with Daddy that she doesn't push it. I think I have some Methodist blood on my mother's side. I asked Daddy about it, but he said I didn't have to believe in God if I didn't want to.

Daddy and I tried to avoid the Caldwells, but they have a daughter who is always sitting on the front porch and she looks so happy to see us that we wave at her. Their house is far back in the woods, so she never gets to meet many people. She must have asked Mr. Wentzel my name because one day when Daddy and I got there, she smiled right at me and said, "Hey, Fay, how are you today?"

I didn't know what to say, so I said, "Fine," and kept walking.

Mr. Wentzel said, "I think she wants you to go over there and talk to her. She's a crippled girl and can't come over here." I was scared to go up on that porch, but Daddy made me.

I was surprised at how pretty she was, up close. I had never talked to a crippled person before, so I stood behind Daddy, who answered all her questions about me—how old I was, what grade I was in and all that stuff. Daddy talked to her for a long time. Her name is Betty and she's been crippled all her life. She is eighteen years old.

She doesn't look like what I thought a crippled girl would look like. Daddy is very upset over her and one time tried to talk to her mother and daddy about her. Her mother wears her gray hair in tiny waves and she has ugly gold-framed glasses and an old, ugly, flowered housedress. She never uses any makeup and looks like a prune. My mother wears Merle Norman makeup every day of her life, makeup base, rouge, powder, the whole thing, even when she's staying home.

Mr. Caldwell always has on khaki work clothes and is the tallest man I've ever seen, and they are both real country. Daddy told Mr. Caldwell he should take Betty to see some good doctors to help her walk. Mr. Caldwell got real funny and started saying how it was evil to tamper with God's will, that her affliction was a sign from the Lord. Mrs. Caldwell stayed behind the screen door, looking mean, telling her husband to come on back in the house and get away from us. He finally left, but I stuck my tongue out at Mrs. Caldwell before I went.

Afterwards Daddy said it was a damn shame that poor girl had to waste her life with those two rednecks. He told me that people like the Caldwells would shoot you in the head and swear that they had read somewhere in the Bible to do it.

One person on the river who is great is Mr. Wilbur Donnally, who has the most famous curio collection in Harwin County. He keeps it in his living room and it costs a quarter to see it. He has a baseball that in 1932, in Tallahassee, Florida, had bounced off a first baseman's head and had been caught by a fielder and was counted as an out. He also owns the Mystery Sea Freak. Nobody knows if it's a fish or a bird.

My favorite is the old bullet that had been shot through the face of a Choctaw Indian chief by an Indian enemy. After he found out he wasn't killed, he spit the bullet out into his hand, loaded it into the muzzle of his gun and shot his enemy dead.

Daddy's favorite curio is the stuffed chicken with ten toes. That's what gave Daddy the idea to become a taxidermist. He figured after the summer months were over, it would be nice to have something to do. So he had a sign made up to go in the window that said "Bill Harper, Certified Public Taxidermist." He is going to take a course by mail and collect things to stuff when the season is over. It's lucky we have a big ice cream freezer to keep the dead animals in.

We need to hire help for the malt shop, so we went up to Beulah Heights, the colored quarters, to look for a dishwasher and found one named Mattie Mae.

According to Mattie Mae, there is a real live albino living in Beulah Heights. Her name is Ula Sour. She has pink eyes and never goes out in the daytime because she is spotted. Nobody knows where she lives and she's so ugly she would scare you to death. Somebody saw her once in the night picking flowers. I would give anything to see her.

I love to go to Beulah Heights. Daddy buys me the best barbecue from the man on the corner, who makes it outside his house every day. I go into the Elite Nightspot for an Orange Crush. I love the Elite Nightspot. Little colored Christmas lights are all around and it has a jukebox and everything. I never heard any of the songs before because they are race music from Africa and Chicago.

The lady who runs it is named Peachy Wigham and has gold teeth and lives on a liquid diet. Peachy said I could come to see her anytime I wanted and gave me a dead chicken foot for good luck. I showed it to Momma and she said for me to throw it out right away, it might give me a chicken disease. I washed it real good and hid it in a Luden's cough drop box.

We are now looking for a waiter. There is a sailor base up the road, and a lot of sailors have applied for the job. Oh, and I forgot to tell you the best thing. My picture is being used as an advertisement, just like Kay Bob Benson's. Daddy took a photo of me looking real sad and pale. Then he made me up with Momma's Merle Norman kit, mascara and all, and curled my hair and took another picture with me looking very happy. He put them both on a sign and under it printed "Which twin eats at Harper's Malt Shop?" Momma says it is false advertising, but I think it will bring in the customers like crazy.

Daddy has been practicing his short-order cooking. I get all the cheeseburgers and chocolate malts I want. He is a wonderful cook. He and Momma are having a big fight because he wants to sell beer and Momma doesn't want him to. She is afraid he will drink up the profits and that the beer will bring in a rough crowd. Daddy thinks beer is where the big money is. If he does win, I hope we get Miller High Life because it is my favorite. Daddy likes Budweiser a lot and Momma hates it all.

There is a real nightclub here called the Blue Gardenia Lounge that's going to have live acts. Daddy and I went up to meet the owners, a man named Harold Pistal and his brother, Claude. We only met Harold and his wife, though, because Claude is in Detroit. They have a little girl named Angel, who is five.

Angel has real big ears that stick way out. When the season starts, Mr. and Mrs. Pistal have promised to pay me twenty-five cents a night to come up and tape her ears back before she goes to sleep. They will be busy working in the lounge and can't do it. I can see all the acts for free, too. Angel is OK for a small child, even if she does get confused about how old I am and says "Yes, ma'am" to me a lot.

All the beach balls, inner tubes and floats that we ordered have come. I have to go and blow them up.

June 6, 1952

Momma got scared and called the doctor again. I didn't have polio, just hyperventilation from blowing up all those inner tubes. Daddy is going to buy a bicycle pump.

Mr. Romeo brought Michael over to meet me when I was sick, and he is great! I was sorry my face was so red. Michael is going to take me crabbing and fishing and everything. He is a junior lifeguard, which will come in handy since I can't swim. He already has a suntan, but it might be his natural color.

Yesterday Connie, the Sunshine bread truck man, let Michael and me ride to Cotton Bayou to a grocery store where he had to deliver bread. Connie gives Michael all the day-old doughnuts and saves me some, too.

Cotton Bayou is way down in the swamps. The people there are Cajuns. That means French and something. The bayou is real beautiful, lots of pine trees and sand. There was someone Connie wanted us to meet. We drove up to an old white wooden grocery store that was falling down. It had a sign on it, "Cotton Bayou Grocery and P.O." It didn't look to me as if anybody lived there at all, but Connie told us there were a lot of people way back in the bayou that you never see. A mailman delivers their mail in a boat once a week. I would hate to be waiting on a letter for a week. What if the boat sank, or an alligator got the mailman?

The inside of that grocery store was so old it looked to me that those cans of peppers from Cuba and all kinds of funny foods had been there for a long time. Mrs. LeGore ran the place and was the postmistress. She must be a Cajun because she talked funny. I bought a strawberry drink from her and a Buddy bar. Michael had already eaten six day-old doughnuts, so he just had an RC.

Connie asked if we could see Jessie. Mrs. LeGore said for us to wait until she had cleaned him up a little. I wanted to know if Jessie was a person or an animal. Connie said that Jessie was a person about twenty-five years old who hadn't been out of his room since he was fifteen because of elephantiasis. I had never seen anyone with elephantiasis, and neither had Michael. I was willing to go back there only if I couldn't catch it.

We waited a long time. Mrs. LeGore had over a dozen old calendars on the walls and she must have sold a lot of chewing tobacco because there was a bunch of it. She even sold tobacco in a bag with papers if you wanted to roll your own.

I didn't finish my Buddy bar. It was too stale. Pretty soon Mrs. LeGore came back in. Connie picked out five loaves of bread and three day-old coconut cakes for Jessie. We went in the back of the store and there was Jessie, lying on a mattress on the floor, with one leg propped up. He must be the fattest man in the world. I couldn't even see his eyes good. His momma had wet his hair and combed it down for him. He was wearing a flowered shirt without buttons that was fastened together with big safety pins, and he had on what looked to me like pajama bottoms. He was friendly and glad to get the cakes and ate them without a knife or fork. His room was little, and there was a collection of red and blue satin pillows that said "Mother" and "Sweetheart" on them with yellow silk braided fringe all around them and a pillow from Nashville, Tennessee, and one from Charleston, South Carolina.

Grapico, Dr Pepper, Orange Crush and Buffalo Rock signs were all over the walls along with a cross, a Goodyear tire and some Chesterfield and Kool ads from the store. A whole bunch of Christmas pictures of Santa Claus drinking Coca-Cola and a Last Supper picture were stuck right in the middle of them.

Jessie asked if we wanted to hear him sing. I said I would love to hear "Shrimp Boats Are a-Coming," but he only knows patriotic and religious songs, so he sang something about Jesus. He had a pretty good voice, too.

He gets a wonderful program on his shortwave radio from Del Rio, Texas. They mentioned his name on the air once and sent him a fan with a picture of Jesus Christ dressed like a shepherd standing around with a staff and some sheep.

Jessie asked Michael if he was going to marry me when we grew up. I told him my daddy wouldn't let me marry an Italian boy because he didn't want me to work in a grocery store, and Jessie laughed so hard he shook the whole room. Then he started to sweat a lot and asked Connie to put his leg down. His leg was the size of a truck tire and didn't have any knees. Laughing must have tired him out because he was breathing real heavy.

We had to go, so I told him good-bye and it was nice meeting him. Michael never did stop staring at him. At least I looked at the room. Connie told us Jessie weighed more than 500 pounds and can't get through the door of the room or get up at all anymore. His momma has to feed and bathe him there. Every week two or three men come to turn him over on his side so he won't get sores. All he cares about is his radio, his momma and food. If I ever catch elephantiasis, I am going to get a bigger room.

We were in the "Dashes from Dot" column this week. "William Harper at the new Harper's Malt Shop is busy preparing for a successful summer and little Daisy Fay Harper is going to be the newest member of the Jr. Debutantes' Club that will have its first meeting of the summer season in two weeks at the live bait store." Mrs. Dot also reported that Kay Bob Benson was still up in the air over her plane trip to visit her grandparents in Columbus, Georgia, where she had attended a pajama party.

Mrs. Dot's husband, Mr. Dot, is mad at me. When we were coming home with them from the dog races at Pensacola, I tried to throw what was left of my hot fudge sundae out the window and accidentally hit him with it. He's the one who wanted to stop at the Tastee Freeze in the first place.

Mrs. Romeo told Momma that Mrs. Dot married beneath herself and comes from a very wealthy family in Memphis, Tennessee. When they lost all their money, she had to marry Mr. Dot. She used to go to cotillions and everything.

Did you know that the dogs at the racetrack caught the rabbit once because it was too slow and when they found out that they had been chasing a stuffed rabbit all those years, they were so disgusted they all retired right there, never to race again? Mrs. Dot was there the night it happened.

Daddy hired a waiter for the summer, Hank Turner. Hank is about twenty years old and has a crew cut and green eyes and the biggest muscles I have ever seen. On top of that, he's got real tattoos, an American flag on his right arm and the Statue of Liberty on his left arm, and when he flexes his arm, the flag waves. A map of the entire state of Minnesota, where he comes from, is on his chest. He and his twin brother were famous football players for the university there. When he got in the Navy, he developed his muscles and entered a Mr. Universe contest. He came in second.

He can pick me up with one arm and walk around with me that way. I bet he can kill a person with one blow. Momma says I have to quit pestering him so much. I can't wait until someone says something smart to me and I can get Hank after them.

Momma finally gave in and Daddy got a beer license. To celebrate, Daddy, the Romeos and some more people drank seventy-eight draft beers, and we played the jukebox all night. Momma even had some beers and jitterbugged and sang "Blue Champagne."

Some people are starting to come down to the beach already. I can't wait. Everything is going to be great. Daddy already has a dead flamingo and a fox that died of rabies in the ice cream freezer to stuff in the fall. Michael and I are looking for dead animals all the time, but they can't be dead too long, they lose their shape.

Oh, and guess what? A man named Roy Grimmett is going to rent the land on the side of the malt shop from Daddy and put in an archery range and bring his wife and live in a trailer, right on the property.

Momma says anybody that lives in a trailer is trash, but I have never been in a trailer myself.

It doesn't look like I am going to get my pony soon. Daddy has to build a stall for it and he doesn't have time right now.

I have to go eat some cheeseburgers. . . .

June 30, 1952

The malt shop opened and I got so sunburned my nose almost peeled off. Momma took me to some hillbilly doctor that scared her to death about skin cancer and gave her some white junk out of a navy survival kit. She mashes that stuff on my face every day. It looks like lard, and you can't get it off for anything. The thing that makes it so bad is that other kids come down here for a week and tan like crazy.

I am staying inside most of the daytime because nobody will play with me. I have done every number painting they put out and the one of the Persian kitten twice. I sent one of them up to the crippled girl, Betty Caldwell.

Momma and Daddy are busy all day and night until they close up at ten. I have to go into the shop and get my breakfast like a customer. Hank takes my order and Daddy fixes it, only I don't have to pay for it. Momma is working at the cash register. Our place is always full and she is raking in the money, so I guess we will be rich. I never get to see Michael because his daddy has him working at the store. Those Italians start them early.

Poor Lassie bit the garbage man and we had to give her away to a farm that has lots of children and land for her to play, but isn't that what they always tell you?

Roy Grimmett's archery range is wonderful. He made it out of a big wall of straw. He said I could have the straw to feed my pony when the summer is over. I went into his trailer and their air conditioner sure works good. It's like living in an icebox. He has taught me to shoot the bow and arrows. At the archery range you get ten arrows for a quarter and if you can hit three balloons, you can win yourself a free hamburger or a hot dog at my daddy's place. The trick is people will buy a cold drink to go with it.

Roy's wife, Mava, has the biggest bust I've ever seen. She says it's so big from shooting those bows and arrows for so many years.

Mr. Grimmett pulls a seventy-five-pound bow that he made himself. It has a sight on it like a gun. He uses special steel arrows and never misses. He went up the road to the Mississippi state park and shot a wild boar in the head. Now it is in our ice cream freezer.

Sometimes he lets me help him attract business by shooting balloons out of my mouth. That was a great business getter until my momma looked out the window and saw me do it. She got real mad and told Mr. Grimmett to shoot balloons out of his wife's mouth.

I am spending most of my time digging tunnels in the sand under the malt shop. I have four tunnels dug so far. I never get to play with Hank Turner. He is too busy, but I'm glad he's here because of onions.

Daddy is allergic to onions. When he was little, he had a bad case of the measles and his mother fed him too much onion tea. So if anyone orders onions on their hamburger, Daddy comes out of the kitchen and has an argument with them. It's good to have Hank stand behind him because Daddy is so little.

I have been making money taping Angel Pistal's ears back before she goes to sleep. Her daddy lets me go into the lounge, have a Coca-Cola and see the acts.

The Blue Gardenia Lounge is dark blue with white flowers on the wall. There's a live band and a microphone, a spotlight and everything. I saw Bean Curd Butler, a comedian who talks country, and Miss Mary Kay Hurt, a one-woman band, but the act that's here now is a singer named Sheila Ray. She is famous. Her ad says she has appeared in night spots in Biloxi and Gulfport, Mississippi.

She is real skinny and has white hair and black eyebrows. I think she dyes one or the other. Her big number is "Tweedlee Dee." She uses a lot of personality in that one. I like her all right, but as far as I'm concerned, nobody can touch Doris Day for singing and personality. I have a record of her singing "It's Magic," which in my opinion is one of the finest recordings ever made.

If truth be known, Sheila Ray is trying to copy Doris Day's

style and looks, but she can never compare to Doris Day. I understand Doris Day is a natural beauty.

Pretty soon, Pegleg Johnson is coming. He tap-dances with one leg missing. I can't wait to see him.

I love the acts. The only bad part about going up there is that Claude Pistal, Angel's uncle, is back from Detroit. And boy, is he mean and ugly. You should see him. He has bad skin and greasy hair and pop eyes, a real Peter Lorre type, only taller and skinnier.

He hates me. I was up there one night and I saw a group of men sitting in one of the back rooms playing poker. I went in and asked if I could play a hand or two. They said fine, so I sat down and ordered a Coke.

You may not know this, but I happen to be an expert poker player. Daddy taught me all his tricks. I was sitting there, minding my own business, working on an inside straight, when Claude Pistal came in and picked me up by the back of my shirt and threw me out the door and slammed it right in my face, just when I was winning, too. On top of that, when I got home, I smelled so bad of cigar smoke Momma found out where I had been and threatened to cut my heart out if I ever did it again. Too bad, I could win a fortune.

I told Angel what Claude had done and she said that Claude hates everybody in the world except her, including her daddy, and not only that, he carries a gun.

Claude bought her a real live miniature grand piano and all kinds of things from Detroit. She even has a dollhouse you can sit in. She said he would buy her a pony if she wanted it.

We are selling those shells in plaster of paris with the cross on them so fast we can hardly keep them in stock.

Everyone says Daddy has the best hamburgers on the beach if you don't like onions. He sells a lot of beer and at night, when the malt shop closes, he drinks a lot of it, too.

He has made some new friends. One is a short bald man named Billy Bundy, who is a famous radio preacher. Billy got in a lot of trouble once in the Midwest, selling autographed pictures of the Last Supper. Imagine, him thinking you could forge Jesus Christ's signature. He promised to get me an autograph of Sue Sweetwater, who has a radio program at his station. Another friend of Daddy's is Al the Drummer, who plays the drums at the Blue Gardenia Lounge. Momma said he looks like a weasel and that Daddy ought to put him in the freezer and stuff him in the fall!

Jimmy Snow brought Daddy a dead bobcat and do you know what Jimmy Snow told me? He said that the finest perfumes in the world were made out of bobcat pee, especially Blue Waltz perfume. No wonder it smells so bad.

My momma only uses Shalimar, which is very expensive. I think Shalimar is made out of some other kind of pee. Momma won't fix any malts or ice cream cones because she said all those dead animals in the freezer make her sick.

Momma doesn't like Billy Bundy, Al the Drummer and Jimmy Snow much. She said Daddy was being friendly with people he wouldn't even talk to if it wasn't for that beer.

The worse thing that has happened is that the Jr. Debutantes have started and I have to go to the meetings with that white stuff on my face. There's nobody good in the club, just Kay Bob Benson and a bunch of shrimpers' daughters that won't talk to me on account of they are real religious and found out that Daddy is a drinker.

The first meeting Kay Bob got to stand up and explain the charms on her add-on charm bracelet. Who cares? All we did is learn to pour tea and curtsy. I already knew how to do that. We have to wear plastic barrettes in our hair with the club colors, seafoam green and oleander pink, and make ashtrays and tea plates out of shells.

We are supposed to do good deeds. Next week we are going to clean up the debris at the end of Highway 3, weather permitting. I can hardly drink my tea and eat my cookies, that live bait shop smells so bad. Those shrimper girls are used to it, but I'm not.

Mrs. Dot always ends the meeting with a thought for the day. Mrs. Dot's thought for the day was: "You can get through life if you realize at an early age that the only two books in the world that really mean anything are the *Memphis Junior League Cookbook* and the Holy Bible, in that order."

Momma and Daddy are fighting a lot and they are always tired. A carnival is coming here soon. I don't feel well. My neck hurts and my back hurts. My legs are real stiff. I probably have polio and will have to go in an iron lung and be a crippled girl, like Betty Caldwell, or maybe it is appendicitis or TB even.

P.S. I also have been exposed to elephantiasis!

July 1, 1952

I didn't have polio, but I did have to have an enema.

Momma is definitely not happy with Daddy's actions this summer. The other morning I was witness to one of the greatest temper fits of all times. Daddy hadn't been home all night because he was running up and down the road with Jimmy Snow and Al the Drummer. It was about seven o'clock in the morning when he finally did come home, and Momma and Hank were trying to get the place ready to open. I myself was trying to have a quiet breakfast.

When Daddy did come in, Momma took one look at him and saw he was still drunk. On top of that, he was wearing someone else's clothes. All hell broke loose.

Momma was holding a white platter known as a seafood platter, but they are good to serve breakfast on, too. She took that platter and smashed it on the floor, hollering at him she was sick of him acting like a horse's ass. Then she broke another platter and another. Every time she said something, she'd break another one. She went through every platter we own and then started through the cups and saucers, breaking two or three of them at a time. Daddy ran out the door. I didn't move. After all, she wasn't mad at me and I sure wasn't going to miss this fit for anybody. I figured it was the best one I'd ever see in real life. Hank and I didn't take a chance and say anything, though. You never can tell about these fits, she could have turned on us.

After Daddy ran out, she finished breaking everything, including the shrimp cocktail cups. She was starting on the display table and was smashing all our shell arrangements until she came to the ones with the crosses in them and she just stopped.

She went in the back and didn't come out for a long time. The only person that can match her throwing a fit is Barbara Stanwyck.

Harper's Malt Shop didn't open that day or the next. It took us two days to clean up the mess and get more dishes.

The only thing left were some ashtrays under the counter that Momma didn't see. Daddy said she cost him about $350 in dishes. I think he is going to behave himself from now on. It is too expensive otherwise. He explained to Momma why he had on someone else's clothes. They had all decided to take a swim and had taken their clothes off. Sheila Ray, as a joke, had dug a hole and hid them in the sand, then couldn't remember where she had buried them. It was true because we saw Sheila Ray on the beach all day digging up holes and crying.

Daddy said Sheila Ray was Al the Drummer's fiancée. Momma doesn't believe him. She thinks Daddy likes her. The only peace and quiet I can get is under the house.

Sometimes Momma forgets to put that white stuff on my face, but not often.

They are setting up the carnival across the street. I went over there and met a man named Mr. Kowboski, a Polish Gypsy. He said his wife and children are coming down in a week and I will have someone to play with. They will be Yankee children, but I am not going to let that stop me.

I haven't been doing much. I have been digging my tunnels under the malt shop every day. I have about sixteen tunnels dug and I've been going on the fishing pier. I kick the fish back in the water. People ought not to catch fish they are not going to eat.

I go every morning and every afternoon. George Potlow, the man who runs the pier, gives me a cold drink for free.

We don't have Mattie Mae as a dishwasher anymore. She got into a fight with another girl over her boyfriend, Jerry, and was bitten in the face. Her head swelled up like a poisoned dog's. Daddy and I went to Beulah Heights to see her.

Peachy Wigham had the Elite Nightspot lit up with blue Christmas lights. She told us that she had another colored woman who didn't have a boyfriend that would be a good dishwasher. Peachy said Mattie Mae was crazy about that Jerry and wouldn't be any good for nothing now that he was back from Korea.

The new dishwasher is a little old skinny woman named Velveeta Pritchard. She is the blackest woman I ever saw, so black she looks blue, which is a sign of royalty among Mississippi colored people.

They hate albinos with a passion, which I don't think is fair. I still am dying to see a real albino in person. I asked Velveeta if there was one living up there in Beulah Heights and she said no, there wasn't and it was just a story someone made up. But I think she was lying. I just know there is an albino up there. I can feel it in my bones.

Velveeta has only worked for us a little while and she hates Daddy already. Momma is crazy about Velveeta and they talk and talk all day. Momma won't let me say "jig time" anymore. I don't like Velveeta at all. She is a one-woman person and will take Momma's side against anybody.

One of Momma's gold loop earrings got stuck in my nose and she ran in there and told her as fast as she could. She finds all Daddy's hiding places for liquor and runs and tells Momma. She knows she won't get fired because Momma thinks she is wooonnnderfullll!!!!

Hank is having a terrible problem with women. They won't leave him alone. He's too sweet to say no. There is this one girl who is after him all the time, Tommie Jo Harris. Her daddy owns a truck stop four miles up the road and she hangs around here day and night.

Mrs. Dot said that her heart is just like the moon, there is always a man in it. Tommie Jo is a real wild girl and every local boy is crazy to get her to go out with them. They like her because she is so mean. She drives a convertible and goes every place by herself. Mrs. Dot believes everybody wants to catch her and tame her, which seems silly to me if what they like about her in the first place is that she is wild.

The story I like about Tommie Jo is the one where she went out with this guy that thought he was a big deal with the women, a lady-killer in Mrs. Dot's term. Well, he got her into a car and tried to sweet-talk her, not caring a thing in the world about her but just trying to win a bet he had made with the other guys that he could kiss her. And then she took her knee and pushed in the cigarette lighter and at the very moment he thought he had won the bet, she stuck the lighter on the end of his nose. She took the wind out of his sails! Now he doesn't dare show his face too much and he sure doesn't play with the emotions of any other young innocent girls.

Tommie Jo wears colored scarves around her neck, a real Jennifer Jones type. She doesn't talk to me. I don't think she likes young children. She sure likes Hank, though. I know this for a fact because the people that rent a room to Hank at the Hammer's Christian Motel have a vicious grandchild named Gregg. He made me hide outside Hank's room one night because he had seen Tommie Jo go in there. She turned out the lights and got into bed as a surprise for him when he came home from work.

All I can say is that I feel sorry for Hank because he works very hard and I know he was tired. But when he came home and saw her in the bed, he was a perfect gentleman about it. We could see in the window, he pretended to like her. I'm never going to act like that and throw myself at anyone, not even Cornel Wilde if I ever meet him. Anyway, they are going to get married.

Yesterday the Jr. Debutantes cleaned up the debris at the end of Highway 3 because weather was permitting. Mrs. Dot's thought for the day was: "If you make friends with the phone and frozen food, then life will be a bowl of cherries."

In her opinion, Alexander Graham Bell and Clarence Birdseye are the two greatest Americans that ever lived excluding Robert E. Lee. She believes we never lost the War Between the States, that General Lee thought General Grant was the butler and just naturally handed him his sword. Her family in Memphis had some heirlooms from General Lee, but the only thing General Grant left behind was empty whiskey bottles.

July 12, 1952

Momma got a call from Jackson today. Grandma Pettibone hit the jackpot at bingo and had a heart attack. They took her to the Baptist Hospital and told her not to smoke because of the oxygen tanks in the rooms, but Grandma hid one of her Camels in her hair and smoked one after everybody left. She blew out all the windows in the right wing of the Irondale Baptist Hospital. She wasn't hurt, but the explosion made a lot of people on the other floors go into heart failure. Anyway, Momma has gone to Jackson and put her in the Methodist Hospital. Grandma says that's just fine with her because the Baptists are too strict.

Mr. Honeywell and his all-girl army got a bazooka gun, but none of them are strong enough to hold it up. They put it on a wheelchair, but the wheelchair won't roll in the sand. Too bad, I wanted to see it shoot.

At the Jr. Debutantes' meeting this week Mrs. Dot said we are going to adopt a poor child overseas and be foster parents. Whoever it is will write us every week and thank us. I hope it's a girl. Imagine growing up and coming over here to meet its parents and seeing me and Kay Bob Benson and the shrimpers' daughters!

I tried to talk them into adopting an albino child, but Kay Bob Benson had a squealing fit. She gets whatever she wants. She is always having baby-doll-pajama-spend-the-night parties. I sleep in my swimming trunks and I don't want to go anyway.

Mrs. Dot's thought for the day was: "Nothing endures like personal quality." Next week we are going to have a talk on accessories, whatever they are, from a woman from the Magnolia Springs Dress Shop. If Momma is still in Jackson, I'll miss that one for sure.

Angel Pistal is getting to be a pain. I have to put paper sacks on her hands because in her sleep she pulls the tape off her ears and she wants to hear a story every night.

Mr. and Mrs. Pistal are getting their money's worth. Momma doesn't like to go to the Blue Gardenia Lounge, but even she couldn't resist seeing Pegleg Johnson's act last week. He was wonderful.

There was a singer on the bill named Ray Layne and he was good, too. You should have seen Momma's face when Pegleg Johnson came over to the table after his act and asked her to dance. She looked so funny. They danced to "Dance, Ballerina, Dance" by Nat King Cole. They did twirls and dips and everything. He picked Momma over everyone in the room!

I wondered if the leg that Kay Bob Benson's mother found washed up on the beach was Pegleg Johnson's. Momma said for me to hush. She was sure it wasn't, but I think maybe it was. It's too bad they didn't save it so he could see. I wanted to ask him where he lost his leg, but Momma said she would kill me if I did, it's not the sort of thing you ask.

That singer, Ray Layne, came over to the table and sat with us for a while. He is real lonesome, being down here by himself. I found out he is only seventeen years old and he's from Hattiesburg.

Momma likes Mrs. Pistal a lot, but she's never going back to that place because there were sleazy people there, lounge lizards she called them. Claude Pistal and all his friends looked like criminals to her. I didn't tell her that those were the men I had played poker with.

The next day that boy Ray Layne, the singer up at the Blue Gardenia Lounge, came to the malt shop and asked Daddy if he could see me. Daddy came and got me out from under the house where I was digging tunnels.

He asked me if I could go swimming with him and I said sure.

He is so handsome and has curly hair. He has a girlfriend named Ann who wears glasses. He has gone with her for a long time and misses her. I sure wish he was my boyfriend. I would never let him go anywhere without me. I think he is wonderful and the best singer I have ever heard in my whole entire life.

And guess what? He kissed me good-bye and said he had enjoyed meeting me! He should be a movie star, a real Rory Calhoun type. Momma has got to get my tooth fixed.

The Kowboskis are here with their carnival. There are seven of them and two are my age. They have a big school bus they live in, that is better than Roy Grimmett's trailer. At the carnival they have a penny arcade and a Ferris wheel and a machine that takes your picture four times for a quarter, and they sell cotton candy and caramel apples. Momma told me never to eat any candied apples because those carnival people buy rotten apples and put candy on them. I know I shouldn't eat them, but I can't help myself. However, I do make it a point to look for worms.

Mr. Kowboski lets me sweep out the penny arcade anytime I want to and be the money changer. It's great over there! Music plays all the time, and you can hear it over at our place. I like them very much even if they are Gypsies. I don't believe they steal children, but I wouldn't care if they did steal me. It would be fun to live in that bus. Michael comes over sometimes and we ride the Ferris wheel. You can see the whole beach from way up there.

Kay Bob Benson came once, but she got scared when I rocked the seat and she won't go back on the Ferris wheel for nothing.

Billy Bundy, that radio preacher, finally brought me a picture of Sue Sweetwater, who has a radio show on WHEP. She signed it "To Dottie Fay," so how can I show it to anyone?

Billy Bundy is a funny preacher if you ask me. Daddy and I see him almost every day in the back room of the Bon Ton Café, the only place he can get alcohol after church. He comes in and sits down at a table all by himself and orders his drinks. Then he takes out his red plastic letter opener and opens all the money envelopes he gets from the Christians that listen to his radio show and stacks the money up in neat little piles all over the table. Every once in a while you can hear him say, "Praise the

Lord," when he gets a $20 bill. Ten-dollar bills only get a "Bless you, brother." Five-dollar bills get a "Thank you, sinner" and a dollar just gets "Every little bit helps." Once he got a $50 bill and he said, "Hallelujah, Jesus!" real loud. But mostly he gets fives and tens.

July 21, 1952

A terrible thing happened. The malt shop fell three feet and is sticking up in the air on the right side! I ruined the foundation by digging so many tunnels. It happened overnight. Daddy noticed it because all his hamburger patties kept sliding off the grill into the french fries. I didn't mean to do it. If you ask me, this place is cheaply built. I hope my mother doesn't notice what I did when she comes back from Jackson. I told Daddy I wouldn't tell her that he has been drinking if he doesn't tell her the malt shop fell.

He had to build a ledge on the grill so the eggs and hamburgers don't slide off into the french fry grease. Other than that, I don't think it is too noticeable. I'll be glad when Momma gets back because Daddy is in a bad mood.

Daddy went with Hank when he got married to be Hank's best man. Daddy said the wedding was sad. It took place in an office and the bride didn't wear a wedding gown, just a suit with a mum corsage. There wasn't even a honeymoon. Hank came to work the next day and didn't look any different. Daddy gave him $50 and I gave them some shell napkin holders and some oyster shell ashtrays I had made at Jr. Debutantes.

The wedding was written up in "Dashes from Dot." So was the fact that the Harper's Malt Shop is all cattywampus, but Mrs.

Dot saved my hide by writing it had been a natural act of God that caused it. I think she didn't want to print the fact that a Jr. Debutante had dug tunnels under the house, what with her liking us to be social and all.

Michael has been reading Mickey Spillane's book *Kiss Me, Deadly* and thinks he's big stuff. He says it's only for boys and adults. I read it last year and it's not all that hot.

The only good thing that happened is the woman who was going to talk to the Jr. Debutantes on accessories got sick, so we sang "Row, Row, Row Your Boat" instead. Mrs. Dot's thought for the day was: "Remember if people talk behind your back, it only means you are two steps ahead!"

Daddy and Jimmy Snow have been on a drunk the whole time Momma has been gone and poor Hank is running the malt shop by himself.

Jimmy is drinking because his girlfriend, Iris Ann Moody, who he has been engaged to for eight years, is marrying someone else. I don't know what Daddy's excuse is.

Mrs. Dot must have found out that Daddy was drinking because she wanted me to go stay with her, but I told her I was fine. I like her very much, but I can't stand her husband. He is mean to her and insults her in front of people all the time. I'm glad my hot fudge sundae went down his back.

July 30, 1952

Momma's home from Jackson and the first thing Velveeta did was tell her I had caused the malt shop to fall. She also told on Daddy. When he came in drunk, Momma was so mad she socked him all over the back room. Every time he would get up, she would hit him again, but she did turn the lights off so that the neighbors couldn't look in.

I could only see shadows and hear them. It was like watching *Flamingo Road* with Joan Crawford. During the whole fight the carnival music was playing a real nice song, "Give Me a Kiss to Build a Dream On."

Momma was accusing him of fooling around with a roller derby woman. When she broke the phone over his head and he started to bleed, she got scared and made me run over to the Romeos and call the doctor. He came and said Daddy was all right, but we would have to order another phone. He said to Momma, "Fay, you better be careful. If he had been sober, you would have killed him."

Momma is being real sweet to Daddy because I think she was afraid she might have killed him. I would have been the daughter of a famous murderess, and when she went to the electric chair, I would have been an orphan and everyone would feel sorry for me.

I guess I could get a job and live in a hotel and wear black, but I would be marked for life. I would rather be a shut-in, like Jessie, only I want a better disease than elephantiasis. All of this trouble began because Velveeta is a squealer. She should see what James Cagney does to squealers.

Grandma is fine. She has already started having bingo parties at her house again. Momma is disgusted with her because she won't give up her Camels. She said she would die anyway if she couldn't smoke her Camels and play bingo.

Grandma has some old man as a boyfriend and Momma thinks she is going to get married again. According to Momma, he is so decrepit he can hardly stand up and Grandma is acting like a silly, old woman. The only problem is that she can't find my real granddaddy so she can get a divorce. Grandma is trying to have him declared legally dead because it's been nine years that the Bureau of Missing Persons have been looking for him and they gave up. If Grandpa isn't dead, he sure is going to be mad when he finds out he is dead in the eyes of the law.

Grandma sent me a letter and said for me not to worry about her but to be sweet to my momma because she thought Momma was headed for a complete and full nervous breakdown and no wonder, being married to that little worm, Bill Harper. She also sent me a head scarf with the map of Mississippi on it.

The biggest news around here, besides my daddy getting his head busted, is that I am a real bona fide hero. I may get a medal from the VFW. Last Sunday, Michael and Angel and I decided to go fishing in the lagoon. We were sitting in the boat, fishing for toadfish so we could blow them up and hang them in our rooms when all of a sudden Michael hooked something on his rod and his hair stood up on end. He started hollering and jerked the biggest, blackest snake I've ever seen right into the boat. As soon as that snake hit the boat, all three of us jumped out into the lagoon. I was so busy yelling at Michael for pulling a snake in the boat I must have forgotten I didn't know how to swim because I made it to shore in NO time. When Michael got there, we looked around and Angel wasn't anywhere in sight. Then I remembered she couldn't swim either. I was so scared at having to tell her momma and daddy their little girl had drowned that I jumped back in the water.

Michael and I were diving and looking for her, but we couldn't find her anywhere. Finally I saw her standing on the bottom of the lagoon, and I dove down and went under her and grabbed her feet and pushed her straight up in the air so her head would stick out of the water.

I was standing on the bottom and sinking fast, knee-deep in the mud. Michael saw the top of her head and grabbed her by the ear just in time. When I tried to get back to the top, I was stuck in the mud and couldn't move. Michael was so busy saving Angel he forgot about me. Some junior lifeguard he is!

I thought I'd just have to go ahead and drown at an early age, but then I remembered that black snake. When it hit me that some more of them might be in the water, I must have got the strength of a hundred, because I got loose and saved my own life.

Angel was real sick. I never saw somebody throw up so much in my life, and we had leeches all over us just like Humphrey Bogart in *African Queen*. Ugh! We took Angel back up to the Blue Gardenia Lounge and told her momma and daddy what had happened.

Claude wasn't there, thank goodness. He's crazy about Angel. He probably would have killed Michael and me for almost getting her drowned. Mr. and Mrs. Pistal hugged her and were so glad she was all right that it didn't seem to matter I could have been drowned myself.

Michael and I took Mr. Pistal and showed him that black snake. And guess what? It wasn't a snake at all. It was a big electric eel. That was why Michael's hair had stood up on his head.

Mr. Pistal took me home and told Momma and Daddy I had saved Angel's life and he would never forget what I had done. Momma and Daddy acted proud of me in front of him, but when he had left, Momma pinched me real hard and wanted to know what in the world I was doing, jumping in the water like that when I couldn't even swim. She was about to hit me when Daddy said, "Well, Fay, she can swim; she isn't drowned, is she?" He had a good point. So we finally did prove Daddy's theory that small children can swim if they are scared enough. Daddy is happy about the whole thing because he put that dead electric eel in the ice cream freezer and is going to stuff it in the fall.

At the Jr. Debutantes' meeting I had to stand up and tell how I had saved Angel's life. After I was finished, one of those shrimpers' daughters made a snoot at me. Creep. Mrs. Dot said that I was a natural-born storyteller and very brave on top of that. She is going to put it in her "Dashes from Dot" column.

I guess I should have told them Michael had been there, too. Oh, well, I don't think he reads the paper anyway. Mrs. Dot's thought for the day was about snakes in honor of my story. She said, "Never be rude to a rattlesnake because he is the gentleman of the snake world. He always announces his comings and goings with a rattle."

I want to go to Magnolia Springs and see the double feature that is playing there now. Listen to this ad:

"THE COMMIE NAZI SHOW" . . . HITLER'S CAPTIVE WOMEN AND SLAVES OF THE SOVIET, FILMED IN MOSCOW. ALL WOMEN MUST SERVE THE STATE. FACTS ABOUT THE STATE CONTROL OF LOVE, PAGAN BIRTH RIGHTS, DEPUTY HUSBANDS, TORTURE FOR GIRLS THAT REBEL, DEGRADING AND SINFUL.

and the other film that is playing is called *Prehistoric Women
. . . They Feared No Beast, Only the Beast in Man*. I can't wait.
Mr. Honeywell and his all-girl army are taking me as a reward
for being a hero. Mr. Honeywell believes that this double feature
is something that every American woman should see.

Jimmy Snow got put in jail for crashing his plane into his old
girlfriend's house and waking her up. We went to see him and
he seems right at home. The policemen like him a lot and give
him beer and everything. I found out from one of those policemen that Jimmy Snow is a war hero for shooting down Japanese
planes. Daddy told me that's why he drinks so much, he misses
the war.

Jimmy was raised in an orphanage in Tennessee and doesn't
know who his parents are. I can't get over him having snow
white hair and eyebrows when he isn't even that old. He may
have been scared real bad once or else he could have albino
blood, like Ula Sour, and not even know it! But I'm not telling
him!

August 3, 1952

Guess what? Hank and Tommie Jo are going to have a baby.
I hope it's a girl. If it is, they should name it Claudette after
Claudette Colbert.

I wrote and told her that I thought she was wonderful in *The
Egg and I*. I haven't received an answer yet, but as you know, she
is one of the busiest film stars in Hollywood. If it's a boy, they
should just call it Hank, Jr.

I don't go out much anymore. I had my feelings hurt real bad.
I was over at the Kowboskis' carnival, sweeping out the penny

arcade for Mr. Kowboski, when one of his daughters came in and told me to go home, that I didn't belong there, the carnival was a family business.

Then she hit me, so I hit her back, and all of those kids jumped on me at once. Big families really stick together. Mr. Kowboski got them off and took me for a long walk. He told me not to feel bad. They were just jealous because I was an only child and didn't live in a school bus. And I shouldn't cry because I don't fit in anywhere. That is what is going to make me special and it will all work out OK someday.

I went to see the movie about the Communists. Boy, I don't ever want to be one of those. Daddy and Mr. Honeywell are having a fight because Daddy thinks Mr. McCarthy, the Commie fighter, is wrong, but Mr. Honeywell says he is right to get all those Reds out of the country. After seeing that movie, I agree with Mr. Honeywell. Besides, I sure don't want to stand in line forever to buy my groceries. I want to be rich, but I will be a good rich person.

I'm in charge of the friendship basket for the Jr. Debutantes. I am going around all over Shell Beach and getting everyone to put stuff in it for the poor. I wonder who these poor people are. I never get to see them. I wanted to take that friendship basket up to the colored quarters and get them to put things in it and at the same time try and see if I couldn't find that albino woman, Ula Sour. It would have been a perfect excuse to knock on all the doors, but Momma wouldn't let me. She said the colored people don't want to be bothered with a Jr. Debutante and besides, they need everything they have. But I did ask Peachy Wigham to contribute. She gave me a bottle of Thunderbird wine. Peachy won't tell me where that albino woman lives for nothing.

We got a letter from that little girl we adopted in South America and she writes letters better than I do. I think someone else wrote that letter. I can't write in South American, so how come she can write in American? It's fishy to me.

Mrs. Dot's thought for the day was: "Sincerity is as valuable as radium."

Michael's mother is furious. For her birthday she got a pair of false teeth, uppers and lowers, and Mrs. Dot put it in her "Dashes from Dot" column. She didn't want anybody to know, but Mrs. Dot prints the news while it is still news, and anything else you hear is just plain gossip.

Everybody down here is upset as they can be and I know why. George Potlow, that man who runs the fishing pier, has a colored woman living with him. I heard Momma and Mrs. Romeo talking about it. They are afraid that because he was originally a Yankee, he might be married to her. I've seen her at that pier when I go up and kick all the fish back in the water. She's real shy and nice, not at all like Velveeta. I asked her about where the albino woman lives and she won't tell either. Velveeta stepped on a catfish and hasn't been to work for a week. I'll bet the catfish died!

Jimmy Snow is out of jail. He said he was going to take me crop-dusting with him, but he made the mistake of saying it in front of Velveeta. Momma and Velveeta are still thick as thieves. Momma likes her better than me or Daddy and we are white people.

I was in the malt shop the other night, washing dishes, when I discovered that if I stuck my head around the partition and the people in the place saw it was just a small child washing those dishes, they were very surprised.

Because of my theatrical background, I took advantage of this and pretended I was an orphan that the Harpers had stolen. I told those customers I had been washing dishes for three years and my hands were withering away. Since some of the people were friends of Momma and Daddy and knew I was kidding, I got great laughs, especially when I asked them to contact the men in charge of the child labor laws.

Momma saw me and wanted to know what in the world did I think I was doing, making such a racket. I guess I got carried away because I put a frying pan at the back of my head and made a halo and said, "Woman, dost thou not know that I must go about my father's business?" Jesus said it to His momma when she was bothering Him at the temple. I got a great laugh from everybody. Momma seemed to think it was funny, too, until the last person was out the door. Then she started after me. I tried to run, but I got cornered on the back porch that leads to where we live.

I was wedged in between the Coca-Cola boxes and couldn't move to the right or the left. She beat the living daylights out of me. Daddy kept saying to her, "Now, Fay, calm down." I embarrassed myself by pleading for mercy, a thing you never know you'll do until the time comes.

The boy Jesus didn't get smacked when He said it. Mary just went on home and let Him alone. You sure can't trust the Bible for guidance.

It came home to me that night that Momma has certainly lost her sense of humor. From now on, I plan to walk softly as far as Momma is concerned.

August 8, 1952

I found out I got ringworm from Felix. If it gets in my head, they will have to shave off my hair. I'll be bald just like Eisenhower, and I am a Democrat.

The doctor said it's one of the worst cases he's ever seen. Momma has to put purple medicine, called itch-me-not, all over me. I have purple circles everywhere.

That woman who is crazy over accessories finally came to the Jr. Debutantes' Club. You wouldn't believe it. Everybody was getting excited over a bunch of scarves and gloves and pearl collars. She said with the right accessories you can dress up any outfit. She had on a black dress and she kept adding pop beads and all kinds of things.

She thought it changed the way she looked, but it didn't. She said the well-dressed woman had a complete wardrobe of accessories for every occasion. At the end of her talk she set up shop and tried to sell us things.

I might have bought something from her, but Kay Bob Benson screamed, "She's got ringworm," and they wouldn't let me try anything on. That woman stayed away from me because I had white stuff on my face and purple rings all over me. I would liked to have had some pop beads, but you can't buy anything unless you try it on.

Kay Bob Benson won't get anywhere near me because she is afraid of getting ringworm in her hair and she is crazy about her hair. Her mother takes her to Magnolia Springs to Nita's Beauty Box every week and gets her hair fixed like Jane Powell's. She looks as much like Jane Powell as I look like the Queen of Sheba. I'm not invited to her stupid birthday party because of the ringworm, so just as I was leaving Jr. Debutantes, I went over when she wasn't looking and said, "Happy birthday," and gave her a big birthday kiss right on the face. She about squealed her head off and ran in the live bait store to the sink and scrubbed her whole head and ruined her Jane Powell hairdo.

Momma is going to make me send her a birthday present. I am going to find out what perfume has the most bobcat pee in it. Or maybe I could give her a jar of Daddy's hemorrhoid medicine with the rubber finger in it.

Mrs. Dot's thought for the day was: "Fashionable people never wear evening clothes in the daytime unless, of course, they are being buried."

August 13, 1952

Jessie LeGore, the fat boy on Cotton Bayou, died. He sent me a sweetheart pillow because I had made him laugh once. I wish I had gone back to see him. I could have told him some jokes or done my Mario Lanza impersonation. He never hurt anyone. I don't think anyone should have to die.

Sometimes in the middle of the night, I wake up and remember that I am going to have to die and it scares me so bad that I break out in a cold sweat and I go get in the bed with Momma and Daddy. Maybe by the time I grow up, they will find a cure for dying and I won't have to worry.

If anything happened to my momma or daddy, I couldn't stand it. I saw *Bambi* when I was five and when Bambi's mother got burned to death after she said, "Run, Bambi, run," I started screaming and crying so loud they had to take me out of the theater. I wouldn't let go of my mother for days. I can't think about that fire without getting sick to my stomach. If I do die, I hope it is the end of the world, so I won't be alone.

Connie said they couldn't get Jessie out of his room. He was so fat they had to tear the house apart, and it took fifteen men to pull him to his grave.

This sweetheart pillow is the first gift I ever got from a dead person. He must have known he was going to die, but he couldn't get up and run. I would run so fast that nothing would catch me. I believe you can outrun death. I don't even want to think what my momma and daddy would do if I died. Momma said I am the only reason she is living and if she didn't have me, she would take a gun and blow her brains out. She stays with Daddy just so I will have a father. If it wasn't for me, she would have left him a long time ago.

Daddy said he wouldn't want to live if anything happened to me. I take very good care of myself for that reason.

When I told Michael that Jessie had died, all he wanted to

know was how much did he weigh and how big was the grave. I don't think Michael ever saw *Bambi*.

August 16, 1952

You won't believe the act they have coming up at the Blue Gardenia Lounge after Pegleg Johnson. Her name is Tawney the Tassel Woman and her act is for adults only. She is billed as an exotic dancer and has played clubs in the French Quarter in New Orleans. I saw her picture. She must do a western dance because she had on a short cowgirl outfit.

I've got to see her act somehow, but I don't know how I'm going to arrange it after what happened the other night. I was standing around in the lobby of the lounge, talking to some of those poker men, waiting to get paid for taping Angel's ears back, when Claude Pistal came in and told me to get the hell away from there and quit hanging around. I answered back I was an employee and I wasn't leaving until I got paid. He called me a smart-ass brat and said if I didn't watch out, he would kick me in my little butt.

I told him if he so much as touched me, my daddy would beat him to a pulp. My momma would scratch his eyes out and if that wasn't enough, Hank, who was a runner-up in the Mr. Universe contest, would knock his head off. And if that didn't work, I would wait till he was asleep and stab him in the heart.

Harold Pistal came around the corner and stopped him from clobbering me. They had a big argument. Claude said if he finds me hanging around there again, he will wring my neck.

Harold led me inside his office and paid me and warned that I better not come up there anymore because his brother was pretty mean. Since Claude owns half the place, he gets his way. Harold asked me not to tell my daddy because ever since Claude's wife died, Claude's been crazy and might do anything.

I said, "Your brother has no manners and is ugly to boot."

Claude Pistal is a creep! He is lucky I'm reasonably mild-mannered like Clark Kent.

I got a ride up to the colored quarters and went in and had an Orange Crush with Peachy Wigham at the Elite Nightspot and told her how rotten Claude Pistal was. According to Peachy, he is so mean he would stick a knife in you and walk around you with it. What's more, he is nothing but white trash and mean as snake shit, and I asked her what had happened to Claude's wife and she told me that a lot of people down here think that he killed her himself. I was sorry I told him Daddy was going to beat him up after I heard that.

August 18, 1952

Michael and I went to the Magnolia Springs Theater and saw Johnny Sheffield, who plays Bomba, the Jungle Boy, in *Elephant Stampede, The Hidden City, On Panther Island.* He is great. I love his brown curly hair. My two favorites are Cornel Wilde and Johnny Sheffield. I hope I marry someone with curly hair. Michael has straight black hair. Too bad. The best thing was the theater announced a Coming Attraction for next month. They gave everybody there some ads to give out to get business. It says in big red letters;

HEY KIDS, COME TO THE SMILEY BURNETTE PICTURE PARTY . . .
IN PERSON, AT THE MAGNOLIA SPRINGS THEATER . . . DIRECT
FROM HOLLYWOOD, SMILEY BURNETTE, ROTUND COMIC OF THE
WESTERN SCREEN FAMED FOR HIS CLUMSY ANTICS.

There's a big picture of him and he is going to play an electric organ with a tone just like a huge pipe organ. And he's awarding a free pony to some lucky boy or girl! He's bringing a Hollywood photographer and every single boy or girl who comes to the show will have their picture taken with him free of charge. When he gets back to Hollywood, a group of judges will pick the picture they consider the most individual from an advertising point of view and the lucky boy or girl who is picked will receive free of charge a pony from Hollywood as payment for the use of their picture in Smiley Burnette's advertisement.

I know I am going to win that pony. Michael and I took as many of the ads as we could and hid them. We figure the fewer kids there, the better my chances will be. I paid Michael a dollar not to have his picture taken. He said OK. He didn't want a pony anyway.

I am going to make Momma take me to Nita's Beauty Box and get a good hairdo, but if my ringworm doesn't clear up, it might hurt my chances to win the pony.

Jimmy Snow thinks I have a real good chance and so does Hank. Momma believes I shouldn't get my hopes up, but she always says that, even about Christmas and I always get a lot of stuff. I am going to wear my swimsuit and my seersucker shirt. It might be bad luck to change outfits. Grandma Pettibone wears her lucky polka-dotted dress for the big bingo parties. She says you have to pull for things. I am going to take at least an hour a day and just sit and pull for this pony. They could even take me to Hollywood. You can never tell about these things.

Johnny Sheffield might be a friend of Smiley Burnette's and see my picture and want to meet me. Mrs. Dot says I'm darling. So does Michael's mother. When Rose Mary Salvage comes across my picture in the Hollywood magazines, she is going to die!

Everybody says if you could have a cheeseburger and a malt anytime you wanted it, you would get tired of them, but that's not true. I've had about three cheeseburgers and two chocolate malts every day and still like them.

The only thing bad about it is I don't meet as many people as I thought I would. Most of the tourists stay a week and just as you get to know them, they leave.

I miss Lassie very much and I have to hide Felix in the dirty clothes basket whenever the man from the health board comes. It is against the law to have an animal living where you serve food, particularly one with ringworm.

Daddy has to sit on the ice cream freezer where all the dead animals are so the health inspector won't look in it, but I don't think they have any germs.

Everybody is still very busy. Michael is going to go with me to see Tawney the Tassel Woman next week.

Mrs. Dot let me help her with the women's club plastic sale. Other than that, life is pretty dull. I can't wait for Smiley Burnette to get to town.

Michael and I went up there yesterday and saw an old movie, *Test Pilot*, with Clark Gable and Spencer Tracy. I hated it. Clark Gable and Spencer Tracy were friends and they went everywhere and flew planes. Myrna Loy, Clark Gable's wife, sat at home and waited and didn't do anything except at the end of the movie when she had a little boy. Every time they have somebody born in the movies, it is a little boy. They never have little girls being born. What makes boys so great and woooonnnderfullll? I can do anything a boy can do. I can even beat up Michael. It must be terrible to be born a girl and know that your daddy really wanted a little boy.

I just got back from a trip to Florida and Jackson. Grandma Pettibone called Momma in the middle of the night. She and that old man had eloped and gone to Florida. They hadn't been there one night on their honeymoon when he got sick. So Momma had to go take them home to Jackson. She didn't want to leave me behind because she knew Daddy would get drunk with Billy Bundy and Jimmy Snow while she was gone.

When we got there, Grandma was waiting for us at the door. The first thing she said was: "I should have known better than to marry some old man." We took the Greyhound bus to Jackson.

Those seats are rough and made the back of my legs raw. Momma said to Grandma, "How could you marry again when you don't know if Grandpa is dead or not? What if he shows up and they put it in the paper that you have two husbands?"

Grandma thought about it for awhile and then she said, "I'd rather have two husbands than be married to one little worm!" I told you Momma never could get anywhere with Grandma.

When we got home from Jackson, Daddy was sober as a judge, but he did smell like Listerine and was taking a lot of B.C. headache powders.

Roy Grimmett's wife, Mava, had her sister come to the trailer and live with them. Her name is Edna and she is beautiful, a real Betty Grable type. She likes me very much. She was married to a sailor and he got killed and she is going to have a baby. Isn't that sad? She works at the archery range and has a real big bust, too. I think she must be lonesome because she lets me spend a lot of time with her.

Tonight, after Michael gets off work, he and I are going down to the Blue Gardenia Lounge and see Tawney the Tassel Woman.

We talked about the Smiley Burnette picture contest coming up and he has a great idea. We can take that pony all around and let children sit on it and take their picture and charge them a dollar. Michael has a camera. The only thing I was wondering is if that pony came with a saddle. I would think so, all the way from Hollywood.

August 23, 1952

Last night Michael and I walked up to the Blue Gardenia Lounge the back way and snuck around the side of the building and waited for the ten o'clock show. I didn't want to run into Claude Pistal again.

We waited and waited and finally, we heard the band start up. We stood on the wooden Coca-Cola boxes we had brought and had a good view of the stage from the window. Michael was so excited he had to run around to the back and go to the bathroom. Aren't boys lucky? Every time I have to go to the bathroom, the sand fleas get me bad.

Pretty soon Tawney the Tassel Woman came on and do you know what? She isn't even a dancer at all. She had two tassels on her brassiere and one down below. She started shaking around. She got one tassel going one way and the other one going the other way. The one down below was going a different way. Michael's eyes about popped out of his head. I don't know how she did it. Then they put out all the lights and put a blue spotlight on her and she just walked around and bent over and shook herself at the audience.

Tawney's a lot older than her picture and her hair is the color of a carrot. She must have gone crazy over her applause because she took off her top right there in front of everybody.

I thought Michael was going to faint, but she had another little brassiere on underneath. Then, just as she was starting to take off her bottom, I heard someone coming around the back, cussing up a blue streak. It scared me so bad I fell off my box and pulled Michael down with me.

We made such a racket I was sure we were goners. Whoever it was got closer and closer and was cussing louder and louder.

We were under the bushes and all we could see were feet. He got right in front of us and guess who it was? It was Pegleg Johnson. I recognized his leg. He was carrying a suitcase and he was mad as hell because his pegleg kept sinking into the sand.

He cussed up a storm and threw his suitcase down and started back around the building where he had come from. I told Michael we better get out of there fast because he might go and get Claude Pistal and I wasn't taking any chances.

We ran as fast as we could. Michael is still mad at me because I made him miss the end of the act. Grandma is right. She says all men are fools over women. The more I think about it, the more I am convinced that Tawney had little motors in her brassiere. A real fake!

August 26, 1952

Velveeta told Momma I was at the Blue Gardenia Lounge and had seen Tawney the Tassel Woman. Nobody in the world knew that but Michael and he wouldn't tell for nothing because he would get into big trouble for being there himself. Besides, I made him swear not to tell on a statue of the Blessed Mother that the Romeos have in their front yard. Catholics never go against the Blessed Mother. She is very popular with them. Saint Joseph is nothing compared to her.

The point is I caught Velveeta red-handed. She has been

reading my papers. That is the only way she could have found out.

I told Daddy Velveeta had been into my private papers. He asked me what I write about so much. I told him just things that happen. He wanted to know if I ever put things in my papers about him and I said, "Oh, yes, it's mostly about you." So he went out and bought me a big tin box with a combination lock on it. I don't trust Velveeta as far as I could throw her. I didn't know colored people could read that well. People who say they are stupid are wrong. With my luck, Velveeta is probably a college graduate posing as a maid.

My momma has private papers. She should have locked them up. I looked in the top of the closet and found a lawyer's paper that told where my daddy was in a paternity suit. I know what that means, too. The woman that sued him was named Billie G. Thweatt. I hope it is true. If it is true, that means I have a brother or sister out there somewhere.

When I get to be on *This Is Your Life*, maybe they will come out from behind the curtain and surprise me. I'm dying to ask Daddy who Billie G. Thweatt is, but I am saving that name to use when I need it.

And bad news for the fish. George Potlow came over to the malt shop and told Momma and Daddy they would have to keep me from going on the pier and kicking the fish back in the water because the fishermen were getting mad.

I saved twenty-five whitefish and three croakers the other day.

Edna, Roy Grimmett's sister-in-law, and I are having a good time. We take walks and do a lot of things. She thinks I am real funny. I try to do everything to make her laugh. Momma says I am making a fool out of myself, but Edna doesn't think so.

Roy Grimmett is making me mad. He is always trying to get Edna dates with sailors so she can get married again. I wish he would leave her alone. I could get a job and take care of her and that baby.

Daddy got his taxidermy kit in the mail from Wisconsin and a certificate. You should see it. It has every kind of eye you can imagine: deer eyes, rabbit eyes, fish eyes, but no eel eyes and no flamingo eyes. But he can use the rabbit eyes for the flamingo because they are nice and pink, and he can stuff the eel with its eyes closed.

Curtis Honeywell and his all-girl army traded in the bazooka and got a machine gun that really works. The other day they shot our window out by mistake. Momma says we are lucky we weren't all killed in our beds because Mr. Honeywell thinks Daddy is a Commie anyway.

We were in the "Dashes from Dot" column this week. It said, "As the end of the season approaches, it is no doubt that Harper's Malt Shop is the busiest place on the beach," and she was happy Little Daisy Fay Harper's ringworm is clearing up. Kay Bob Benson was in it, too. She was "Thrilled to receive a Madame Alexander walking doll from her grandparents for her birthday." She is a little old for dolls if you ask me.

I wonder how that crippled girl, Betty Caldwell, up at the Bon Secour, is doing. She liked the number painting I gave her. I am going to send her an oyster shell ashtray from Jr. Debutantes.

Poor Jimmy is heartbroken over Iris Ann Moody whose house he crashed into because she went and married someone else.

The other night Peachy Wigham called Daddy and said for him to come get Jimmy. He was sitting in the Flite Nightspot drunk and wouldn't go home and her customers don't like white people in their colored nightclub.

When we got there, Jimmy had passed out and Peachy had put him to bed in her back room. It took Daddy and two colored men to carry him to the car. The whole time I was back there where Peachy lived, I heard someone moving around in the other room. I tried to open the door, but it was locked.

Maybe Peachy has a boyfriend living with her. She isn't very pretty, but she is real rich. I bet her boyfriend is just after her money. She sells bootleg whiskey. Daddy says if there was ever anything you need, just ask Peachy. She can get it and will be happy to sell it to you.

Besides being real rich, she knows a secret about the white sheriff's daughter, so she never gets arrested like the other coloreds do.

Most of her money comes from the colored mortuary she owns, which is the only one in Harwin County. She even has a layaway plan.

August 28, 1952

I wish those two would make up their minds. One minute Momma hates Daddy and the next minute they both gang up on me. She tells me he is a no-good rotten father and I don't have to mind him. Then she gets friendly with him and ignores me. I never know what to think.

I have to go in their room to get to the bathroom and all I did was come in to go to the bathroom when both of them jumped on me. Daddy even hit me. It was in the middle of the afternoon and Daddy must be crazy because there isn't any door to knock on, except the screen door.

I didn't know they were taking a nap and besides, my mother didn't have any clothes on. I asked her what she was doing and she said she was showing Daddy her hysterectomy scar.

She lied to me. Daddy has too seen her naked. To hell with them!

I have checked and they don't have a girls' town where I could go and live at all, just a boys' town. Boys get all the attention!

August 29, 1952

Do you think that Ann Blyth has false teeth? The beauty operators up at Nita's Beauty Box do.

I had my hair fixed for the Smiley Burnette picture contest today. Earline, the one that did my hair, said that Ann Blyth had enough china in her mouth to set a table for ten.

The Beauty Box is decorated all in purple. They have purple leather chairs and all the operators wear purple uniforms with purple plastic name pins. The woman who owns the Beauty Box, Mrs. Nita Beaver, must be crazy over purple.

Edna took me there because Momma was working. They let me look in the movie magazines and pick out a hairdo, free of extra charge. I chose one that Lizabeth Scott wore in the movie *Dark City*.

My ears about burned off from sitting under that dryer. They didn't put enough cotton on them. Those bobby pins get red-hot and I still have marks on the back of my neck where they burned me. When Earline combed me out, she nearly killed me and broke some teeth in her comb. She said, "Girl, you've got hair like a horse's tail." According to Mrs. Dot, true aristocrats have hair as thin as a bee's wing, so I guess that lets me out. When she finished, Edna said it looked exactly like Lizabeth Scott's hair, but Daddy said I looked more like Betty Furness.

The hairdo cost me two dollars and a half, plus tip. Momma said I had to tip my operator. Only white trash don't tip. If it had been up to me, I wouldn't have given her anything for breaking a comb on my head.

I made a mistake because the Smiley Burnette picture contest isn't until tomorrow morning at ten o'clock and I am going to have to sit up all night. If I don't, I will mash my hairdo.

Earline told me Kay Bob Benson had made a special seven-thirty-in-the-morning appointment so her hairdo will be fresh for the picture with Smiley. I didn't know you could get an appointment at seven-thirty in the morning.

Dumb Michael has the measles and can't go at all, so I wasted that dollar I paid him not to have his picture taken. He said it was only fair because I made him miss Tawney the Tassel Woman's act. He's got a memory like an elephant.

Daddy and I have been working all week to fix my tooth for the picture. He got some white candle wax and glued a piece on with airplane glue so you would never know I had a chipped tooth.

I can't wait until tomorrow morning. I hope the saddle goes with it. Jimmy Snow is going to pick me up in his Henry J at nine and take me to the theater because Saturday is Momma's and Daddy's busy day and they can't leave.

August 30, 1952

I was out in front of the malt shop at eight o'clock this morning, ready to go. I waited and waited, but Jimmy Snow never showed up.

When it got to be ten o'clock, I started walking so if I met Jimmy on the highway, we could save some time.

I walked ten miles to Magnolia Springs, but he never came down that highway.

By the time I got to the theater, the wax had melted off my tooth. It didn't matter, though, because the movie had started and Smiley Burnette had already left.

I had to get a ride home with Kay Bob Benson and her mother. She never stopped talking about how it had been a real great show and how she was sure she was going to win that pony because all the other kids had been real ugly. I thought ugly is as ugly does. Maybe she will win the pony and I can ride it or something.

Jimmy Snow is in big trouble. Momma hopes he is dead because he will wish he was by the time she gets through with him, disappointing her little girl like that.

I am so sunburned from walking up the highway that I can hardly move. Maybe they will feel sorry for me and call Peachy Wigham and order a pony, but no luck so far.

August 31, 1952

Guess why Jimmy Snow didn't come and get me? He was in jail because he found out that Iris Ann Moody and her new husband were home from their honeymoon and he flew over their house and dumped DDT all over it.

It's amazing how he was able to hit their house and miss all the neighbors. We went to see it and it looked just like Christmas. Jimmy is a Champion Crop Duster.

The Kowboskis left today, so I went over and said good-bye. I am still mad, but I wanted to have my picture made in that machine for the last time. You get four pictures for a quarter and I had my pictures made thirty-two times, smiling and not smiling; but Michael stuck his face in four and ruined them. I am saving those pictures for *This Is Your Life*.

Hank is going to quit in two weeks and go to work for Tommie Jo's daddy for the winter. I sure will miss him, but he said he would come and see me.

Woooonnnnnnderfulllll Velveeta is going to leave. We can't afford to pay her after the season is over. Hooray!

School is getting ready to start. Momma doesn't want me to go to school in Magnolia Springs. It is too country. She wants me in Catholic boarding school and talks about putting me in the Ursuline Academy in New Orleans.

We are going to New Orleans and take a look at the school pretty soon. Momma hired an accountant to go over the books and tell us how much money we made. His name is Mr. Lilly and he has one hand missing, but instead of having a hook, like Harold Russell in *The Best Years of Our Lives*, he's got a rubber hand that looks just like a baby doll hand.

Momma is mad at me because I keep looking at it, but I can't help myself. He keeps it in his lap most of the time, though.

I wonder where he got that hand. It must have come off a big doll. The fingers are stuck together and it is yellow. What if someone went to shake hands with him and it came off, or if he left it on a restaurant table by mistake?

September 2, 1952

Momma is mad at me. I pulled the bathroom mirror off the wall in that cheap motel we stayed at in New Orleans. It wasn't my fault. It looked like a medicine cabinet to me and I wanted to see if anybody had left anything. Momma's afraid we are going to have seven years' bad luck because of it.

When we got home, Mr. Lilly told Momma we hadn't made any money. We are in debt. Daddy spent a lot buying that liquor license. We used ice cream in the malts, instead of malt base like we were supposed to, and Daddy hadn't mixed his hamburger with bread the way everyone else does.

He believes Quality is better than Quantity, but in this case, we are in a lot of trouble. We have a big payment in November and no money. The minute I broke that mirror, Momma knew everything was going to turn out bad.

She is doubly mad because when we were in New Orleans, she bought my uniforms for the school and now I can't afford to go. I guess I will have to wear a blue skirt and a white blouse for the rest of my natural life.

I'm glad I'm not going to that school in New Orleans. The mother superior said my roommate would be a nice girl from Colombia, South America. I sure didn't want to be roommates with a headhunter.

Now I will get to ride the school bus with Michael. Kay Bob Benson's mother takes her to school. Of course!

When I got back from New Orleans, the first thing I did was go and look for Edna, but she was out with some sailor who wants to marry her. When she came home, she told me that she had decided to accept his offer. She feels she should get married again, so her child can have a father. I don't want her to marry him. He is a Yankee. I asked her why she couldn't stay here with us, but she said she couldn't.

It's Roy Grimmett's fault. He pushed her into it. Now she is being friendly with Momma. I heard Momma say to her, "Mr. Harper and I did, up until the fifth month." I came over and said, "Did what?" And Momma said, "Danced." I know she's lying. She hates to dance with Daddy. I don't even want to think about it.

At Jr. Debutantes this week, Mrs. Dot gave a talk, "How to Handle Colored Help." She says beware of being too familiar and that everyone must know their place for a house to run smoothly and a well-bred colored person doesn't want to mix. It is only the ill-bred coloreds that try to be friendly. You must always be properly dressed when a colored man is on your property so as not to drive him crazy, and if a colored man is within two blocks of your home and can see in the window, you must put a robe on at once.

It is our Christian duty to see that colored help get all our old clothes and anything else you want to give them, but never anything new except at Christmas and never, never, under the threat of death, say the word, and she spelled it out, "N-I-G-G-E-R." Only white trash calls them that. I never said that word but once. It doesn't count, though, because Velveeta didn't hear me.

It's all right to touch or hug a colored woman, but never a colored man. Most important, though, never sit and eat at the same table with them. They don't like it and you must give them their own jelly glass to drink out of. Colored people don't respect you unless you respect their right to privacy.

I wish Momma could have heard that talk. Velveeta drinks out of any glass she wants to and sits down at the table with Momma and everything. Momma better watch out. Velveeta won't respect her if she keeps this up. I never knew that white people weren't supposed to drink out of a jelly glass. I have a Welch's grape jelly glass I drink out of all the time.

Mrs. Dot's thought for the day was: "Good manners are your round-trip ticket to the world."

September 4, 1952

Roy Grimmett is a liar and I hate his guts. I hope he shoots himself in the heart with his own bow and arrow and if he asked me to pull the arrow out and save him, I wouldn't. I hope he gets locked in his trailer and freezes to death, or it falls off a cliff with him in it. I wish I had that machine gun that the Mississippi Maidens have. I would shoot him full of holes and pour acid on them.

He and Mava were taking Edna to Pensacola to get her married today. She started to cry and I know she didn't want to go.

Roy came back from the wedding about six o'clock and was laughing his head off. He threw Edna's old wedding ring on the counter and asked if anybody wanted to buy it. He said he bought her that ring himself. She never did have a husband in the first place; she was just some dumb old country gal that got herself in trouble and he was glad he finally got her married off.

I threw my cheeseburger and fries at him and told him he was a dirty liar and lower than snake shit.

Momma said how dare he say something like that in front of me and took me in the back room. She also said she was shocked at my language. Daddy came and put a cold rag on my head and said I might as well know the truth. Edna never was married. They had known it all along. Momma started shaking her head and said no that Daddy was wrong. She had been married. Then they got into an argument. Daddy was stupid enough to believe Roy against Edna. Men always stick together.

They went outside and screamed at each other for a while and then Daddy brought me some orange juice, which I threw up. I don't know why he always brings me orange juice when I'm upset. I hate orange juice. I would rather have a malt. Daddy told me he had talked it over with Mother and she was right. Roy Grimmett was a liar. Roy said those things just to be a big shot. I knew it.

CREEP . . . CREEP . . . CREEP . . . SNAKE SHIT . . . CREEP.

September 6, 1952

I got a letter from Roy Grimmett today, telling me he was sorry he lied to me and that Edna had too been married. As a matter of fact, her dead husband was a war hero, like Jimmy

Snow. So there. I'll bet it killed him to have to write that letter. I still hate him and on top of that, he writes just like my mother, real little with curlycues. I write exactly like my daddy. We have the same color of blue eyes and the same color hair. We could be identical twins if we were the same age.

Momma says I am beginning to act more and more like him every day in every way. I was sweet when I was little, but when Daddy came home from the war, he played too rough with me and turned me into a tomboy. What's so bad about that? I can't stand sissy girls for nothing. The initials K.B.B. come to my mind.

School doesn't start until the middle of September because most of the kids that go to school at Magnolia Springs live on potato farms and have to help pick potatoes. Just think, I'll be socializing with shrimpers' daughters and potato farmers.

Mr. Romeo said Shell Beach is deserted after Labor Day. I can't wait. I am tired of tourists with mean children. Speaking of mean, I am so mad at Felix I don't know what to do. She chewed all the yellow fringe off the sweetheart pillow that Jessie LeGore left me. My one and only inheritance is ruined. I guess she is just bored.

Daddy and I are excited because the Big Speckled Trout Rodeo Contest is next week and he and I are going to enter and we are going to win. I know that for a fact.

Daddy already bought the winning fish off of Harvey Underwood a month ago and put it in the freezer. He told Momma it was a fish, he was going to stuff later on this year. It weighs twelve pounds and two ounces. I don't see how anybody could catch a fish bigger than that. The all-time record holder weighed thirteen pounds and that was six years ago. Our chances are excellent!

The person, us, who catches the biggest speckled trout during three days of fishing wins first prize and first prize is an Evinrude outboard motor, valued at $146.90 and second prize is a Ply-Flex fishing rod valued at $36. Now all we need is a boat to go with it!

September 13, 1952

Boy, wait till you hear this. I have some top-secret information about Kay Bob Benson. Momma and Mrs. Romeo get together every day for coffee and talk, talk, talk. Today I just happened to be under the window when Mrs. Romeo told Momma that the reason Kay Bob Benson's mother spoils her so bad is because she is a special-order child.

When Mrs. Benson was forty years old and hadn't had a baby yet, she went to the doctor and found out she was fine and that something was the matter with Mr. Benson. She didn't have the nerve to tell him so, Mrs. Romeo said, Kay Bob Benson is an artificial incinerator child that Mrs. Benson got from a doctor in New Orleans! Since Mr. Benson has prostate trouble and she can't get another one without Mr. Benson being suspicious, Kay Bob is the only child she will ever have.

Mrs. Romeo was getting ready to tell Momma about some woman that Mrs. Dot's husband was running around with, but she slammed the window down before I could hear any more. Ha! I knew there was something funny about Kay Bob Benson!

September 15, 1952

Tomorrow is the last day of the Speckled Trout Rodeo and everything is going just as Daddy and I planned. We went down to the Speckled Trout Rodeo Headquarters the first day and registered early in the morning and headed on up to our spot on the river. Daddy made a big show of how he didn't expect to win, but thought it would be fun for his little girl since he had been so busy all summer and hadn't had a chance to spend any time with her. He made me paddle up and down the river for a while every day so people could see us fishing.

Then every day we went and napped and didn't even fish at all. I took my Red Ryder BB gun and shot at snakes. I ate candy and Daddy drank his beer and told me war stories. At five o'clock we would go back to the Speckled Trout Rodeo Headquarters at the live bait shop. Daddy would say, "Well, no luck today. Those fish just aren't biting," and act real disappointed to throw them off the track.

I got to wave at the crippled girl, Betty Caldwell, the first day we were there. She said, "Hey, Fay, how are you?"

I said, "Fine." Then her mother marched down to where we were and handed me the oyster ashtray that I'd sent Betty and told me she'd thank me not to send any more ashtrays because they don't drink or smoke and turned around and left. She could have used it for bobby pins or something. Bette Davis smokes. I don't see anything wrong with it.

While I was shooting my BB gun killing time, Daddy told me all about when he met Momma and how they would go out to the roadhouses and have fun. They went to one called the Silver Slipper and one called the Casa Loma and one called the Dew Drop Inn. Daddy's story of their romance is different than Momma's. He made it sound like she was after him to get married, but I know better. Daddy said he could have had any girl in Jackson, but he chose Momma because she was so shy. He went to pick her up one afternoon to take her on a date in his blue DeSoto convertible and didn't know she had burned her legs on the seat until she started to cry. She was too much of a lady to say anything. I know my momma is a lady. Everybody says so, but I don't think she is shy anymore.

We are going to take the winning speckled trout out of the freezer tonight before we go to bed so it will be good and thawed for tomorrow.

September 18, 1952

That trout was still frozen stiff as a board when we took it out of the freezer. So Daddy put it in a pan of boiling water and locked it in the trunk of the car. When we got up to the Speckled Trout Rodeo Headquarters, Daddy carried on some more how he had not caught one fish and how he hoped he caught something today. What kind of fisherman would his little girl think he was? We rowed up and down the river long enough for everyone to see us, just as we always did. Then we went back up to our spot and waited for that trout to thaw out. Daddy sure got his money's worth when he bought those freezers. About two o'clock in the afternoon the trout finally thawed, but putting it in the hot water had turned his eyes all cloudy. It didn't look like a fresh fish to me. Daddy didn't think so either and started cussing. Then he got an idea.

He said, "Don't move from this spot. If anybody comes up here, tell them I have gone to the bathroom." I sat there and waited and I tell you nothing smells worse than a dead trout.

About an hour later he came sneaking through the bushes and nearly scared me half to death. He had me drag the fish up to the bushes where he'd brought his whole taxidermy kit, right down to the artificial eyes, and some airplane glue. It took us forever, but we found some trout eyes. They were a little too big and the wrong color, but he said he didn't think the judges would notice. He cut the real eyes out of that trout and glued those plastic eyes in their place. We sat there and blew on them so they'd dry and at about four o'clock that fish started to look pretty good. The glue had dried funny, but Daddy said it made it appear like the trout had died terrified. I told you my daddy likes to see the bright side of things.

We were just getting ready to go when some old country man came by in a boat and saw us and yelled out, "I heard Emmet Weaverly caught a thirteen-pounder this morning." Our trout was only twelve pounds and two ounces. I thought Daddy was going to be sick. But he's a quick thinker. He grabbed my box of BBs and stuffed every one of them down that trout's throat. By the time we got to the headquarters, everyone had weighed in but us.

So far the winner was Emmet Weaverly's fish that weighed twelve pounds and eight ounces, not thirteen like that man had said.

When Daddy got in the room, do you know what he did? He handed me that trout and said, "Hey, folks, look what my little girl just caught."

I couldn't believe it. I said, "Oh, no, Daddy. You're the one who really caught it."

He said, "No, honey, you caught it. Run up there and have it weighed."

If looks could kill, he'd be deader than that fish with the plastic eyes. I knew what he was doing. He was acting like he really caught it, but he was letting his little girl get all the glory. I tried to hand it back to him, but by then everybody thought the idea was so cute they pushed me up to where the scales were. I put the fish down on the scales very carefully. I didn't want those plastic eyes making a noise if they hit anything.

Our trout weighed twelve pounds and nine ounces. I did some fast figuring in my head; that was seven ounces of BBs. Everybody started applauding and saying, "Bill Harper's little girl won." I looked around and there was Daddy, smiling, getting patted on the back, taking all the credit. Just then Mrs. Dot ran over and grabbed and kissed me and said how proud she was that a Jr. Debutante had won first prize and to come and have my picture taken for the paper.

I never took my eyes off the trout. Just as a judge was about to pick it up, I grabbed it in the nick of time. The official Speckled Trout Rodeo photographer started posing me for the picture for the paper. They said for me to hold it up by the tail and smile real big. It was hard to smile because if one of those plastic eyes fell out on the floor and they found out that fish had been dead for a month, I would go to jail. Mrs. Dot would die if one of her Jr. Debutantes became a jailbird. The more I thought about it, the worse it got. My heart started pounding and my lips began to tremble. I couldn't smile if my life depended on it. They made me stand there longer and said, "We're not going to let you go until you give us a big smile. So smile big, honey." My hands started to shake and that trout was shaking like crazy, too. I just knew those eyes were going to fall out. One had slipped a little anyway, but I needn't have worried about the eyes because at that moment the BBs started coming out of that trout's mouth one by one all over the floor. I was in a cold sweat, but you never saw anybody smile as big as I did.

I knew they had to get that picture fast! Mrs. Dot said, "Oh, look she caught a female fish, it's just full of caviar!" I sure was glad she didn't know the difference between BBs and caviar. Thank goodness Daddy came over and grabbed the fish out of my hand and turned it right side up and said, "I'm taking this trout home and stuffing it to make it into a trophy to donate to the Speckled Trout Rodeo as a gift." Everybody thought that was a fine idea, especially me. He said he had to get it home right away before the trout went bad.

Momma was waiting up for us. Daddy said, "Look what Daisy caught," and didn't even give her time to look at it good before he threw it back in the freezer. He told Momma not to open the freezer until at least twenty-four hours because it would ruin the trout if she did. She believed him. She was so proud of me for winning, it was all worth it.

Daddy won't have a hard time stuffing that fish. He's already got the eyes in.

You should have seen that picture they took of me. The first time I have my picture in the paper and I look awful, not like Celeste Holm at all. In the "Dashes from Dot" column, Mrs. Dot said, "Jr. Debutante Daisy Fay Harper is the champion fishing woman," and then she devoted the rest of the column to discussing the rules of etiquette for men and women while fishing. Did you know that a lady never baits her own hook?

My daddy has the outboard motor in the shack out by the side of the malt shop. He doesn't have a boat yet, so I don't know what good it is doing him. Momma and I want him to sell it. We need the money for the payment on the malt shop, but

Daddy says as soon as he starts stuffing his animals, he will have enough money to pay the note and buy a boat besides. Not one word about a pony. He's already started stuffing the electric eel.

Mr. Romeo was right about this place being deserted after Labor Day. There is not a single person down here anymore and most everybody has left for the winter except Michael and myself and the shrimpers' daughters. Kay Bob Benson has gone to visit her grandparents and to get another doll out of them, I guess.

September 21, 1952

Momma and Daddy went deep-sea fishing with Mr. and Mrs. Dot today, but I stayed home because they were afraid I would throw the fish back.

I was playing around by myself up by the highway when I saw a car parked a block up the road and there were two people in it, kissing and carrying on in broad daylight. Puke!

About an hour later they drove up to the malt shop and I went over to tell them we were closed. When I got there, guess who was in that car? CLAUDE PISTAL!!!! I almost fainted. He asked me where my momma and daddy were and I told him that they were right up the road and would be back any minute, which was a lie, they weren't coming back until six, but he must have forgotten he hated me because he asked me if I would let his friend Ruby use our bathroom. No wonder she had to go to the bathroom, that car was full of empty Jax beer cans.

When I helped her around the side of the malt shop and showed her the bathroom, she asked, "Whose little boy are you?"

I said, "I am a little girl" . . . she must have been really loaded, I have a ponytail and everything. She has long brown hair and isn't bad-looking, but she must be pretty hard up to go out with someone as ugly as Claude Pistal.

After she finished with the bathroom, she decided to comb her hair and put on some lipstick. I figure she's pretty rich because she had on the biggest, reddest ruby ring I have ever seen. I asked her if it was a real ruby and she said it was. She told me her name was Ruby Bates and she has a twin sister named Opal. Her daddy had given her that ruby ring and gave Opal a big opal ring when they were both twenty-one. Then she started crying over her daddy and said he had been the sweetest man that ever lived. I didn't know what to say, but she must be a little crazy because she stopped crying just as fast as she started. She did a terrible job of combing her hair and put her lipstick on all crooked. My mother applies her makeup perfectly.

Ruby asked me what my name was and I told her Daisy Fay Harper. She acted as though that was the funniest name she had ever heard and about laughed her head off. I told her it wasn't my fault that I was named after a vase of flowers that happened to be in my mother's room. I didn't have anything to do with it. When I got her back to the car, I told her, "Nice to meet you," and took off. I wasn't taking any chances with Claude Pistal. Now that I think about it I don't think being named after a vase of flowers is any funnier than being named after a ring!

September 22, 1952

Jimmy Snow came down to see us and Daddy had to tell him that he didn't have his half of the payment on the malt shop. Jimmy said that was OK, he didn't have his half either. He is a great guy. Momma is worried to death, but Daddy said he would figure out something.

He is busy stuffing that electric eel, but it has lumps all over it. Momma wants to know who in the world is going to buy an electric eel anyway. If Daddy can't get the eel right, he will start on the flamingo.

That preacher Billy Bundy came down and tried to sell Momma a religious sewing machine. Daddy asked Billy what made that sewing machine so religious and Billy said, "Because if you buy one, God will bless you." He's sold a lot of them over the radio, but Momma didn't want one and we can't afford it anyway.

Last week was the last meeting of the Jr. Debutantes for the season, and Mrs. Dot put in her "Dashes from Dot" column that an hour of Mexican folk dancing led by Corky King of the Corky King School of Dancing was enjoyed by all. This is false reporting. I didn't enjoy it one bit. Kay Bob Benson thought it was the grandest thing in the world. She claims she is Corky King's best student and that Corky King told her she could be a professional dancer when she grows up.

Do you know what Kay Bob Benson called me when I accidentally stepped in the middle of that big hat we were dancing on? A beach rat! I didn't say anything, but she was walking on a thin line. I could have called her an artificial incinerator, but I didn't. And as far as that stupid hat dance goes, what good is learning a foreign dance? Just how many times do you think we'll be going to Mexico anyway? Besides, I hate anything Spanish, especially Spanish mackerel. Momma and Daddy caught about 300 Spanish mackerel when they went deep-sea fishing. If I eat one more, I'll throw up.

I'm glad it was the last meeting. All Mrs. Dot does anymore is talk about when she was a girl. She has told us the story of her coming-out party in Memphis at least ten times. I always enjoy it, but the rest of the Jr. Debutantes are mean and laugh at her behind her back. When Momma and Daddy went fishing with Mrs. Dot and her husband, all Mr. Dot did was make fun of her all day until she started to cry. He's a jerk. She must be getting pretty upset because at the last meeting she didn't even have a thought for the day for us. She just told how happy she had been when she was a young girl, without a care in the world and going to party after party with so many nice young men. Then she looked at us kind of sad like and said "I wish someone could take all those days, hours and minutes and put them in an envelope and slip them back under my door."

September 30, 1952

School has started and am I glad. All Momma and Daddy do is Fight Fight Fight . . . I usually don't like school, but I am crazy about my teacher. Her name is Mrs. Sybil Underwood and she is beautiful, a real Gene Tierney type. And guess what? She is related by marriage to Mr. Roy Underwood, who raised the chicken with the ten toes.

The schoolwork is easy compared to the school I came from. These potato farmer children aren't as smart as the fifth grade in Jackson. I won't even have to do homework, but I am having a very hard time with shyness. Mrs. Underwood winked at me once and I turned so red that I had to put my head down on the desk. It's terrible to have light skin that shows when you blush. I don't know what's the matter with me. If she calls on me to read out loud, I think I will die.

I almost always know the answers to the questions, but I can't put my hand up at all. My arm gets as heavy as lead. People that put their hands up all the time are pushy and Yankeelike anyway.

Mrs. Underwood called Momma after the second day and asked her if I had always been so shy and Momma said no, I had never been that way before and that she and Daddy had had trouble with me the other way around. Mrs. Underwood is concerned that I'm not talking to the other children, but I would rather talk to her than them. I don't know anything about potatoes and shrimp and I don't want to.

It's still hot here. Kay Bob Benson's mother brought a big electric fan to the classroom the other day and turned it right on Kay Bob. I was nearly dying of the heat, but I wouldn't sit next to her if they paid me.

Michael got the surprise of his life this morning on the school bus. His momma packs him a lunch every day. He is such a pig that he starts eating it before we even get to school. This morning he took a hard-boiled egg out of his paper sack and broke it over his head, showing off the way he always does, but Michael's mother must have forgotten to boil it because the egg was raw and it ran all over him. On top of that, it was rotten. He had the funniest look on his face I've ever seen.

I went up to Mrs. Butts, the bus driver, and told her she better stop because Michael was sitting back there with a rotten egg on his head.

Mrs. Butts stopped the bus and made us open all the windows because it stunk so bad. Michael had to sit in the back of the bus while she drove him home. Everybody was late for school, but I didn't care. It was worth it just to see his face.

I went over to Michael's this afternoon because he never did come to school. He said by the time Mrs. Butts got him home, the egg had dried hard as a rock and his mother had to wash his hair eight times with Halo shampoo.

Daddy had to give up on stuffing the flamingo. The neck was too long and he couldn't get it to stand up right. He used a coat hanger and everything, but it still didn't work, so he is working on the bobcat that Jimmy Snow brought him.

October 21, 1952

I've been in school three weeks now, and I still can't look at Mrs. Underwood. I'm liable to get a double chin from looking down so much. She gave us a reading test and I made the highest score. I am only in the sixth grade and I am already reading at a ninth-grade level so I figure I can just coast until I hit the ninth grade.

Momma is mad at me. She doesn't pack me a lunch to take to school because she says it's very important children have a hot lunch, and since they have a cafeteria at school, she gives me lunch money. But someone with the initials K.B.B. told her mother, who told Mrs. Romeo, who told my mother that I was going over to the Pig and Whistle Barbecue Stand at lunchtime and getting me a barbecue and a Coke. First of all, this is a lie. I get cheeseburgers. Second of all, Mrs. Dot, who I admire, said she wouldn't be caught dead in any cafeteria ever since her uncle, Willis B. Crenshaw, choked to death on a catfish bone in the Red Star Cafeteria in Selma, Alabama, in 1936. And third of all, here is the menu for the school cafeteria for this week alone that they print in the Magnolia Springs paper. You be the judge.

MONDAY ....spaghetti and meatballs and ice cream
TUESDAY ....meat loaf, potato sticks, succotash and a peach half
WEDNESDAY ......cheese wiener, rice and gravy, buttered spinach, coconut pudding
THURSDAY ....tuna salad, pickled beets, macaroni and cheese and a banana
FRIDAY ....beef stew, snap beans and Jell-O

Puke.

Daddy finally finished stuffing that bobcat. It has a big smile on its face. Momma said nobody was going to buy a stuffed bobcat grinning from ear to ear and that's what Daddy gets for learning how to be a taxidermist through the mail. Momma is right. That bobcat doesn't look mean at all. In fact, it looks like it is tickled to death to be dead.

I don't know what is wrong with boys. I can play baseball as good as any of them, but they don't want girls to play with them. Up until the sixth grade, boys were nice. Now they are acting like jerks. All they do is giggle about Patsy Ruth Coggins wearing a training bra. You're never gonna catch me wearing a bra. Michael's mother said I should tell my momma to get me a bra, but I didn't.

I wish I had a black satin jacket from Japan. Amy Jo Snipes's brother sent her one from Korea. It has a dragon on it and everything.

Momma and Daddy stopped fighting over money and are now fighting over some woman she thinks he is running around with. Kay Bob Benson said her momma and daddy saw my daddy at some beer joint with a woman, but I don't believe it. Momma must have believed them because when he came home late the other night, she got the gun out and told him she was going to shoot him dead. He was on the back porch holding the screen door closed with all his might so she couldn't get out there and get a good aim at him. He was in a bad spot because if he ran, she would shoot him in the back, and if he stayed where he was, there was a chance she would shoot him through the screen door. He was between a rock and a hard place. He said for me to help him, so I ran in between him and Momma since she didn't want to shoot me.

She was mad as hell. She reared back and kicked the door so hard she knocked it clean off its hinges and Daddy was thrown eight feet out in the yard. She chased him all over that beach but never did catch him.

Mrs. Underwood took me aside at recess and said she heard my momma and daddy were having some trouble. I said it wasn't true, that everything was fine. Kay Bob Big Mouth Benson had better shut up! Anyway, Mrs. Underwood said anytime I wanted to talk to her, I could, I was her favorite sixth grader, and she wished I wouldn't put my head down on my desk so much. I knew all along I was her favorite. I don't have much competition in that class, but it sure makes me feel good to hear it.

Sometimes I think about the school catching fire and Mrs. Underwood being trapped inside the schoolroom. When I run in and drag her to safety, she is so happy she gives me a big kiss and a hug. I wish there was some way she could know I saved Angel Pistal's life without me having to bring it up. I tried to get Michael to tell her, but he won't. I guess it's just as well; to hear him talk he saved Angel and me at the same time and swam the English Channel to boot. That lagoon is only fifteen feet across.

I wish I had a Buick Super 8, Dyna Flow, with the holes on the side. I would take Mrs. Underwood for a ride.

October 27, 1952

Kay Bob Benson said to me today, "Don't you ever change your clothes? You have worn that same outfit every day since school started."

I told her, "Yes, I do change my clothes every day; it's just that I have a lot of white blouses and blue skirts that look alike." She was a pain in Jr. Debutantes and she's getting to be a bigger pain in school.

We are having a big sixth-grade Halloween party and you should have heard what those dumb sixth graders thought would be fun to look for on our Halloween scavenger hunt. My suggestion was the best. I wrote down "an albino," but Kay Bob Benson squealed out she knew that suggestion came from Daisy Fay Harper. The suggestions were supposed to be anonymous. Mrs. Underwood thought finding an albino would be too hard, but I told her one named Ula Sour was right up the street in the colored quarters. Even so, she didn't think it would be a good idea for us to be running around the colored quarters at night. Rat's foot! I'll bet some of those country kids could find that albino. My one big chance to see her ruined by you know who!

I think when I grow up, I am going to be a Republican. We had to vote on the Ten Best Items to Look For. Mrs. Underwood said it was the democratic thing to do. I could have given them ten great things to look for. Instead, we are going to look for things like a toothpick, a cigar butt, a powder puff and an empty lipstick case. Easy stuff like that.

I went to Elwood's Variety Store and bought my Halloween costume and it is terrific, a red devil suit with horns and a tail that stands up. The rubber pitchfork that came with it is not too good, but Jimmy Snow said he would bring me a real one.

Listen to this ad that was in the paper today:

HALLOWEEN NIGHT AT THE MAGNOLIA SPRINGS THEATER . . . COME ONE, COME ALL, SEE ONE OF THE SCARIEST STAGE SHOWS OF THE CENTURY. THE MAD DOCTORS' BLOODCURDLING VOODOO SHOW. THE MAD DOCTORS' VOODOO SHOW FEATURES BLOOD-SPATTERED THRILLS, SAID TO MAKE FRANKENSTEIN LOOK LIKE A SISSY. INHUMAN MONSTERS WILL RUN FOOTLOOSE THROUGH THE AUDIENCE. GHOSTS, GHOULS AND WEREWOLVES WILL LEAVE THE STAGE AND COME SIT WITH YOU.

YOU WILL SEE ONSTAGE IN PERSON GIRLS SACRIFICED TO IN-HUMAN CREATURES! HEADS CUT OFF WITH A BUZZ SAW! YOUR TONGUE MIGHT BE RIPPED OUT! VAMPIRE PEOPLE WHO DRINK YOUR BLOOD! MURDER BEFORE YOUR OWN EYES! WARNING . . . GIRLS SHOULD NOT COME ALONE! ALL SEATS . . . 50 CENTS. UNDERTAKERS AND GRAVEDIGGERS WILL BE ADMITTED FREE.

Too bad it is a white theater. Peachy Wigham could get in free because of her mortuary.

But I'm not going. Do you know why I am having to miss this show, probably the best show to ever come here as long as I live? Because when Mrs. Underwood asked the class if we would rather have the Halloween party the night before Halloween or on Halloween night, a certain party stood up and said, "Oh, no, Mrs. Underwood, it just wouldn't feel like a real Halloween party unless it was Halloween." I pointed out that there were some of us who might be interested in going trick or treating Halloween night or to a movie, and if we had the party the night before, we could kill two birds with one stone.

Mrs. Underwood said, "Let's have a vote. How many want it Halloween night?" Kay Bob Benson threw her hand up so fast it's a wonder it didn't fly out of its socket. And then all those potato farmer children and the shrimpers' daughters voted yes. Michael and I were the only ones that voted no. I'm going to get even with Miss Kay Bob Benson if it is the last thing I ever do.

As much as I would like to, I can't go to the Halloween show at the theater because I would disappoint Mrs. Underwood if I wasn't at the party. Besides, I have never seen her at night.

October 29, 1952

Today I put my plan in action!

I asked Mrs. Underwood if Michael and I could do a show at the Halloween party. She said, "What kind of show?" And I told her we wanted to do a house of horror. The customers would come in one at a time. She thought that was a fine idea, so Michael and I have been working on it all day.

He wanted to call it "The Hall of Blood and Guts, Enter If You Dare." I wanted to call it "The House of a Hundred Horrifying Horrendous Horrors," but Michael said, since we couldn't think of more than eight horrors, his title was better. I let him have his way because he is my partner in one of the all-time great revenges in the world.

Daddy made us a sign that says "HALL OF BLOOD AND GUTS . . . ENTER IF YOU DARE" and it is dripping with blood!

I've already written the script for the show. Michael and I are busy testing out the props. Daddy bought me an ugly rubber mask. I am going to be Madame Bodini, the ugliest woman that ever lived. Michael is to be my faithful assistant, Grondo the Gruesome. Someone will blindfold the customer and lead them into the HALL OF BLOOD AND GUTS . . . ENTER IF YOU DARE and I will say in a scary voice, "I AM THE FAMOUS MADAME BODINI, THE UGLIEST WOMAN IN THE WORLD. . . . YOU ARE BLINDFOLDED BECAUSE NO MORTAL CAN LOOK UPON MY FACE AND LIVE. . . . MY FACE IS GUARANTEED TO CAUSE HEART ATTACKS." Then I say, "WELCOME TO THE HALL OF BLOOD AND GUTS. . . . ENTER IF YOU DARE. . . . BE WARNED, THERE IS NO TURNING BACK. . . . YOU ENTER AT YOUR OWN RISK. . . . THE MANAGEMENT IS NOT RESPONSIBLE IF YOUR HAIR TURNS SNOW WHITE FROM FEAR, BUT WE WILL GIVE YOU A DISCOUNT ON HAIR DYE. FEEL THE HIDEOUS HUMP OF MY FAITHFUL ASSISTANT, GRONDO THE GRUESOME." The hump will be my sweetheart pillow, which Michael will have under his shirt.

After they move a step, I'll say, "YOU ARE NOW IN THE HALL OF BLOOD AND GUTS, ENTER IF YOU DARE, WHERE MONSTERS CHEW UP AND SPIT OUT SMALL CHILDREN." Michael will make growling and spitting noises and I will do a scary laugh. Then I say, "FEEL THE HEART OF A SMALL CHILD, STILL WARM, JUST RECENTLY RIPPED OUT." We are going to put a piece of raw liver in their hand. "DIP YOUR HAND INTO A BUCKET OF WARM BLOOD FROM THE SAME CHILD." Campbell's tomato soup in a bucket feels just like blood. "HERE IS THE EYEBALL OF A MAD FIEND WHO WENT SO CRAZY FROM FEAR WHEN HE LOOKED UPON THE HORRIBLE FACE OF MADAME BODINI THAT HIS EYEBALLS POPPED RIGHT OUT OF HIS SOCKETS. BE CAREFUL, WE ONLY HAVE ONE LEFT. I ATE THE OTHER ONE FOR BREAKFAST. YUM, YUM, GOOD TO THE LAST DROP." And I'll give them a peeled grape.

Then we are going to put this big rabbit's-foot key chain in their hand and say, "HERE IS A DEAD RAT WHO GRONDO JUST BIT

THE HEAD OFF OF AND IS CHEWING ON AT THIS VERY MINUTE." And Michael will make chewing noises and I will do my scary laugh again.

We will move them another step and I say, "AS YOU CONTINUE DOWN THE HALL OF BLOOD AND GUTS, ENTER IF YOU DARE, YOU ARE WALKING BY THE SPIDER WEB OF THE GIANT THREE-FOOT SPIDER, WHO, AS I AM TALKING, IS WALKING ON YOUR ARM, LOOKING FOR A PLACE TO BITE YOU." What will happen here is I drag a hairnet I got from Nita's Beauty Box over their face and Michael will put his mother's fox fur on their arm.

"HERE IS A DISH FULL OF WITCHES' MOLES THAT FELL OFF FROM FEAR." We haven't found anything that feels like moles yet, but we are still looking.

"STAND PERFECTLY STILL, THE FAMOUS WATCHDOG SNAKE OF MADAME BODINI IS CRAWLING UP YOUR ARM." We got five wieners and put two toothpicks at the end for teeth. We are going to wait until the night before and glue them together so it will be a long snake.

"AND NOW FOR THE ULTIMATE, ULTIMATE SUPERHORROR OF ALL TIMES . . . GET READY AND REMEMBER, THE MANAGEMENT IS NOT RESPONSIBLE FOR HEART ATTACKS . . . A HANDFUL OF WORMS AND MAGGOTS JUST TAKEN OUT OF THE STOMACH OF A PERSON WHO DIED OF THE BLACK PLAGUE." This is going to be the Kay Bob Benson special!

"CONGRATULATIONS. YOU ARE STILL ALIVE. BUT YOU HAVE NOT YET LOOKED UPON THE FACE OF THE HORRIBLE MADAME BODINI." Michael is going to pull their blindfolds off and I am going to shine a flashlight under my chin and scream. How about that! Pretty good, huh! It is going to be authentic. We are even going to have a hot plate in the room to keep the heart and blood warm.

Michael's mother is still mad at him, though, because when we were over at his house trying out things to use as blood, before we settled on Campbell's tomato soup, we tried out some beet juice, but it was too thin. Michael threw what was left of the beets and the juice in the toilet and a few minutes later Michael's mother went in and used the bathroom. After she was finished, we heard her scream for Michael to get his daddy quick, and she kept yelling, "Oh, my God," over and over. His daddy ran in there to her and began yelling, too. What had happened was Michael had forgotten to flush the toilet and she thought she was dying or something.

November 1, 1952

On Halloween, Daddy and Jimmy Snow came up to the school after class and made a great room out of blankets and quilts and put up the sign. It was nice and dark in there. We took all the horrors inside and got the hot plate ready to warm up the blood and the heart of the small child. I made Michael rehearse his part five times. I knew mine. Jimmy kept his word and got me a real pitchfork.

Daddy stopped by the Elite Nightspot and I picked up my packages I had ordered from Peachy Wigham. You can always depend on Peachy. She is a good businesswoman. I was in my devil costume by five o'clock and I couldn't sit down for two hours because I would ruin my tail if I did. Michael's mother took us to the party and I finally saw his costume, which he had been keeping a surprise. He went as a pirate with a black patch over his eye. Not very imaginative if you ask me. We had a hard time getting that pitchfork in the car, but we finally made it. I stood up in the back seat all the way to protect my tail. Since I'm pretty tall for my age, I had to lean over a little. Michael's mother drives as slow as a snail, and I thought we would never make it. When we got there, dumb Michael got so excited he couldn't wait for me to get my package and pitchfork out of the car. He slammed the door on my tail and ruined it before Mrs. Underwood even had a chance to look at it.

You should have seen the costumes those potato farmers' and shrimpers' children showed up in. If there was one ghost, there were a hundred. One stupid boy was dressed like a Pilgrim. There was a witch and a scarecrow and the little bald boy in my class, Vernon Mooseburger, came as a mean potato. Those people sure have potatoes on their mind.

Kay Bob Benson was the Good Fairy, in a costume made especially for her in Meridian. It took first prize, of course. What can you expect with a broken tail, but Mrs. Underwood told me I looked darling. She was beautiful in a blue sweater with her initials S.U. sewn on.

They had a grab bag set up for a nickel and I got a bat-the-ball paddle and a tin frog you can click that I swapped Michael for a set of jacks and some wax lips. He nearly drove everyone crazy clicking that thing all night.

We had popcorn and red and black licorice, which I hate. Mrs. Underwood had put up paper skeletons and black and orange crepe paper and black cats and witches all over the room. I bet she could be a professional decorator if she wanted to.

They had a big tin washtub full of apples for bobbing. I wouldn't get near it because Mrs. Dot had told us at Jr. Debutantes that her cousin had married a very wealthy banker from Mobile and at their wedding party he'd drowned accidentally while bobbing for apples. Just think, Mrs. Dot's cousin was a bride and a widow on the same day. Mrs. Dot won't touch an apple to this day.

When the other kids went out on the stupid scavenger hunt, Michael and I got ready to open up the HALL OF BLOOD AND GUTS . . . ENTER IF YOU DARE. We made the witches' moles out of corn candy that I had eaten the white tips off of, which is OK with me because that's the only part I like. We warmed the blood and the heart and waited for our first customer. Amy Jo Snipes was the hostess for the HALL OF BLOOD AND GUTS . . . ENTER IF YOU DARE . . . and was in charge of putting the blindfolds on. I used my scarf with the map of the state of Mississippi on it that I got from my grandmother for the blindfold. I told Amy Jo Snipes when Kay Bob Benson was coming through, she was to say, "Here Comes the Good Fairy," so I could get ready.

Our first customer was Herbert Holk. We about scared him to death. He squashed the eyeball and almost ruined it. After he got out, I told Michael when he made his chewing and spitting noises, not to spit on the customers because it was not sanitary. And I added to my speech, "BE CAREFUL NOT TO SQUEEZE THE EYEBALL." Michael looked scary because he went bobbing for apples with his eyepatch on and the black dye was all over one side of his face.

Our next customers went better. You should have seen their faces when I screamed at them at the end. We had a lot of customers, but we had to stop for an intermission because the blood got cold.

When I told Amy Jo Snipes we were ready to resume business, Michael, who was in charge of heating up the heart, got the liver so hot he dropped it. Vernon Mooseburger got cheated, and I like him. It took us forever to find that piece of liver. Have you ever tried to find a piece of liver in the dark? Then guess who our next customer was? I near about died. It was Mrs. Underwood. I was nervous and my voice didn't do right. And by that time the snake had turned into only one wiener—the rest had fallen off—and the witches' moles had all stuck together. I hope she didn't notice. She acted real scared, but I know she wasn't. And when Michael tried to pull the blindfold off, he couldn't reach her and he botched it up and she had to take it off herself. It ruined my timing, so I just said, "BOO." She must think I'm dumb.

Customers kept coming like sheep to the slaughter. One girl peed when I shined the flashlight on my face and screamed at her. I was getting worried, so I went to the edge of the entrance and said to the hostess, "Where is the Good Fairy?"

"The Good Fairy isn't coming," she said in her hostess voice. "Why not?" I said. She said, "I don't know. Your next customer is ready, Madame Bodini." I said, "Get in here." She said, "What?" and I said, "Get in here." Then I heard her say, "Wait here, I must go into the HOUSE OF BLOOD AND GUTS . . . ENTER IF YOU MUST for a talk with Madame Bodini." I forgot she didn't know my Madame Bodini face and she jumped three feet when she saw me. I told her to go and find out why the Good Fairy

wasn't coming. And I told her it's the HALL OF BLOOD AND GUTS
. . . ENTER IF YOU *DARE*, not ENTER IF YOU *MUST*.

She came back a few minutes later to say that the Good Fairy
thought the whole thing was silly and childish and all a fake.
She wasn't going to let two idiots get tomato soup on her specially
made Good Fairy costume. I instructed the hostess to go back
out and tell her we would skip the soup, but if she didn't get in
there, I would tell Mrs. Underwood she had cheated on her
arithmetic test, which she hadn't, she is as smart as a whip. Even
so, Kay Bob Benson knows I am Mrs. Underwood's favorite and
she might believe me. Pretty soon the hostess called out, "Here
comes the Good Fairy now," and in she came. I WAS READY FOR
HER.

The first thing she said was, "Daisy Fay Harper, your daddy's
a no-good, two-timing drunk and you're nothing but a beach
rat and if you so much as get one drop of anything on me, my
mother will see you pay for it." We made her feel the hump and
when we handed her the heart of the dead child, just recently
killed she acted like she was bored with the whole thing. She
said, "That's nothing but a piece of liver." We skipped the
bucket of blood; I am a person of my word. With the dead rat,
she said, "That's nothing but a rabbit's-foot key chain. I can
feel the chain." We should have taken that chain off. And as
she held the eyeball, she said, "This is a grape." She was batting
1000 so far.

I said, "YOU ARE WALKING BY THE SPIDER WEB OF THE THREE-
FOOT SPIDER, WHO, AS I SPEAK, IS WALKING ON YOUR ARM LOOKING
FOR A PLACE TO BITE YOU." She didn't even let me finish.

She said, "It is not. This is a hairnet and that's some old piece
of fur." She would make a great blind person.

I skipped the witches' moles; she was enjoying guessing everything too much. She got the wiener right and when she got to
the bowl full of guts and veins, she said, "This is macaroni and
cheese."

I said, "That's right, Good Fairy," even though it was spa-
ghetti. Then I said, "GET READY FOR THE ULTIMATE, ULTIMATE
SUPERHORROR OF ALL TIMES . . . A HANDFUL OF WORMS AND MAG-
GOTS TAKEN OUT OF THE STOMACH OF A DEAD PERSON THAT HAS

JUST DIED OF THE BLACK PLAGUE . . . AND IT IS VERY CONTAGIOUS."
"This is just more macaroni and cheese," she said. I said,
"Madame Bodini and her faithful hunchback assistant beg to
differ with the Good Fairy." She stomped her foot and said,
"You're not fooling me. It is macaroni and cheese just cut up
in smaller pieces. I ought to know, I eat enough of it." That was
true. They are very big on macaroni and cheese at the school
cafeteria.

I said, "Madame Bodini bets the Good Fairy five dollars that
it isn't macaroni and cheese." Then she got mad and pulled
her blindfold off and by that time those worms and maggots I
had gotten from Peachy Wigham had crawled halfway up her
arm.

You never heard anyone scream so loud. She tore down the
whole side of the HALL OF BLOOD AND GUTS . . . ENTER IF YOU
DARE running out of there. Madame Bodini closed for the night.
All I can say is I got the worms and maggots from Peachy Wigham on special order and if you remember, she owns the colored
mortuary.

November 4, 1952

In the "Dashes from Dot" column today, it said, "The hit
of Mrs. Underwood's sixth-grade Halloween party was a horror
show put on by Jr. Debutante Daisy Fay Harper and little
Michael Romeo. It was so good and scary that one little girl was
seen running, screaming in terror, from the booth. Congratulations on a job well done!"

Guess who's not speaking to me? Even Mrs. Underwood said
Kay Bob Benson is too emotional for her age.

Momma is angry at Daddy again because he doesn't have enough money to pay that note coming up on the fifteenth. She said to me, "Ask your father where are his drinking friends now?" Al the Drummer was gone. Jimmy Snow lost all the money he had playing poker with the Pistal brothers and when Daddy went to Billy Bundy, the radio preacher, to borrow some money, he just quoted him a speech. "Neither a borrower or a lender be."

Daddy said, "They find something from the Bible to fit every occasion, don't they?"

Momma says, tell your father this or tell your father that, when we are all in the same room. I have to say, "Daddy, Momma says this or Momma says that." They are driving me crazy!

Mr. Curtis Honeywell and his all-girl army got new camouflage uniforms for guerrilla fighting. They are green, spotted, baggy shirts and pants and a helmet with a net on it to match. I didn't want to poke my nose in, but it seems to me if they are going to do most of their fighting on the beach, they would be better off wearing white. You can't see anything white on the beach. I know; I was over at Michael's house one day and my mother called me to come home and get my Spanish mackerel. I took off running as fast as I could behind the cottages and all of a sudden I flipped up in the air and did a complete somersault and landed like a ton of bricks flat on my back. I was so surprised at being on the ground I just laid there. It was a puzzle to me until I looked up and saw Mr. Romeo's white rubber clothesline. I was running so fast I didn't see the clothesline and it caught me under the chin and flipped me over. Momma is going to get my eyes checked.

Mrs. Dot is driving all the Jr. Debuantes and Michael, who is an honorary Jr. Debutante, and Angel Pistal to a town called Daphne to the Rainbow Roller Skating Rink that has a real live organist. Her name is Princess White Cloud and she has a Hunkpapa Sioux father and a Chippewa mother and she is billed as the Most Musically Accomplished American Indian in Public Life Today. It says that she has played the organ in Broadway theaters all over the country. I wish she was a Blackfoot Indian. I would give anything to see a Blackfoot Indian in person, almost as much as I would give to see an albino. I've never seen a Chinese person or an Eskimo or a person from Lapland, the Land of the Midnight Sun. I have never seen snow and the people in Lapland have it all year round. I have a glass paperweight that has a house in it and when you shake it up, it snows. I could just look at that thing for hours!

Wouldn't it be great if I could grow up and marry Johnny Sheffield, who plays Bomba the Jungle Boy, and go to live in Lapland? I would keep a Christmas tree up all year round and Momma and Daddy and Mrs. Underwood and maybe Jimmy Snow could come and visit on holidays. I would have to get across the ocean first. There are some big boats that go all the time because Mrs. Dot's sister got molested on one once. Mrs. Dot said her sister didn't feel so bad when it happened because she thought it had been a foreign man and you know how they are. But when they caught the man and he spoke English and turned out to be a used car salesman from Wheeling, West Virginia, she had a complete and total nervous breakdown and won't ride in a boat to this day.

November 8, 1952

Tommie Jo, the girl who married Hank Turner, called Daddy on the phone just crying her eyes out. She said Hank had gone out to the store and hadn't come back for three days. They hadn't had a fight or anything, and there is no trace of him at all. Daddy called the long-distance operator in Minnesota and got the number of a Mrs. H. Turner. When she answered the phone, she said yes, she had a son named Hank, but she had not seen him in six years and they had been looking for him because he had a wife and children in Minnesota, too. He had never gone to the University of Minnesota and didn't have a brother. Hank had been in a bad accident and has a steel plate in his head and she thinks that is why he forgets to go home and forgets that he is married and has children. I never saw a steel plate in his head.

Tommie Jo is having a fit because he took her car with him and she is pregnant. When Granddaddy Pettibone left, he did it on purpose, but Hank is so sweet I know he didn't mean to. Momma hopes he doesn't get somewhere and forget again and marry some other woman.

Mrs. Dot took us to the Rainbow Roller Rink the other night and we had a great time. Princess White Cloud, the organist, was sitting out there in the middle of the rink in an Indian dress and a feather bonnet, playing up a storm. I wore blue jeans, but Kay Bob Benson showed up with a whole skating outfit and her own skates with blue pompoms. She can skate backwards, wouldn't you know it. I can hardly skate forwards and Angel can't skate at all. Mrs. Dot pulled her around the rink. We had to do a sweetheart skate. Michael and I fell down about eight times. Kay Bob Benson and Amy Jo Snipes didn't fall once. She would stick her nose up in the air every time they went past us. We were usually on the floor. On top of that, she went and told the manager there were two children out on the rink that were hazardous to the other skaters. At one time in my life I thought I might grow up and be an ice skater like Sonja Henie, but I have changed my mind. If it's so hard to skate on wheels, imagine how hard it would be to skate on ice. I admire Sonja Henie even more than Esther Williams, who I heard has plastic hair.

The Jr. Debutantes missed the circus completely because Mrs. Dot is scared to death of elephants. This fear comes from when her second cousin parked her red Studebaker in front of the library while she was in looking up her family tree. When she came out at six o'clock, the whole front of the car was smashed to the ground. Some men who were standing there were with the circus and told her that this elephant named Judy had walked by and, before they could stop her, had just sat down on the car. In her act she used to sit on a red stool and put her feet up in the air and when she saw the red car, she got confused and thought it was her stool. Mrs. Dot's cousin made those men go home with her because she said her husband never would have believed that an elephant sat on her car. But we are going to get to go to the Harwin County Fair and Agriculture Show that is coming up pretty soon. They don't have any elephants, just cows.

November 10, 1952

You will never believe what has happened. Harper's Malt Shop has burned to the ground. I am homeless. Daddy is having a fit because the insurance is not half as much as he thought it would be.

A week ago Momma and I were up at Buddy's Café having dinner. I got tired of sitting around waiting on Momma to smoke her cigarettes and drink her hundred cups of coffee, so I left and started over to Michael's when I saw smoke coming out of the wooden shack on the side of the malt shop. A whole bunch of rags that smelled like gasoline were starting to burn. I grabbed a bucket that was in there, ran outside and filled it full of sand about four or five times. The fire was almost out and I was hollering for my daddy and when he got around to the side of the house and saw what I was doing, instead of being proud of me, he yelled at me to go over to Michael's and he'd take care of the rest.

Michael and I were playing old maid and just when I was sure Michael was going to be the old maid, some men ran up and started banging on the door and yelling, "Harper's is on fire." I sat there for a minute before it dawned on me that I was a Harper. I ran out the door and sure enough, our place was burning again as big as you please. Daddy was sitting across the street, drinking Pabst Blue Ribbon beer, and everyone else was running around like chickens with their heads cut off. A few minutes later Momma came home from Buddy's and when she saw what was happening, she sat down in the road and started crying about her silver fox fur. I was so excited about her silver fox fur I forgot about Felix. As soon as I thought of her, I took off, no matter what Momma said. I started calling her and calling her and pretty soon I heard Felix meow from under the house. I crawled under there as fast as I could and grabbed her. It's a good thing the malt shop had shifted up on that side. Some men in the house were throwing stuff out the window, so I ran up and asked them to get my birth certificate and my baby pictures that were in the bottom drawer of the dresser. Those men wouldn't listen to me at all. I told them over and over I needed those pictures for *This Is Your Life,* but all they saved was the television set, which they broke when they threw it out the window, and a mattress and some sheets and pillowcases.

Men that try to act like heroes and use their brute force on little children sure are stupid. Our car would have burned up, too, but Michael, who is only twelve, got in it and backed it away. I climbed in with him and noticed some of my school books in the car, so I took them out and threw them in the fire. I figured it would save me from doing a lot of homework, but unfortunately under the headline in the paper the next day that said HARPER'S MALT SHOP BURNS TO THE GROUND IN TRAGIC FIRE it also said that seen throwing her school books in the fire was little Daisy Fay Harper. Rat's foot! No wonder Hollywood stars hate reporters, and after all that some busybody do-gooder has already bought me a new set of books.

We lost everything we owned, including all the animals in the freezer, but Daddy and I try to look on the bright side of things. All those blue skirts and white blouses burned up and what was left of those Spanish mackerels. Thank goodness I was wearing my jeans and my red and white flannel shirt I like so much. A friend of Momma's and Daddy's named Mr. White who has some cottages down on the beach let us stay in one for a while, so that's where we are living. About a day or so after the fire Daddy took me out to the car and opened the trunk and said, "Well, look what just happens to be in the trunk." It was my tin box of private papers with the combination lock, my sweetheart pillow and that stuffed bobcat. All I can say is that I am sorry that my birth certificate and my baby pictures didn't just happen to be in that trunk. Momma is furious her silver fox fur and her alligator purse weren't in the trunk either.

She is not speaking to Daddy at all again. According to her, Daddy is a "stupid son of a bitch from hell without the good sense God gave a pig." If she ever finds out the fire was his fault, she will kill him for sure, especially when she knows what we're getting from the insurance company.

The day after the fire Daddy sent me to where the malt shop had been to wait for the insurance man. I had to stand up the whole time because the sand was still so hot you couldn't sit down. A lot of people from Magnolia Springs came to see the ruins and Kay Bob Benson had the woman who works for her mother bring her. She parked right in front of our place and just sat and laughed. When I told Momma on her, she said not to worry, every dog has its day. Mrs. Dot came and cried and cried. She said she couldn't believe that this terrible tragedy had befallen one of her Jr. Debutantes. She took it harder than anyone and devoted her entire "Dashes from Dot" column to us. She said that I was the bravest soul, standing on the disaster site the next day, like a good little soldier waiting for the insurance man, my little chin held high trying not to cry. I never did think about crying, I was too happy over those white shirts and blue skirts burning, not to mention the Spanish mackerel, but it made a good story.

Everybody is being real sweet and Michael's mother made him give me a pair of his blue jeans and a shirt. Boys' blue jeans are the best. People are trying to give us a lot of things, but Momma won't take hardly anything. She is too proud to accept charity. I think she ought to wait and see what people offer and then make up her mind. When I told her it would be a terrific time to go on *Queen for a Day* because she had a great sad story, she started to bawl. She and Mrs. Dot ought to have a crying contest. My mother doesn't know this, but I am going to get a job as soon as I finish the sixth grade and buy her a brand-new silver fox fur that is not worn out on the elbows. Boy, I can't wait to see her face and if I can make enough money, I will get her an alligator purse, too.

November 14, 1952

Momma left today to go live with her sister in Virginia. She told me she just couldn't stay with Daddy anymore and when I get older, I would understand. She wanted me to go with her. I love my mother very much, but I can't see leaving my daddy. Besides, I am having too good a time in the sixth grade. Mrs. Underwood is reading us *Nancy Drew and the Clue in the Crumbling Wall*. I am very interested to see how this one turns out. Boy, one chapter at a time can sure make a nervous wreck out of you. When Momma left, she didn't even have a bag to pack or anything to put in it. Mrs. Dot picked her up and took her to Magnolia Springs to catch the Greyhound bus. She'll come back, she always does. She made me promise to write her every week and if Daddy gets in jail, I'm to go up to Mrs. Dot's house.

The night she left, Daddy got on a real mean drunk. When I asked him to stop drinking so much, he told me to shut up and leave him alone and get on the bus and go to Virginia with my mother, he couldn't stand the sight of me. He said he had never cared anything about me, which is a lie. He was saying that because he's upset over Momma. It hurt my feelings anyway, but I didn't let him see me cry. I fixed him the next day, though. Before I went to school, I left him a note that said, "Billie G. Thweatt called you up on the phone last night."

November 16, 1952

Mrs. Underwood took me in the cloakroom today and asked me if my momma and daddy were fighting again. I said no, which was the truth because she's in Virginia. She said, "I know something is wrong." I said, "What has Kay Bob Big Mouth Benson been saying now?" Mrs. Underwood said Kay Bob Benson hadn't said anything, she could just tell by the way I was acting. I don't know how. I have been real funny lately and have cracked a lot of good jokes and made the whole class laugh, so she didn't get it from me. It had to be Kay Bob Benson that spilled the beans!

November 19, 1952

I got a letter from Momma today. She is fine. She has got a job as a waitress and will send for me whenever she can. I am surprised that she hasn't come home yet. She must have been madder than I thought. This is the longest she's ever been gone, and I miss her.

Do you remember the little bald boy, Vernon Mooseburger, who came to the Halloween party as a mean potato? You wouldn't believe how cruel people can be just because he doesn't have a hair on his head. Kids call him ugly names like cue ball, Daddy Warbucks and Henry, after the bald boy in the cartoon funny papers. I call him Vernon. He is poor and got a disease when he was little that made all his hair come out, including his eyebrows. His momma bought him a brown leatherette hat with flaps that he wears even in summer. The only time I ever saw his hat off was when he was the potato. I always choose him to be on my side if ever we play softball because the other kids choose him last.

Mrs. Underwood made us all write an essay on what we would like to be when we grow up. I wrote one called "Why I Want to Be Bald When I Grow Up." Mrs. Underwood picked it out with three others to go to the Harwin County Fair and compete with essays from children all over Harwin County. I said how great it would be in the summer to be able to put a cold rag on top of your head. You would never have to go to Nita's Beauty Box and get a comb broken in your hair. When you went out, all you had to do was take a rag and polish your head a little; and if you got into a fight, nobody could pull your hair; and when you got old, you would never have to turn gray and dye your hair purple. Vernon didn't know how lucky he was. Most of the essays were pretty dull, but wait until you hear what Kay Bob Benson wants to be. She wants to grow up and be Miss America, just like Yolanda Betbeze, or the mother of Jesus if He ever comes back. Oh, brother. You were not supposed to be two people, and if Jesus Christ ever does come back, I would want to be Him, not His mother. Daddy says always go for the top prize.

November 21, 1952

Get ready for this. This is even better than the HALL OF BLOOD AND GUTS . . . ENTER IF YOU DARE. Michael and I were on the beach after school, and he was shooting his .22 rifle at pilings and tin cans, like he always does. He got that gun for his birthday . . . which deep in my heart made me jealous because girls don't ever get a real gun. Michael only let me shoot his stupid gun once, even though I am a mascot for the all-woman army. He pretends he's Roy Rogers, which is all right with me, except that he always wants me to pretend that I am Dale Evans, which I can never bring myself to do. He says there can't be two Roy Rogerses, so I have to be Hopalong Cassidy, second best.

He was shooting up and down the beach when he saw that something had washed up in front of Hammer's Christian Motel. It looked like a sack of potatoes, but Michael ran over and found it was not a sack of potatoes at all. It was a dead woman with a bullet hole right between her eyes! Michael hadn't meant to shoot her. We hadn't even seen her. Who would have thought someone would be on the beach this time of year? Here I was, just eleven and already a witness to murder. Since there was nobody around, I decided Michael shouldn't have to go to the electric chair because of one accident. I chose my friend against the law and I'm still not sure what that says about my character, but we made a blood pact that neither of us would tell.

So I went home and watched *Our Miss Brooks* with Eve Arden, Gale Gordon and Richard Crenna, and about an hour later some men banged on our door. It seems to be men that carry bad news, doesn't it? They had found a dead woman on the beach by the pier. I didn't know what else to do but to go with Daddy to see it. After all, a dead body is a big event and if I said that I was not interested, that would have made me look suspicious. I had a duty to protect Michael from the law.

When we got there, it was almost dark. The wind was blowing the sea wheat and it was making a weird noise. The moon was full and turning orange. The police had the place roped off and were looking at the woman with flashlights and were doing a lot of mumbling that police do at this sort of thing just like in the movies.

The Hammers, who were lording it over everybody because the body had been found on their property, have a vicious grandchild named Gregg. Do you know what he did when everybody's back was turned? He ran up there and tried to get the dead woman's watch and rings off of her before he was stopped. Personally, I think he had a lot of courage to touch a dead body in the dark. They should have let him go ahead and keep it, even though the watch probably wouldn't run unless it was a Timex. They put one in a washing machine on television once.

Pretty soon the hearse from Magnolia Springs came. Right at that moment Michael and his mother and daddy came down. I found out later that Michael had run home and hidden under his bed and made his momma and daddy wonder about him. Michael was white as a sheet and he is an Italian person. He looked at me, but I kept a blank look. I was sticking to our blood pact. Michael, however, after being there three minutes fell down in the sand and started screaming and hollering that he was the murderer and had shot the woman dead that very afternoon. I kept my mouth shut. His confession, however, didn't hold much weight with the police since they said she had been shot with a pistol and had been dead for about three days.

It was real sad to see someone confess like that when they didn't have to. To make him feel better, I told him it could have been him, if she hadn't already been killed. I looked over and little Gregg was getting the tar smacked out of him by his grandmother. She had to wrestle him to the ground to get whatever it was away from him. He let out a scream and tried to bite her in the leg. Mrs. Hammer marched right up to the police and said, "Here, my grandson took this off that dead woman," and handed them a ring.

The minute I saw that ring I knew the dead woman was RUBY BATES! I hadn't recognized her without her makeup. I yelled, "I know who that dead woman is. She's Ruby Bates and she's a friend of Claude Pistal's." This policeman said, "What did you say, little girl?" and I said, "That woman is Ruby Bates and she's Claude . . ." but before I could get anything more out, Michael's mother slammed her hand over my mouth so hard I saw stars. She told the police I didn't know what I was talking about and was hysterical at seeing a dead body. I tried to tell them again, but she pinched me so bad that I couldn't have said anything if my life depended on it.

She pulled me up the road and asked me where in the world did I get the idea that woman was a friend of Claude Pistal's. I told her he had been parked in a car with her smooching one afternoon and I had taken her to the bathroom for him. She said, "How do you know that's the same woman who was with Claude Pistal?"

I said, "I recognized the ring . . . I'd know that ring anywhere."

She thought for a minute and then she said, "You didn't see that woman with Claude Pistal."

I said, "Yes, I did."

She said, "No, you didn't."

I said, "Yes, I did."

And then she said, "Daisy Fay Harper, believe me, you didn't see any woman with Claude Pistal. Do you understand me?"

I said, "All right, but I did."

She said for me not to mention his name under any circumstances because Claude Pistal is the meanest man in Harwin County and there was no telling what he would do if I said he knew that woman. I suddenly realized she had a point and that Peachy Wigham had called him mean as snake shit. Mrs. Romeo asked me if I thought he would remember me seeing them together. I said I didn't think so, he was pretty drunk. She asked me who else knew I had seen them. I said, "Nobody." I hadn't told anybody, not even Daddy, which is a miracle because I usually tell everybody everything. She made me proimse not to open my mouth and to never say Ruby Bates's or Claude Pistal's name out loud again as long as I lived or she would call my mother and make her come get me and take me to Virginia.

Daddy asked me what Michael's mother and I had been talking about and I said, "Female trouble." That always shuts them up. Momma used that one all the time.

The papers are full of stories about the dead woman. The police said her name was Mrs. Ruby Bates. I told you so! She was from Meridian, the wife of a Mr. Earl Bates. She is survived by her sister, Mrs. Julian Wilson, who must be Opal, and a brother, Mr. Lee Halprin, who lives in Las Vegas, Nevada. She had been killed by a single bullet in the head and had been dead approximately sixty-eight hours when the body was found. They even knew what her last meal had been—peas and carrots. I sure wouldn't want my last meal to be peas and carrots.

The police found the gun that killed her up on the beach about two blocks from where Harper's Malt Shop used to be. She had taken a cab all the way from Meridian. I'll bet she was surprised when she saw the malt shop had burned down and she didn't have any place to use the bathroom. The police called it a suicide and said she had walked out in the water and shot herself in the head. Then her body had drifted down the beach in front of the Hammer's Christian Motel. What I wonder is this. After she had shot herself between the eyes, how had she enough time to turn around and throw that gun way up on the beach before she died. Daddy pointed out if she had drifted down the beach from where the malt shop was, she would have had to pass under George Potlow's pier. That pier has barnacles on the pilings that would have ripped her up, but she was in fine shape except for the hole between her eyes.

At school, Mrs. Underwood let me stand up and tell how Michael and I had found the dead woman. I did it great with gestures and everything. Afterwards, she let the class ask questions. You should have heard those questions! Some of them didn't even believe that we found the dead body at all. And of course, Kay Bob Benson got up and told the story about how her mother had found the leg. So what! We found a whole body. Stay away from sixth graders if you can.

At recess I go across the football field to the high school and a senior boy named Marvin Thrasher gives me a Mounds candy bar every day and sometimes an Almond Joy. He is a big fan of the Peter Paul candy company. I talk to the high school teachers a lot, too. I am getting plenty of attention being a victim of a fire disaster and the product of a broken home at the same time.

November 23, 1952

Mrs. Dot comes down to see me once in a while and she sure has been acting funny lately. She wears the Jr. Debutante pink and seafoam green barrettes all the time now, and she made me sit down and listen to a talk called "Fun with Rayon" that I already heard her do in Jr. Debutantes. Sometimes she does baby talk to me. Mrs. Romeo said that her "Dashes from Dot" column last week didn't make a lick of sense.

In school Mrs. Underwood told us a story about a little girl who had gotten rabies and gone mad. They had to feed her by putting a tray under her door. When anybody in her family got close, she said, "Don't get near me because I'm liable to bite you." Well, you should have heard the class just roar at that one, including Michael. Mrs. Underwood told them there was nothing funny about rabies. That little girl knew if she bit any member of the family, they would get rabies, too, and she died without ever having been petted. I cried so hard Mrs. Underwood had to take me to the school nurse.

When I was in the school nurse's office, a high school girl came in and said, "Oh, Mrs. Smith. I feel awful. I've got my period and my stomach is all hot." Mrs. Smith went over to a big icebox and got her a Coca-Cola. I wondered why I didn't get a Coca-Cola. I told Patsy Ruth Coggins, the dumbest girl living, I knew a way to get us a free Coca-Cola. So at recess we went over and I said, "Oh, Mrs. Smith, my stomach is burning up something awful and so is Patsy Ruth's." She said, "Do you have real bad cramps?" I said, "No, we just have a period and I think I might have to have a Coca-Cola and Patsy Ruth wants one too." Patsy Ruth said, "I would rather have a Dr Pepper if you have it." I could have killed her. Sure enough, Mrs. Smith gave us both a Coca-Cola and two aspirins. I told her I didn't want any aspirins, but dumb Patsy Ruth took the aspirins. We finished our Coca-Cola and thanked her and left.

Today I went back over there. Mrs. Smith said, "Do you still have your period?" I said, "Oh, yes, and now it's worse than ever. My stomach is so hot I can't touch it with a ten-foot pole."

But she didn't give me my Coca-Cola. She went over and looked at some papers and said, "You are going to the doctor right now. This is not normal, you having a period for a week."

I said, "Listen, I don't even go to school here. I was just passing through. I live in a school bus and I am on my way to Wisconsin."

That lie didn't do me a bit of good because she had my name and Mrs. Underwood's name written down on a paper from the time I had been there for a crying fit. She took me right back over to the grammar school and told Mrs. Underwood I had my period for over a week and, not only that, it had gotten worse. Mrs. Underwood looked real surprised and asked me if it was true. I said, "Well, I didn't know for sure if I had it for a week or not, but my stomach is hot." Mrs. Underwood looked at me funny, thanked the nurse and told her she would take care of it.

She gave the class a longer recess and took me in the classroom, sat me down and said, "Now are you sure you have your period?" I said I couldn't say for sure, but I thought so.

"What makes you think you have one?"

I said, "I was craving a Coca-Cola."

Then she asked me if I knew what a period was. I said if she meant in grammar, I knew what a period was and I knew what a comma and an exclamation mark were. She said, "Daisy Fay Harper, didn't your mother tell you what a period is?" I said, "I guess not or I would have remembered." Caught like a rat in a trap in a lie in front of Mrs. Underwood!

She said, "Do you know what a Kotex is?"

"Sure, Momma has a box of them at home."

She said, "Do you know what they're for?"

"I sure do," I said. "My momma told me they were for dusting in hard-to-reach places."

Mrs. Underwood settled back, crossed her legs and said, "I guess I'm going to have to tell you about your period." And she did. She told me all about it and it meant you were a woman and all. I thought I was going to die right there on the spot. I've never heard anything so terrible in my whole life. I hope she is wrong and I never get a period. I am eleven years old and entirely too young to hear about it. Can you imagine my mother not knowing what Kotex are for and dusting the house with them? Well, her mother can just tell her what they are for, I'm not getting into the facts of life. I haven't heard one fact of life that I liked yet.

November 24, 1952

I AM IN BIG TROUBLE! Yesterday at school I was sitting there listening to Mrs. Underwood read us, *The Clue of the Whistling Bagpipes*, Chapter 14, "Trouble on the Mountain," when someone knocked on the classroom door. Mrs. Underwood stopped right at the best part and went to find out who was there. She came back and said, "Daisy Fay, your aunt and uncle are here to see you. They're waiting for you in their car."

I got all excited because it had to be my Aunt Mignon and Uncle Raymond all the way from Virginia and I just knew Momma was with them. They had brought her home as a surprise!

Mrs. Underwood said to get my things, I could be excused early and not to forget to do page 57 in my arithmetic book. I got all of my stuff, ran out and jumped in the car. And guess what? It wasn't my Aunt Mignon and Uncle Raymond at all. I had never seen these two people before in my life. I said, "Hey, I think you've got the wrong little girl."

The woman said, "You're Daisy Fay Harper, aren't you?"

I said, "Yes," but by that time they had driven off with me. I said, "Wait a minute, I don't know you."

She said, "You were named after a vase of daisies that were in your mother's room, weren't you?"

I started to get nervous. I said, "How did you know that?" And then I saw that ring on her finger and I knew who she was, Opal, the murdered woman's sister! I started screaming they had better stop and let me out of that car or I would tell the police. I tried to jump out, but the man had locked all the doors.

Opal said, "Don' be afraid. We won't hurt you. We just want to talk to you about my sister Ruby."

I said to the man, "Who are you?"

He said, "I'm her husband." He pointed to Opal.

Then Opal said, "Wouldn't you like some ice cream?" That sounded like a good idea and besides, I thought if we went to a public place, I could run if I had to. But they took me up the road to the Tastee Freeze, a drive-in, and I had to stay in the car. When the waitress came, I screamed that I was being kidnapped and to call the police. She laughed because she knew me. One time I had gone up there with Michael with a saucepan on my head and had told her that I was Johnny Appleseed. She just kept laughing, so I gave up. I ordered an orange crush and a banana split, but I wasn't saying anything to those people. I had made a promise to Michael's mother not to ever mention the names Ruby Bates or Claude Pistal out loud as long as I lived.

Opal said, "I wanted to meet the little girl my sister told me about. Ruby liked you a lot, and we hope you'd like to help us find her killer. We know it was Claude Pistal, and we've tried every way in the world to get a case against him, but Claude lies and says he never knew a Ruby Bates. Ruby had told me all about Claude, though I warned her against ruining her reputation by going with him, but Ruby just told me not to worry, the only person who had ever seen them together was a little girl named Daisy who lived on the beach and had been named after a vase of flowers. That was how I found you."

Well, I hope everybody is satisfied they gave me such a stupid name! If they had named me something simple like Mary, this would have never happened.

Then the man started to talk and asked me to think about

Ruby's four little motherless children. He must have thought I was stupid. I said, "Mister, I am in the sixth grade and I can read obituaries, and she didn't even have any children, so there." That shut him up. I said, "You better take me home now."

He tried a different story. "Don't you feel bad about letting Ruby's killer run loose when you could put him in jail where he belongs? How would you feel if it had been your momma and somebody knew the killer and wasn't telling?"

He was beginning to get me with that mother stuff, so I just clamped my lips shut and looked out the window. I did feel bad, but not bad enough to get myself killed in case they didn't arrest Claude in time.

Opal started to cry and said, "Please help me, Daisy. You are the only one who can."

Then he started up again. "Daisy, I want you to think about this. If Opal and I found out about you seeing Claude and Ruby together, don't you think eventually Claude Pistal's going to remember you saw them together. Think what he might do to you."

"You're not going to tell him, are you?"

I could have choked myself. I still hadn't admitted anything, but I should have kept my mouth shut. The man pretended like nothing had happened and just kept on talking. "Now, we don't want to, Daisy, but the time will come when we might have to tell the police." They kept talking to me like that for over an hour, but I never said another word except to order a hot fudge sundae with nuts.

They finally gave up and took me back to school in time to catch the school bus home.

Mrs. Underwood better check out who she lets take her students out of class. She should ask to see some identification. I was as sick as a dog on that bus. Mrs. Butts had to stop three times for me to throw up. When I got home, guess who was sitting there with Daddy? Opal and her husband, the very ones that had kidnapped me.

Daddy looked worried. The man said, "Daisy, I'm Mr. Kilgore from the FBI." He had lied and told me that he was Opal's husband! FBI men are not supposed to lie. On top of that, he had a tape recorder and was playing the tape of what we had been saying in the car that afternoon. They made me sit down and hear it.

"Listen to this, Mr. Harper. This is where we got her."

He played the part where I asked if they were going to tell Claude Pistal on me. I sure do have a southern accent. He played some more of the tape, but all you could hear was them talking and me eating my banana split.

He said to Daddy, "This tape will hold up in court as evidence, Mr. Harper, because the child had no way of knowing Ruby had a sister named Opal unless she had talked to her because her name appeared in the obituaries as Mrs. Julian Wilson."

Daddy looked at me. "Is this true?"

I didn't know what to answer without incriminating myself. I said, "I want to talk to my lawyer," which was the wrong thing to say because Daddy grabbed me and about shook my head off.

He said it was not funny and I better quit acting like a horse's ass and tell him everything before he beat the living daylights out of me. Mad as he was, he might have killed me before Claude Pistal got a chance.

Mr. Kilgore told him to calm down, I was probably just scared. So I told them the whole story, but I never once said Ruby Bates's or Claude Pistal's name out loud. Only used "he and she" and they would say "Ruby" and "Claude Pistal" and I would nod my head yes. I wasn't taking any chances of them fooling me and taping my voice again.

I told them all about when I was up at the Blue Gardenia Lounge waiting to get paid for taping Angel's ears back and how he threatened me and how Harold Pistal had warned me not to tell my parents about Claude being so mean. Then I told Mr. Kilgore about the afternoon Claude brought Ruby up there to use the bathroom. It was when Momma and Daddy had gone fishing with Mr. and Mrs. Dot and caught all those rotten Spanish mackerel. When Mr. Kilgore asked for the exact date, Daddy called Mr. Dot on the phone to find out. Mr. Dot remembered, and also reminded Daddy that he still owed him money for half the rental on the boat. I'll bet Daddy was sorry he made that phone call.

After I finished my story, Mr. Kilgore admitted that taping my voice had been illegal. Tricked! But he did it for my own protection, Claude is dangerous and the FBI suspects him of a lot of murders all over the country, but they haven't been able to pin anything on him until now. All I had to do was to sign a paper stating I had seen Ruby Bates and Claude Pistal together on the afternoon of September 21 and for us not to worry, that I would probably never be called to testify. That's right, I'll probably be dead.

My daddy must have read my mind because he said, "Now, wait a minute, how do I know my little girl will be protected?"

Mr. Kilgore said, "Mr. Harper, trust me. We know exactly where Claude Pistal is at this very minute."

"Where is he?" I asked.

Mr. Kilgore answered, "I'm not at liberty to say, but don't worry. I'll be back tomorrow with legal papers for you to sign. Meanwhile, don't discuss the case with anyone, not even Mrs. Romeo."

Opal said she could never thank me enough for what I was doing, I had made her the happiest woman alive. Sure, I thought, she wasn't the one that Claude Pistal was going to kill.

Daddy and Jimmy Snow sat up all night and didn't sleep a wink and didn't have one drink.

This morning before I went to school, Mr. Kilgore came back with that paper to sign. Before he left, he said, "Miss Harper, I just want you to know, I have cross-examined a lot of pretty tough customers, and you are the hardest nut I have ever had to crack. My hat's off to you."

I felt great until I started thinking on the bus that he said that just to make me feel good because it had only taken him one afternoon to make me spill my guts. I had sold out for a banana split and a hot fudge sundae and, on top of that, I hadn't done page 57 on my arithmetic book.

It's not that I don't trust the FBI, but in case there is a slipup, I have written down the combination to my lock that goes to the box where I keep my private papers and put it in a Luden's cough drop box and put it in a sock, and put that in a cigar box. I glued that shut with airplane glue and put it in a sack and buried it on the beach. I have given Michael the map of where I buried it. He is to go dig it up only if I am killed. There are two parts to the map. I made Daddy take me up to the colored quarters and I gave Peachy Wigham the other half. I told her under no circumstances is she to give it to Michael if I am living, and she said she wouldn't. She asked no questions. That's why she's so popular.

This is my farewell note just in case.

To Whom It May Concern:

If you are reading this, I am dead. Claude Pistal has killed me. Don't think for one minute that I died from natural causes, no matter how good it may look. Trust me, he murdered me in cold blood.

I, Daisy Fay Harper, being of sound mind and in the sixth grade, do solemnly swear I saw Claude Pistal and Ruby Bates together on the afternoon of September 21 of this year, kissing, and that they did know each other. If you don't believe me, ask her sister, Opal, who is known as Mrs. Julian Wilson, and Mr. Kilgore of the FBI.

Good-bye Mother and Daddy. I loved you well. You were wonderful to me when I was alive and I appreciate it very much. And, Daddy, don't feel bad about not getting me that pony. I probably wouldn't have taken care of it anyway. Try not to go to pieces.

Good-bye Michael Romeo, my trusted friend. Tell Mrs. Underwood a special good-bye for me and that she is the best teacher I ever had in my whole life.

Good-bye to Mrs. Dot and to Jimmy Snow and to everyone in the sixth grade except Kay Bob Benson and she knows why.

Good-bye to Peachy Wigham. Thanks for the maggots and to everyone else who liked me when I was alive, including Mr. Curtis Honeywell and his all-girl army.

Good-bye to my grandmothers and granddaddies and to one step-granddaddy and Aunt Bess and Sue Lovells and to Edna, who is married to a sailor in Pensacola.

Good-bye to Angel and your mother and daddy. I hope

your ears get better. Mr. Pistal, I am sorry I am putting your brother in jail and probably in the electric chair, but fair is fair.

Oh, and good-bye to Hank Turner if they ever find you.

This is my last will and testament and I am sorry it is so small, but as you know, most of my stuff burned up. I leave my sweetheart pillow to my mother. I leave my clothes to Michael, even though he will probably not want to wear that one pair of girls' blue jeans. If not, give them to Patsy Ruth Coggins.

I leave my cat, Felix, to my daddy.

And the last thing I have to say is that I am responsible for burning down the malt shop. I did it by mistake, so don't try and take the insurance money away from Daddy. It wasn't enough anyway.

Daisy Fay Harper

November 25, 1952

Daddy, Jimmy Snow and Billy Bundy went up to the Blue Gardenia Lounge today to tell Harold Pistal to get a message to his brother, Claude, that if he dares come within 100 miles of me, Daddy will kill him. And if Claude kills him, Jimmy Snow will kill Claude and if he kills both of them and Billy Bundy, there is a whole group of other people that will kill him. I don't think Daddy has another group of people, but it made a good threat!

Harold said for Daddy to calm down. Nothing was going to happen to anybody. Claude is in South America for good and is never returning because some men in Detroit are mad at him. When Daddy got home, he called up Mr. Kilgore, and Mr.

Kilgore said yes, Claude was in South America, and if he ever tried to come back, the FBI would pick him up so fast it would make his head swim. Daddy was happy as a clam over this news and so was I. I am too young to die.

I better write that little girl we adopted in Jr. Debutantes who lives in South America and tell her if she ever runs across a man named Claude Pistal not to talk to him because he is bad business.

November 26, 1952

When I got to school this morning, there was a substitute teacher. Mrs. Underwood was in the Magnolia Springs Clinic and had her appendix out Saturday morning. She would be back in two weeks. Here I had been so worried about myself while poor Mrs. Underwood was sick. We wrote her a get-well note. Mine was six pages long and I put a joke in it. When I was over at the Pig and Whistle Barbecue at lunch, I decided I had better go see her in person and make sure she was doing all right. I don't trust that other teacher. She might be trying to take Mrs. Underwood's job.

When I arrived at the clinic, the nurse said they didn't allow any children visitors unless they had an adult with them. It took me forever to find an adult to take me in. Finally, this retarded man named Leroy that always hangs around the Big B Drugstore went with me, but I had to buy him an ice cream sandwich before he would do it.

I said to the nurse, "Here is my adult," but the nurse looked up and said, "Leroy, you get out of here now and go on home."

I don't know what was the matter with her. He was an adult, wasn't he?

I finally went around the back and found another way in. I looked in all the rooms, and most of the people were old and asleep. I went by one room and there were four people standing outside the door. One was a preacher reading from the Bible. Whoever was in that room was dying. What if it was Mrs. Underwood? I ran up and down the halls, but I couldn't find her. I was yelling, "Mrs. Underwood, Mrs. Underwood," when that nurse caught hold of me, but as she was dragging me to the front door, I heard Mrs. Underwood's voice coming out of a room way down at the other end of the hall.

She said, "Is that Daisy?" I got away from that nurse and ran to the room and there was Mrs. Underwood, sitting up in her bed with a beautiful blue lace bed jacket on. She wasn't dying at all. Then, all of a sudden, that nurse was right on top of me and she was mad. I had woke up all her patients making such a racket.

Mrs. Underwood asked if I could please stay. That nurse wasn't going to let me, but the other patients were all ringing their bells, so she said, "Oh, all right, but just five minutes."

Mrs. Underwood looked surprised to see me. She said, "Daisy, what in the world are you doing out of school?" and I said I thought I'd better come up and see if she was really OK because I had a terrible time in the hospital once when they took my tonsils out. She said she was fine and for me not to worry about her. I told her we had all written her a get-well note and then, like a dummy, told her everything I had written in my note, including the joke. Now it won't be a surprise when she gets it.

After I left, I realized that was the first time I'd seen Mrs. Underwood without her makeup on. She is a natural beauty, just like Doris Day.

November 28, 1952

Mrs. Dot took us to the Harwin County Fair. I had $15 and I knew I was going to win a terrific prize for Mrs. Underwood. We were all packed in that car like sardines. Angel Pistal had to sit on my lap. She is the boniest little girl I have ever met.

Amy Jo Snipes and her sisters were yacking away about what rides they were going on. Even Kay Bob Benson was excited because she forgot herself and asked me a question. She broke her silence from Halloween, but when I answered her and she realized what she had done, she looked at me and said, "Who are you?" and stuck her nose in the air.

When we got to the fairgrounds, the sky was all lit up, and Mrs. Dot had to park a mile away. It was freezing cold outside with a big brown ring around the moon. We went up to this huge archway that said "Welcome to the Harwin County Fair and Agriculture Show." We had to wait forever for Mrs. Dot to buy our tickets and Michael was so excited that he bought a Kewpie doll on a stick from some man who was selling funny buttons and all kinds of stuff before he even got into the fair. They had the biggest Ferris wheel I have ever seen. Kay Bob Benson bought herself a white wooden baton with glitter pasted all over it. There was a caterpillar ride with a green and white canvas top on it that closed up when you rode it, and a loop-the-loop, and bumper cars that Michael couldn't wait to ride on, and a huge merry-go-round, and every ride had a different tune playing on it.

Mrs. Dot made us all stay together and we had to visit the exhibition halls before we could go on any of the rides. I got me a corn dog and we went into this big barn, full of livestock stalls, with cows, and sheep and pigs, and some of them had ribbons on them, where they had won a prize. After them came a display of John Deere tractors and farm equipment that I didn't care a thing in the world about. I never saw so many Future Farmers of America in my life. That place stunk to high heaven.

Then we went into this big building that had squash that

weighed twelve pounds and some real big ears of corn. They were selling fruit jars full of jams and jellies and pickles and little tiny corn, and a bunch of homemade clothes that came from the home economics departments all over the county. I wouldn't be caught dead in those clothes. I buy all my things at Elwood's Variety Store. A lot of churches had made quilts, but I prefer an electric blanket myself. We saw an art show by some school kids with some of the ugliest pictures you ever laid eyes on, and then we came to the essays. I looked for mine, but it wasn't there. The winning essay was from somebody from Loxley and was entitled "When I Grow Up, I Want to Be a Good American." Who doesn't?

I was having a fit to get out of there and go ride the rides and play the games and win some prizes and so was Michael. Finally, when Mrs. Dot got to the garden club section, we had our chance. Her entry, "Marshland Magic," had won a ribbon, but all it looked like to me was a stuffed duck sitting in some weeds. She was so busy carrying on and telling everyone that went by about her arrangement that Michael and I snuck away and ran back out to the midway. The first thing we did was to buy ourselves a hat that a woman sewed your name on right there, any color that you wanted. I got a black one with "Daisy Fay" written on it in pink thread. Michael got a red one, with purple thread. He has no taste at all.

We rode the bumper cars. Crazy Michael crashed into everyone. Some boys got so mad that when they bumped us back I hit my tooth on my candied apple and nearly knocked it out. One's already chipped; I don't need to lose another. We spun around about six times and I had to get out before I was sick. Michael wouldn't leave. He said he was going to wait for a better car. I told him I would meet him at the Ferris wheel in thirty minutes, and went over to the booth where they have stuffed black and white cats you knock over with a baseball, three tries for a quarter. The prizes were watches and radios and a lamp with a hula girl. When you turned it on, the skirt moved up and down. I spent five dollars trying to win that lamp for Mrs. Underwood, but I never could knock more than two of those cats down at a time. Those balls were not heavy enough if you ask me because I am a real good aimer.

I finally gave up and went over to the next booth where water was running in a little stream with little yellow plastic ducks floating down it. You could pick a duck out of the water for a quarter and the man would look at the number on the bottom of the duck and tell you what prize you had won. I stood there and watched for a long time and nobody ever won a big prize. He always reached under the counter and gave them some dinky prize, like a tin horn or a rubber spider, so I decided to skip that one. By then it was time to meet Michael at the Ferris wheel, but he didn't show up until twenty minutes later.

When he did show up, he had Vernon Mooseburger with him. The three of us rode the Ferris wheel and got off just in time, because some little girl waited until she was on the very top and threw up all over everybody. We also rode the caterpillar and the crazy mouse. Michael kept grabbing handfuls of cotton candy off of the small children's paper cones when their parents weren't looking. You should have heard them scream, but by that time Michael would be long gone. In one sideshow they had a two-headed sheep in a bottle, but I think it was rubber, a real gyp! We saw the fat man and we wasted our money on that because Michael and I both agreed Jessie LeGore had been fatter, but Vernon thought it was great and wonderful.

My favorite was the half man, half woman. One side of him was dressed in a black suit with a sock and shoes on one foot, and the other side of him had on makeup and a high heel with one leg in some red pedal pushers. He had a half of a mustache. I tried to talk to him so I could see if he had a man's or a woman's voice, but the man inside told me I wasn't supposed to talk to the act. I think for fifty cents I should have gotten at least a sentence.

We walked around looking for a game I could win at when I saw just the thing I wanted to get Mrs. Underwood. A black and white plaster cocker spaniel with sparkle on it. It was on the shelf of the man who guesses your weight. He claimed he could guess your weight within three pounds. I went up there and gave him my quarter. He looked at me and said, "Little girl, I think you weigh ninety-two pounds." I was hoping and praying he would be wrong, but I got on the scale and weighed ninety-three pounds. I made Michael and Vernon do it too, but he guessed right both times. He must have been an expert. I was disappointed because Mrs. Underwood sure would have loved that black and white cocker spaniel.

I had only about $2 left because I had to pay for Michael and Vernon to have their weight guessed. There was one booth where you try and throw a wooden ring around a stick with a prize on it, but none of the prizes looked good to me. It was mostly packs of cigarettes and Mrs. Underwood doesn't smoke. Then I saw the one I was going to try next. All you had to do was to throw a penny into an ashtray and you could win yourself a goldfish in a little round bowl. I made that man give me $2 worth of pennies.

Do you know how hard it is to throw a penny into a simple ashtray? They bounce right out. After I tossed $1.68 worth, my penny bounced out of one ashtray and into another. Hooray! I picked out the biggest and the goldest goldfish they had. Mrs. Underwood was going to be crazy about this. Did you know they don't give you the bowl! That man poured my fish into a little white cardboard box with a wire handle and gave it to me. I said, "Don't I get the bowl?"

He said, "No."

"Why not? What good is a fish without the bowl?"

He said, real disgusted like, "Read the sign, girlie, it says win a goldfish. It doesn't say anything about a bowl."

"Then why do you put them in bowls and fool people into thinking that they are going to get a bowl?"

"Do you want the fish or not?"

I took it.

You have to watch those carnival people all the time. As we turned around to go, Vernon Mooseburger gave him the finger. I had thirty-two cents left, so we decided to ride the merry-go-round. I picked out a beautiful white horse with a red saddle. Michael picked out a black one with a gold saddle and Vernon had to settle for a brown one. When the merry-go-round stopped, we had to run like everything for our horses before anyone else grabbed them.

Michael and I got ours, but Vernon missed his and wound up with a little white one on the other side. We were having a fine time and my horse went way up in the air, much higher than Michael's. All the little kids were waving to their parents, and some of the parents stood on the side of the horse and held them so they wouldn't fall off. We had been around about fifteen times when I looked out and guess who was there in the crowd. *Claude Pistal!* I nearly had a heart attack. We came around again and he was still there, staring right at me.

I was so scared he was going to kill me my hair stood up on my head. I jumped off of my horse and started running. I went over two of the benches where the parents sit with small children and flew off the other side. I looked back and there he was coming right after me. I must have knocked down ten people in my way out the entrance gate and on towards the parking lot. I nearly went crazy trying to find Mrs. Dot's car. My heart was pounding so hard I could barely breathe.

When I found the car, it was locked and somebody was coming up behind me. I ran to the last car, which was a pickup truck, and it was locked, too. Nothing but an open field was on the other side of the parking lot and I knew if I ran out in that field, Claude Pistal could shoot me. All I could do was climb in the back of that truck and hide under some potato sacks. I heard someone opening car doors, shutting them, and getting closer and closer. Pretty soon I couldn't hear anything but my own heart sounding like a bass drum. All of a sudden somebody was walking around my truck. I said a Hail Mary. Whoever it was got in the truck and drove it out of the parking lot onto the highway, with me in it. All I could think of was: "Thank you, Blessed Mother," and I'm not even Catholic. Then I got to wondering what if it was Claude Pistal's truck. When whoever was driving stopped at an intersection, I peeked in the back window and saw it was some old man who had a little boy with him who was sound asleep. I started banging on the window and yelling, "Let me out of this truck!" I woke his little boy and nearly scared him to death.

The old man stopped the truck and wanted to know why I was there. I don't think he believed I was hiding from a killer, but since he lived just outside of Magnolia Springs, he agreed to let me out when he got to town. He asked whether I didn't want to sit up front with him, and I sure did. Those potato sacks smelled as bad as that livestock barn.

After he let me out, I ran all the way around the back roads and came up behind the Elite Nightspot. I banged and banged on the door until Peachy Wigham finally answered in her nightgown. She said, "Lord, honey, we're closed on Monday nights," but by that time I was already inside. She said, "Child, what is the matter with you, you are as white as a ghost."

I started babbling as fast as I could, not making any sense, just like Mrs. Dot's column. I knew what I wanted to say, but I couldn't get anything to come out right. Peachy made me take a drink of whiskey to calm me down. I told her she had to call my daddy and the FBI because Claude Pistal was here and was going to kill me. In about twenty minutes Daddy and Jimmy Snow arrived.

After I told them Claude Pistal was not in South America but right here in Harwin County and had chased me and almost caught me, too, Daddy went in the next room and had a talk with Peachy. She unlocked a closet and brought out two paper sacks with something in them. She gave Daddy one and Jimmy Snow one. Daddy came over to me and said, "I want you to stay right here with Peachy and don't worry about anything." It wasn't until after they left that I realized that I had lost my hat with my name on it, but I still had the goldfish.

Peachy got a big shotgun out of the closet and put her chair right in the middle of the room and sat down. I was so tired by this time I could hardly see straight. She told me to go in her room and go to bed, that everything was going to be all right, she would take care of my goldfish. It was dark in the back room and there was another person in that bed! I hoped it wasn't Peachy's boyfriend because Mrs. Dot said you were not supposed to touch a colored man, but at that point I didn't much care. I crawled right up against whoever it was and went to sleep.

The next morning I opened my eyes, and for a minute I forgot where I was. Then I turned over and looked right into the face of ULA SOUR, THE ALBINO WOMAN! I started hollering for Peachy to come in right away. Peachy came running with the shotgun and said, "What's the matter?"

I said, "There's an albino in your bed."

Then Peachy laughed because Ula Sour was sitting up looking at me, as surprised as I was to see me in her bed. Peachy said, "Honey, you got in the wrong bed."

"I said, "You didn't say what bed to get in. I didn't know you had two beds."

She introduced Ula and me. She's the one I heard walking around in that back room when I went up there to get Jimmy Snow. I told her I was sorry I scared her but I was real happy to meet her, I'd been wanting to for a long time. She was very nice and she wasn't all white. She had two big brown spots on her like that cocker spaniel dog at the fair, not scary-looking at all.

We got out of bed, and Ula made us a cup of coffee. I asked Ula why she never went out. She said people had made fun of her since she was little because she was an albino and she was tired of it. And guess what else I found out? She works for Peachy in the colored mortuary as an undertaker and a maid at night. Imagine a colored person having a maid. Peachy said she was the best undertaker she had ever hired. I'll bet she's who I got those maggots from. We played the jukebox waiting for Daddy and admired the goldfish that Peachy had put in a pickled pig's feet jar for me.

About nine-thirty Daddy came to get me. I introduced him to "Ula Sour, the famous albino and undertaker," and he thanked them for taking care of his little girl. He handed those two paper sacks to Peachy and she put them back in the closet. I asked Daddy what was in those sacks and he said, "Never mind. Just come on, we are going home." I got my goldfish and I told Ula I'd like to come back and see her sometime. She said I could.

When we got to the car, I asked Daddy when I was going to have to testify against Claude Pistal and he said, "You're not."

"I'm not?"

"No, you're not."

"Why not?"

"You're just not, so don't worry about it."

"Why not?"

When he just kept on driving, I asked again, "Why not?"

He said, "Because Claude Pistal is dead, that's why."

"He is?"

Daddy said, "Yes."

"Are you sure?"

"Yes, I'm sure."

I thought for a minute and said, "How do you know?"

He said, "I just know."

"You knew he was in South America, too, and he wasn't."

Then Daddy said, "When I tell you he's dead, he's dead. Have I ever lied to you before? Now just shut up about it." I did, but he has lied to me before, plenty of times. What about the time he told me that Santa Claus had been killed in a bus accident?

He took me to the Tastee Freeze and bought me a malt while he went across the street for a beer. When we got home, Mr. Kilgore from the FBI was waiting for us. Daddy turned to me and said, "Just shut up," but I hadn't even opened my mouth.

Mr. Kilgore said, "Mr. Harper, we've been looking all over for you. I wanted to inform you that Claude Pistal was found shot to death up at the landing strip outside Magnolia Springs."

Daddy said, "Thank God. Do you have any idea who did it?"

Mr. Kilgore said, "We are pretty sure it was a gangland killing. There were ten bullet holes in him. We found out he was involved with a dope ring operating out of Cuba. In fact, a lot of the gang had been hanging around the Blue Gardenia Lounge. We've been waiting to make arrests."

When I heard that, all I could think was I had probably been up there playing poker with murderers and killers. Thank goodness I hadn't tried to cheat like I do with Daddy sometimes. Mr. Kilgore said Claude had flown out of South America into Cuba and had taken a small plane and landed it at an old airstrip up the road that nobody uses much anymore except crop dusters. As a matter of fact, it had been a crop duster named Jimmy Snow that had discovered the body and had called them.

Daddy thanked him for telling us. Mr. Kilgore was sorry I had been so scared.

After Mr. Kilgore left, I looked at Daddy and he looked at me. I was wondering how he knew Claude was dead at ten o'clock when the body hadn't even been discovered yet. But just then we heard the police sirens coming down the highway. Three police cars skidded up in front of the house and stopped. About five policemen jumped out and started banging on the door, saying, "Open up, it's the police."

Daddy went to the door and the policeman said, "Is Daisy Fay Harper here?"

I said, "Here I am," wondering what in the world they were going to do to me.

The policeman said, "Are you all right?"

"Yes, I'm just fine, why?"

"Thank God, little girl, we have been looking for you since last night. A woman named Mrs. Dot is almost crazy with worry." She had called the Harwin County Highway Patrol and the police department with some story about this little girl being kidnapped by a white slaver at the fair and had dealt them a fit all night, threatening to put all their names in the paper and ruin their reputations if they didn't find me.

Daddy said, "I'm Bill Harper, her father, and maybe I can explain the misunderstanding. My little girl spent the night with a friend of hers and forgot to tell Mrs. Dot."

And the policeman said, "Where were you, Mr. Harper? We had somebody here looking for you all night."

Daddy said, "Well, it's a little embarrassing. Could I talk to you for a second over here?" And the policeman and Daddy went over to where they thought I couldn't hear, but I heard what Daddy said because his voice had gotten real high.

He said, "Uh, fellow, do you know a woman named Rayette Walker?" The policeman must have, because he started to laugh, and Daddy said, "You see, I am separated and . . ."

The policeman said, "Don't worry, buddy. I figured it was something like that."

Daddy said, "Thanks."

Then the policeman said, "OK, boys, it's all right. Let's go," and he turned to me and said, "Don't ever do that again, little girl. That poor Mrs. Dot is hysterical."

I said, "Where is she?"

He said they had her up at the sheriff's office lying down, with a doctor and Michael's mother putting ice on her head. After they left, Daddy looked at me and I looked at him.

I said, "Who is Rayette Walker?"

He said, "Nobody."

I said, "Are you sure?"

He said, "Yes, I'm sure."

I said, "How do you know you're sure?"

He said, "Have I ever lied to you?"

I gave up.

I visited Mrs. Dot and was she glad to see me! If anything happened to one of her Jr. Debutantes, she would have just died. I didn't tell her what really happened. That would have sent her into another fit.

After that, I made Daddy take me up to the Magnolia Springs Clinic to give Mrs. Underwood her goldfish. This time I went in the front door because I had an "ADULT." That ole nurse was rude as could be. She said it was against the rules to bring an animal into the clinic. Daddy told her if she didn't let me take that goddamned goldfish in there to Mrs. Underwood, he would tear the clinic apart, brick by brick, even though it was wooden.

The nurse said, looking real mean, "All right, but I can certainly understand why your little girl is the way she is, after meeting you."

You should have seen Mrs. Underwood's face. She was as happy as she could be with that goldfish. She said it was beautiful and she would rather have that than a black and white plaster cocker spaniel with sparkle on it any day.

After we left, I asked Daddy if he didn't think Mrs. Underwood looked like Gene Tierney. He said, "Yes, she looked just like her." I told you so. I am writing Gene Tierney a letter and telling her she has a look-alike living in Magnolia Springs, Mississippi. You never know when she may need a stand-in!

Michael and Vernon Mooseburger said Mrs. Dot made them

stay at that fair two hours after it closed and had everybody that worked there looking for me. Even Kay Bob Benson had to go in a search party, with the alligator man. I missed his act. When Michael and Vernon asked me why I went all funny and jumped off of the merry-go-round before my ride was up, I said I had to go to the bathroom real bad, and got a ride home because I didn't want to use a public bathroom that freaks used. Do you know what? They believed me!

You should see the papers . . . the front page is all about Claude Pistal. They even ran a picture of Jimmy Snow pointing to the spot where he discovered the body. Jimmy sure looks like an albino in that picture. The article said that ten bullets from three different guns had been used and that three bullets from a .22 caliber pistol were found in his liver. Somebody was a good shot unless they had been aiming for his heart. Claude's real name was Claude Piastelia and he had been in jail on all kinds of things, including manslaughter. Boy, I am glad he is dead. The only thing I can't figure out is how Daddy knew Claude was dead at 9:30 that morning when the paper said Jimmy Snow didn't discover the body until 10:08.

December 6, 1952

Today Harold Pistal brought Angel down to the house to say good-bye. They are moving away because of all the stuff that was in the papers about Claude. Thank goodness Angel can't read yet. She had on a Davy Crockett hat that she is just crazy about. I don't think she even knows that Claude is dead. When we all took a walk on the beach, I told Harold I was sorry his brother had been killed. Because I wasn't going to lie, I also said that since Claude was trying to kill me, I wasn't as sorry as I should be, and after all, I was an only child and was needed at home. Harold thought maybe it was better he was dead. Angel was making a crooked sand castle and couldn't hear, so he confessed to me that Claude had killed his wife in a jealous rage and was never the same after that. I wasn't surprised to hear it. When I asked him if Claude had killed Ruby Bates, he said probably. What's more, Harold already knew from Claude about me seeing Ruby and him together. I almost fainted on that one. Claude had remembered after all. I said, "I knew he was trying to kill me that night up at the fair."

"He wasn't trying to kill you, Daisy."

"He wasn't?"

"No, he was just looking for Angel and thought she might be with you."

"I think he was out to kill me."

"He would have never killed you. Because he couldn't is one of the reasons he left the country. He thought you might remember seeing him and Ruby."

"I still think he was out to kill me."

"He would never have hurt you, you saved Angel's life."

"That didn't stop him from hating me."

"He didn't hate you, he just didn't think you should be hanging around the nightclub talking to those friends of his. He didn't trust them."

"Well, anyway, he never thanked me for saving Angel's life."

"He couldn't, he didn't want anyone to know . . ."

"Know what?"

"That Angel was his little girl. We took her after her mother was killed when she was about six months old."

You could have knocked me over with a feather.

Harold made me swear not to repeat anything he had told me to anybody, and I promised I wouldn't. I asked him if he had any idea who had killed Claude and he said no. I am beginning to have an idea, but I don't want to think about it.

Angel hugged me good-bye and promised to write when she

learned how. I couldn't help thinking how lucky for me it was that she fell out of the boat that day. Poor Angel. I will miss her. Just think she has to go through life with big ears and on top of it she doesn't even know she is an Italian person. . . .

December 15, 1952

I'm Mother Goose in the Christmas play! I am so mad. Everybody in my class gets to be in their own play, but I have to be in the first and second graders'. I have no choice because Mrs. Underwood told them I would. I wanted to do my imitation of Vaughn Monroe singing "Racing with the Moon."

When the curtain goes up, I say, "I am Mother Goose, and I am in a tizzy. It is almost time for me to take all my little Mother Goose characters to the manger to see the Baby Jesus, who has just been born under the Star of the East."

Then the Star of the East walks across the stage and takes a bow.

The first-grade teacher, Miss Florence, rings a bell backstage, and I say, "There goes the magic bell." I go up to where they are going to have this big papier-mâché book and after I say, "Oh, look, here are Jack and Jill," these little first and second graders walk out of the book, all dressed like whoever they are supposed to be. I have to announce all of them.

When Tom, the piper's son, the last one, comes out, I say, "Now, children, we must be off to Bethlehem to see the Baby Jesus, who has just been born under the Star of the East." Then the Star of the East walks by again and takes another bow and we all walk off in the same direction as the Star. At the end of the whole pageant we are discovered standing in the manger.

That's stupid. Mother Goose didn't even live at the same time as Jesus.

Mrs. Underwood is having a problem casting the manger scene. She is trying to be democratic and let everybody vote who they want to be Mary and Joseph. I can't even vote because Kay Bob Benson said I shouldn't because I wasn't going to be in their part of the show.

I didn't even get to take part in the Thanksgiving parade. I didn't have anybody to make me a Pilgrim outfit. It was a dumb parade anyway. They had a float that was supposed to be Washington crossing the Delaware, but it wasn't nothing but George Crawford wearing a black hat, sitting in a rowboat his daddy had put in the back of their pickup truck that said "Crawford's Septic Tanks." This boy named Jimmy Beck was a float, but he was just riding a bicycle with crepe paper on it, with a dog in the basket. Kay Bob Benson was the Statute of Liberty with a silver cardboard crown. The Magnolia Springs High School Marching Band was there, too, but they are terrible. Not a one of them can march in a straight line and they have too many trumpets. The best thing in the parade was the Mississippi Maidens, Mr. Curtis Honeywell's all-girl army.

At Jr. Debutantes, we are painting magnolia leaves oleander pink and seafoam green to decorate this Christmas tree that Mrs. Dot has sticking in a sand dune to beautify the beach for the holidays. We have to pin the decorations on because they keep blowing off. The whole tree blew over the other day.

I got a real nice letter from Momma. She is going to try and visit me at Christmas. I can't wait to see her. I wish I could get her that silver fox fur.

We drew names in school and we have to get whose ever name we got a present. We are not to spend over a quarter. I drew Reba Quigley, but I swapped it with Patsy Ruth Coggins, who got Vernon Mooseburger's. I wonder who got my name! I hope it wasn't one of those potato farmers' children. I don't want anything homemade. I am going to get Mrs. Underwood a bowl for her fish so she can take it out of the pickled pig's feet jar Peachy Wigham gave me.

Michael and I were in Elwood's Variety Store yesterday shopping for our presents. We were in the back of the store in the boys and girls' ready-to-wear department when I saw a little boy dummy they had dressed up in a checked suit. He had on a blond wig that would be just perfect for Vernon Mooseburger's head. It has a part in it and everything. He wouldn't ever have to comb it because it was all stuck together, real neat like. If I could get him that wig, then he wouldn't have to wear that brown leatherette hat when he played the shepherd.

I asked the manager, Mrs. Hilda Jinx, how much that blond wig was, but it was not for sale. I told Michael I had it in my mind to snatch that wig off of that little boy dummy's head when nobody was looking. Vernon Mooseburger could get a lot more wear out of it than that dummy and needed it much worse because that dummy wasn't going to be in a Christmas play. Michael says he won't help me get that wig because he doesn't want to spend Christmas in jail. I told him he wouldn't go to jail. I was the one who was going to take it. Robin Hood used to steal from the rich to give to the poor, and this way we were stealing from a dead dummy and giving to the living, so it would be all right. I reminded him about Tawney the Tassel Woman. If he was being so honest, it was my duty to tell his mother the whole truth and nothing but the truth. I hated to do this to Michael, but I was forced to. When we got home, I made Michael practice having an epileptic fit all night, until he got it right.

Today after play practice, I said to Miss Florence, "I'm going to walk around in this Mother Goose outfit a little and I'll be right back."

She said, "Don't you dare go outside and get that Mother Goose dress dirty."

I was stuck, so I said, "OK, but I have to go to the bathroom," and took off before she could stop me.

Michael was outside waiting on me. We headed downtown, and on the way we went over the plans again. He went into Elwood's and started shopping while I waited in the Big B Drugstore. Then I followed him into Elwood's.

Michael was walking around the store, talking out loud, saying, "Let's see, who can I buy this for?" and picking up stuff and putting it down again. Then he'd say, "I wonder if my mother would like this?" He always overdoes things.

Mrs. Hilda Jinx looked at me funny. I got back in the children's department without her stopping me and waited for Michael to have his fit. Pretty soon he fell on the floor and yelled, "I'm having an epileptic fit. Help. I'm having an epileptic fit." He wasn't supposed to say anything! Everybody ran over to see him and I snatched the wig, but somebody had glued the stupid thing to the dummy's head. I finally peeled it off and got out the door without anybody seeing me.

I met Michael back up at the school and he was bragging on himself about how good he threw fits. When I got home, the wig was a mess from being in my geography book all afternoon. I worked on it for hours and then stuffed it with newspaper to keep its shape.

I can't wait until Vernon Mooseburger sees his present. He is going to have the best Christmas. At Jr. Debutantes, Mrs. Dot said when you get someone a gift, make sure it is something that they can enjoy and something that fits their personality. What could be more perfect for a bald boy than a wig? He needs eyebrows, too, but the dummy's eyebrows were painted on. Too bad. Maybe I can get him eyebrows next year.

December 23, 1952

We exchanged presents today in school. I gave Mrs. Underwood a goldfish bowl and a box of Mary Ball candy and some Blue Waltz perfume. George Crawford drew my name. He gave me five packs of Wrigley's spearmint gum . . . twenty-five cents . . . cheapskate! You should have seen Vernon Mooseburger's face when he got his wig. He ran into the bathroom and put it on. It looks great, except it pokes out at the back and on the sides, but I told him he could glue it down or put Scotch tape on it and then it will be perfect. Everybody loved it except Kay Bob Benson, who said it looked cheap, but I'll bet it is worth a lot more than a quarter.

Just after we had opened all our presents and Mrs. Underwood was reading us *Nancy Drew and the Hidden Staircase*, Chapter 1, "A Clue for Nancy," someone knocked on the door. She went to see who it was and came back with a big smile on her face and said, "Daisy Fay, there is someone to see you." I thought, I'm not going to go through that again. I asked Mrs. Underwood to find out who it was and get a positive identification. Mrs. Underwood said, "Daisy, it's a surprise." I told her I was not interested in any surprise visitors. She said, "All right, I'm not supposed to tell you, but it's your mother."

I said, "Does she have green eyes and funny eyebrows?"

Mrs. Underwood said, "Daisy, I know your mother."

I went out in the hall and there was my momma, all the way from Virginia. Boy, was I glad to see her. Yeah! She is going to be here with me until the day after Christmas, staying at the Magnolia Springs Hotel because she still isn't speaking to Daddy. She will come and see me in the Christmas play tomorrow night.

I'm home getting my pajamas and things and she is up visiting Velveeta Pritchard in the colored quarters. Momma still thinks Velveeta is wooonnderfullll. I feel sorry for Daddy. He is very upset that Momma is here and won't even see him. He and Jimmy Snow are in the other room, tying one on. I hope they sober up in time to see me in the play.

Momma told me all about her job in Virginia. She is not a waitress anymore, she got a promotion. She is now the Official Hostess in a very important pancake house in Charlottesville called the Pancake House and she can wear her own clothes instead of a waitress uniform. When I come to Virginia, I can eat all the free pancakes I want. I like every kind except buckwheat. They taste like nails.

We are in the "Dashes from Dot" column. It says that: "Mrs. William Harper, Jr., and her darling daughter, Daisy Fay, are wintering at the Magnolia Springs Hotel." We are only going to be there four days.

December 27, 1952

Momma left this morning. I hated for her to go. For Christmas, Momma got me a new outfit, some underwear, socks and a picture of her she had made in a department store. My present to her was some new Merle Norman makeup. They have a card down there with the color Momma wears, natural beige. She said that she had been running out and it was the perfect present. I must have a natural talent for picking out gifts.

Grandma mailed me some crocheted doilies and she and Aunt Bess sent me $5 apiece. Momma said Daddy was lazy because he gave me a $20 bill instead of going shopping. I got a box of handkerchiefs from Jimmy Snow. Blah! I gave him a six-pack of Budweiser, his favorite, and I gave Daddy Pabst Blue Ribbon. I had to buy the beer from Peachy Wigham. Nobody will sell beer to a child in Mississippi even for a present. Peachy and Ula Sour bought me a big Bible with pictures of Jesus and Mary and Joseph as colored people. I felt real bad because I didn't have anything for them.

The play went OK except when I came out on the stage. I was looking in the audience to see where my momma was sitting. Daddy and Jimmy Snow were standing in the back. So were Mr. Curtis Honeywell and his all-girl army, but I couldn't find Momma. When I did locate her, she was sitting right beside Mrs. Hilda Jinx from Elwood's Variety Store! It made me forget my lines because Michael and I had gone to the movie *I Was a Shoplifter* with Mona Freeman right after we had stolen that wig. You should have seen what happened to her! But when Miss Florence rang the magic bell backstage, I said, "Oops, there goes the magic bell now," and I remembered my words. Jack Be Nimble's candle blew out before he got two steps through the storybook, so he started to cry; and little Miss Muffet pulled her dress up over her head, but other than that, it went OK.

I got the biggest hand of anybody, even bigger than Saint Joseph's. Momma and Daddy were careful to take turns praising me after the play so they wouldn't have to talk to each other. I was hoping they would get together, it being Christmas and all and having a child in common, but they didn't. All Momma said to Daddy was: "How's your new friend?" What new friend?????

December 29, 1952

Don't ever shop at Elwood's Variety Store. They employ a group of mean and evil people who torture young children. Last night Mrs. Hilda Jinx called Daddy on the phone and told him I had dressed myself up as Mother Goose and stolen a wig off a dummy's head in the children's ready-to-wear department while some poor little boy was having an epileptic fit. The terrible thing was there was not one part of her story I could deny. She said that if Daddy brought me to the store and I returned the wig, she wouldn't press charges. She didn't want to have a bald dummy in the children's ready-to-wear department during the after Christmas sale. Daddy had to take me over to Vernon's house to get the wig back. So now Vernon is bald again.

This morning at seven-thirty Daddy had me out in front of Elwood's Variety Store and I had to stand there until eight o'clock when they opened. Finally, Mrs. Jinx came. I tried to hand her the wig, but she made me put it back right where I had gotten it in the first place. It was terrible. There wasn't a customer in the place and all the salespeople were standing behind their counters staring at me. You could have heard a pin drop. I had to walk by notions and paper supplies, and when I walked by the Butterick's sewing pattern counter, the old woman who works there said, "Shame on you, and so close to Christmas, too." That store must be a mile long, and the children's ready-to-wear department was all the way in the back. After I put the stupid wig on the stupid dummy, I had to walk past all those people again, and that woman in sewing patterns said, "Shame, shame." I was never so glad to get out of anywhere in my life. And I will tell you this, the Elwood's Variety Store has lost my business forever, and I have always been a good customer. Imagine them ruining a poor bald boy's Christmas like that.

December 30, 1952

Today I went to the Big B Drugstore and bought Peachy Wigham and Ula Sour Christmas presents with my Christmas money. I got Peachy some Royal Crown hairdressing and some Tangee rouge and Ula Sour a pair of beautiful white plastic sunglasses with mirror lens in them that you can see out of but nobody can see your eyes. I bought myself a pair to wear to Jr. Debutantes next month. We are going to have a talk on "How to Set a Party Table," and now I can sleep through it if I want.

When I got back to school, after Christmas, there was a new boy in our class, Flicka Hicks. He's been at military school and hated it, so he came back here. You wouldn't believe it. He looks just like Johnny Sheffield and has curly hair and everything.

Some people may have thought I was bragging about me getting the biggest hand at the Christmas play, but this is what Mrs. Dot said in her "Dashes from Dot" column, word for word:

Today I have a dramatic review of the annual Christmas pageant put on by the Magnolia Springs Grammar School, and I want to say, good work, children! As always, I have an inside scoop for you. You know theater is the same all over the world, and dramatic temperament is not peculiar to Broadway. I understand there was a small tiff between Miss Kay Bob Benson, Miss Patsy Ruth Coggins and Miss Amy Jo Snipes, who were all vying for the part of the Virgin Mary, and I want to say that their pageant director, Mrs. Sybil Underwood, handled the problem beautifully, by cutting the part of Mary from the play and assigning the ladies the parts of the Three Wise Men. However, Mary was sorely missed in the ever-popular no-room-at-the-inn scene. Michael Romeo, who took the part of Joseph and some of Mary's lines, was wonderful. The Star of the East was played by little Lettie Hawkins, whose mother, Gracie, is the president of the local chapter of the Eastern Star. Lettie was stunning in tinfoil. As always, the pageant ended with the famous manger scene and the highlight of that scene was a surprise visit by Santa Claus, played by our own beloved principal, Mr. J. T. Vickory, who was accompanied by the Easter Bunny, played by his wife, Honey. And I understand that her entire costume consisted of multicolored Kleenex. But the star performer of the entire evening was Daisy Fay Harper, a Jr. Debutanter, who took the part of Mother Goose and introduced us to some of the most darling youngsters you will ever see here or on Broadway. Daisy Fay was precious and kept us laughing with her wonderful and versatile expressions. It was truly an Oscar-winning performance and I hope there were not any famous producers in the audience, or surely our little Daisy Fay will be rushed away to stardom. It was a wonderful show and special thanks to Jimmy Beck, whose rat terrier, Lady, took the part of a camel. I was asked to announce frankincense and myrrh were supplied by the Hatcher Feed Store.

Noel.

I'll bet Kay Bob Benson is kicking herself. She looked so stupid with a beard. I hope Flicka Hicks reads the "Dashes from Dot" column. Maybe I'll send it to him anonymously.

January 2, 1953

Saturday, Michael and I went up to the Magnolia Springs Theater to see the double feature *Superman and the Mole Men* with Georges Reeves and Phyllis Coates and *Bandit Queen,* "EVERY MAN WAS A TARGET FOR HER LASH, HER BULLETS, HER KISSES" with Barbara Britton and Willard Parker. As we were buying our candy, in walked Flicka Hicks in his military school uniform. Guess who he was with! Kay Bob Benson! Going to military school must have made him stupid if he thinks Kay Bob Benson is good-looking. He bought her popcorn and everything. I was so disgusted I left Michael right in the middle of *Bandit Queen* and went down to the colored quarters to give Peachy Wigham and Ula Sour their presents. Peachy liked hers a lot. Ula was at the mortuary. When I told Peachy I needed a drink, she gave me an Orange Crush. I wanted Wild Turkey, so I had some and chased it with Orange Crush. I sure wouldn't want to go to the movies with some boy named after a horse.

January 23, 1953

Yesterday Daddy and I were watching the *Mickey Mouse Club* and when we looked up, two FBI men were at the door. I knew they were from the FBI because they dressed just like Mr. Kilgore, real neat, like the men on *Gang Busters*.

The short one said, "Mr. Harper, we'd like to know your whereabouts on the night of November fifth."

Daddy had an answer right away. He said he had spent the night with Rayette Walker, who lived at 212 Division Avenue, and that Jimmy Snow had been with him.

The men wrote it down and said, "Well, Mr. Harper, that coincides with Miss Walker and Mr. Snow's story." They said they were sorry to have bothered us, but they had to do some routine checking.

Boy, was I mad. Daddy had told me that Rayette Walker was nobody and now I find out he spent the night with her! I'll bet all the times he was spending the night with Jimmy Snow, he's been with her. And Daddy said he never lied to me. Ha!

Today when I went over to the high school and got my Almond Joy from Marvin Thrasher, I asked him if he had ever heard of a woman named Rayette Walker. He asked me how in the world did I know her. I told him she was not an acquaintance of mine, but of Daddy's and Jimmy Snow's. He just laughed and said he didn't doubt it, because Rayette never met a man she didn't like. He said for me to stay away from her because she would ruin my reputation. Rayette Walker must be the woman Momma and Daddy were fighting over and the one Kay Bob Benson's mother saw Daddy with at a beer joint. I am going to call on her tomorrow and tell her she has broken up my mother and daddy.

January 24, 1953

I took that picture of Momma she gave me for Christmas and the colored Bible to school today. After school I walked over to Division Avenue and found 212. It is a little white house with a front porch that looks like it is getting ready to fall down. Real low-rent, as Momma would say. I went up on the porch and knocked on the door. Nobody was home but a toy chihuahua that barked its head off.

I waited there until six o'clock. Finally, some woman came. When she saw me sitting on the porch, she looked scared and said, "Daisy Fay, what are you doing here" She knew my name. I asked could I come inside, and she let me. By that time I remembered I had seen her working up at Nita's Beauty Box. She looks a lot like Yvonne De Carlo, only a little heavier.

When we got inside, she asked me if I wanted to sit down, but I wasn't sitting in anybody's house that was a home wrecker. I showed her my mother's picture and told her my daddy was married to this woman and I was their child. I told her I knew she and Daddy had been fooling around. It was all over town and my mother knew it, too. What's more, my reputation was ruined forever because I was a Jr. Debutante and needed a good reputation. And my school is having a mother-daughter supper, and now I have to go by myself all because of her.

She looked real sad and said, "Daisy, your daddy has told me everything about you since you were born. I even saw you in the Christmas play."

I said, "You did?"

And she said, "Yes, you were wonderful."

I asked if she had noticed that I had forgotten my lines, and she hadn't noticed it at all.

To get back on the track, I said, "If you know all about me, how come you stole my daddy away from a perfectly good wife and made her leave?"

She didn't have an answer for that one. She just said for me not to be mad at Daddy because he loved me very much, and they had never meant to hurt me or Momma. Then she added, "When you grow up, maybe you will understand," the old famous line that they always give you.

I told her I was in the sixth grade and read at ninth-grade level and I understood a lot, and I hated her guts for hurting my momma, and I was never going to Nita's Beauty Box again, and for her to stay away from my daddy and leave him alone and to go out with single men, all in one sentence. She asked me if I wanted a Coca-Cola. When we went in the kitchen, she had Mrs. Dot's review of the Christmas play stuck on her refrigerator. I'll bet she wasn't there at all but just read the review.

I made her swear on the colored Bible she would leave my daddy alone. She said if I hated her so bad, she would. I said I did. Then I gave her back her Coca-Cola bottle and left.

January 25, 1953

Oh, brother, am I in trouble again. When I got home from Rayette's last night, Daddy wasn't here, so I just made myself a peanut butter and jelly sandwich and watched a little television and went to sleep. But today after school, he was home, drunk as a skunk.

Daddy was so mad at me for going up to Rayette's and making her swear not to ever see him again I think he would have killed me if Jimmy Snow hadn't been there. He was crying and carrying on and saying I didn't know what I had done and why didn't I just stay out of things I didn't understand. I told him I had a patriotic duty to protect Momma and he wasn't going to hurt my mother over any beauty operator. He just sat there and cried in his beer. I sure thought it was funny, him acting like that over somebody he told me was nobody.

He and Jimmy Snow talked for a while and then Jimmy came in my room and said for me to go for a walk with him on the beach. I told him it wouldn't do any good because I was mad at him, too, for going up to Rayette's house with Daddy in the first place when he knew Daddy was a married man. After we got to the beach, Jimmy said, "Daisy, your mother and daddy are going to get a divorce."

I said, "They are not!" Even if they said it, it didn't mean a thing. They have been getting a divorce since before I was born. Momma will get over being mad at Daddy and come home any day now.

Jimmy said, "I know you want to believe your momma's coming back, but it's just not going to happen."

I said, "Even if it is true, which it isn't, Daddy doesn't have any business running around with some old beauty operator that is trash, and everyone says so, too."

Then Jimmy said, "Now, Daisy, Rayette Walker has been a good friend to you, me and your daddy."

I almost had a fit on that one. I said, "She isn't any friend of mine, breaking up my home and making Momma leave home. I hate her and I wish she was dead in the grave with maggots eating her stomach."

Jimmy didn't answer me for a long time. Then he said, "Daisy, sit down. I have something to tell you." I didn't want to sit down because of the sand fleas, but he took off his jacket and put it on the beach. It was a bright clear night and I could see his face in the moonlight. He'd been drinking, but I don't think he was drunk. He looked at me. "Daisy, can I trust you?"

"Yes, of course, you can. I am capable of keeping life-and-death secrets to the grave. I even have some information about Michael Romeo and a certain exotic dancer that I have kept from his momma."

"You're a pretty smart girl, Daisy, and you're old enough to understand what I am going to say."

I agreed with him about the smart part and told him to get on with it.

He said, "I hate to see you make a mistake about Rayette you will regret. Now I'm only going to tell you this once, and I want your word of honor that you will never ask me or anybody about it again."

I said, "Yes, now tell me."

He said, "Are you sure?"

And I said, "Yes."

By this time I was being eaten alive by mosquitoes and sand fleas. I thought if he didn't say what he had to say, I was going to itch to death. Besides, the suspense was worse than *Nancy Drew*.

"Well, Daisy, if the police ever trace some of the bullets they found in Claude Pistal's liver to a certain woman's gun, then maybe you'll understand what a good friend she was to you and your daddy."

I just sat there. I forgot about the sand fleas and mosquitoes. I had suspected it, but now I knew for sure what had been in those paper sacks Peachy Wigham gave Daddy the night before Claude was murdered. Rayette, Daddy and Jimmy Snow had killed Claude Pistal trying to protect me! Rayette had lied to the police, a crime in itself, about Daddy being there all night. Not to mention hurting her reputation. I didn't say a word. Pretty soon we went back in the house and found that Daddy had already passed out. After Jimmy left, I went to bed, but I couldn't sleep. All these people in trouble, even Peachy, because of me. And Claude hadn't even been trying to kill me!

I may read at a ninth-grade level, but I sure can be dumb sometimes. I was sorry I had been so mean to Rayette. I just pray she keeps her mouth shut and they don't trace those bullets to her gun. There is such a thing as knowing too much.

January 26, 1953

I went into Nita's Beauty Box this morning and asked Rayette Walker if she would go with me to the mother-and-daughter dinner next week. She started to cry right there in her stall and with her customer's head half rolled up. Her customer sure was mad because her hair was drying all funny. I've got to go and get me a dress to wear to the dinner, but I'm not shopping at Elwood's Variety Store, you can be sure of that. When I grow up, I hope I don't bawl at the slightest little thing. It's embarrassing. I've seen enough crying the past two days to last me for a long time.

When I got home from school this afternoon, Daddy was as happy as he could be. Rayette must have called him up. He asked whatever made me do such a nice thing, but I couldn't tell him because I promised Jimmy Snow. I will do anything to make Daddy and Jimmy happy after what they did for me. I can never repay them for as long as I live. If Daddy wants to date Rayette, he can. When I get rich, I am going to buy him another outboard motor and the boat, too. The three of them are the only real live heroes I know in person.

I hope my momma doesn't find out I am taking a beauty operator to the mother-and-daughter dinner in her place.

February 2, 1953

The night didn't start out very well. The first thing that happened was when we went to pick up Rayette, her toy chihuahua, Trixie, bit Daddy on the ankle and made him bleed. It goes to prove Mrs. Dot's theory: Toy chihuahuas are dangerous. One time her mother was on her way to a DAR meeting and her toy chihuahua, who she loved better than life, was in the car with her. As she came to a stoplight, that dumb dog ran under her brake looking for its ball, and Mrs. Dot's mother had to make a life-and-death decision, whether to slam on the brakes to keep from hitting two people that were crossing the street or to mash her dog's head under the brake. She chose the dog over those two people and knocked them eight feet up in the air, and one of them was in a wheelchair. It cost her mother a fortune in hospital bills. It's a good thing one of those people was already crippled or it would have cost her more.

Rayette had on a royal blue wool dress and shoes to match. When we got to the dinner, Kay Bob Benson came right over to us and said, "That's not your mother, that's Rayette Walker who works at Nita's Beauty Box."

I said, "I know what my own mother looks like, don't I? Rayette Walker is just pinch-hitting for my mother, who is a very successful hostess in Virginia."

Mrs. Underwood was about the only one who was nice to Rayette. Everybody else ignored us the whole evening. The dinner was Chicken a la King with English peas. I hate the dreaded English pea and wouldn't eat one if my life depended on it, ever since I found out that Ruby Bates's last meal had been peas and carrots. Mrs. Dot gave a speech entitled "Mother, The Best Friend a Girl Can Ever Have," and some old woman named Geneva Corsset sang a song called "Mother." What a stupid song. I know how to spell "mother." Then we had to sing the Mississippi state song and Billy Bundy said a prayer, and the dinner was over.

Daddy was late picking us up. He had been to some beer joint and was half loaded. I hate to be the last one to leave. Rayette said she had a wonderful time, and I guess she did because she ate everything on her plate, plus three of the red Jell-Os.

Kay Bob Benson and her mother wore mother-and-daughter dresses and acted like they had just come in style. Fashion hits slow down here.

It sure was funny to see Billy Bundy praying in front of all those mothers and daughters.

I'm making all my own valentines this year. I am going to make Flicka Hicks one with a horse on it. He still spends all his time with Kay Bob Benson, and if that isn't bad enough, a man came to school and made us look at an eye chart and I couldn't see anything but one big *E*. So I'm going to have to get glasses. A chipped tooth and glasses. I might as well give up!

February 6, 1953

Today Rayette and I went to the glasses store and got me a pair. I wanted some brown ones like Grace Kelly's, but Rayette picked out a pair of blue plastic wing tips I'm not too crazy about. She says they go with my eyes and the shape of my face. I put them on and I can see for miles and read every sign they have in Magnolia Springs. I think I have the same kind of vision that Superman has. I went by and showed Peachy Wigham and Ula Sour my glasses. They thought they were great.

Poor Jimmy Snow is in the Magnolia Springs Clinic because he crashed his plane on some telephone wires and broke his arm and his shoulder in two places. Daddy said he was going to be up there in traction for a long time. I am going to visit him and tell him he better have his eyes checked because he might need glasses like I did and that may be why he is crashing his plane so much.

I got a letter from Momma and she wants to know if Daddy is taking good care of me and all that stuff. She wrote she would feel better if I came to Virginia to live with her, but I can't leave Daddy because he needs me.

Even though Rayette and Daddy are fussing over something, she is still friendly to me.

I told Daddy he'd better make up with Rayette real soon. I didn't say why I thought so, but if she gets mad enough at him, she's liable to blow the whistle. It's real brave of Daddy to even have a fight with her. If it was me, I sure wouldn't. I'm wearing these ugly blue glasses, aren't I?

Kay Bob Benson said I look like a hoot owl.

February 14, 1953

Mrs. Underwood loved the valentine I made her. It has a Shell Beach, Mississippi, gold decal on it. I made twenty-six valentines. I had two left over, so I sent one to the little girl in South America that the Jr. Debutantes adopted and one to Van Johnson. I only got three, from Michael Romeo, Vernon Mooseburger and Patsy Ruth Coggins. Daddy forgot it was Valentine's Day and Momma's hasn't come yet.

February 16, 1953

This morning about six-thirty, Mrs. Hammer, who owns Hammer's Christian Motel, looked out her window and saw a woman naked as a jaybird skipping up and down the beach picking up seashells. She grabbed a blanket and ran out to cover her up and that woman was Mrs. Dot! She had reversed herself back in time and thought she was a little girl again. Mrs. Hammer called Mr. Dot and he said that last night she had gone crazy and stabbed him eighteen times with a penknife and run out the front door naked. He wasn't killed because the knife was so little. They called an ambulance and took her to the crazy ward in Meridian. I told Daddy for us to go get her and bring her here to live with us, but Mr. Dot had already signed the papers and there was nothing we could do. To tell you the truth, everyone here is disappointed that she didn't use a bigger knife on him.

February 18, 1953

I hate all those rotten shrimpers' daughters and Kay Bob Benson so bad I could throw up. Michael's mother got us all together and said we should buy Mrs. Dot a gift for her to take when she went to see her. Those girls said they didn't want to spend any money because she was crazy and wouldn't appreciate the present. Can you believe that? Kay Bob Benson claimed she knew Mrs. Dot was crazy all along. I asked Michael's mother if I could go too. I can ride with her, but I can't go in because they don't let children visit. I had gotten Mrs. Dot a box of Whitman's candy. Maybe after she eats the candy, she can use the box for a purse. I had seen Olive de Havilland do that in a movie called *The Snake Pit,* where she was in a crazy ward.

When we got there, I was surprised to see that the building looked just like a real hospital anybody would be in. Mrs. Romeo went in, and about an hour later she came back and was very upset. She was shaking so bad she had to have five cigarettes before she could drive home. She was still holding the box of Whitman's candy. They wouldn't let Mrs. Dot have anything at all. Mrs. Romeo said they walked her down this long hall that had doors with bars on them. People out of their minds were screaming their heads off. Mrs. Dot was in a room with five or six other women. She was sitting on her bed in an old gray dress and her hair had not been combed for days. She kept trying to fix her hair the whole time and thought Mrs. Romeo was her sister or something and started to serve her tea with lemon and cream and sugar. She handed Mrs. Romeo an invisible cup and didn't even know where she was. She thought she was at her home in Memphis and those other people in the room were visiting her. When she left, Mrs. Dot was trying to give all those crazy people a cup of tea and one of them took it. The nurse said Mrs. Dot was in a bad way, and she didn't think she would ever get out of there, but not to worry because she was perfectly happy and was not suffering. There was nothing we could do but eat the candy ourselves.

February 20, 1953

Sunday, Daddy and I were up at the Bon Ton Café and Daddy
kept watching Billy Bundy count his money. According to Billy,
to make real money in the religious game, you need a Glory
Getter. A Glory Getter is someone who can make people think
they can get them to glory. The best Glory Getters are little
children and platinum-blond-haired women. Billy had a platinum-blond-haired woman once whose specialty was handling
snakes. She could get more money in that collection box than
you could shake a stick at, but she got mad at him because one
of her snakes bit her, so she ran off with a mechanic. There was
some little preacher boy over in Louisiana he wished he could
get his hands on because he was a gold mine. But the boy's
momma and daddy had him all tied up and weren't letting anybody have any part of him. I'll bet that little boy has curly hair.

Billy averages about $150 a week, and that sounds like a lot
to Daddy and me, but Billy says it is only peanuts. At one time
he made over $500 a week and he can hardly live on $150. He
has to pay alimony to two women and child support for five
children. He doesn't dare not to pay it because he is still in
trouble with the law for selling autographed pictures of the Last
Supper.

Daddy asked Billy Bundy if it was hard to preach and if you
had to go to Bible school before they would let you get up in
front of people and take up a collection. Billy said no, all you
got to do is tell people what they want to hear, and then scare
them into giving you their money. Then he went back to count-
ing and stacking his money.

Daddy is worried because the insurance money is almost gone,
and we have another payment to make on the land where the
malt shop used to be. Maybe that is why he thought up the
miracle.

Today when I got home, Daddy and Billy Bundy were both there. Daddy pulled me in the house, shut the door and closed all the windows. I didn't know what was going on, but I knew it wasn't bad because they sure looked happy to see me. They sat me down at the kitchen table and asked me if there was anything I wanted before they started to talk to me. I ordered a Coca-Cola and a liver cheese sandwich with mustard and mayonnaise that I got in a hurry. Billy Bundy looked at me and said, "Yes indeed, you are a very lucky little girl because your smart daddy has thought up a miracle that will make us all rich and maybe make you famous."

The miracle is that I am going to pretend to drown and then come back from the dead as Billy Bundy's new Glory Getter. Daddy is convinced he can make a machine that can shine a cross on the sky. The deal is Billy is getting sixty percent of the profits and I am thrown in for nothing. When I heard this, I told Daddy I didn't think he made such a good bargain. Daddy said for me not to worry, we will still make a bundle. Billy Bundy is a very sharp businessman.

Billy wants to keep me dead for three days, but Daddy said no, I was only going to be dead for twenty-four hours. He didn't want my momma to hear about it or to worry her on any account. Daddy stuck to his guns on that point, and we all shook hands. Daddy is to get to work on that machine and I am to keep my mouth shut.

February 22, 1953

Yesterday Daddy went to Meridian and bought himself an old movie projector. He has a little piece of plywood with a cross cut in it over the hole in front of the projector where the light comes out. Last night about three o'clock in the morning, when everyone was asleep, he woke me up and we went out on the beach with an extension cord. Sure enough, when he turned it on, there was this cross shining in the sky as big as you please. Boy, is he smart. Now all he has to do is figure out a way to get the machine to work on batteries because on the day of the miracle I am going to have it in a boat and after everybody sees the cross, I am going to sink the boat with the machine in it so nobody can find any evidence. The timing of the miracle is very important because a lot of people should see the cross. Daddy and Billy Bundy think we should do it on a cloudy day. There are a lot of technical things involved in a miracle you wouldn't even dream about.

Plans for the miracle are moving right along. We need a rowboat. Billy Bundy pointed out that Mr. Wentzel, who lives up on the Bon Secour River and has a lot of rowboats for rent, might not miss one. Last night Billy borrowed a truck from somewhere, and about one o'clock this morning Billy and Daddy and I drove up there. We parked the truck by the river about two miles up from Mr. Wentzel's boat dock, and Billy told Daddy to stay with the truck while he and I went and got the boat. The trip up was an easy one for Billy because he had a bottle of whiskey he was swigging on the whole way, but I was just eaten alive by those Bon Secour mosquitoes. To me, it would have been easier if Daddy had let us off closer to the boat dock, but they are not listening to me. I don't even have a percentage of the miracle.

When we finally got down to where the boats were, we picked

us out a rowboat and were busy trying to untie it when all of a sudden we looked up and Mr. Caldwell, the crippled girl's daddy, was standing right there and shining a big heavy-duty flashlight on us. He said, "Hey, what's going on?"

I thought we were goners for sure, but just then Billy grabbed me by the neck and stuck me under the water and said, "It's just me, Brother Caldwell, baptizing a poor sinner, a real emergency case, who needs to be saved." He made up this whole story about me and how I had come to him that night, begging to be saved from a life without Christ. He went on and on, but I wasn't hearing much because he was drowning me and I was having to fight for my life.

Billy used my fighting for the benefit of his story. He said, "See, Mr. Caldwell, how some sinners fight salvation." Mr. Caldwell must have believed him because he wished Billy good luck with God's work and went on back up to his house.

I was mad as the devil at Billy for holding me under that water for such a long time. I told him that I was for the miracle as much as he and Daddy were, but I sure didn't want to be killed at such an early age because of it.

We had to wait in the water until Mr. Caldwell turned out his lights, a fact that didn't make me too happy because everybody knows that the Bon Secour is full of water moccasins. To make matters worse, when we did get that boat untied, Billy made me row all the way up to where Daddy and the truck were. The boat was heavy and it took us forever to get it in the back of that truck. When I told Daddy that Billy had made me row, Billy claimed he had done it because it was good practice since I would have to use rowing in the miracle. Anyway, we have got that rowboat in the living room and I can't have anybody over.

I was so tired in school today I slept through Chapter 14, "George Gets Lost," of our *Nancy Drew* story.

Daddy has been painting that stolen rowboat all week. It is now the same color as the Gulf of Mexico, so if a plane comes over, they can't see it. He has the machine working on batteries real good. We tried it out last night. He has also come up with a great idea he got from working at theaters.

A lot of times the people from Hollywood would send life-size cardboard figures of the stars to put outside the theaters. Daddy's idea is to make cardboard figures of Jesus Christ, His mother and the Apostles to stand up behind me in the revival meetings. Each one will have its own spotlight, he is going to put clothes on them and then use fans so the clothes will blow in the wind. Daddy says this will be a very dramatic sight and should bring in more money. He is going all out.

The miracle is set for next Tuesday, when the *Farmers' Almanac* says it is going to be cloudy. Late Tuesday night I am going to put on a white choir robe that Billy stole for me from his church. We will get the boat in the water and I'll row out as far as I can until I can't see land anymore. Daddy will then run up and down the beach and wake everyone up and carry on about how his little girl has drowned in the Gulf of Mexico because of his drinking. In the meantime, Billy is just going to happen to have a camera in his car so he can take a picture of the cross for the paper. At 6:45 A.M. on the dot, I turn the machine on and pull the nail out of the hole Daddy drilled in the bottom of the boat. Daddy figures it will take about thirty minutes for the boat and the projector machine to sink, so the cross will still be on when I get to shore on my inner tube. Once I can see people, I am to let go of the inner tube and dog-paddle all the way in. As soon as my feet touch bottom, I will stand up and walk out of the water with my hands in a praying position and my eyes cast upwards. According to plan, this should be at five after seven when Daddy will make a big fuss and get people to look at the spot where I'll be.

When I get to the shore, I'm supposed to say, "I have been with my Father in heaven, and He let me come back from the dead to deliver a message to my daddy to quit drinking, and I have something very important to tell all of the other sinners in Harwin County. . . ."

After that, Daddy and Billy Bundy will grab me and take me up to the house and keep me there for three days, and Friday I will make my first appearance after being dead at a revival meeting. It sounds good to me.

The little girl from South America the Jr. Debutantes adopted is still sending us letters, but nobody will answer her, so I am going to write and tell her Mrs. Dot is sick, but not to worry, we will keep sending her money.

I'll bet she looks just like Carmen Miranda!

March 2, 1953

I am back from the dead, and you wouldn't believe what happened.

Last night at one o'clock I put on my choir robe, and Daddy and Billy and I dragged the boat out in the water. I got in it and rowed away. In the boat with me were the projection machine, a flashlight, an inner tube, a pair of pliers and an assortment of Peter Paul candy bars. Billy let me take his Timex waterproof, shatterproof watch, which I was to throw away when I left the boat, because he didn't think a person coming down from heaven would be wearing a Timex. I had to agree with him, although I would have loved to have it for myself if he didn't want it.

I also had a list of instructions in case I forgot what to do. Daddy said if you know how to read instructions, you can do anything in life, and he taught me how to read them real good. I rowed and rowed as far out as I could and ate all my candy in the first hour.

It sure was cold sitting in that boat in the dark for five hours. I started doing a lot of thinking about sharks and I hoped I wasn't going to be drowned for real.

To tell you the truth, I almost rowed back a couple of times, but I knew if I did, Daddy would kill me. When the sun came up, I looked at the shore and I had drifted all the way down past the pier, so I had to row like crazy to get back to where I was supposed to be in time for the projection machine to go on.

By then it was six forty-five. I was exhausted, but I turned the machine on and pulled the nail out with a pair of needle-nosed pliers, threw the perfectly good watch away, and jumped out of the boat and headed for shore on my inner tube. I could begin to hear voices on the beach as I got closer and helicopters were beginning to fly all over the place. I thought I never was going to make it, but I let go of the inner tube when I was supposed to and started dog-paddling in.

When I got to where I could walk and looked up, I never saw so many people in my life. It's hard to walk in the water with your hands in a praying position, looking up. I fell down three times. We should have practiced that part. When I reached the shore, everyone started screaming and running toward me, Mr. Curtis Honeywell and his all-girl army, Michael and his whole family, the police and the Coast Guard, and just about the entire town.

Daddy grabbed me first and did a great scene, just like Cary Grant's in the movie *Penny Serenade* when he thought he was going to lose his little girl. Billy Bundy was running up and down the beach, screaming, "Look at the cross, look at the cross," to make sure that everyone saw it. I said my line about coming from heaven with an important message and I had to repeat it twice so everyone could hear me. Then Daddy took me straight up to the house and put me in the bedroom.

Daddy hadn't told Jimmy Snow about the miracle and he had come down to the beach with his arm still in a cast to look for me. When he saw me alive, he just sat right down on the beach and cried like a baby. He wasn't paying any attention to the cross at all. All day long, reporters and people kept coming, but Daddy and Billy Bundy won't let me talk to anyone until the revival meeting.

I heard what Daddy was saying to them through the door, promising he would never touch a drop of liquor again because God had let his child live. Daddy was real corny, especially when he would tell them he had to check on his little girl and then walk in here and take a drink. Mrs. Underwood came down to see me and I felt real bad that I couldn't see her, but Daddy said that it would be bad for business. The room is full of cardboard figures, fans and spotlights and signs that say, "Come see the Little Girl who came back from the dead, with a message from God," and she might get suspicious.

Daddy promised to tell Jimmy Snow that I wasn't really drowned. I don't like to see Jimmy upset. I will probably be in the paper since this is the most exciting news that has happened here since the malt shop burned up.

March 23, 1953

I'm still not sure what went wrong. Daddy rented the dance hall across the street for the revival meeting. Billy Bundy announced on the radio where the revival meeting would be held and at what time. He also announced he had photographs of the cross that had appeared on the clouds and he would send them to anybody in his listening audience for a donation of $5. He did a sermon based on how a little child shall lead them and threw in "unless a person becomes as innocent as a child, they cannot enter the kingdom of heaven." It was great.

That afternoon we went over to the dance hall to set up the cardboard figures with their fans and their spotlights, and to rehearse. I was to stay in the ladies' room until Billy had finished his sermon and told about how he was an eyewitness to me coming back from the dead. Daddy had rented an organ and had hired Miss Irma Jean Slawson to play "Let Us Gather by the River" when I was brought up on the stage. He thought a song about water was best since I had been drowned. Irma Jean had made quite a name for herself at the Future Farmers of America Convention that had been held in Robertsdale earlier this year.

Daddy had already taken care of arrangements to charge a dime for parking, but he never dreamed how many people would show up. There were so many people he didn't get his dime from a lot of them. A man he'd hired to sell cold drinks and hot dogs ran out of hot dogs before the revival ever started. By seven o'clock Daddy's folding chairs had been rented and people were still coming. Billy Bundy had gotten me a maroon choir robe from the Magnolia Springs Baptist Church and a rhinestone cross to wear. That was going to be my official uniform. Daddy put some rouge and some Maybelline mascara on me he had borrowed from Rayette Walker, who wasn't mad at him anymore. All I was supposed to do was to walk on the stage, look real holy, talk a few minutes about my trip to heaven and go into the audience with my buckets and get money.

At first everything went real well. Billy Bundy had on a black suit with a string bow tie and preached like crazy about the burning fires of hell and how God had sent this child to lead everybody to salvation. He said things like "Suffer the little children to come unto me." I couldn't hear it all from the bathroom, but the people seemed to like it because they said "Amen" a lot. Then he got to the part where I had been in heaven and had returned from the dead to talk to them. The cue for me to enter was to be three knocks on the bathroom door from Miss Irma Jean Slawson. I was to count to ten to give her enough time to get back to her organ. I was getting real nervous waiting for my cue when all of a sudden Miss Irma Jean ran into the bathroom and used it and ran back out, and then she knocked three times on the door.

I counted to ten and entered the stage with my eyes pointed upwards just like Daddy had told me to do. Even though Miss Slawson had made me nervous giving me my cue, she was well worth the money Daddy paid her. She sure played loud. The minute I came out Daddy hit me with a spotlight and I had to stand there a long time before I could make my talk. Those people were taking my picture and screaming out things like "Praise the Lord" and "Hallelujah" and stuff like that. Daddy blinked the spotlight a couple of times before I got enough nerve to speak.

I put both my hands up in the air like Daddy had told me to and sure enough they quieted down. He knows his audiences. I started my talk with how I had been in heaven and that God was real nice-looking. He and the angels had told me to come back to earth and stop my daddy from drinking and to tell everyone how much we needed money so I could carry the Lord's work all over the whole state of Mississippi. They seemed to like what I was telling them. Then I got carried away with myself and forgot my planned speech. I started talking about how wrong it was to catch fish that they weren't going to eat and leave them on the pier to die and that catfish have souls and I had seen a lot of them in heaven and it was evil to kill them. I went on about how wrong it was to be mean to colored people and especially little children and albinos. I had a lot to say that night about meanness no matter what form it took.

I was having a good time when all of a sudden I could feel that they were no longer listening to me. Even though I was supposed to keep my eyes upward, I looked down in the audience and saw Mr. Caldwell, that man from the Bon Secour River, come walking up the aisle carrying his crippled daughter, Betty. Miss Irma Jean Slawson must have gotten scared. She stopped playing the organ and everything became real quiet. He walked right up the stairs and onto the stage and said, "Touch my little girl and make her whole." I didn't know what he was talking about, so I just stood there too scared to move. I looked at my daddy, who was by the spotlight, but he was just staring at Mr. Caldwell and Betty. I looked over for Billy Bundy, but he had dropped his Bible on the floor and froze on the spot. I was getting no help from my partners, who sure hadn't told me what to do in this situation. Then Mr. Caldwell looked up towards heaven and said in a real loud voice, "Let the angel of the Lord touch my child." I didn't know what he was talking about and I would have been standing there to this day if Betty hadn't said, "Fay, help me. Put your hands on me and help me."

Well, there was something so sweet about the way she said that that even though I was scared to death to touch a crippled person, I went right over and put my hands on her legs. When I did, I felt very strange, as though electricity was going through my body and through my hands and into her.

The whole time I was hoping I wouldn't catch a crippling disease from Betty. My mother would kill me if I did. Her legs were real skinny and she had on hose. Why in the world would you put hose on a crippled person? I must have stood there for about five minutes before her daddy put her down and stood her on her feet. He said to me, "Angel of the Lord, make her walk."

I was the Angel of the Lord he was talking about. I didn't know what else to do, so I said, "You'd better walk now," and I touched her again for good measure!

Once Mr. Caldwell let go of her, sure enough, she put one foot in front of the other and started to walk, and after she got going good, she was walking and running all over that stage. It was great until her daddy fell on his knees, crying and screaming and praising the Angel of the Lord who had cured his little girl. He was carrying on something fierce, just trying to get attention if you ask me.

When he did that, the people in the audience went crazy and four or five of them began rolling up and down the aisles and a lot of the others stood up and started babbling in the unknown tongue that was very popular with religious people. You should have heard them, "Gobble, gobble, gobble." I was enjoying that until some old woman threw her hearing aid at the stage and hit me in the head with it, screaming, "I can hear, I can hear, praise God, I can hear."

No wonder the way everyone was yelling. All of a sudden the whole audience was knocking over Daddy's rented chairs and was headed right up on the stage after me, hollering, "Heal me, heal me." Daddy always told me that Christians were dangerous and I believed him, so I picked up my choir robe and started running. Miss Irma Jean Slawson must have gone crazy, too, because at this point she began to play "If I Knew You Were Coming, I'da Baked a Cake" that isn't even a religious number.

Just as I reached the ladies' room, they caught me and were jerking at my clothes and pulling my hair so I couldn't get away. Someone ripped my rhinestone cross right off. I was yelling for my daddy, but he wasn't there. I swung and hit two or three of them, and I bit a man with a withered arm that I was sorry for later. But I think they had it in their mind to kill me. I was on the floor kicking as many of them as I could when I saw Jimmy Snow socking those Christians left and right with the cast he had on his arm and there was Daddy, swinging the cardboard picture of the Apostle Paul.

Jimmy got to me first and picked me up with his good arm and ran through the crowd with me just like I was a football. Daddy was in front of him swinging what was left of Paul, and Billy Bundy hit one of those Christians in the head with his Bible. Just as we got to the front door, someone grabbed Jimmy by the leg and he fell down. He yelled at me to keep going and get the hell out of there, so I did. It's a good thing I had on my tennis shoes under my robe because I must have run four miles up that beach as fast as I could. I never even took the time to look behind me until I got to the pier, where I bought me an Orange Crush and a Baby Ruth on credit, and ran in the bathroom and locked the door to wait for my daddy.

I must have waited for two or three hours while some fisherwomen kept banging on the door, trying to get in, but I wouldn't open up. How did I know that they weren't Christians in disguise? You should have heard them cuss. Anyway, if they weren't Christians in disguise, they were fisherwomen and were taking the lives of innocent fish, so they could just use the men's room. Serves them right.

Finally, Daddy came to get me. He said we had to hurry because the police were after him for disturbing the peace. I didn't even have time to pack my things. We jumped in the car and were halfway up the road before I noticed that Daddy was all beaten up and only had half of his glasses left. He was driving with one hand and nearly wrecked us about four times. Finally, I had to steer.

We turned off the road and headed towards the airfield where

Claude Pistal had been killed and where Jimmy Snow was waiting for us in his plane. Just as we turned off, we heard the sirens. The Highway Patrol was right behind us. That scared Daddy so bad that he lost what was left of his glasses turning around to look.

We almost rammed Jimmy's plane because Daddy couldn't see to find the brake and kept stepping on me instead. I couldn't move because I was steering. Finally, I found the emergency brake and pulled it, which caused us both to crack our heads. Daddy said, "Get out and run like hell," which I did. Jimmy had driven the plane over to where we were, but I had to guide Daddy because he couldn't see. When I got him to the plane, Jimmy grabbed him and pulled him in, and pulled me, but by then a highway patrolman had me by the foot. As Jimmy drove off across the field, my tennis shoe came off right in the policeman's hand! You should have heard him cuss. He said, "Halt, goddammit it, halt!" I didn't think officers of the law were supposed to cuss, but they do.

Daddy just kept hollering, "What's happening, what's happening?" I was sorry he couldn't see because Jimmy did a wonderful thing. He pushed a button and all of a sudden DDT came out of the back of the plane and covered the Highway Patrol car. They had to slam on their brakes and when they did, Jimmy turned that plane around, revved up the motor and we took off. We flew all the way to Key West, Florida, dusting crops when we felt like it.

The first thing Daddy did when we got here was to buy himself a pair of glasses and get me a new pair of tennis shoes. I ate so much key lime pie I made myself sick. After Jimmy got back, he called to say Peachy Wigham was keeping Felix for me. So anyway, here I sit in some old, ugly motel in Key West, Florida.

Daddy has a job running the pictures in a theater, but this is the bad news. Momma called up and she is furious. Somebody sent her the Magnolia Springs paper and she read about me drowning and coming back from the dead. I'll just bet it was Kay Bob Benson's mother. She said Daddy is crazy to have done such a sacrilegious thing and I can't stay with him anymore.

If those Christians hadn't gone crazy, I could have made a lot of money and bought her a silver fox fur and an alligator bag. I'll bet she wouldn't have been so mad then.

Anyway, she's on her way down to put me in a Catholic boarding school in Bay St. Louis, Mississippi. Now I wonder who is going to write to that little girl in South America. Kay Bob Benson and the shrimpers' daughters won't.

June 22, 1956

Momma died a week after my freshman year in high school so I won't be going to boarding school anymore. Instead, I am back in Shell Beach with Daddy, who has taken her death pretty hard. The thing of it is we didn't even know she was sick. I hadn't seen much of her in the past three years because I was staying in school for the summers, too.

The last time I saw Momma was when she came to visit at Christmas and all I did was complain about how much I hated the school. She looked a little thin, but I didn't imagine she was sick. In June my grandmother called to tell me she was in the hospital, but by the time I got to Virginia she was dead of cancer. I'll never forgive myself for not going up there and seeing her sooner.

At the funeral I never did go look at her, I just couldn't. I knew it wasn't Momma in that coffin. That couldn't have been my momma in a little box like that.

Every time the phone rings I keep thinking it's her, or maybe I'll get a letter from her. I can't believe she's gone.

A preacher stood up and said a lot of things about her at the funeral, but he didn't even know her. I wanted to kill him. I started to scream at him to shut up and to get away from Momma, and they made me leave the church. I didn't go to the graveyard. I couldn't have watched them put her in the ground.

A week later, I went to see her grave. There wasn't even a gravestone there, nothing but a bare plot of land, and I didn't leave Virginia until she had one. I never did buy her that silver fox fur and her alligator purse. I could have if I had tried harder; I just didn't. All I have left is her dinner ring and a picture she gave me when I was eleven.

This is the last letter I got from her:

Dear Daisy,

I am sorry I was not able to be with you on your birthday. I can't believe my little girl is fifteen. Hope the things fit. Wish it could have been more. I hope this is the best birthday ever. Did your daddy send you anything? Wanted to get you a coat, but this job just barely pays the rent. Daisy, I hope you will learn from me and not be foolish. Get an education. As you grow older, I hope you understand that your daddy and I just couldn't ever go back together and it has nothing to do with you. We both love you very much. We didn't mean for it to happen. I married your daddy because I thought he would take care of me, but he couldn't. Now I find I can barely take care of myself. Try to be more like Grandmother. Don't depend on anyone. I learned too late for me. But it isn't too late for you. Momma has always thought I was stupid and I guess she's right. I believed if you loved a man and was a good wife, things would work out, but that isn't always the case. About all I can give you right now is love. Miss you every day. Sorry you broke your glasses. How did you sit on them? If the tape doesn't hold them, tell your daddy. Remember you are the best thing that ever happened to me. I am so proud of you. If I didn't have you, I couldn't go on. Try not to be so disappointed about your daddy and me, honey. No matter what, you are the best part of both of us. Sorry to be so serious, but it is hard to believe my little girl is growing up so fast. I love you.

Your Mother

I've been home about a week now and today is the first time I felt like going out.

Michael and his mother came to see me. He looks great and has grown up a lot. He said how sorry he was about Momma. He is going to become a priest. We had a laugh about Tawney the Tassel Woman, and I told him when he gets to be a bishop or something, I will come and blackmail him. He won't be going to the Magnolia Springs High School with me but to Spring Hill Seminary in Mobile, Alabama. I'll miss him.

Of course, I always have Kay Bob Benson to look forward to.

I went up to Peachy Wigham's this afternoon. She and Ula Sour were very glad to see me and I sure was glad to see them. They said that I hadn't changed a bit, just a little taller, that's all. My old cat, Felix, is fat as a pig and didn't even know who I was. They asked me if I wanted her back, but I told them, no, they could keep her. It would break their hearts if I took her back. Felix sleeps on the bar and is spoiled rotten.

Daddy lost the land he had, so he is running the Flamingo Motel for a man who moved back to Tupelo. I have my own motel room. It's OK except it's right by the bar, which gets pretty noisy.

Guess who the motel maid is? Velveeta Pritchard! She finds it hard to look at me without crying because of Momma. I've been nice to her, which is the least I can do because Momma loved her so much. I told her that Momma had asked about her all the time.

Nobody has been able to do anything with Daddy and his drinking. He's trying, but it's hard for him, especially since he's the bartender in the motel. Almost every morning when I get up, someone is taking him back to his room. It seems Daddy can't make anyone a drink without having one himself.

Crazy old Jimmy Snow is living in the motel with Daddy. He's having a hard time getting crop-dusting jobs because he's had three more accidents. I don't guess he'll ever change, and he's drinking as bad as ever. He and Daddy make a fine pair. Daddy heard from Mr. Wentzel that Betty Caldwell had married a nice boy who's a dentist. They live in Meridian and have a little girl. Guess what her name is? DAISY FAY! Why in the world would someone name their child Daisy Fay if they didn't have to?

Thank heavens, the police never did find out who shot Claude Pistal. I have worried myself sick over it. Every day I half expected to hear the police had taken Daddy and Jimmy to jail. Rayette Walker moved to Pell City, Mississippi. I hope she never talks. Daddy and Jimmy Snow never say anything about the murder even when they are drunk, and I have never said a word either. Mrs. Dot is still in the hospital. Other than that, Shell Beach is about the same. They've built a few more motels and cottages, but not very many. Everyone still wants to go to Florida. Daddy believes that the people who built up Florida are going to come to Shell Beach and then we will all be rich. They better hurry up.

I don't know how I feel about going to the Magnolia Springs High School this year. I'd really gotten to like the boarding school, now that I think about it. I don't know what made me tell Momma I didn't. It's called Mother of Mary Academy. I was the oldest boarder there. There were only twelve others; the rest were day students. I didn't like not being able to go home at night, but it was quiet and I never had to do homework because my teacher was in charge of my dormitory and said I didn't have to because she knew I could do the work. Her name was Sister Jude. I am convinced she is really the movie star June Haver. I read where June Haver went into a convent, and I kept asking her if she had been June Haver, but she told me she wasn't. I still think she is, though.

She slept in my dormitory right by my bed. We all had curtains on steel rods that we were supposed to pull around our beds at night. Nobody but the nuns ever did. I looked in Sister Jude's curtains. All she had was a bed and a dresser without a mirror. Nuns aren't supposed to look at themselves in the mirror. It's a sin or something. I asked her how she put her habit on in the morning and she said she learned to feel how to do it. There was this Greek girl, Patula, in the seventh grade, who claimed nuns take a bath with their clothes on. Do you believe that? She also told me that the nuns shave their heads. I tried every which way to see Sister Jude without her habit on to find out if her head was shaved.

Patula was so crazy she asked the nuns if they wore brassieres. Do you know what Sister Jude said when she asked her? She said they do if they need one.

The thing about Sister Jude is, I don't think she really wanted to be a nun. I'm not sure, though. She came from a very poor family, and they more or less made her go into the convent. I don't know if that is true, or if she is really June Haver and made that story up to confuse me. She showed me a picture of her as a young girl, and she looked exactly like June Haver with brown hair.

The first week I was in school I had to clean the chapel and I put the mops and brooms in the confessional by mistake, thinking it was the broom closet. The next day, when Father O'Connell went in to hear confessions, he stepped in a bucket and fell over the mops. Sister Jude took up for me right away and said that I wasn't Catholic and what could you expect.

The other kids were nice, but they were dating and going to dances that I wasn't invited to, so I really didn't get to know them well. I was glad Sister Jude was my friend. Every time there was a party, all the girls wanted to do was to go on the football field and make out. The priest was no better. One little girl came running out of the church one day and told me that he put his hands on her bosoms. When I repeated that to the mother superior, she said for me not to say anything about it because he was from Ireland. They do things differently over there. Remind me not to go to Ireland!

I hate the way the priests act. They think they are so smart. Did you know they don't allow women on the altar except to clean because they don't think they are good enough? Sister Jude nearly genuflected herself to death at the altar. Watching her made me so mad I had to leave. The next day I went in and walked all over that altar and didn't genuflect once. Who says that priests are better than nuns?

September 21, 1956

School started. Pickle Watkins will be my best friend as long as I live. The first day of school this girl named Dixie Nash called me a dirty mackerel snapper because I came from a Catholic school. I called her a Baptist baboon. After school, when she and a friend of hers started to push me around, Pickle came over and told them to lay off. Nash called Pickle a redneck. Pickle kicked the shit out of her and said, "You date sailors and are nothing but white trash." I kicked the other girl. We had them both down on the ground when some teachers broke it up. Those girls were pretty tough. The thing that saved Pickle and me was that I had on saddle oxfords and Pickle had on white loafers, with taps, while both the other girls had on cardboard ballet slippers that didn't hurt at all.

Dixie Nash scratched my face a little with her nails. Pickle made me come home with her because I might get hydrophobia or even a venereal disease from that girl. She put some Mercurochrome on my face.

Pickle has red, curly hair and freckles, and is the same height as I am. We can wear the same clothes! Her family moved her from Opp, Alabama, three years ago. When I told her my name, she said she had heard about me coming back from the dead and always wanted to meet me. She has a brother, Lemuel, and a little sister, Judy, who they call Baby Sister. They live on a farm about four miles from town. She plays in the band and wants me to be in it, too. I don't have to read music. They just need good marchers to make the band look bigger. Most of the others can't play either. Pickle is first chair trombone.

She is never getting married, just like me. Maybe we can go to the same college and get an apartment together in New York City. I spent the night with her. Her mother is very nice and her father is OK, but he makes them say grace at the table. He's a deacon at the church. They seem afraid of him. Today Pickle let me wear her new pearl collar. I turned my sweater around so the buttons would be in the back.

We went to see Miss Philpot, the band director, who'll be glad to have me; all that was left was a saxophone, so I had to take it. I wanted a tuba. I'll have to wear an old blue uniform from the forties because the band can only afford twelve new gold ones, and those go to the people who can read music. Pickle wears a gold one. I hate my uniform. I look like a bus driver. Pickle is a big deal in school and is going to try out for cheerleader and wants me to try out with her. I had to change my sixth-period study hall to go with her to the Future Homemakers of America. I told her I didn't want to be a Future Homemaker. She doesn't want to either, but her daddy makes her. She says we can have a lot of fun because the teacher is real old, and we can sneak out a lot.

I saw Vernon Mooseburger and Patsy Ruth Coggins, and Amy Jo Snipes is in love. How boring! All she talks about is her boyfriend, Nathan Willy, and how she is wearing his gold football that is just as good as an engagement ring. You should see Nathan. Pickle says he's so dumb he couldn't pour pee out of a boot.

Flicka Hicks is a big football player. He doesn't even remember me. The worst news of all: Kay Bob Benson is head majorette! When she saw me, she said, "Daisy Fay Harper, you haven't changed a bit," which is an insult because I am older and have new glasses. She is giving a "back to school, cement mixer, putty, putty party." Naturally I am not invited, so Pickle is not going either. Kay Bob goes home for lunch every day and irons her clothes for the afternoon classes and she and Flicka are in the school paper all the time as a current walk-to-class couple. Double Barf!

September 27, 1956

I went over to the grammar school to see Mrs. Underwood, who sent me a note about my mother. I love Mrs. Underwood, but I didn't want to talk about Momma. I don't even talk about her to Pickle. I still think about her and miss her and wish there was some way I could tell her how much I loved her. I don't know if she knew it or not.

If I ever thought for a minute there was a God, I sure don't now. My Daddy was right about that one. Pickle wishes her father had died instead of my mother. She hates him, and so do Lemuel and Baby Sister.

Lemuel is crazy about me and wants to date me. He's tall and skinny and has a flattop, and is not bad-looking. Pickle said I could go out with him until we find someone better, but if he tries anything funny, she will kill him because we are going to college together. Whenever I spend the night with Pickle, he drives us crazy, trying to see me in my pajamas. Pickle thinks he is a degenerate. Her father doesn't like Pickle to come to the Flamingo Motel. He is very strict and hates my daddy because Daddy won't join the White Citizens' Council, which is just another name for the Ku Klux Klan.

Michael Romeo has decided he doesn't want to be a priest after all and is back home. He said the food was terrible. His mother is mad, but I'm glad. Besides, I need his vote for Pickle and me to be cheerleaders. The football team decides. We already have Vernon Mooseburger's vote and Pickle's brother, Lemuel's, and all his friends', and Amy Jo Snipes, who is also trying out, assures us her precious Nathan will vote for us because if he doesn't, she won't do "you know what," whatever "you know what" is. If "you know what" is what Pickle and I think it is, we are sure that Nathan will get us elected.

We try out tomorrow. Here is our cheer:

RICKETY, RICKETY, RACK
RICKETY, RICKETY, ROO
MAGNOLIA SPRINGS, WE LOVE YOU
TWO BITS, FOUR BITS, SIX BITS . . . A DOLLAR,
   ALL FOR MAGNOLIA SPRINGS,
STAND UP AND HOLLER.

October 2, 1956

Pickle lied to me. Mrs. McWinney, the Future Homemakers of America teacher, is not that old. You couldn't get out of her room dead in a paper sack. So far she's lectured on "How to Use Starch to Your Best Advantage," "How to Freeze Eggs," "How to Dust Using Both Hands." Today we had to look at colored slides of different cuts of meat. Pickle has gone crazy. She wants to win the Betty Crocker Homemaker of Tomorrow pin they are going to award in home economics, and I have to help her. In exchange she is teaching me the saxophone. It is hard. My chipped tooth keeps splitting the reed. She says I'm going to learn to play "Lady of Spain" if it kills her.

And we are cheerleaders. Yeaaaaa! Pickle found out that every one of the boys voted for us, including Flicka Hicks. Amy Jo Snipes was right. "You know what" was powerful enough to get us elected. Nathan looks happier, and our first game is coming up soon. Every day when the band marches downtown at band period, all the people close their doors and shut their windows because we sound so bad. I'm playing "Lady of Spain" to all the marches, and it fits pretty well into "Stars and Stripes Forever" and "Semper Fidelis."

Miss Philpot is a nervous wreck and chain-smokes. Since she is sensitive to loud noises, you wonder why she ever became a band director. She is in love with Mr. Narney, the football coach, but he looks like a gorilla to me. He told the boys not to have anything to do with girls during football season because they will lose their strength. The boys also are not to play with themselves, but according to Pickle, Lemuel breaks training all the time. That is really gross. I'm never going to let Lemuel even hold my hand. What's the matter with boys? Pickle knows all about them, and she will never let any one of them do anything to her. They'll say anything to you to get you to do it, but afterwards they tell everybody and won't respect you. You should hear how they talk about Dixie Nash, that girl we kicked so bad.

Your reputation is worth everything. Pickle and I have real good ones. Her brother would tell us if we didn't. The boys looked in Mr. Narney's billfold one time and found rubbers! Nobody says anything much about Amy Jo Snipes and Nathan, who are doing it because they are in love. Besides, Nathan will kill anyone who does.

Pickle told me there was a car parked somewhere and this boy and girl were petting and when a car hit them from behind, the girl's nipple was bitten off and she had to go through life with only one nipple.

Pickle won't take a drink from a boy because they put Spanish fly in it, which will make you go crazy and go all the way. Her story about a girl at the drive-in and a gearshift is just too gross to repeat.

October 9, 1956

I moved to a double room down at the end of the motel. I can't stay by the bar because of all the screaming and hollering. I got so mad I went in and swiped a bottle of Jack Daniel's whiskey to help put me to sleep. Last night some drunk drove around the motel in a convertible playing a trumpet.

When Jimmy Snow's here, he tries to keep it quiet. He got a crop-dusting job in Macon County. If he makes enough money, he'll buy me some new clothes, not a minute too soon. It's important how you look. I can't go on wearing Pickle's things all the time.

We hang around with the seniors, and if we want to stay in good, we have to look neat. Pickle says we should only date senior boys. She has one on the string named Mustard Smoot. She's not in love, though. She just needs a senior to be seen with. Marion Eugene, Mustard's friend, is going to ask me out so we can double-date.

Our first football game was a disaster. During the first quarter Vernon Mooseburger's helmet flew off when he was tackled. It hit Mudge Faircloth, our best cheerleader, in the right knee, and she had to be carried off the field. Vernon should wear cotton in his helmet to help keep it on his head.

Five minutes before half time, when Pickle and I ran to the band room to change from our cheerleading costumes into our band uniforms, some idiot had locked the door. We ran around the outside and I had to break the window so we could get in. Pickle is one of the few players who can read music, plus we were both important parts of our band formations, particularly when we formed the word "GO." Anyhow, we changed clothes as fast as we could and got back just as the band was entering the field. Miss Philpot was nervous and gave the "enter the field" command too early. We marched out before the game was over and messed up a field goal for our side. The bass drummer lost his drumsticks trying to get out of the way, and he had to hit his drum with his fist.

We formed a bell and played "School Days" and "Ring, Ring, Goes the Bell." It went all right. Then we played "Teacher's Pet" and formed a big apple.

Just as I marched by, Edwina Weeks, who plays the cymbals, screamed at me, "Look at your hand." It was all bloody from breaking the window and the blood was dripping on my saxophone. I hoped I wouldn't die while forming an apple on the Magnolia Springs Football Field. What a way to go.

I didn't have time to think because we had to form the word "GO" while they played "Mr. Touchdown U.S.A." and I played "Lady of Spain." Then we had to form a big football with the majorettes in the center simulating the laces. Every time Edwina Weeks passed by, she screamed, "Look at your hand!" and pretty soon she started screaming for everyone to look at my hand. We had to stand there for what seemed like forever while Kay Bob Benson in her trashy blue sequined majorette outfit did her tricks, twirling two batons at one time, throwing up her baton and catching it behind her back. She didn't miss once.

By this time my whole arm was bloody. I thought, if I have to die, let it be during Kay Bob Benson's baton number so I can ruin it. When we got off the field, Edwina Weeks threw up, and Pickle tied my arm with my sock to keep the bleeding down. It ruined the look of my cheerleader outfit, just having on one sock, but we didn't know what else to do. We got through the game and won.

Afterward all the cheerleaders are supposed to run up to the football players and hug them and tell them how great they did. Boy, did they smell! No one ever told me how stinky and sweaty they would be. I guess I don't have much school spirit.

Today my wrist is taped and it looks great, just like I tried to commit suicide. I wore sunglasses to school and Pickle told everyone that I had experienced a great personal tragedy and not to ask me about it. You should have seen those people looking at me. We are going to make up a great personal tragedy to spread around tomorrow. I think it will have something to do with Tony Curtis and his recent marriage.

October 11, 1956

Jimmy Snow came home and gave me $25. Pickle and I went shopping with a copy of *Seventeen* magazine. I bought a pair of white loafers and more collars, including a fur one for winter. I hate it, but Pickle wants to wear it, and some sweaters plus two new skirts.

Pickle is sure that when it gets cold, we will be accepted at the Senior Radiator. The seniors have a special radiator they stand around at the end of the hall by the principal's office and maybe, even though we are only sophomores, we might, if we're real popular, be accepted at the Senior Radiator. We have to work hard at being popular and smile at everyone in school, even people we think are real spastics.

We went out with Mustard and Marion Eugene to the Hub Drive-In to see a double feature, *The Earth vs. Flying Saucers* and *Shack Out on 101* with Terry Moore and Frank Lovejoy. We were having a good time, until *Shack Out on 101* came on the screen. The boys were drinking beer and thought "shack-out" was so funny that they giggled and screamed every time anybody in the movie said it. Pickle made Mustard get in the back seat with Marion Eugene and I got in the front seat with her and watched the picture. It was a good movie, all about blackmail and crime.

Pickle and I have decided to write Terry Moore and tell her she has been in too many movies about crime and shoplifting. We would like for her to make a film that is funny, maybe a musical, because all these crime movies might begin to affect her personality.

October 15, 1956

I can never face anybody at school as long as I live. I have never been so humiliated in my whole life. I might as well quit and go back to work at the potato shed with the retards. My best friend is supposed to stand by me in my moment of need, but Pickle is in the other room sound asleep. This is all her stupid brother's fault for bringing that stupid mule down to the stupid swimming pool in the first place.

Pickle and I were having a perfectly good time swimming. I was wearing my flowered two-piece suit and my rubber swim hat with the flowers that match. Then Lemuel brought that stupid mule over and said, "Come on, I'll give you a ride on Molasses."

I told him I was afraid to ride horses. He said not to be afraid, that he'd just lead him around the park.

My dear friend Pickle said, and I quote, "Oh, go ahead and ride him; he is as gentle as a lamb."

I got up on that thing and it had an Indian blanket in place of a saddle. I asked Lem what I was supposed to hold onto.

He said, "Hold onto the mule."

I said, "Won't that hurt him?"

He said, "No, mules can't feel a thing."

He led me around the park, but I got scared when I remembered the story Mrs. Dot told me about some girl in Memphis who fell off a horse. It stepped on her right boob and mashed it flat. Now she is one-sided, so I told Lem to let me down.

About that time a bee stung Molasses, who they had just told me couldn't feel a thing, and he took off, running as fast as he could go. He galloped out of the park and right straight down Highway 3. I had to hold onto his mane for dear life with one hand and onto my glasses with the other. I must have been bouncing up in the air three feet. I kept saying, "Whoa! Whoa!" but that stupid Molasses wouldn't stop. About a half mile down the highway, I saw a convoy of jeeps filled with soldiers coming towards me. They had to pull off the side of the road to keep from hitting me, and as I went by, they all started yelling and whistling and hitting the sides of the jeeps. Just then I realized the top to my bathing suit had fallen down and there I was naked, flopping up and down the highway. I must have ridden by 200 jeeps, but I couldn't let go 'cause I would have killed myself. I had to choose between modesty and death, and I'll tell you, I almost chose death. You should have heard those soldiers carrying on. You'd think they'd never seen a naked girl on a horse before. Even I've read *National Geographic* for heaven's sake.

Molasses ran off the highway through three fields and all the way to Pickle's house. When he finally did stop, it was in front of Lem and half the members of the Magnolia Springs football team. When I looked up and saw Flicka Hicks standing there, I ran in the house and hid in Pickle's room, but she was still down at the pool waiting for me. When she did come home and I told her what happened, she said she was sure that the boys didn't notice my top was off, they were probably looking at my flowered swim hat because it is so pretty.

I hope she is right, but I still could die of mortification. What if the Army gets my name and puts it in the paper that I was riding down the middle of Highway 3 bare-breasted? It will ruin our chances of ever being accepted at the Senior Radiator, even though Pickle is prepared to swear on the Bible it wasn't me.

I have never been so sore in my whole life. I'll probably never be able to sit down again, but I certainly have a lot more respect for cowboys now. All I can say is Mr. Lemuel Watkins is going to be very sorry when he wears the jockey shorts Pickle and I put poison ivy in.

October 18, 1956

Pickle got into terrible trouble for spending the night with me. Her daddy was waiting for her when she came home from school and accused her of being with a boy. The only reason I found out is when we were dressing out for gym, I saw huge red welts on her back. She said it was nothing, but I asked her sister about it and she said that her father is always beating them if he thinks they've been with boys. She told me one night Lem tried to kill him when he was beating up on Pickle. Lem nearly got sent to a reform school. Now they just put up with it until they can get away from him.

I wonder why Pickle never told me. I guess she is too embarrassed. My daddy may drink, but he never hits me. I was so upset over Pickle I forgot I had exposed myself until Kay Bob Benson came down the hall with three of her friends and said, "Well, here is Lady Godiva."

I know Flicka Hicks told her. I just know it!

October 26, 1956

We won another football game and the band was OK. We did a jungle show, and we formed the African continent and played "Abadaba Honeymoon." We formed two jungle drums and they turned out all the lights on the field while Kay Bob Benson twirled two fire batons in the air. Then we formed a hunter's hat and played "Searching," made a skull and bones and played "Witch Doctor."

During the game Nathan Willy was hurt and Amy Jo Snipes got hysterical and ran out on the field with the water boy and the coach and they had to pull her off of Nathan's body. He only had a sprained ankle.

After the game we went to the Spinning Wheel and I got in the trunk of Patsy Ruth's car and let my arm hang out dripping with catsup, but nobody saw it and I ruined my sweater. Nathan was walking around using Amy Jo Snipes as a crutch. She loved it. She will make the perfect wife. I think she has braces on her brains. If I have to hug those football players one more time, I will SCREAM. Why can't they lose?

Velveeta found a whole bunch of empty whiskey bottles under my bed and asked me where they came from. I told her they were Daddy's. I hope she keeps her mouth shut. I am still having a hard time sleeping. I never see Daddy anymore. Jimmy is worried about him and made him go to the doctor. Daddy is throwing up blood, but he won't stop drinking for anything.

Pickle is driving me crazy. All she thinks about is the Senior Radiator. She is very good at math and I am failing algebra. Who cares if x equals z or whatever? It seems to me I am learning a lot of useless stuff. The only thing I like is English, but not the grammar. Pickle can even diagram a sentence. I wish they would let me take shop, but they won't. I am taking driver's education, but I am failing that because I had a head-on collision on the driving machine.

Pickle's daddy went out of town for a White Citizens' Council meeting, and Lem and she and Baby Sister and Michael and I drove their tractor to the Hub Drive-In where we saw *The Beast with a Thousand Faces* and *The Cult of the Cobra*. Nathan and Amy Jo Snipes were there. They never watch the movie.

Pickle is after me all the time to smoke Kents because the senior girls do. They taste awful. I told her smoking Kents was like smoking Tampax. She smokes every chance she gets.

The TB bus came to the school the other day. In the study hall over the loudspeaker, they announced the names of all the girls who had to go back to have their X rays done over. Their X rays didn't take because they were wearing rubber falsies and that great and wonderful majorette Kay Bob Benson was one of the first names called. Ha-ha.

November 1, 1956

Patsy Ruth Coggins sewed her own skirt into the sewing machine in Future Homemakers of America class. When the bell rang, she jumped up and ripped the arm right off the sewing machine. Her father has to pay for the whole machine. Tomorrow we have a lecture about small appliances and how to use them.

We had another football game. The band did a salute to Stephen Foster and played "Beautiful Dreamer" and we formed a bed. Then we played "My Old Kentucky Home" while the majorettes slowly pranced like horses. We finished up with "I Dream of Jeanie with the Light Brown Hair." We formed a comb. Miss Philpot is running out of ideas if you ask me. We won the game again and Pickle is still pushing for Senior Radiator.

We can't wait until next week because Madame Ramona is coming to town. Listen to this ad:

MADAME RAMONA DOESN'T MAKE HOUSE CALLS . . . FIRST TIME IN YOUR COUNTY . . . TELLS EVERYTHING YOU WANT TO KNOW WITHOUT ASKING ANY QUESTIONS . . . GIVES YOU NAMES OF ENEMIES AND FRIENDS . . . GIVES TRUE AND NEVER-FAILING ADVICE ON ALL AFFAIRS OF LIFE . . . CONSULT HER ON BUSINESS . . . LOVE . . . MARRIAGE . . . WILLS . . . DEEDS

. . . MORTGAGES . . . LOST AND STOLEN ARTICLES AND SPEC-
ULATIONS OF ALL KINDS. DON'T BE DISCOURAGED IF OTHERS
HAVE FAILED. SHE DOES WHAT OTHERS CLAIM TO DO. ONE VISIT
WILL CONVINCE YOU THIS MEDIUM AND DIVINER IS SUPERIOR TO
ANY READER YOU HAVE CONSULTED. THIRTY YEARS' EXPERIENCE
PRIVATE AND CONFIDENTIAL READING DAILY AND SUNDAY FOR
BOTH WHITE AND COLORED . . . HOURS 9 A.M. TO 10 P.M.
YOU MUST BE SATISFIED OR NO CHARGE. LOCATED AT THE SID-
WELL SERVICE STATION ON ROUTE 19 . . . LOOK FOR A SIGN
WITH A HAND . . . ATTENTION. SHE IS STRICTLY AN AMERICAN
PALMIST, NOT A GYPSY OR AN INDIAN.

November 5, 1956

Last night Pickle and I had to ride back from the football
game in Robertsdale with Mustard and Marion Eugene. We have
to be nice to them so we can have dates with seniors for the
Homecoming Dance. Marion Eugene about drowns himself in
Old Spice and all he wants to do is kiss-kiss-kiss. It wouldn't be
so bad if he kept his mouth shut.

We won the game. I hugged Vernon Mooseburger because he
hadn't played at all and smelled nice. Marion Eugene got mad.
Amy Jo Snipes is mad as hell because when Nathan made a
touchdown, she got all excited and jumped up and down and
cracked her tooth on his gold football she wore on a chain around
her neck. It was just a hairline crack, not chipped like mine, so
I don't know what she was carrying on about.

November 6, 1956

Today after school Patsy Ruth Coggins, Amy Jo Snipes, and Pickle and I went out to see Madame Ramona at the filling station. All of Amy Jo Snipes's questions were about Nathan. She wanted to find out if he truly loved her. I wanted to know if I was going to be famous and rich, and how long it would take, and when Pickle and I are gonna get to New York City or Hollywood.

Pickle went in first and was in there a long time. When she came out, she was all smiles. Madame Ramona had told her she was going to win a prize, and Pickle was sure it was going to be the Betty Crocker Homemaker of Tomorrow pin. I didn't want to disappoint her, but the bread she made was the worst in the class, even worse than mine. At least mine rose up a little. Then Amy Jo Snipes went in and came back in a fit. Madame Ramona told her her sister, who is a member of Curtis Honeywell's all-girl army, was going to get married before she did. Patsy Ruth Coggins chickened out altogether because she said it was against the rules of the Rainbow Girls to believe in anything but God.

So I went next. Madame Ramona was in a dark curtained room in back of the filling station. A little dirty girl was on the floor playing with paper dolls. Madame Ramona claims she isn't an Indian or a Gypsy, but she is something foreign. She had on lots of greasy makeup, tons of bracelets, and was smoking Chesterfields. I had to sit down at this old card table with pictures of dogs on it and shuffle some cards. I was so scared I forgot my questions for a minute. When I remembered to ask her if I was going to be rich and famous, all of a sudden she stopped playing with those old cards and said, "Did you just receive an inheritance?"

I said no, I was not from a rich family. She might have me mixed up with Patsy Ruth Coggins, whose daddy owns the Chevrolet dealership, but is a Rainbow Girl and isn't going to come in.

She said, "You got an inheritance from somebody."

I said, "No, ma'am, I didn't."

She said, "Yes, you did."

I said, "No, I don't think I did."

She said, "It is shiny."

I thought and thought, but I couldn't think of anything. I told her the only thing I ever got was a sweetheart pillow from Jessie LeGore and a ring that belonged to my mother. She jumped at me and said, "That's it! Your mother wants you to wear that ring so she can help you." My heart stopped.

"Your mother wants you to stop grieving over her and let her go. She is fine and she wants you to be happy. She is worried because you aren't sleeping and you need your sleep."

I said, "Really?"

"Yes, that will be five dollars."

I gave it to her. I was sweating. How did that woman know about me not sleeping and that ring? I didn't tell anybody anything. When I got home, I put Momma's ring on and I'm never going to take it off. And I threw out what was left of my Jack Daniel's whiskey.

November 21, 1956

Here's the latest news. We got dates to the Homecoming Dance with Mustard and Marion Eugene. Amy Jo Snipes is going to make Nathan marry her during the Christmas vacation, and we all have to be in her wedding. Pickle is going to be the photographer for the school annual, and she signed me up to be on the staff. We all have to do our science projects so we can enter them in the county fair. Pickle is heartbroken because Judy

Ashwinder won the Betty Crocker Homemaker of Tomorrow Award pin. Now she is sure she is going to win a prize for her science project.

Pickle says I shouldn't be seen with Vernon Mooseburger because he is bald and not a senior. Vernon's problem is that he is very shy.

I cut an ad out of the paper for the Dale Carnegie Course. It says that Dale can turn you into a confident and forceful speaker. I talked to Jimmy Snow, who agreed to loan Vernon the money for the course. I told him to consider it as an investment. Vernon could turn out to be the President of the United States or something. Vernon will go if I don't tell anyone.

I am still failing algebra. That teacher hates me because I walked in and saw her washing her false teeth in the ladies' room. Daddy thinks people who are good at math are Nazis.

Pickle's daddy was just named some big deal in the White Citizens' Council. His speech was in the paper. Mr. Watkins said the NAACP is not the enemy of the white people, they are only stupid. The enemies of the white people are the Democratic party and the Republican party. He is a Dixiecrat and has proof that eighty-seven different organizations of the Communist party are working with the southern Negro to take over the United States and kill all the white people in their beds. Rock and roll is a Communist-inspired plot to get white children to lower their moral standards and if it isn't stopped, we will all go crazy and be hypnotized by the African drumbeat that is in rock and roll. When the time comes, we will turn on our parents and kill them. He said he has proof that Fats Domino is in cahoots with Russia.

Anyway, this Assembly of God preacher came up to the school and made Miss Philpot take "Blueberry Hill" out of our band show because it is a Communist number. So we had to do the salute to Stephen Foster again. Puke.

We got in the school paper. It said in "Teen Talk":

What cute, blonde sophomore, with blue glasses and eyes to match, has Marion Eugene keeping his white bucks clean as a whistle?

Everybody knows it is me. And it said:

> Mustard Smoot and Pickle Watkins have been seen sharing
> a malt and sweet talk at the Spinning Wheel.

Mustard and Pickle. They sound like a hot dog!

November 23, 1956

When I came home from school today, Daddy had some
woman in his motel room. She answered the door and said he
was asleep. Her name is Ruth, and she looks like an old drunk
to me. Jimmy Snow said Ruth was divorced from some air-
conditioning man. No wonder I haven't seen much of Daddy
lately. And I thought he was still so upset over Momma!

Jimmy Snow and I go out and eat almost every night, but
Daddy never comes with us. Well, I hope he's happy. I'm not
talking to Ruth. She's worse than Rayette Walker.

Grandma Pettibone said most men won't wait until their
wives are cold in their graves before they find another one.
Daddy's a real jerk. I would go live with my grandmother if I
could, but the man she married is in bed with another heart
attack. Daddy's daddy still won't talk to him so I guess I'll stay
here until I can graduate and Pickle and I can go to New York.
Stupid jerk!

We had to take an aptitude test for the Harwin County Board
of Education. It had a lot of math on it, so I copied Pickle's
answers. My test said I was suited to be an Artistic Mechanic.
What's an artistic mechanic?

November 24, 1956

Jimmy Snow and I went with Vernon Mooseburger to his first Dale Carnegie lesson at the Elks Lodge. We waited for him to make sure he didn't leave. Afterwards he said he liked it, even though there were mostly old men in there. He thinks he can go through with it, and I'm glad. He still needs a wig, though.

Pickle decided we need to become Rainbow Girls because all the senior girls are in it. Your daddy has to be a Mason or your mother has to be in the Eastern Star. She talked Patsy Ruth Coggins into getting her mother to sponsor us. I asked Patsy Ruth what the Rainbow Girls do. She said it was pretty easy. All you do is sing hymns. Just what I want! Thanks a lot, Pickle!

We bought our formals for the Homecoming Dance. Pickle's is a pretty aqua net with a big satin bow. Mine is a white ballerina-length net dress with little red polka dots. We had to buy strapless bras. Pickle's has lots of padding. We're both on the decorating committee. Our theme is "Rhapsody in Blue" because the Blue Flame Butane Company is sponsoring the dance. I hope I never see any more blue crepe paper and blue toilet-paper flowers. That crepe paper stains your hands something awful. Everybody knows that Amy Jo Snipes is going to be the Homecoming Queen because she is getting married and Nathan is the captain of the football team and a senior. Besides that, she threatened him with "you know what" if she didn't get to be queen. Pickle and I are in the Homecoming Court.

It looks like we will be county champions in football. We haven't lost a game yet. We're going to have a slumber party at Patsy Ruth Coggins's house the night of the Homecoming Dance.

Yesterday Daddy's girlfriend, Ruth, packed her bags and left. She slammed the door so hard it sounded like a cannon going off. About five minutes later Daddy opened the door and it fell off the hinges. When I walked by him, he said, "The bookkeeper I hired for the motel hasn't worked out, so I had to fire her."

Does he think I'm stupid or something?

November 25, 1956

Poor Pickle. Her daddy won't let her go out with Mustard Smoot anymore. He thinks she is letting Mustard go all the way. He beat the hell out of her last week. He must be crazy. Pickle is going to go to the Homecoming Dance with her brother, and Lem will have to meet his date at the dance. She is always having to sneak around because he won't let her do anything! I can't spend the night there anymore because he says I am a bad influence. It's just as well. He looks at me funny and makes me feel dirty. I feel sorry for Pickle's mother. She has to do everything he says, and he won't give her any money. She sews some clothes for people so the kids can have money. I'm lucky. When I want money, I go get it out of the cash register or ask Jimmy Snow for some. Nobody checks to see how much is in there. Jimmy says that the bartender that Daddy has working for him takes money all the time anyway.

I read in *Photoplay* that June Haver left the convent and married Fred MacMurray. I'm writing Sister Jude and if she isn't there anymore, I'll know for sure she's June Haver. Why in the world would anybody leave the convent and marry Fred MacMurray?

Daddy and Jimmy and I had Thanksgiving dinner at the Romeos' house. I don't think you are supposed to have lasagne on Thanksgiving, but it was good, a lot better than Jimmy's cooking.

Guess what? We lost the Homecoming Game. It's all Michael Romeo's fault. He made a touchdown in the first half and turned around to see if everybody was looking and ran into the goalpost and hurt his throwing arm so bad they had to take him out of the game. He was the only one on the team who could pass. Every time Mustard threw the ball, the other team kept catching it and made three touchdowns.

Our band show stunk! It was all about Thanksgiving. We formed a turkey that looked like a chicken. On top of that, it rained and our pompoms got wet and soggy. At the end of the game I ran up to hug the players. It was the least I could do after they lost and those boys were crying their eyes out. Can you imagine getting so upset over a stupid football game? All the cheerleaders were crying except me. Pickle worked herself up into a fit. I know she didn't care that much. She told me I didn't have any school spirit and to pretend. So I pretended to cry for her sake.

We changed into our evening gowns at Patsy Ruth Coggins's house and I was the only one whose eyes weren't red and puffy. Amy Jo Snipes said we had to be happy for the boys' sake, to help them get over the tragedy of losing. It was our duty as southern women and cheerleaders. When the boys came to get us, Patsy Ruth's mother made us all pose for pictures in front of the fireplace. Not a one of their tuxedos fit. Lemuel's pants were three inches too short. Marion Eugene looked like a pigeon, his shirt stuck out so far in front. Pickle could have killed Mustard Smoot because he brought her a purple orchid, which didn't match her aqua dress.

When we got to the auditorium, most of the crepe paper had fallen down. The boys were drunk before the dance even got started. By the time the Homecoming Queen and her court were presented, half the boys couldn't walk straight. Amy Jo Snipes and Nathan led the parade, and the band played "Blue Velvet," which is "their song." Amy mooned all over Nathan, who didn't even know where he was. Somebody spiked the punch. Miss Philpot must have had some because all night she crawled over the dance floor with a flashlight looking for a cameo that fell off a black velvet ribbon she wore around her neck. Pickle made me take off my glasses, so I didn't get to see much. Those glasses looked awful with my new dress.

Guess who showed up at the dance? Crazy old Jimmy Snow. He wanted to see me in my formal. I tried to get him to dance with Miss Philpot, but he wouldn't. He said I was the prettiest girl there! The strapless bra I bought was the most uncomfortable thing I ever had to wear in my life. With that and the girdle, all I remember is pain. None of the boys know how to dance, so I wound up dancing with Pickle and Amy Jo Snipes most of the night. They're not much better. I am the only person in the Magnolia Springs High School who can lead. Kay Bob Benson and Flicka Hicks came in late. She had on a black dress her mother got her in Meridian and looked like the poor man's Virginia Mayo, but all the boys thought she was wonderful.

After the dance at the pajama party, Amy Jo Snipes made us swear we would give her a wedding shower. Then she passed out slips of paper with what she wanted on them. She said she did it so we wouldn't be embarrassed and two of us get her the same thing. I have to buy her a colander, whatever that is.

I still have marks on me from that strapless bra. I'm throwing that thing away.

December 3, 1956

I am so disgusted. I got a letter from Sister Jude, she's not June Haver, and my science project failed even before it got started. Mr. Leeds, our teacher, said whoever won would get a prize and a trip to Tupelo. I wanted to mate a flounder and a stingray and see if I could come up with a whole new breed of flounder that could sting you if you tried to gig it. I feel sorry for flounders lying there on the bottom of the Gulf getting gigged. Jimmy Snow got me a flounder and a stingray, but nobody could tell what sex they were. When we put them in the washtub, they hated each other and the flounder died. I killed a fish. I didn't mean to, but we ate it, so I guess it was all right.

I told Mr. Leeds, and he gave me another project. I have to do one on the "Effects of Chemicals on Fire Ants." Patsy Ruth Coggins is doing "The Blowfly Maggot in Harwin County" and Michael is doing "Islets of Langerhans, Your Liver's Best Friend." Kay Bob Benson is doing "The Human Circulatory System" and Vernon Mooseburger is doing "The Incredible Life-Span of the Potato Bug." Now that he is in Dale Carnegie School, he shouts and uses funny gestures. He is going too far, and everybody thinks he is obnoxious.

Pickle is cheating. She is doing "The Study of the Chick Embryo." Her brother, Lemuel, did it last year and since we have a new science teacher, she is using his old charts. Ever since Madame Ramona told her she was going to win a prize, she's been impossible.

We attend Rainbow Girls every week down at the Masonic Hall on top of Tally's Furniture Store. We have to sit outside while everybody else goes in to the secret meeting. All those Rainbow Girls have secrets. I can't wait until we are initiated to find out what they are.

December 4, 1956

Pickle and I saw the best movie ever, *All That Heaven Allows,* about a tragic love affair. Jane Wyman is in love with a gardener, played by Rock Hudson. I like him almost as much as Cornel Wilde. Pickle and I think Jane Wyman should go to a better beauty parlor, her hair is too short in the back. We are going to write and tell her. We never did hear from Terry Moore. Rock Hudson and Jane Wyman are really in love. I don't think they could act that well if they weren't. I wish them both a lot of luck. Pickle says if it wasn't for my glasses and my tooth, I could pass for Celeste Holm's sister.

At the Rainbow Girls this week, we sang "Softly and Gently,

Jesus Is Coming" and "Pass Me Not, O Gentle Savior." Not only that, we had to listen to Mrs. Coggins tell about the history of the hymns. She belongs to a garden club and Patsy Ruth told me they answer the roll call with the name of a flower. Can you imagine having to say "Begonia!" It's bad enough being named Daisy.

Mrs. Snipes, Amy Jo's mother, is having all the bridesmaids' outfits made and we are going to a million fittings. I hate them.

The motel is failing. In the past month only two people stayed there. The only reason they came is they were lost and thought they were in Florida.

I finished reading *Great Expectations* for English. Estella is my favorite character. She is as mean as a snake.

December 5, 1956

Kay Bob Benson's mother brought her science project to school today. It is a see-through plastic body with a heart and veins. When you plug it in, blood runs up and down the veins. She won first prize. Pickle is sick over it. Lemuel didn't win with the chick embryo last year, I don't know why she thought she would win this year. One girl brought in a big tooth with cavities. It is gross. I didn't win anything. You just can't kill those fire ants. The only thing that will kill them for sure is Dr Pepper and Coca-Cola. I hate my project.

Vernon Mooseburger is now on the debate team and I have to go listen to him debate. He always wins because nobody else can get in a word.

At the Rainbow Girls, we sang "Guide Me, O Thou Great Jehovah." Patsy Ruth Coggins is an officer called the Outer

Observer, and she makes sure no one observes the secret ceremony. She takes it seriously, giving four official raps on the door whenever she goes in and someone inside gives three.

I'm doing all this to be accepted at the Senior Radiator. During my book report on *Great Expectations,* all the girls laughed every time I said the name Pip because that's what they call their period. Real mature!

December 7, 1956

Pickle signed us up to raise money to buy sewing machines to send to Korea. Whoever raises the most money gets a brand-new Eureka Supermatic vacuum cleaner with a new double-sized throwaway dust bag. It has cyclone air action and seven attachments and is worth $69.95. I don't know why she wants a vacuum cleaner, but she is determined to win a prize.

I came up with a way for us to make a fortune. It came to me the other day while I was up in the plane crop-dusting with Jimmy Snow. Why not take a picture of a farm from the air and put the picture in the paper under the heading MYSTERY FARM? When the people who own it recognize the picture and call in, we can sell them the picture of their farm for $10 to use on Christmas cards. People will eat that up. Pickle is going to get the school camera and Jimmy is going to take her in the plane tomorrow. After we win the vacuum cleaner, we might be able to make enough money so we could buy a car and get our own apartment. I would feel better if Pickle was out of that house. She won't tell me, but her daddy is still beating the daylights out of her. I can see the marks. Lemuel says she sasses him and it makes matters worse. She is very brave. I think if anybody ever beat me with a strap, I'd get them when they were asleep.

December 10, 1956

Yesterday afternoon Jimmy and Pickle went up in his plane and flew all over Magnolia Springs taking pictures. We have fifteen MYSTERY FARMS and one mystery filling station. We stayed up all night developing those pictures in her darkroom. They turned out great except for one thing. Dumb Pickle didn't find out whose farms she took pictures of. They are a MYSTERY to us, too! Can you believe someone would be that dumb? Sometimes I wonder about her. Now we don't have any more money for film. I can see when Pickle and I go into business, I will have to be the brains. Since she is on the honor roll, it makes you wonder about the Mississippi school system.

Today Pickle decided that because we only have five more days left to make money, we will rent ourselves out as slaves after school and all day on Saturday. They are going to announce it on the radio show—two slaves are available but only as a pair. We don't want to be a slave by ourselves. Some man might try and hire us. Pickle says we can charge $2 an hour. If we work hard, she's sure we can win the vacuum cleaner.

December 11, 1956

A woman named Mrs. Clayborn hired us as slaves to change all the drapes in her house. Mr. and Mrs. Clayborn are about the richest people in Magnolia Springs and have the biggest house in town. Mr. Clayborn owns the tractor dealership and a lot of farmland. I didn't want to hang curtains, but Pickle was thrilled to death because she always wanted to get into that house and try to see Virginia Clayborn, who they keep locked up. Virginia is the little girl the Clayborns adopted a long time ago and she never grew up right, so they don't let her out at all. She is twenty-two years old and four feet two inches tall, but she isn't a midget or a dwarf. She just has fits and foams at the mouth. That's why they live so far from town. Pickle told me all this, but I don't believe a word of it. She's just trying to get me to feel good about being a slave. She'll do anything to win a prize.

The Clayborn house is a huge, dark, red-brick thing that looks like nobody lives there. But when we knocked on the door, some woman answered.

Pickle said, "We are the two slaves you ordered."

Mrs. Clayborn invited us in and took us to the living room. On a table sat a real stuffed turtle with red lights in its eyes. Weird. She had on some opera music and she had been sitting there reading poetry books to herself. She called her colored maid and told her to help us get started with the drapes and then she went back to reading her poetry. The whole house was funny. I never saw such old furniture. There wasn't one new thing. I prefer Danish modern.

While we were taking down the drapes, Pickle asked the maid, "How is sweet little Virginia getting along these days?" The maid just looked at her like she was crazy. I knew Pickle had made up that story about Virginia and I told her so after we left.

The next day, when we went back, Pickle was determined to prove to me that girl lived there. Every time the maid would leave for a minute, Pickle would run around as fast as she could opening all the doors, looking for Virginia. I told her to stop it, she was going to get us in a lot of trouble. Pickle thought the crazy girl was either in the basement or up on the third floor. One time Pickle pretended she had to go to the bathroom and went down to the basement looking for her, but she said there wasn't anything there but more old furniture. Through it all, Mrs. Clayborn sat in the living room and listened to her music and read her poems.

Saturday was our last day, and all I wanted was to finish hanging the drapes and get out. We were on the second floor in one of the bedrooms when Mrs. Clayborn called the maid downstairs. Before I knew it, Pickle ran to the third floor looking for Virginia and started jerking all the doors open, leaving me standing there holding about fifty pounds of red velvet drapes. All of a sudden I heard Pickle scream bloody murder and she came flying past the bedroom and kept going out the front door. I didn't know what happened, but I figured I'd better get out of there, too. So I dropped the drapes and started to run down the stairs. Just then Mrs. Clayborn was running up them, screaming, "Virginia, get back in your room." I looked around me and this girl with fuzzy hair and pop eyes was coming down behind me. I was right in the middle between her and Mrs. Clayborn, and Mrs. Clayborn was yelling at me, "Stop her, stop her!" I didn't have much choice because that girl ran straight into me, and when Mrs. Clayborn grabbed both me and the girl, I was stuck between them and couldn't get loose.

The girl was screaming, "I hate you!" and was trying to hit Mrs. Clayborn, but she was missing her and beating hell out of me.

When we got her back to her room, Mrs. Clayborn said to me, "See that she doesn't hurt herself. I'm going to get the doctor," and locked me in there with her! I tried, but I couldn't get out for love or money.

I looked around, and there wasn't anything in the room she could hurt herself with. There wasn't anything in the room at all as a matter of fact. But she sure could have hurt me if she had a mind to. I was about to be killed by a crazy person just because Pickle Watkins wanted to win a stupid vacuum cleaner.

When Virginia sat down on the floor and started to holler and beat her fists on her head, I said, "Hey, you better stop that."

She looked at me and said, "Who are you?"

I said, "I'm Daisy Fay Harper, and I'm hanging drapes downstairs. You must be Virginia. How do you do?"

She looked at me and said, "I want hillbilly music."

I said, "What?"

She said, "I want to hear some hillbilly music," and began to hit herself in the head again.

I was hoping she wouldn't start to foam at the mouth. I didn't know what else to do, so I sat down and sang her a little bit of "It Wasn't God That Made Honky Tonk Angels" and then a little bit of "Kaw-liga" and "Your Cheatin' Heart." I was just starting in on "Happy Trails to You" when she got mad and said that was a western song. She may have been crazy, but she wasn't stupid. I sang her bits and pieces of every hillbilly song I could remember from my daddy's jukebox. I was singing "I Fall to Pieces," a Patsy Kline hit, for the second time when the door opened and this doctor with a black bag came in and said, "Well, how's little Virginia today? Your mother tells me you're not feeling well."

Can you believe that? She almost kills me and the doctor thinks she's not feeling well. I'd hate to see her when she's really sick.

When I got downstairs, Mrs. Clayborn was standing there wringing her hands and saying over and over, "I'm sorry about what happened. I don't know how she could have gotten out." I knew how she got out, but I wasn't saying anything because I wanted to get paid. She asked me to forgive Virginia because she was not well.

When I said I didn't think Virginia would be so mad if she could just listen to some hillbilly music, Mrs. Clayborn told me they'd tried that but she breaks any radio or record player they get her and hurts herself with it. Just then I remembered the outhouse joke that my daddy played on Momma, so I suggested Daddy could go in Virginia's room and put a drive-in speaker on the ceiling where she couldn't get at it. He could hook it up to a radio or something.

When the doctor came downstairs and heard my idea, he

thought it was a good one and said for Daddy to call Mr. Clayborn and make arrangements to do it as soon as possible.

Mrs. Clayborn went to her purse and gave me a $20 bill. I told her that she only owed us $12, but she said for me to keep the change and hugged me good-bye. When I got outside, my dear best friend, Pickle Watkins, who had been hiding in a four-o'clock bush, ran up. "What happened to you?" she asked.

I looked at her. I said, "What happened to you?" and kept walking. I'm never speaking to her again. I would never leave her like that no matter what. I gave her the $20 and told her to shove that stupid vacuum cleaner up her stupid nose. She cried and carried on, but I will never forgive her as long as we both shall live and that's that.

Daddy will probably make a lot of money installing those speakers, and the Koreans aren't going to get one red cent of it.

When I got home, I told Daddy and Jimmy Snow that if Pickle calls me, I'm not in.

Now that I think about it, Virginia is not four feet two inches tall. She is the same height I am. I knew Pickle didn't know what she was talking about.

December 15, 1956

Sunday, Pickle came down to the motel and knocked on my door. I was sitting on the roof, and she didn't see me. I sit on the roof a lot. People never think to look up. Anyway, she knocked and then she slipped a letter under my door and left.

I went down after she had gone and read the letter. It said how sorry she was for leaving me, but that girl had scared her so bad she just ran and thought I was right behind her. A likely story! I got all the things she's ever given me, including some clothes she had loaned me, and put them in a box.

Monday morning, at school, Lemuel met me when I got off the school bus, and I gave him the box. He said Pickle was heart-broken and couldn't eat all day Sunday and wouldn't I please make up with her. I told him Pickle had cut me to the quick, hurt me too bad to ever make up, but I was not mad at him or Baby Sister and would continue to remain their friends if they wished.

When I got to class, I never looked at Pickle once. By lunch it was all over school that we had broken up. Everybody fluttered around her like she was the injured party. I wondered if she told them about leaving me to be killed. Patsy Ruth Coggins gave me a long, tearful talk on how best friends should never fight and wouldn't I send Pickle a message of some kind she could deliver. I told Patsy Ruth Coggins to tell Pickle that we were definitely not a current walk-to-class couple.

Amy Jo Snipes drove me crazy all through lunch, running on about how it would absolutely ruin her wedding if two of her bridesmaids were not speaking to each other, and wouldn't I make up just for the wedding. Afterwards I could go back to not speaking if I wanted to.

Vernon Mooseburger wanted to have a debate on the pros and cons of making up with Pickle, but I told him to mind his own business. Then he wanted to debate the pros and cons of minding his own business. That debate team has got him crazy!

I held out all day until sixth period, Future Homemakers of America, and then I looked at Pickle by mistake. She was looking right at me. I started to laugh and so did she. We ran up to the ladies' room and cried and hugged and kissed and made up. We said we loved each other and Pickle promised never to leave me again. How can you stay mad at Pickle?

Daddy put those speakers up for the Clayborn girl. He came home and told me he thought Virginia was crazy as a loon. I could have told him that.

December 19, 1956

This Saturday we went to Amy Jo Snipes's shower. She got all kinds of kitchen things. I never could find a colander. I don't know what it is. I just gave her some money so she can buy it herself.

Kay Bob Benson and Patsy Ruth Coggins won the vacuum cleaner for raising the most money for the Koreans. That's the second prize Kay Bob Benson has won this year.

Pickle found out the Magnolia Springs paper is going to give away an Esterbrook fountain pen for the best human-interest photograph. She dragged me out to the old folks' home to get a picture of this man who was having his hundredth birthday party. When we got there, his family had come from all over the country. It was awful. He just sat in a wheelchair all slumped down and every once in a while one of them would go over and try to sit him up and say, "Look, Big Poppa, here's little Larry, or Aunt Somebody or other." He couldn't hear or see, much less recognize people. They had him in a suit that was four times too big. Pickle said he had a diaper on underneath. They thought Pickle and I were part of the family and talked to us about how Big Poppa used to hide under a pile of leaves whenever any of them would visit. After meeting the relatives, I don't blame Big Poppa.

They put a cake in front of him, lit the candles and sang "Happy Birthday, Big Poppa." He almost fell over right in the cake, but a nurse caught him in time. Pickle got a picture, so she is happy. After a while they just wheeled him in a corner and visited with each other. It was terrible. That old man didn't get one present, but Pickle said what would you give a hundred-year-old man? I guess she's right.

December 28, 1956

Well, Miss Amy Jo Snipes is now officially Mrs. Nathan Willy. I hope she'll live. That was the first wedding I have ever been to and I don't care if I never go to another one. I couldn't believe Pickle. She kept snapping pictures all through the ceremony, and she was a bridesmaid. She shouldn't have gotten in the bride and groom's face like that, but she is desperate. Her picture of the old man didn't turn out, it was all blurred. I told her, "What do you expect, trying to take a picture of one hundred lit candles with a flashbulb?" Even I know better than that, and I'm not a photographer.

A wedding is supposed to be serious, but I laughed all the way through because when Miss Philpot played "Here Comes the Bride" on the organ, Mr. Snipes and Amy Jo started in the door at the same time and couldn't get through together. He stepped back to let her go first and dumb Amy Jo stepped back to let him go, and they both went at the same time again. I guess she forgot she was the bride.

Nathan looked like he was going to faint dead away. He was sweating and his hands were shaking so bad that she had to put her own ring on. She seemed very calm. After it was over, the preacher said, "You may now kiss the bride." He missed her mouth completely. When she got out on the church steps, Amy Jo threw her bouquet right at her older sister for meanness.

This is the write-up that appeared in the paper. I'm in the last part of it:

SNIPES-WILLY UNITED

Love between Miss Amy Jo Snipes and Mr. Nathan Willy was solemnized in marriage on December 22. The Calvary First Baptist Church, where the bride's mother is a member, was the lovely setting for the double-ring ceremony. The romantic aura enhanced by candlelight and huge pedestal vases of white gladiolas dramatized the wonderfulness of the occasion at which Rev. Chester A. Matts so beautifully officiated. Strains of nuptial music filled the air, as Miss Ina Philpot expressed her congratulations to the couple from the console of the Hammond organ, with the song "Blue Velvet" reflecting the couple's sentiments to each other. The melodic soprano of Mrs. Lady Ruth Buckner reiterated the couple's sentiments with "I Love You Truly," by Bond. Best man was Mustard Smoot. Maid of honor was Miss Linda Lou Snipes, sister of the bride. For her daughter's wedding, Mrs. Joe Snipes chose a dress of Nile green with jeweled illusions and matching Nile green shoes. She wore a white carnation corsage. The bride's mother looked poised and stunning throughout the occasion. The groom's mother chose a dress of blue shantung with blue jewels and satin trim. The bridesmaids looked very feminine in full-length gowns of petal pink chiffon, feathering bodices of curly red lace. Bridesmaids' gowns were worn with head-pieces of pink bows designed by Mrs. Snipes. They carried bouquets of pink daisies and lilies of the valley, attached to pink chenille hearts, tied with tulle, and all wore organdie mitts pointed at the wrists. They entered to the tune of Mendelssohn's Wedding March of *A Midsummer Night's Dream*. Prettier than a rose as it bursts in bloom was lovely little Karla Kay, the bride's niece, wearing a gown simulating that of the bridesmaids', copied by her maternal grandmother. The familiar "Here Comes the Bride" announced the triumphal entry of the bride with her father, Mr. Joseph E. Snipes. The bride looked radiant through her finger-tipped veil of illusion and in a full-length gown of white silk organza and Venetian lace. The fitted high-rise bodice featured a Juliet neckline and bishop sleeves trimmed in lace. Her corsage was an orange mum nestled in net and carnations with knotted streams of white satin ribbons. She carried a white Bible covered with Chantilly lace. Her some-thing old was her lingerie; her something new was her wedding dress. Her something borrowed was a string of pearls from her Aunt Mildred, and her something blue was a frilly laced garter, presented to her by her mother. She wore a penny in her shoe.

As the bride walked down the bridal path to meet her groom, she observed the presence of many relatives, friends and well-wishers, including the bride's own hairstylist, known professionally as Miss Ethel, who was in the third row. A reception for the happy couple was held at the Elks Hall, where dainty tea refreshments were served from a silver tray, including petits fours and bridal mints and nuts. Also, souvenir rice balls in white tulle with green ribbon designed by Mrs. Jule Lewis were given each guest by Miss Patsy Ruth Coggins. Mrs. Willy's wedding guest book was officiated by Miss Pickle Watkins and Miss Daisy Fay Harper. The bride and groom plan a honeymoon in Panama City, Florida, and will reside in Magnolia Springs.

Christmas was gruesome. Every place was closed. The Romeos went to Jackson. Daddy, Jimmy Snow and I stayed home and watched the *Perry Como Christmas Special* with Rosemary Clooney. We missed Momma a lot. Neither Daddy nor I said anything, but I could tell he was feeling pretty bad. Pickle and Lem gave me a great ID bracelet and Grandma Pettibone sent me some underwear. Jimmy Snow bought me a pair of red suede fruit boots I wanted and Daddy gave me $20, but I already spent it getting everybody presents.

I hate Christmas anyway. Who wants to put Christmas lights on a motel? I'll be glad to go back to school. We get to be initiated into the Rainbow Girls in January.

Kay Bob Benson got a car. I'll be glad when Pickle and I are out of here. I hate the beach in the winter.

I wish Daddy and Jimmy could make it through one night without getting drunk. Jimmy knows Daddy is supposed to stop, but he keeps drinking right along with him. I asked Jimmy if he wouldn't stop so maybe Daddy would. He stopped for one day and then went back. I think they are both alcoholics. I read an article in *Reader's Digest* and it said the alcoholic is the last one to admit it. I am going to try and get them to go to the Alcoholics Anonymous or they will both wind up in a rescue mission. Momma always believed Daddy could quit if he wanted to. He loved alcohol better than he did her and better than he does me because he gets real mad every time I ask him to give it up. Jimmy Snow is going to kill himself flying while he's drunk.

January 8, 1957

I never wanted to be a Rainbow Girl. It was Pickle's idea. We had to wear evening gowns for the initiation and I had to buy a new strapless bra. We waited outside the secret room at the Masonic Hall while they voted on us.

Pickle and I had five sand crabs apiece in a handkerchief. I made her promise that if we did get in that secret room, we would throw them on Patsy Ruth Coggins for being so silly. We sat outside forever. Patsy Ruth told us they had a box they all go and put a ball in. If we got a black ball, it meant we couldn't be Rainbow Girls.

Finally, this big senior girl, Becky Bolden, came out to get us. She was the Sister of Faith, our conductress in our journey to the end of the rainbow. She did a secret knock and somebody inside did another knock. The door opened. Becky made the sign of the rainbow and we were led in.

You should have seen the inside of that room. They had stars and rainbows on the wall, a huge cardboard Eastern Star, and in the middle was a stand with an opened Bible on it. They sang "Onward, Christian Soldiers" and marched us around the room in front of some big chairs where these dumb girls were sitting with crowns on their heads. Our conductress made us stop at each one. She would say, "This is the station of the Sister of Hope." She took us in front of the Sister of Love and the Sister of the Moon. They had Sisters of everything you can think of.

A group of old Eastern Star ladies were standing in the corner with their hands over their hearts. After we had marched around some more and stopped at the stations again, the Sisters said some kind of mumbo jumbo, and the first one asked, "What seek you here?" and the Sister of Faith, our conductress, said, "We travel in search of a pot of gold which ancient tradition says is at the end of the rainbow." I figured they must keep all their secrets in the pot I saw over in the corner of the room. I couldn't wait to find out what was in it.

When we stopped in front of the Worthy Adviser, she asked us if we would make our town a kinder and gentler place in which to live, remembering that meekness and gentleness are those virtues which a woman can most effectively use. We said we would and I dropped my first sand crab right by Patsy Ruth Coggins's feet.

As they led us around again, they said a lot of stuff like "The Mission of True Womanhood is to be a wife, mother or sister." I think we had to promise to be virgins and, in time of war, kiss the soldiers good-bye or something or another. I was too busy dropping my sand crabs to listen much. Finally, we got up to the pot of gold. This old woman in a white evening gown was standing there and said, "My dear girls, I am happy to welcome you into our assembly. We sincerely hope your initiation into the Order of the Rainbow Girls will be one of your happiest memories." She lifted the top off the secret pot and was getting ready to show us what was in there when all those Eastern Star women started screaming and picking up their skirts and running all over the room, like chickens with their heads cut off. All ten of our white sand crabs were scurrying sideways over that red rug. The Sister of Patriotism was standing up in her chair screaming her head off. The Sister of Faith grabbed us and threw us out of the room and slammed the door in our faces. We could hear all kinds of commotion going on in there. Pickle was having a fit.

She said we shouldn't have dropped those sand crabs because there had been a Bible in the room. We would probably both go to hell and she would be thrown out of her church in disgrace. We would never be accepted at the Senior Radiator now, and it was all my fault.

I told her nobody told me they had a Bible in there, and they shouldn't have had so many secrets. She made me so nervous that I backed into a gas heater in the hall and my net dress caught on fire. I could hear it burning and it scared me so bad that I took off running, which made it worse. By the time I got downstairs the back of that dress split right in half and fell apart in the street. I was a block away before I noticed and stopped. When I did, I was standing in front of the Magnolia Springs Bakery in my underwear. Pickle came flying around the corner and brought me what was left of my dress, but it was just a handful of burned net.

We had to walk all the way back to the Masonic Hall. You should have seen the looks on the faces of those men in the pool hall when we went past the window. If things weren't bad enough, they ran out and followed us to the hall, staring at me. I guess by now there isn't a man in Harwin County that hasn't seen me half naked.

As we turned the corner, all the Rainbow Girls and Eastern Star women were standing in front of the Masonic Hall. They had smelled the fire and come out, and there I was in downtown Magnolia Springs in my strapless bra and panties. I thought those women were going to faint. Someone ran upstairs and got me a coat, but we're not going to be Rainbow Girls and Patsy Ruth Coggins won't even speak to us.

Here's the thing. You would think they would have been glad I didn't burn up, but no, they would rather that I died in a fire so they could have given me an official Rainbow Girl Funeral. They claimed I besmirched the pure reputation of the Rainbow Girls forever. It wasn't my fault that dress was so cheap. The hell with them! My ponytail is also burned on the ends, and it will take forever to grow out. I never did get to see what was in that pot of gold!

Half of the school isn't speaking to Pickle and me. Those Rainbow Girls are supposed to be gentle and meek, according to the Worthy Adviser, but they called us some of the ugliest names you have ever heard, including daughters of Satan.

Pickle got a terrible beating from her father over the whole thing, but the worst thing happened today. We walked by the Senior Radiator and guess who was standing there laughing and yacking her head off? KAY BOB BENSON! Horse pee!

February 16, 1957

Jimmy Snow didn't come home the other night. We called up the hospital and sure enough, that's where he was again. I sat down with Daddy and told him I was leaving if he and Jimmy didn't go to Alcoholics Anonymous. I'd never been so mad and it must have worked because Daddy promised to go and take Jimmy with him when he gets out of the hospital.

Alcoholics Anonymous has a very good record, and they both might meet some nice people there for a change. You should see the scuds they run around with. One of them tried to get in my room once and banged at the door all night. If he had gotten in, Jimmy and Daddy were so drunk they wouldn't have been any help.

I felt bad after I had gotten so mad at Daddy because of what he and Jimmy had done for me, taking a chance on going to jail, but it is for their own good. Sometimes you have to treat them like children. We called Alcoholics Anonymous and if Jimmy Snow is out of the hospital, they are going to their first meeting on Friday night. I'm keeping my fingers crossed.

March 12, 1957

Daddy and Jimmy Snow attended two Alcoholics Anonymous meetings, and I am proud of them. They both look better, and they say they feel better. Things are looking up.

Today in Future Homemakers of Tomorrow, we had to learn

how to lay a pattern. Who cares? I buy all my clothes at the store. Next week we are going to learn how to pack a suitcase correctly. That may be something Pickle and I can use for when we leave.

They showed *The King and I* at the Magnolia Springs Theater and Vernon Mooseburger has decided he is the King of Siam. All he does is strut around and every time you ask him a question, he will answer you and say, "et cetera, et cetera, et cetera," from the movie. He is full of himself. Who would have ever thought there would be a bald-headed movie star!

The only thing I have to look forward to is the band is going to march in the Mardi Gras parade in New Orleans. I wish I knew something besides "Lady of Spain." Pickle is going to teach me "Glow Little Glowworm" if she has time.

Do you know what Lemuel told me? That all the girls in the Future Nurses of America Club are nymphomaniacs, which means they are all crazy for sex and can't get enough.

You should hear Amy Jo Snipes talk about how wonderful marriage is and how she and Nathan do their homework together. It is just too romantic! They live with her mother, so she doesn't have to cook or clean or anything. I can't imagine being married and going to high school. Oh well, at least she always has a date.

We went to the drive-in with Marion Eugene and Mustard. That boy is all hands. I have to keep eating candy and popcorn so he will leave me alone. After the movie they always want to go parking. Mustard and Pickle sit and smooch. Pickle says she doesn't like it but she will do anything, short of going all the way, to get a date to the Senior Prom. I am tired of fighting Marion Eugene off. Someone told him when a girl says no, she really means yes. I'd love to get hold of the person who started that one.

April 1, 1957

I think Kay Bob Benson ought to pay for a dentist, but she said she isn't going to because it's my fault my other front tooth got chipped. I should have gotten out of the way.

We were marching in the Mardi Gras parade in New Orleans, and Kay Bob Benson was showing off. Every time we stopped, she did all her stupid baton tricks, throwing that stupid thing way up in the air and catching it behind her back. Once, when Miss Philpot gave the whistle to march, her baton came down and hit my saxophone and chipped my other front tooth. Now I have two chipped teeth. I could kill her. Not only that, it bent my keys and my saxophone won't play at all. I had to march all day pretending to be playing.

We had a terrible time in New Orleans. The bass drummer was hit in the head with a Coca-Cola bottle, and right after we got off the bus, some man called Edwina Weeks over to his car and exposed himself to her. That parade is dangerous if you ask me. They throw all kinds of stuff at you, and we had melted candy all over our uniforms. It will cost a fortune to have them cleaned. The only good thing that happened is that some drunk spit on Kay Bob Benson!

P.S. "Glow Little Glowworm" doesn't fit into any march.

April 10, 1957

Last night, before we went to the drive-in, Marion Eugene stopped by the pool hall to get some money from his brother. When he came out, he said, "Guess who is in there shooting pool?"

I said, "Who?"

"Your daddy and Jimmy Snow."

I said, "I don't believe you. They are at the Alcoholics Anonymous meeting."

He told me to go see for myself. I went in and sure enough, there they were, drinking beer. I am disgusted with both of them. It turns out they only went to Alcoholics Anonymous one time. Daddy made Jimmy leave, saying he wasn't going to stand up in front of a bunch of reformed drunks and give his name and say, "I am an alcoholic." Besides that, all they did was pray. They have been out every Friday night shooting pool. I give up. If I had some money, I would get my own apartment or go live in the Magnolia Springs Hotel.

They should be ashamed to be setting such a bad example for me. And Daddy should wait up for me when I have a date. Jimmy is the only one that won't go to sleep until he sees if I'm all right.

Pickle told me the worst story about these two people parked in Lover's Lane in the town where she came from. They were sitting there smooching when on the radio it said that a sex maniac with a hook on the end of his arm had escaped and was running around loose. Well, the girl got real scared and wanted to go, but the boy wanted to stay. They had a big fight over it. Finally, the boy got mad and drove off. When they got home, he opened the door and there was a hook hanging from the handle.

Daddy and Jimmy don't ever talk to me about boys and sex. I think somebody should tell me about it. I worry, because if kissing can get you pregnant, Pickle is in trouble. I know she won't take a bath after her father or her brother have been in the tub because she's heard of a girl that did that and got pregnant. I told her to take showers.

Pickle is in love with Tab Hunter. I had to sit through *Battle Cry* eight times. She wrote him a letter and told him he should star in a movie with Piper Laurie and asked him for a picture.

We are going to be in the senior play. I get to play a waitress. I go over to wait on a table and Billy Hamp says to me, "How old are these eggs?" I say, "I don't know, mister, I just laid the table." I don't think that's funny, do you?

Pickle gets to do four daffy definitions. They ask her, "What is a neighbor?"

She says, "A person who's here today and gone to borrow."

"What is a dentist?"

"A bridge builder."

"What's an Eskimo?"

"A person who has to undress with an ice pick."

"What is a zebra?"

"A horse behind bars."

She has all the funny lines.

Mustard Smoot is doing an imitation of Tennessee Ernie Ford. And there'll be a takeoff on *Your Hit Parade*. Miss Philpot is directing.

We were in the school paper. I was named the Wittiest Girl in the sophomore class. Pickle was named the Girl with the Most School Spirit. Kay Bob Benson got the Best Dressed, naturally. Michael was named the Cutest Boy and Vernon Mooseburger was named Most Likely to Succeed. Patsy Ruth Coggins was the Sweetest. Oh, brother, they should have heard what she said to Pickle and me when we threw the sand crabs at the Rainbow Girls. She is not mad anymore, but her mother won't let her take Pickle and me in her car. We have had to walk everywhere. What a drag!

The Senior Prom is coming up and Pickle and I are going to get appointments at Nita's Beauty Box and a full makeup at the Merle Norman Studio the afternoon of the prom. I couldn't buy a new dress, so Pickle is loaning me her old aqua one and she is wearing one of her cousin's. We are going to stay up all night and see the sunrise, and then we will all have breakfast at the Magnolia Springs Hotel dining room. It will be the first time Pickle and I have ever stayed up all night on a date. All the seniors do it. I can't wait. Kay Bob Benson is not going to the Senior Prom because Flicka Hicks is not a senior. Too baddddd! But, as Miss Doris Day says, "Que Sera Sera."

May 22, 1957

The theme of the prom this year was "Red Sails in the Sunset" and the crepe paper decorations were red and orange. Everybody said Pickle and I looked beautiful. I wish you could have seen Becky Bolden's face. She was dancing and the pin to her corsage got stuck in her inflatable bra. One side totally collapsed. She screamed like she had been shot, and all her friends rushed over and escorted her to the ladies' room, pushing everybody out of the way. It was a riot. She never did come back. Patsy Ruth

Coggins got sick and couldn't come to the dance. Pickle made the band play "Rocking Pneumonia and the Boogie Woogie Flu" in her honor. After the prom a whole group of us drove down to the beach. The boys brought blankets so we could sit and watch the sun come up. Marion Eugene gave me his senior ring to wear and Mustard gave Pickle his. Pickle must have known because she had adhesive tape in her purse and wrapped it around Mustard's ring so it would fit. I did mine the same way. That ring must weigh five pounds.

We were eating breakfast over at the hotel when all of a sudden in walked Pickle's daddy, who picked her up by the arm and said, "OK, young lady, let's go," and practically dragged her out the door. We didn't know what to do. I am sure Pickle was embarrassed to death. Poor Mustard just sat there. He was so furious he was about to cry.

Today Pickle wouldn't dress out for physical education so I know her daddy had beat the hell out of her. I asked her how he found out where she was and she said she had told him she was spending the night with Patsy Ruth Coggins. He had called there late and Mrs. Coggins told him Patsy Ruth had the flu and nobody was spending the night there. He went to all the motels and hotels looking for her. She said he had sex on his mind.

Today was Kid's Day, when all the seniors dress as little kids. Lemuel was acting like a real nut and stood up in his seat. His foot went right through it and he couldn't get out. He was stuck there for about two hours until the janitor came and took the whole desk apart.

We got our school annuals today. Pickle's photographs were terrible. You can't tell who is who. Everybody signed my book. Listen to this:

> *When you get married*
> *And have twenty-five*
> *Don't call it a family*
> *Call it a tribe*
> *Yours till the pillowcases*
> *Come to trial*
> *(Patsy Ruth Coggins)*

Love is a funny thing
It's shaped like a lizard
It runs down your spine
And tickles your gizzard
(Mustard Smoot)

When you get married
Don't marry a fool
Marry a boy from
Magnolia Springs High School
(Mrs. Nathan Willy)

Roses are red
Stems are green
You've got a shape
Like a submarine
(Michael Romeo)

When you get married
and live in a tree
Send me a coconut
COD

      —and—
When you get married
and have twins
Don't call on me
For safety pins
      —and—
When you get married
And live in a truck
Order your children
From Sears, Roebuck
(Edwina Weeks)

I love to be naughty
I hate to be nice
So I'll just be naughty
And sign my name twice
(Vernon Mooseburger, Vernon Mooseburger)

First comes love
Then comes marriage
Here comes Daisy
With a baby carriage
(Mudge Faircloth)

When the golden sun is setting
And you lay beneath the sod
May your name be written
In the autograph of God
(Becky Bolden, Sister of Faith)

For my best friend
I love you little
I love you big
I love you like
A little pig
(Pickle Watkins)

One night as I lay on my pillow
One night as I lay on my bed
One night I stuck my feet out the window
The next morning my neighbors were dead
(Lemuel Watkins)

When you get married
And live up a stair
Don't come to me
For your kitchen chair
(Judy Ashwinder)

Remember M
Remember E
Put them together
And remember ME
(Baby Sister)

Too sweet to be forgotten . . .
(Miss Philpot)

Sugar is sweet
Salt is strong
My love for you
Is forty miles long
(Marion Eugene)

I just wrote my name, upside down. . . .

May 29, 1957

Do you know that I failed algebra? On top of that, I failed civics and driver's education. I didn't even know I was failing civics. I worked so hard passing Spanish it slipped up on me. They don't have summer school here. I'm going to have to go to Jackson and stay with my Grandmother Pettibone so I can be a junior with Pickle next year. I could just kill myself. Pickle and I were planning to have so much fun this summer. We were going to get a deep tan and peroxide our hair and everything.

Since I can't be here this summer, Pickle is going to get a summer job at Elwood's Variety Store to make some extra money for clothes.

I leave for Jackson next week, and Pickle will accompany me to the bus station. She promised to write every day and tell me what's happening. We will have a great time next year, I just know it. Juniors have all kinds of privileges and Lem is getting a car. If he lets Pickle borrow it, we can play hookey all the time. I can't wait.

1958

_____

January 22, 1958

I had been in summer school two months when Pickle stopped writing me. I sent her letter after letter asking what was wrong, but never heard a word. About a month later Patsy Ruth Coggins wrote and told me that Pickle was pregnant.

How Pickle let that happen I will never understand. We were supposed to go to New York together. No matter what, I am getting out of Mississippi as soon as I can. I failed algebra again in summer school.

Daddy and Jimmy Snow and I are living in Hattiesburg, Mississippi now. The man who owned the motel Daddy was running fired him because he rented a room to some colored people and the White Citizens' Council found out about it and came down and shot out all the windows. Daddy is working in a beer joint here called Jonnie's, and Jimmy is still crop-dusting whenever he can.

Our apartment house is called Milner Court. My room is a screened-in porch. I hope we move soon.

The school I am going to is Blessed Sacrament Academy, and the catechism teacher, Father Stephens, is driving me crazy trying to get me to become a Catholic. A lot of rich girls go to the school. They are all in sororities and are debutantes. Sally Gamble, whose daddy runs the biggest department store in Jackson, is in my class. I haven't made any friends, but I don't want any, I just want to graduate and get out of here.

February 3, 1958

Grandma Pettibone hit the jackpot at bingo and sent me $15.

There is a theater called the Azalea Street Playhouse where they put on live plays a block from where we live, so I went over to buy myself a ticket to see a show. While I was in the lobby, I overheard this man saying that the spotlight worker had gotten mad and quit and they had to have someone for the show that night. I told him I could run a spotlight because my father and grandfather were spotlight workers and had taught me, which was a lie. They never taught me, but it always looked pretty easy to me. The man said great, and for me to be at the theater that night. I got on a bus and went downtown to the Melba Theater where a friend of Daddy's was working as a projectionist. He got out this old spotlight and taught me how to work it. I was right, it is easy. All you have to do is point it and turn a knob to make the light bigger or smaller.

After the show that night, the director of the theater, Professor Teasley, came up to the light booth and said I had done a wonderful job. The other person they had couldn't even find the stage half the time, so I am now the official spotlight worker. They don't pay anything, but I can see all the shows for free. Everybody says this is the best community theater in Mississippi. I am invited to the cast party next week and my name is going in the program. I am using Fay Harper because it will look better in print. Even if I had the money, I won't have any time for sororities and stuff. In fact, if I hadn't promised Momma to finish high school, I would just drop out and become a full-time professional spotlight worker.

February 19, 1958

My new friend Mr. Cecil is a famous hat designer here and is the costume designer for the theater. He's tall and skinny and has dyed blond hair and is the funniest person I have ever met. There are ten young boys that work with him at his hat salon and everyone calls them the Cecilettes. They are a riot. We go out drinking together after the show. Mr. Cecil doesn't usually like girls, but I am an exception. He thinks I am pretty and he is going to help me dress better and fix my hair. It nearly killed me when he plucked my eyebrows, but I look a lot better.

A lot of people don't like him, but he is a real tragic figure. When his best friend, who was a hairdresser at Gamble's Department Store, wanted to go to New Orleans for the Mardi Gras, Mr. Cecil worked for three weeks and designed him a great Snow White costume before he put him on the Greyhound bus. He hasn't heard from him since, and that was five years ago this February. Every year he goes to New Orleans to look for him. After losing my best friend, I know just how he feels.

I also like Professor Teasley, our director, a lot. He has long white hair and a daughter who is a professional actress in Chicago. The money to build the theater came from his mother, Mrs. Nanny C. Teasley, who is very rich and a little deaf. On opening nights, which is when she comes to the theater, everyone has to scream their lines. She always wears a long black dress and carries a black cane with a solid gold top on it, but you have to be careful, because she likes to hit people in the knee with it. Mr. Cecil and I went out to her house the other day. She is having an evening of culture in her front yard for the John Birch Society consisting of a dance and a poetry reading, and she wants him to design the costumes for her and me to run the spotlight. We don't know when it will be. Mrs. Teasley says the dance is about moon goddesses and we will have to wait for a full moon.

Her house is a big white plantation, right on the water. She showed me the medal she got from the Hattiesburg VFW in 1943, for single-handedly shooting down two enemy planes over the Mississippi Bay. Unfortunately they were both United States weather planes from Pensacola, Florida, but because the pilots hadn't been killed and she thought they were the enemy, they gave her the medal anyway. Besides, Mr. Cecil says she donates a lot of money to the VFW.

As a hobby she raises crabs. When I saw all those crabs running around, I asked her if she ever got pinched. She said yes, but if you love crabs like she does, they can pinch you and pinch you and you don't feel a thing.

February 26, 1958

The next play we are doing at the theater is *The Crucible* which is about witches in Salem, Massachusetts. Mr. Cecil is sick about it, the costumes are so dull. Since they don't need a spotlight for that play, I am working the light board downstairs.

I took Mr. Cecil over to Jonnie's bar to meet Daddy and Jimmy Snow and you should have heard what stupid Jimmy Snow said. I told Jimmy Snow that Mr. Cecil was a friend of mine and if he didn't like him to shut up. What if Mr. Cecil is unusually graceful for a man? He's a lot nicer than any of Jimmy's friends and a much better dresser and besides that, he knows all the best people in town.

Yesterday Mr. Cecil took me over to meet a friend of his who is a sculptress and comes from a very rich family, but has been disowned. Her name is Paris Knights. She's beautiful and uses a black cigarette holder and wears army pants with pearls.

She also takes snuff and cusses like a sailor. Paris is very sophisticated if you ask me.

You should see her sculptures. I know what they are, I'm not dumb, hundreds of men's things of all sizes. The reason she got disowned was because she donated one to the Hattiesburg Museum of Art to be auctioned off at a big Beaux Arts Ball. One of the women on the committee thought she recognized her husband's thing and threw a martini in Paris's face and caused a big upset. Paris said the resemblance was just wishful thinking on that woman's part.

Mr. Cecil told me that when she lived in New York, she had an affair with Marlon Brando. I wonder if one of those things is Marlon Brando's.

While we were there, Paris served us some wine and a French cheese called Camembert. It is the first foreign food I've ever had except Mrs. Romeo's Italian food and some Chinese food at Joy Pong's Restaurant.

When Paris asked me if I believed in free love, I didn't know what to say, so I said yes. She's had affairs with all kinds of men, including Orientals. She thinks I am at the age where I should be experiencing life. To tell you the truth, *I* think I'd better wait. I haven't even gone to bed with an American man yet. She's looking for an apprentice to help her in her studio, but I don't feel like handling those sculptures of hers. Maybe Catholic school has made me a prude.

Daddy has a new girlfriend. This one is the worst yet. Jimmy Snow said she couldn't help being so ugly, but she could at least stay home. I think she just wants free drinks.

March 11, 1958

Tootie, Helen and Dolores are secretaries that work at the theater. Since they all want husbands, I took them over to Daddy's bar, hoping one of them would like Daddy so he would quit running around with that ugly woman. They didn't like Daddy, but they thought Jimmy Snow was the cutest thing they had ever seen. Jimmy's so shy he wouldn't even talk to them. Tootie did the bunny hop all night and couldn't go to work the next day she had so many blisters.

I wish Daddy's bar looked better. The walls are all fake wood and stuffed blowfish and a fishnet hang from the ceiling.

Mr. Cecil and I are writing a funny sketch for the cast party. He plays a witch and I interview him at home just like the TV show *Person to Person.*

He's mad at Mrs. Teasley. She called us up at the last minute to say there was going to be a full moon and the costumes for the dancers were only half finished. It really didn't matter because it wasn't a full moon after all, and I missed half of the dancers with my spotlight. Nobody told me they were going to use hoops and balls. You should have seen those girls, they were jumping and leaping all over the yard. One girl stepped on some dog stuff and screamed and stopped dancing, but Mrs. Teasley hit her with her cane and made her go back. At the end of the evening everybody read a poem they had written. Mrs. Teasley's was the best.

> *Soon it's gonna rain, soon it's gonna freeze*
> *Soon it's gonna blow all the moss off all*
> *the goddamn trees.*

March 16, 1958

We did our sketch at the cast party for *The Crucible* and it went over great. Professor Teasley said I could be in the next play, it's called *Cat on a Hot Tin Roof*. Mr. Cecil advised me to hold out for a big part. I want the lead, the one Elizabeth Taylor played in the movie, so I am practicing my diction. All you can hear backstage is people saying "Pepsi-Cola, Pepsi-Cola." I am screaming at least an hour a day to strip my vocal cords so I will have a low voice. Since Jimmy Snow sleeps all afternoon, I have to sneak into the theater through the ladies' room window and scream there. It must be working because I am hoarse all the time. If the reviews are good, I'll bet Kay Bob Benson's mother reads them. She was always bragging about how she read the Hattiesburg *Press Register*. I got a funny letter from Grandma Pettibone. She isn't speaking to Aunt Bess since she gave her a party for her sixty-fifth birthday and Aunt Bess got drunk and went up and asked Grandma's preacher if he knew where she could get some birth control pills.

March 21, 1958

Professor Teasley assigned the parts in *Cat on a Hot Tin Roof* today. He says there are no small parts, just small actresses. I think he is dead wrong! Playing the part of a colored maid with only one line, "Storm's a-coming," is a small part no matter what. I have already bought Daddy and Jimmy Snow tickets for opening night. I should have waited. I had more lines as Mother Goose. According to Mr. Cecil, stars start out with small roles. When I asked him to name one, he thought a long time and then said Ann Sothern, but I think he is lying.

April 6, 1958

There is a scene in *Cat on a Hot Tin Roof* where the head maid and the other servants bring in a birthday cake and everybody sings "Happy Birthday" to Big Daddy. I hadn't thought about it before, but on opening night it seemed perfectly reasonable to me a maid would sing along with the family. After all, I was a house maid, not a field hand! At intermission Professor Teasley flew backstage and demanded I get out of my costume because I was no longer in the play. He said I ruined opening night, that maids don't sing "Happy Birthday" and throw kisses and scream, "I love you, Big Daddy." Evidently I was the only one the audience heard. I was just trying to be loud for his deaf mother, that's all. What is the matter with improvising? All the people at the Actors Studio in New York do it. Paris Knights, who was there, thought it gave the play an interesting twist and made it look like Big Daddy was having a hot affair with one of the colored maids. Thank God, Daddy and Jimmy Snow didn't show up!

I am back doing lights for the next play and does it stink! It is an original written by some woman in Jackson named Mrs. Mamie Kole Stafford, called *I Heard a Cry of Despair from the Bougainvillaea*. The play takes place in Macon, Georgia, on the hottest day of the year. Here's page 1:

The day was so hot that the musk scented honeysuckle dropped heavily into the gardenia bushes, sighing like hot honey pouring on flour white buttermilk while lazy yellow winged bees hummed languidly from blossom to blossom.

Oh, brother.

The story concerns a spinster who is afraid of inheriting a bad case of menopause that had caused her mother to go mad.

Cat on a Hot Tin Roof was reviewed in the Hattiesburg *Press Register*, but I wasn't mentioned. The reviewer did say that Mrs. Nanny C. Teasley, the director's mother, was heard to laugh out loud several times during dramatic parts of the play.

April 9, 1958

Today after school I went over to Daddy's bar and there sat Pickle's brother, Lem Watkins. He's been in the Army for eight months and is about ready to go to Germany for two years. When he heard Daddy was running a bar in Hattiesburg, he decided to look me up. We sat there and had a few beers and he told me what had happened. He thought I should know it wasn't Mustard Smoot that had gotten Pickle pregnant.

Pickle had been home alone, ironing some clothes one Saturday afternoon, when her daddy came in from one of his speaking trips for the White Citizens' Council and began screaming at her and accusing her of having sex with Mustard. He started hitting her and calling her names, then he dragged her into the back room and raped her. When Lem got home and found her all beaten up and bleeding, he got a gun and went after his father to kill him, but he never found him. They told Mrs. Watkins what had happened, but she wouldn't believe it and said that if it was true, Pickle had caused it. When Pickle discovered she was pregnant, Mustard married her. Lem said he had to leave home because he knew if he ever saw his father again, he would kill him for sure. He started to cry and made me swear never to let Pickle know he had told me, because she was so ashamed. The last thing he had heard was that his bastard father was home again, saying grace every night.

All this time I was only thinking of myself and how Pickle had deserted me. She must have been going through hell all by herself. What kind of friend was I that she couldn't tell me? I guess I had talked too much about us leaving and going to New York and she was afraid she would disappoint me. I don't hate Mr. Watkins. What I feel for him is deeper. Why does somebody like that go on living and somebody like my mother, who never hurt anyone, die? I'm going to see Pickle tomorrow.

April 11, 1958

I took a bus to Magnolia Springs and got off in front of the bakery. I asked all over town if anybody knew where Pickle was. The woman at the drugstore said she heard she was working at the potato shed. When I got there, some old country woman told me a girl named Pickle Smoot was working in Shed No. 3. As I was walking over, I remembered how Pickle and I always joked about the people that worked at the potato shed.

I saw her before she saw me. She was separating potatoes and my heart was pounding so hard I almost didn't have the nerve to go up to her. I said "Pickle?" She looked at me for a long time and then, as if seeing me was the most natural thing in the world, she said, "Hey, girl, what are you doing down here?" I told her I was just back for a day and thought I'd look her up to say hello.

She told me to wait a minute so she could let some man know she was going to take a break. When I asked how she was, she said, "Just as fine as kind," and that Mustard was farming for his daddy and she had a wonderful little boy named Lemuel. I explained all about the theater I was in, but the whole time I was talking I kept looking at her. She seemed old and tired, and her eyes weren't Pickle's eyes at all.

Pretty soon we just stood there and didn't have anything more to say. Finally, she said, "Well, I better get back to work," and then she asked, "Hey, girl, are you still gonna be an old maid?"

"I guess so."

"Well you ought to give married life a chance sometime."

Just as she was leaving, I asked, "Pickle, do you ever take any more pictures?"

She looked at me sorta funny. "Pictures?"

"You know, photographs, like you used to?"

"Oh, yeah. That was so long ago, I had forgotten. Write me a letter sometime, ya hear."

I walked back to town and got on the bus. The whole way home I was looking out the window. I don't think there is anything in the world sadder than dead things along the side of the road. Do you?

April 16, 1958

Mr. Cecil is back from his yearly trip to New Orleans. He didn't find his friend this time either. He's about to give up hope. He ought to contact the Missing Persons Bureau like they did for my Granddaddy Pettibone when he disappeared.

I am now doing sound for a play called *Anne of a Thousand Days*. It is all about Henry the Eighth and Anne Boleyn, and it is great. All they do is fight, but in the end Anne gets her head cut off and Henry stops being a Catholic.

One of my sound effects is firing a cannon. It's supposed to come in the middle of a speech of Henry the Eighth's to let him know that Anne Bolyn has been killed. Then he goes into a long speech about how he will miss her. At last night's performance my tape machine jammed and Hubert Jamison, the actor playing Henry the Eighth, just sat there and stared at the audience. I was in the sound booth at the back of the theater and there was no way I could let him know the sound machine was not working. He should have figured it out, but he never did, so I finally leaned out of the booth and yelled, "BOOM." Hubert got very mad at me and claimed that I ruined his best speech when everyone in the audience turned around and looked up at the light booth.

Mr. Cecil and I have written this funny sketch for me. I play a very rich society lady who goes to an exclusive restaurant for lunch. I wear a black cocktail dress and have a long black cigarette holder that Paris will loan me. I walk into the room yelling hello to everyone and then I see my husband. I act shocked and say, "Why, George, what are you doing here? Mind if I sit, George? You know, I would just die if word got out that our marriage was . . . uh . . . shaky." I sit down real fast before he has a chance to say anything, and I wave at some other people in the room. "George, you haven't been home in six months now and the dog misses you. Is it something I've done?" I stab myself in the chest with my cigarette holder. I say hello to someone else across the room. I look back at him. "George, you could say something, after all . . ." Then you hear a gunshot. I stand up and grab my stomach. "Is that all you have to say, George?" I notice everyone in the room is looking at me and I laugh and try to pretend nothing has happened. I stuff a handkerchief in my stomach like I am sticking it in my gunshot wound and sit down. "Now, about the funeral. Nothing too elaborate. Five or six hundred and, George, Billy Graham would be nice." I wave at someone else across the room, say, "This will just ruin me socially," flip ashes on the next table and say, "It's not that I mind so much, George. It's just that you didn't even consider the children. What? Oh, that's right. We never did, did we? Well, it's not my fault Mother was so strict!" I yell to someone across the room, "Hello, Kay Bob, you look wonderful, darling," and I turn back to George. "Don't you dare invite Kay Bob to my funeral. I would just die if she showed up." I look back at George. "George, is my makeup all right? Good!" My head hits the table and I die.

I think it's funny and so does Mr. Cecil. He made all the Cecilettes come and watch the sketch, and they loved it. I am going to do it at the cast party for *Anne of a Thousand Days*.

April 23, 1958

My skit went over great. Everyone said it was the funniest thing they'd ever seen. Even Hubert Jamison. Professor Teasley was so impressed he's putting me in the next play called *Yellow Jack* about the war against yellow fever at the Panama Canal.

Mr. and Mrs. Gamble, Sally's mother and father, were at the cast party. Mrs. Gamble asked me if I would entertain at Sally's

coming-out party at the Hattiesburg Country Club for $25.
I told her I would.

Jimmy Snow is dusting crops in Fayetteville and should be
home soon. I wish he would stop doing that kind of work altogether.

I don't see much of Daddy. He and that old woman he's running around with just sit and drink all day long. A lot of the
time he stays over at her apartment. She lives on the south side
in the worst part of town. Oh, well, there is no accounting for
taste.

I am failing algebra again.

April 28, 1958

You should see the Hattiesburg Country Club. It's the most
beautiful place I've ever been to in my life. All the furniture is
real old and the rugs are great. I am going to get into a country
club as soon as I can. Sally Gamble looked gorgeous and all the
boys were dressed up in tuxedoes that fit. There were flowers
everywhere, and the Gamble coat of arms was all over the walls.

I did my number and Mr. Cecil got the gunshot in the sketch
in the right place. Thank God. Mrs. Gamble gave me an envelope with my money in it and told me I could eat in the
kitchen. Some of the girls I go to school with came and talked to
me there. I watched out the window when her daddy presented
Sally to society. It was better than the Rainbow Girls. Daddy
said he was going to give me a coming-out party at Jonnie's Bar.
Very funny. Paris said her coming-out party was the dullest
thing she ever went through.

I found out today Sally Gamble had gotten mad at the girls

that had come into the kitchen to talk to me. She said it wasn't correct to talk to the hired help. Can you believe that? According to Paris, Sally's daddy has paid for her to have two abortions already. I think you are supposed to be a virgin when you come out. She's cheating like crazy, if you ask me.

Mr. Cecil has a new boyfriend and is he happy! I told him to be sure and not make any costumes for him and let him go to the Mardi Gras.

The rehearsals for *Yellow Jack* are great. I play an English noblewoman who comes to the Panama Canal to visit her father and her boyfriend who are both doctors. While she is there she comes down with yellow fever and lets her father and her boyfriend use her as a guinea pig and give her the serum they have been working on. That way she can die knowing she has done something to help medical science. They agree to do it because she is the only one with yellow fever who can speak English. All through the play, she lies there dying, talking about the effects the serum is having on her.

My death scene is fifteen minutes long. This is my big chance. Anyway, after she dies, they are able to get the serum just right and they discover a cure for yellow fever, but too late to save her. Mr. Cecil is helping me with my makeup and my English accent.

May 1, 1958

I am a big hit. This is my very first professional review:

At last night's performance, all the players were especially good, but the performance of Miss D. Frances Harper as the doomed Cecily Bundridge was one of the finest performances this reviewer has seen on the local boards for a long time. Her timing was superb, and as she clutched her throat and waved good-bye to her father and her bereaved lover for the last time, not a dry eye was to be found in the audience. During the play we saw the doomed Cecily Bundridge progress from a gay young English lass into a creature consumed with the dreaded yellow fever. We could hardly believe that the frail, jaundiced, hollow-eyed girl was the same person we saw in the first act. Kudos to Miss Harper.

Hubert is mad at me again, claiming I took too long to die and that I should have warned him I was going to put on makeup at intermission. My makeup was terrific. I mixed yellow and white together in a jar and smeared it all over the parts of my skin that show and painted big dark circles under my eyes. I really looked sick. Hubert told Professor Teasley yellow fever doesn't make you yellow. You only turned yellow from yellow jaundice, and that I looked like a Chinaman. He's just jealous I got such a good review.

But the best news of all is that the play's of such historical interest it was picked to tour all over Mississippi this summer. Professor Teasley claimed that when we travel the highways and byways of Mississippi, "it will be like bringing rain to a thirsty soil." And I don't have to make up algebra. Professor Teasley went to the Mississippi school board and had them fix it so I could graduate anyway on account of I was an artist who was going into show business and didn't need algebra. Kudos to Professor Teasley!

I have twenty-three copies of my yellow fever review. I am sending them to all the big Broadway producers in New York. I can't wait to get there. The first place I am going to is Sardi's and have a martini. Then over to the Algonquin Hotel to sit at the famous round table, where Dorothy Parker sat. And I'll try to get an apartment over the Copacabana nightclub or the Stork Club. I need a big apartment because I want Mr. Cecil and everybody from the theater to come visit. I wish Daddy and Jimmy Snow had seen me in *Yellow Jack*. I don't think they know how talented I am.

May 8, 1958

You could have knocked me over with a feather. Last night Mr. Cecil took me to this party some of the Cecilettes had and I met his new boyfriend. Guess who it is? Father Stephens, the priest who teaches catechism at the school where I go! He didn't have his collar on, but I recognized him and he recognized me. I didn't say anything. I just sat there and minded my own business. Pretty soon I got tired and wanted to go home. When I went in the bedroom to get my coat, he came in and sat down and started to talk to me. He hoped I understood that love wasn't bad, no matter what form it took. He still felt he was a good priest. I told him what he did wasn't any of my business. I wasn't going to tell anybody and to forget it, and I got my coat and left.

I didn't say anything to Mr. Cecil, but I am disgusted over the whole thing. It made me mad as hell because they sure don't let the nuns date and drink. The priests come and go as they please, but the poor nuns live in a convent and are watched all the time. Sister Jude would love to have had her own apartment and go to parties and all, but no . . . just the priests do that. Why do men get to have all the fun?

August 28, 1958

Well, I'm back from the tour. I died of the dreaded yellow jack fever in twenty-three counties and was a hit in every one of them. At the end of the tour my death scene ran thirty minutes.

You should have heard those people carry on in the audience.

The traveling was pretty bad, though. We went in a school bus and it was hotter than hell. We put on the play mostly in high school auditoriums and gyms. The lighting was awful, but all in all, I had a good time.

The play went to Magnolia Springs and Patsy Ruth Coggins came. I asked Patsy Ruth if she had seen Pickle. She had and Pickle was pregnant again. I asked Patsy Ruth to send her my love. I kept hoping that Pickle and Mustard would show up, but they didn't.

My biggest surprise was Mrs. Underwood, who came and brought all her sixth graders. I had to talk to them and tell them I had been a student of Mrs. Underwood's years ago. She looks just the same, only older.

I wish I had had some time to see Peachy Wigham and Ula Sour, but we left the next day. So I wrote them a hello on a program and Patsy Ruth agreed to give it to them for me.

I had become pretty carried away with myself because I was getting so much attention. One night onstage I was crossing my eyes and trying to make Hubert laugh during my death scene. When the show was over, Professor Teasley came backstage and told us not to leave because we had a presentation. I started complaining that I didn't want to hear any more speeches from any more local yokels. And besides, that yellow makeup nearly itched me to death.

I was acting like a horse's ass when all of a sudden Professor Teasley came back with a girl in a white dress. She was about fifteen or sixteen and was carrying a bouquet of roses. Just as I was going to say something smart to the person next to me about being in the sticks, she walked right up to me and I saw the brace on her leg. She reminded me so much of Betty Caldwell, the crippled girl, my heart stopped. I could see that she was very nervous and her hands were shaking.

She looked at me and said, "I just wanted to thank you so much for coming here. This is the first live play I have ever seen. Thank you." When she handed me the roses, I took them, mumbled a couple of words and then ran into the bathroom. I must have cried for an hour. I can't ever do a show again without thinking that someone like that little girl might be out in the audience.

September 16, 1958

Professor Teasley is making me play a seventy-year-old ax murderess in *The Man Who Came to Dinner*. I wanted the lead, but he couldn't find any old lady actress that could stay up late for rehearsals.

We had to move into another apartment. The one we had is too expensive. We are living in the basement of this Christian Scientist woman's house and it is full of pipes. I've hit my head about ten times already. Jimmy Snow knocked himself out the other night going to the bathroom. It may be cheaper, but it is dangerous.

Mr. Cecil has converted to Catholicism. I went to his baptism. I could hardly keep a straight face. All the Cecilettes were there. It sure was funny to see a grown man getting baptized. He had to bend over to get the holy water on his head.

We are working on a new talent number for me. I play a widow who is talking to her dead husband's ashes in an urn. It is pretty funny. At the end I use his urn for an ashtray because I never did like him. I say, "Oh, George, you always did make an ash of yourself."

I only have nine months to figure out how I am going to get to New York. I want to go right after I graduate. I am saving all my money. I didn't buy any new clothes this year; New York is more important. Paris has some friends there I can call. None of the producers answered about the reviews I sent them. I guess

I will just have to go to their offices in person. I am reading a book about Katherine Cornell. She has a cocker spaniel.

September 30, 1958

Listen to this review:

> Playing the seventy-year-old ax murderess, Harriet Standley, was Miss D. Frances Harper, who thrilled this reviewer with her magnificent performance in *Yellow Jack Fever*. She has once again proved to Azalea Playhouse audiences that there is nothing this very talented actress can't do. Her gestures and voice were perfect as the old woman and the added touch of palsy and deafness was very effective. *The Man Who Came to Dinner* is a play with something for the special benefit of everyone in the city limits, that is sure to banish dull care and provides an uproarious evening for the most fastidious and most varied tastes.

Opening night was great. Professor Teasley had a scare, though. After the play was over, he thought his mother had died, but she was just in a deep sleep. I could have told them that. I heard her snoring all through the play.

Daddy and Jimmy Snow came to the show. Daddy thought I looked just like Grandma Pettibone in that old-age makeup. Jimmy Snow was a riot in his suit. He looked so funny. Nobody wears bow ties anymore. I wish Mother could have seen me in a play other than Mother Goose.

Since I had such a small part this time, Professor Teasley is going to give me the lead in the next play called *Private Lives* by an Englishman named Noel Coward. The only bad thing is

I am awfully tired, I'm not getting any sleep at all. But I have to graduate.

I don't have a chance at college. Daddy hasn't saved a penny. He's already borrowed on his life insurance and owes money all over town. My grades are so bad I probably wouldn't be able to get into college anyhow, but I am pretty sure that Katherine Cornell and Gertrude Lawrence finished high school.

October 19, 1958

Do you believe someone would be so inefficient as not to check the scenery before a performance, especially on opening night? J. R. Phillips, the stage manager of *Private Lives,* ruined the entire show. Everything was just fine until the second act when we were in my Paris apartment. Richard Ledbetter, who plays my husband, was supposed to say, "Some women are like gongs. They should be struck, regularly," and make an exit; but when he tried to get out, the idiot door was stuck and wouldn't open. He almost pulled the whole set down before the door-knob came off in his hand. I was looking right at him and I still don't believe it. He left the stage through the fireplace and took the doorknob with him. Not only that, the other two actors came onstage through the window. We all were forgetting our lines and instead of leaving well enough alone, J.R. kept banging the door, trying to get it unstuck. All he succeeded in doing was knocking the pictures off the wall. When he finally got the door open, he couldn't close it, and everyone in the audience saw him standing there during the entire act.

The reviews were all about the scenery. My name was only mentioned once. Mr. Cecil thought the performance was the funniest thing he had ever seen, and it was the first play Mrs. Teasley stayed awake for. But I am collecting reviews and I would have liked a good one. I will never again go on the stage unless I personally check all the doors. I told J.R. not to feel bad, that it could have happened to anyone, but it couldn't happen to anyone, just the retards!

Poor Richard Ledbetter was hysterical because his mother had been in the audience, and he went entirely to pieces after curtain calls. I am beginning to think that no matter what people say, men have more dramatic temperament than women. Richard sure takes longer to put on his makeup than I do. When he comes into the dressing room, he looks at himself in the mirror the whole time he is talking to you. He is nice, but vain. Everyone says that he stuffs socks in his underwear.

October 27, 1958

I am operating the lights for *The Seagull*. Boy, is that one long play, but it got great reviews. Listen to this:

> The play was filled with the gloomy haunting beauty and intense emotion of Russian people and captivated the spectators to such an extent that the atmosphere of the action crossed the footlights and pervaded the entire auditorium filled to capacity.

The reviewer obviously didn't see Mrs. Teasley. She slept through the whole thing. My sentiments exactly!

I am in the next show. It is a musical called *Pal Joey*, and I am playing another old lady, this one on a subway. All she does is chase after three sailors.

Grandmother Pettibone wrote me. She is very sad because her friend Ollie Meeks died. They all got together and had a Memorial Bingo Game in her honor. Grandma had needed O 69 for the jackpot and since that had always been Ollie's lucky number, she felt that it was a sign that Ollie was happy.

November 1, 1958

Thank God J.R. has redneck relatives. After rehearsal he told me he and his cousin Earle were going downtown and watch the police raid the queer bar. His uncle, who is a policeman, tipped him off so he and his cousin could have some fun. I panicked when it dawned on me Mr. Cecil might be in that bar. I made J.R. get me down there as fast as he could and threatened that if he didn't, I would tell everyone in Hattiesburg he was a big queer.

J.R. had been right about the police. They were coming around the corner at the very moment I jumped out of his car and ran in and started yelling at the top of my lungs for Mr. Cecil. I searched all over the room, but he wasn't anywhere around. I was still looking for him when guess who I saw hiding in a corner! Sally Gamble's father! I almost had a heart attack. I ran over and said, "Mr. Gamble, you've got to get out of here," and grabbed him by the arm and pulled him into the men's room with me.

He was as white as a sheet and he kept saying over and over, "This will ruin me!"

I tried to get the window in the bathroom open, but it was nailed shut. We could hear all the commotion going on in the next room, glass breaking and people screaming. Mr. Gamble was shaking like a leaf. I didn't know what else to do, so I pushed him in a stall and told him to lock the door behind him. Just as I was headed for the other stall to hide, the door burst open and two policemen grabbed me by the collar and yelled, "Come on, you stinking fairy," and started pulling me into the other room.

I grabbed onto the door and started screaming, "I'm a girl." I had on blue jeans, so I guess they thought I was a boy at first. They were so shocked to discover I was a girl they let me go. They wanted to know what in the hell I was doing in the men's room there and I had to think fast. "My name is Kay Bob Benson and I am here with my father, Reverend Benson, from the First Calvary Baptist Church. He and I are down here looking for my brother, Lem, who we think went off with some pervert."

They said, "Who's in that other stall?" and started banging on the door and yelling for whoever it was to come on out. I stood in front of the door and tried to stop them.

"Let him alone. The reverend is in there throwing up. This evil place has made him sick."

They pushed me aside and jerked the door open and sure enough, there was Mr. Gamble throwing up all over the place. They looked at him and backed off and said, "Well, all right, but you and the reverend get out of here." They left. I don't think they wanted to fool with somebody who was throwing up like that, so I got Mr. Gamble and we ran out the back door.

It took me forever to find J.R. He had parked the car two blocks away. Big chicken! Mr. Gamble was pretty shook up and could hardly talk. I knew where the Gambles lived, so I made J.R. drive him home and let him out. When he got out of the car, he threw up all over again.

The next day there was a big write-up in the paper. A lot of the Cecilettes were arrested, and so were some very important businessmen. Thank goodness Mr. Cecil hadn't been there, but after the raid Father Stephens dropped Mr. Cecil like a hot potato. He was scared he would get found out if he were seen with Mr. Cecil after they put all the Cecilettes' names in the paper. I never did like him in the first place. Mr. Cecil is heart-broken.

But do you know what he did? He took all his savings and paid the bail for his friends. He said he had to do it because otherwise there wouldn't have been another sequin sewn in the entire state of Mississippi.

Sally Gamble would have a fit if she knew where her father had been, but I'm not going to tell her. I didn't tell anyone, not even Mr. Cecil, and J.R. isn't going to say a word, I'm sure of that.

November 4, 1958

Do you know who is going to be in *Pal Joey*? Ray Layne, the boy singer who I liked years ago in Shell Beach, the one who sang at the Blue Gardenia Lounge. He's twenty-two and is singing with a group of three other guys, called the Four Jacks, and he's broken up with his old girlfriend.

I've never heard anybody with a better voice. I like him more than Eddie Fisher. He still has curly hair and long eyelashes. Why is it the boys always get long eyelashes? He looks like a much nicer version of Rory Calhoun. Was he surprised to see me! He hugged me and said he had often thought about writing me.

Seventeen is not too young for someone of twenty-two. I am very mature for my age. I'll see him again tomorrow at rehearsal. I'd give anything if I weren't playing that stupid old lady. He is probably the best-looking person I know. It is fate that he is in the show. I am probably in love. The only problem is he is a Catholic, but that's no big deal. I can convert. If Mr. Cecil can do it, so can I! Mr. Sandman, bring me a dream!

November 18, 1958

Ray and I are dating. I knew it would happen this way. His mother is wonderful—his father died when he was fifteen, and he has a little brother named Bobby who is adorable but not as cute as Ray. He is real sweet to his mother, and you know what they say: You can tell how a man will act to his wife by the way he treats his mother.

Everyone loves Ray, especially in his sailor outfit in the show. Offstage he wears plaid shirts with buttons on the collars, white wool socks with loafers, and his pants are always pressed. He smells good all the time, and he is the best kisser that ever lived. I never understood why people liked to do that until now.

Ray calls me the most affectionate girl he has ever known. I try to stay away from him, but I can't. I want to be with him all the time. I've looked at every picture that his mother has of him, including him as a baby. There are also a lot of pictures of that girl he used to go with, whose name is Ann. She wore glasses just like mine.

Sometimes after the show, we go down to this nightclub called Canebrake and when they ask him to sing, he dedicates "Because of You" to me and stares right at me until I think I'm going to faint. I still can't believe he is my boyfriend! When he is a big star, we'll live in New York and he'll be on the *Ed Sullivan Show* or have a show of his own.

I hate where we are living. When Ray comes over to see me,

Jimmy Snow and Daddy sit in the room with us and act like he has come to see them. Ray doesn't seem to mind, but I could scream. I wish they'd leave us alone. I never thought I was a jealous person, but now when I see him talking to someone else, I get sick. I asked Paris how you knew if you were in love, and she said, "Don't worry, when it happens, you'll know." The first day I saw him at rehearsal, I knew it. I can't sleep or eat.

Besides being the best kisser in the whole world, he is the best dancer. We slow dance over at the Canebrake and I can follow him. I don't try to lead at all. I told Ray I loved him the second time I went out with him. I know you are supposed to wait until the boy says it, but my feelings just slipped out. If I had a million dollars, I would buy him all the clothes he wanted and a car.

His mother says he's crazy about me, too. I call her up sometimes and get her to tell me stories about when he was young. I wish I had been his mother so I could have been with him from the moment he was born. I love him so much I wish I could cook him up and have him for dinner. I love to brush his hair and look at his hands. Ray Layne! Ray Layne! Ray Layne! Ray Layne! Ray Layne! I wrote Pickle and told her that I was in love.
Ray Layne!

December 28, 1958

This is the best Christmas I have ever had. Ray, his mother and myself and his little brother drove around the city looking at Christmas decorations. The house that won the prize this year was in the Italian section. Pink spotlights were all over the roof and on top was Santa Claus and seven reindeer. The deer looked like they were suspended in air. I never figured out how they got them to stay up like that. A huge red and white ribbon was tied all around the front of the house, it was a big Christmas package. A sign on it said, "Do Not Open Until December 25." On one side of the lawn was a manger with all the figures and plastic sheep and cows standing by, on the other side was a little bench with three of Santa's helpers making toys and a styrofoam snowman with a big card saying, "Merry Christmas from the Pegnellies."

We went to midnight mass and it was beautiful. Ray was an altar boy at one time. Afterwards we opened our presents. I gave Ray three sweaters, a tie, an ID bracelet and a record of Johnny Mathis singing "I'll Be Home for Christmas." I gave his little brother some paints because he loves to paint and Mrs. Layne a mirror and brush set. They gave me some fuzzy slippers and a flannel nightgown. Ray's present was just a box of candy, but I didn't care. Then Ray poured us all a glass of champagne to celebrate. When I looked in my glass, there was an engagement ring! I couldn't say anything. I never dreamed he was going to do that. His mother started screaming and jumping up and down, hugging both of us. He hadn't told her anything about it. I've never been so happy. Thank God I didn't swallow the ring.

I was spending the night with them, so we all got into our pajamas and I put on my new nightgown. Finally, Mrs. Layne and Bobby went to bed. I couldn't wait to grab Ray and kiss him to death. I wanted him to stay with me all night, but he said he shouldn't. When I asked him why, he said the way I was kissing him, we might get into trouble. I didn't care, but he told me he had promised Jimmy Snow he wouldn't touch me. I could have killed Jimmy Snow with a hatchet six times. What Jimmy Snow doesn't know can't hurt him. Finally, Ray agreed! Madame Bodini never tells!

Jimmy Snow and Daddy had a long talk with me about getting married. They wanted me to make sure I knew what I was doing. Jimmy Snow said a singer doesn't make much money, but I can get a job and help Ray until he becomes a big star. And he will be.

January 27, 1959

I am taking catechism lessons so I can be converted to Catholicism and make Ray happy. According to Mrs. Layne, converts usually turn out to be the best Catholics. Oh, brother! You ought to hear. They make you sign not only your life away but your unborn children's lives and their children. They want you lock, stock and barrel. If that priest thinks I am going to have children until I drop dead, he's got another thought coming. But I just sit there and say, "Yes, Father, no, Father." Personally I don't want any children for a long time. I want Ray all by myself. We are going to live with his mother and brother, and that's bad enough. And I'll tell you another thing. If I do get pregnant, I am not going to a Catholic hospital. If there are any complications, they ask the father if he wants the mother or the child. I know Ray loves me, but I am not taking any chances.

Ray is back singing with his group at this nightclub called the Jack O'Lantern that's shaped like a pumpkin. They are wonderful, better than the Four Freshmen. I go over every night. I like the other guys a lot, but Goose is my favorite. He's real silly! They kid Ray about being an old married man soon and will all be in the wedding party.

Grandmother Pettibone can't come because of her sick husband, so the only two people I have to sit on the bride's side are Daddy and Jimmy Snow. Daddy will have to give me away, so that leaves just Jimmy. But I invited everybody from the theater to sit on my side: Mr. Cecil and the ten Cecilettes, and Paris Knights. That should be plenty of people. I just want it to be over with.

February 16, 1959

Yesterday Tootie and Dolores asked me what my pattern was.
I didn't know what they were talking about. It's what kind of
silverware you want. I told them I didn't want any silverware,
but they said you have to have a pattern when you got married,
and you must go down to the store and pick out the one you like.
That way people can come in and ask what your pattern is, so I
made Mr. Cecil go downtown and help me pick one. He's crazy
about silverware. His choice has grapes on the handles and is
called Cornucopia. There is a lot to do in order to get married.

Jimmy Snow is acting like a grouch ever since I got engaged.
All he does is sit around and drink and watch the television set.
Do you believe that a grown man's favorite show is *Howdy
Doody*? Jimmy may not have much education. He never reads
or writes or anything. I am beginning to wonder if he can, but I
would never ask him because I might hurt his feelings. He is
very sensitive where I am concerned. He doesn't have any family
at all except for Daddy and me, which is why I am extra-nice to
him on his birthday. I asked Daddy what was the matter with
Jimmy lately and he said that Jimmy doesn't think Ray is good
enough for me.

I want to spend my honeymoon in the Wigwam Motel, out on
Highway 42. There are about six wigwams in the motel.

Mrs. Layne and I had a long conversation the other night
when Ray was working. Since I didn't have any women in my
family, she wanted to talk to me. She asked me if I had a diaphragm.

I said, "Yes, of course I did."

She seemed shocked and said, "When did you get it?"

I thought she had gone crazy. "I was born with one."

But she wasn't talking about that kind of diaphragm.

"I only had two children and my husband, who was much
more religious than I am, never did know why." She explained
what a diaphragm is and what you do with it and told me not to

depend on Ray if I didn't want any children. It was up to me to protect myself. She asked me if I had ever had a pelvic examination before, and I told her no. She insists I have one before I get married and made an appointment with this doctor next week.

February 28, 1959

I have never been so humiliated since I rode the mule down Highway 3! I went to see that idiotic doctor, and he told me to take all my clothes off but to keep my shoes on. Then he left. This nurse came in and said, "I'm Miss Skipper and I'm here to prepare you." She made me pee in a paper cup and gave me this paper gown and told me to get up on the table. When I did, she said, "Now, scoot down towards me."

I said, "What?"

She said, "I want you to scoot down here and put your feet in the stirrups."

So there I was in brown high heels and earrings, with my legs up in the air. I should have left right then. The doctor came back in and sat down on a stool and started poking flashlights and all kinds of things in me. He even had the nerve to ask if it hurt. That was bad enough, but the nurse stood behind him watching everything. Then he started feeling my breasts all over and at the same time asking me how the weather was outside! Is he crazy? After he was done, I got on my clothes and left. The hell with the diaphragm! That doctor acted like he was a mechanic checking my spark plugs.

April 7, 1959

Ray and his group are going to Panama City, Florida, for a month's engagement at the Lotus Club, but I'll stay here so I can graduate. This is the first time we've been separated. It's a big club and if they do well, they might get a record contract. It's funny. All my life I thought it would be so great to be a senior and here I am about to graduate and could care less.

I hardly ever see Mr. Cecil anymore. I think he's jealous of Ray. He shouldn't be. I still like him as much as I ever did. I didn't get mad when he found a boyfriend. People are funny.

Ray won't be back until a week after my graduation. Daddy and Jimmy Snow will come watch me graduate. I already bought a lot of funny cards to send Ray while he is in Panama City. I am going to be miserable while he's gone and he said he would be too. How could people stand it during the war when they would be separated for years at a time?

I got a letter from Grandma Pettibone. The whole group of Italian women that hit her in the head with a piece of fruitcake and called Ollie an old bat at the VFW bingo party one time finally got their comeuppance. Two days ago they were all on a second-floor screened-in porch playing penny bingo when this big fat woman yelled, "Bingo," and the whole porch collapsed. Grandma said if there is bingo in heaven, she knows Ollie Meeks caused that porch to fall.

May 22, 1959

I should have known something was wrong when Goose called from Florida. He was drunk and not making any sense. He kept saying Ray was a no good son of a bitch. I thought they had been fighting over the act until Ray's letter arrived.

It seems that Ann, Ray's old girlfriend, went to Panama City and they've gotten back together. He wrote he would always love me, but he had never really stopped loving her either. It wouldn't be fair to me because I was so great and he is sorry and so on and so on and so on.

P.S. I graduated and got a watch.

June 8, 1959

Ray's and Ann's wedding picture was in the paper today. It was so strange to see it. I have a picture of Ray and me and he has his arm around me the exact same way and has the same smile as the one in the paper. Is that what love is all about? Just changing a face in a photograph? Very weird.

June 17, 1959

Mr. Cecil came over to the apartment and told me he was tired of me sitting on my behind feeling sorry for myself. He says he's getting me to New York if he has to kill me, and he's entered me in the Miss Mississippi contest, so I can try to win a scholarship to study acting at the American Academy of Dramatic Arts in Manhattan. We're going to write the funniest talent number ever. If Mr. Cecil had the money, he would give it to me, but he spent it all getting the Cecilettes out of jail. He will find me a job so I can afford to get my teeth fixed. His greatest wish was to be a dancer, but he never had the nerve to try and he doesn't want me to wind up like him, always wondering what would have happened.

Mr. Cecil is the bravest person I know. People say terrible things to him and he still goes to work every day and goes out of his way to make people laugh.

We sat down and figured out I need $500 to get my teeth fixed, buy a real pretty gown and bathing suit, and pay my way to Tupelo, where they have the Miss Mississippi pageant. One of the Cecilettes has a secret friend at the television station here, and he found out they are looking for a weather girl. The one they now have is pregnant and they don't want a pregnant weather girl. He is going to set up an audition for me. Mr. Cecil wanted me to get contact lenses. He is sure we can buy them at a good price because another one of the Cecilettes has a friend who is an optometrist. Never underestimate the power of the Cecilettes!

June 21, 1959

I got the job at the TV station! I am the new weather girl on the morning show. All I have to do is to show up at 6:30 A.M., fix the weather map and stand there for three minutes to tell everybody what the weather is going to be. I don't know a thing about weather, but the other weather girl said not to worry, just to remember it always moves to the east. I am surprised I got the job. There were a lot of girls trying out, but Mr. Cecil said he knew I would get it because, in the words of Miss Doris Day, "A certain party was afraid that their secret love would be no secret anymore."

I make $50 a week. If I can get a few extra jobs entertaining somewhere, I will have all the money I need for the Miss Mississippi contest. I go to the eye doctor next week. Ray's mother sent me a long, sweet letter. She hopes I know that she still loves me and she wants me to come over and see her anytime. There isn't a day that goes by that I don't think about Ray, but at least Jimmy Snow is his old self again. He's even been dusting crops. Daddy just won't stop drinking. He'll give it up for a few days, but then he goes back. His girlfriend left him, but he uses any crazy excuse to tie one on.

June 24, 1959

The entrance form for the Miss Mississippi contest came in the mail today. In order to enter, you must be of excellent character and background, talented, ambitious, attractive and never married. Well, I am ambitious and I've never been married. A week of judging will start at the Dinkler Tutwiler Hotel in Tupelo on August 3, and the pageant will be held on the ninth.

I like my job at the TV station. It's pretty early in the morning, but Jimmy drives me in his truck when he's home and the rest of the time I take the bus. At the station they have a big weather board that has these cardboard pictures of things like snow and rain and clouds you can move wherever you want. The job is easy. All I do is move the five o'clock weather girl's weather a few inches to the right. When it all winds up on the East Coast, I start it back in California. The only bad thing is the gospel show that's going on in the studio while I am fixing my weather board. When I come in in the morning, you should see those gospel singers making out on the couch in the makeup room. How they can do that so early in the morning is beyond me. No wonder there are so many Baptists in the world.

I'm in the next play at the theater, *Oklahoma!*, and I get to sing a song entitled "I'm Just a Girl Who Cain't Say No."

The eye doctor gave me some contact lenses and showed me how to put them in. I can only wear them one hour. They hurt like the devil, but I am going to stick it out come hell or high water and will wear them two hours tomorrow. Pretty soon I won't even know they are there. Right now they feel like I have two garbage can lids in my eyes. These are just temporary lenses. I ordered blue-tinted ones. And guess what? Today when I was in the drugstore, a woman came up to me and asked if she hadn't seen me on television. Then she asked for my autograph. How about that? I guess it will be pretty hard for me to go anywhere without being recognized. Now I know how movie stars feel. I like this television work.

July 1, 1959

Oklahoma! opened last night and here is my review:

> Miss D. Frances Harper, an Azalea Playhouse regular, made her singing debut last night as Ado Annie, a role originated on Broadway by Celeste Holm. This reviewer was lucky enough to have seen *Oklahoma!* in New York City, and I must say that Miss Harper, who resembles Miss Holm not only in looks but in talent as well, stopped the show last night as did her famous predecessor with the song "I'm Just a Girl Who Cain't Say No." I am hoping she will take a clue from her song and never say no to sharing her many talents with us.

I am up to eight hours of wearing time with my blue contact lenses.

Mr. Cecil and I are busy with my talent number for the Miss Mississippi contest. I came up with a character who's a cross between Mrs. Dot and Grandma Pettibone. I call her "Susie Sweetwater." I wear a funny hat with flowers and some funny glasses with jewels all over them. I pretend she has a TV show and use an exaggerated southern accent and act real ditsy.

I make believe I am in a TV studio putting on my lipstick and powder when the camera comes on and catches me. I am real surprised and say, "Oh, hi there. Good morning. And how was your morning this morning? And welcome to *The News in the Morning*, your friendly morning news program. Remember, here you get all the news while it's still news. Anything else you may hear is just plain gossip. Well, I have a happy wedding announcement. You know people used to get married in June, but nowadays they get married whenever they have to . . . uh, want to . . . Mrs. Mosell Hicks announces the engagement of her daughter, Quantia, to Seaman Fourth Class Curtis Johnson. Miss Hicks, who attended Central Lee High School, is employed by the Roxy Theater as a candy girl and part-time ladies' room attendant. Mr. Johnson attended New Mercle Grammar School." I pretend to look for a name of a high school but can't find it and give up. "The wedding will take place in the home of the bride and the bride will enter from the kitchen and Curtis and his father, Mr. Willis T. Johnson, will enter from the front porch. The bride will wear a white net ballerina-length dress, with shoes, hat, purse, gloves and ankle bracelet to match. After the ceremony, a reception for the happy couple will be held at the Trailways bus station, where the bride's mother is an employee. After a short honeymoon trip to see Rock City, the couple will reside in the Orange Grove Trailer Park near Mr. Johnson's naval base. Mr. Johnson plans a career in the Navy or one in the trailer park. Well, that's all the time we have for today. And don't forget to tune in tomorrow for *Dateline Divorce* and, as always, I leave you with a thought for the day: Protect your heart as you would your other vital organs. Bye bye."

I just hope Amy Jo Snipes doesn't hear my number. I took a lot of the stuff out of her wedding announcement.

July 2, 1959

It says in the Miss Mississippi brochure that if you get in the finals, you would be judged all over again, so I need two numbers. They judge you on talent and bathing suits and personality. I am too skinny to look good in a bathing suit and my personality is questionable after having been around Daddy all these years, so Mr. Cecil says we should concentrate on talent. I asked Mr. Cecil if I couldn't do my famous death scene from *Yellow Jack* for one of the talent numbers, and do you know what? He said no, because we only have three minutes for our talent numbers, not forty-five! Smart alec! Boo! Hiss! So I am going to do the one about the woman who gets shot as a second number.

July 3, 1959

I am very late with my period and I am scared shitless. If I am pregnant, I will kill myself. Surely I'm not. I can't be. I've never been this late in my life.

Oh, shit!

July 11, 1959

It's been eight days. I don't know what to do, and just when everything was going so good. I asked Tootie if you could get pregnant the first time you did it and she said, "Yes, it happens all the time." How could I have been so stupid? I don't have anyone to blame but myself. I will have to tell Mr. Cecil. I don't know who else I can talk to. I have been horseback riding every day and I have had about a hundred hot baths, but no luck.

July 12, 1959

I told Mr. Cecil I was pregnant and he was very upset for me. He called all the Cecilettes to see if they knew where I could go and get an abortion, but not one of them knew anybody. So we went to see Paris Knights and she said the only one she knew that would do it had died.

Mr. Cecil came over to see me last night and told me he had thought about it, and wanted to marry me and raise the child. He tried to make light of it by saying it was his duty because after all, he had found me the job as the weather girl and the last weather girl had gotten pregnant, too. He thinks pregnancy must be one of the hazards of being a weather girl. I was really touched he would do that for me, but I just can't. I love Mr. Cecil, but not that way. I sat up all night trying to figure out something when I remembered someone!

I placed a person-to-person call to Peachy Wigham and told her. She said for me to hold the phone. And came back on after about two minutes and told me to get down to her as soon as I could. I am leaving tomorrow right after I finish doing my weather report. God bless Peachy Wigham!

July 15, 1959

On the bus I had some time to think about what I was doing.
The idea that I might die down there on the abortion table
scared me to death. I kept thinking about what was going to
happen if I did live through it. How was I going to feel? Would
I be sorry someday? Momma had said having a baby was the
most painful thing in the world. I got to looking at her ring.
Thank God she didn't know I was in trouble.

I must have changed my mind about a hundred times about
whether or not to go through with it. I wrote out a will, then
tore it up. By the time the bus arrived in Magnolia Springs I was
a nervous wreck and my brains felt like scrambled eggs. I went
to the bathroom at the filling station and put some cold water
on my face and sat down on the floor. Then I combed my hair
and used the bathroom and guess who started her period! Me!
I was never so happy in my life. I started screaming and yelling
and carrying on until the man at the filling station banged on
the door and asked if I was all right. And to think I had always
complained about having my period! From now on I will have
a party every month when I start. I couldn't wait to tell Peachy,
but when I got to the Elite Nightspot, only Ula Sour was there.
After I told Ula my good news, she laughed her head off. She
thinks I scared myself so bad I probably stopped myself from
having a period.

Ula called Peachy at the mortuary and told her to come on
home, that everything was all right. I was glad to see Peachy
and she was glad to see me. I found out that Felix, my cat, had
died of old age, but they had a new one they loved a lot even
though it was ugly. I spent the night, and we had a wonderful
time. Peachy serves the best fifty-year-old bourbon in the world.

When I was leaving the next morning, I told Peachy I was
sorry I had caused her so much trouble and would be glad to
pay whoever it was that was going to do the abortion. She said
to forget it.

She wouldn't tell me who the person was who would have performed the abortion, but on my way home on the bus, it dawned on me that the person was Peachy Wigham herself. That's why she hadn't been there when I arrived. She was down at the mortuary getting things ready. Now that it's all over and I have had some time to think, I still don't know if I would have gone through with it or not. God bless Peachy Wigham anyway.

Years ago Daddy told me the reason she never got arrested was because she knew a secret about the sheriff's daughter. Now I know what it was. If only Pickle could have gotten to her!

July 18, 1959

I went to work this morning and the manager of the TV station, Mr. Baers, called me into his office right after my weather report. He said there had been the biggest floods in the Midwest in twenty-five years and asked what the hell was all my weather doing in California where they were having a drought.

I didn't have a good answer for him, so I told him I had just been moving Miss Pat's, the five o'clock weather girl's symbols a little to the right, and it had always worked out OK before.

When he heard that, he turned red in the face! Can you imagine getting that excited over the weather? He buzzed his secretary and ordered her to get Miss Pat in there right away. When Miss Pat came in, he said, "Did you know that this idiot has been moving your symbols every morning and that she doesn't know a damn thing about the weather?"

She just looked at me all surprised and said, "Oh, no. This is terrible because I've been moving yours every night."

You should have heard Mr. Baers! He pitched a fit and said,

"How dare you screw around with the weather! All the farmers are depending on this station to give them the correct weather forecast." He said we two were probably single-handedly responsible for the failure of crops all over the state of Mississippi. Anyway, we both got fired. Some man that plays Bozo the Clown in the afternoon is now doing both reports.

I felt real bad for Miss Pat, getting fired like that, because she is very nice. The only thing the matter with her is she uses too much hair spray. A newsman at the station told me that when a tornado hit Hattiesburg and Miss Pat went outside to get in her car right in the middle of it, her blouse was blown off but her hair never moved.

July 21, 1959

I have a new job at the A to Z Rental Company making $75 a week. I sit in a big warehouse and answer the phone, and if anyone comes in, I rent them whatever they want. We have everything . . . hospital and sickroom supplies, beds, and party supplies, punch bowls, silver, wheelchairs, crutches, even artificial legs and arms. Can you imagine anyone wanting to rent a wooden leg? I've been here for two days and nobody has rented anything yet, so it's very easy. I just go in the morning and stay all day, and at five o'clock I close and go home. The only bad part is it is lonesome, but at least I have plenty of time to rehearse my talent numbers. Sometimes I get in a wheelchair and roll around the warehouse.

Mr. Cecil and I are going down to Gamble's Department Store as soon as we can and buy me a white evening gown for the pageant and a white bathing suit as well. Everything has to be white, according to the Miss Mississippi contest rules. Mr. Cecil has been teaching me how to walk because they judge you on your posture. I go around with a book on my head all the time and I am getting pretty good at it.

If I can just win that scholarship! You should read who all has studied at the American Academy. I wouldn't be surprised if Celeste Holm went there. Mr. Cecil and Tootie and Dolores and Helen and I are planning to celebrate Dolores's birthday at this new Polynesian restaurant that has just opened. Nobody knows how old Dolores is and she won't tell, claiming it is a state secret. Tootie says she rides buses just so she won't have to get a driver's license and reveal her age.

Did you know that they have bedpans made just for men?

July 23, 1959

We got to the Aloha Restaurant about seven o'clock. It was decorated like Hawaii, with Hawaiian music and waitresses in real Hawaiian costumes. Tootie ordered a whole suckling pig for our party, and we had all kinds of funny drinks. My first one came in a coconut. Then I had one called a Mai Tai, and one called a Scorpion.

We were eating our appetizers, shrimp and chicken livers with bacon, and I was having a wonderful time when all of a sudden Mr. Cecil looked like he had seen a ghost. My back was to the door, and he said, "Don't turn around."

I said, "Why?"

He said, "Don't turn around."

Then Tootie said under her breath, "Don't turn around."

So naturally I turned around, and there were Ray Layne and Ann at the door. He saw me at the same time I saw him. I could have crawled under the table. There I sat with four paper umbrellas in my hair and six paper leis around my neck. He came over and said hello and introduced Ann to everyone, including me. I said, "How do you do?" What else would I say?

Helen, who was bombed, said, "Why don't you two join the party?" Tootie kicked her so hard under the table that she spilled her drink. He didn't stay and after he left, Mr. Cecil asked me if I wanted to go. I said, no, there was no reason to ruin the party for everybody. Then I had three more coconut drinks. We never did eat that suckling pig. The poor thing died for nothing. Of all the restaurants in the world, why did Ray have to come into that one?

Afterwards we went to Tootie's apartment. That's where I got the idea of having Mr. Cecil hide me in the closet. I put on Tootie's old winter coat with the hanger still in the back of it, and Mr. Cecil lifted me up and hung me in the closet. At the time I thought it would be the funniest thing in the world for them to find me just hanging there with the coats. What I didn't realize was that Mr. Cecil was so drunk he forgot where he put me. I must have hung in that closet for over an hour before I passed out.

The next morning, when I woke up and saw Tootie's fox furs, I started kicking and screaming. Dolores got to me first and opened the door. I asked her, "What in the world am I doing hanging in the closet?"

She said, "I'm sure I don't know." Nobody had gone home that night, and you never saw so many sick people with hangovers in your life. Those fruit drinks are lethal. I had missed the best part of the evening, though, because Dolores got so drunk she told everybody how old she was, and now they won't tell me.

We sat around the apartment with ice on our heads until about five o'clock that afternoon. Tootie had to call the drugstore to bring us Alka-Seltzer and aspirin and Coca-Cola and ice cream. I will never do that again as long as I live. Thank God it was Saturday. When I did get home, I stayed in bed all day

Sunday. Lucky for me Jimmy Snow was off crop-dusting. If he had played that television set as loud as he usually does, I might not have survived. I don't know what hurt worse, seeing Ray or my head.

July 24, 1959

Daddy had to have the money. I couldn't let him lose the lease on the bar. He tried to borrow all over town, I know he did, but nobody would give him a penny. He wouldn't have asked me for it if he hadn't been desperate. He knew how hard I had been saving.

At first I got mad and didn't want to give it to him. Then I remembered what he had done for me when I was a kid, how he had taken a chance on going to jail for life to protect me, so I couldn't let him down.

I am sure he will pay it back. Besides, I can always go in the contest next year or something. A year is nothing.

July 26, 1959

When Jimmy Snow got home from his crop-dusting job and found out I had given Daddy all my money, he was furious! He screamed, "How in hell could you be so stupid as to give your daddy your money?" and tore into Daddy's room, where he yanked him out of the bed and called him a no-good drunken son of a bitch. He started beating Daddy up until I ran in and stopped him.

Jimmy stormed back into the other room. He had $40 in his billfold that he kept trying to make me take. I didn't want his money, all I wanted was for him to stop acting so insane. He asked why would I give Daddy the money when I knew he would just drink it all up. I told him whatever Daddy does, he was still my father and I owed it to him.

He said, "You don't owe that rotten son of a bitch anything."

And before I thought, I said, "He killed Claude Pistal, didn't he?"

That was the first time I had ever broken my word and mentioned it since I was eleven. I was sorry I had.

Jimmy looked at me real strange and said, "What?"

I said, "Listen, Jimmy, let's just forget about it, OK?"

"Wait a minute. I'm not going to forget it. What the hell are you talking about?"

"I know who killed Claude, so let's just leave it at that, all right?"

"Who do you think killed him?"

"You and Daddy and Rayette. You told me so yourself."

He looked at me like I was crazy and said, "Oh, my God. You didn't believe that story I told you about Rayette Walker, did you?"

"Of course I did."

"Daisy, your daddy and I never killed anybody." Jimmy looked like he was going to cry.

"Of course you did. I saw the sacks with the guns you got from Peachy Wigham."

"What guns?"

"The two sacks you got from Peachy the night Claude was killed. I saw Daddy bring the guns back the next day. You can stop pretending."

"Daisy, there weren't guns in those sacks. That was two bottles of bootleg whiskey your daddy and I bought off of Peachy and took to Rayette's house. He brought the empty bottles back in those sacks."

"Wait a minute. How else would Daddy have known about Claude being dead before the police told him?"

"I went up to the airstrip to get something out of the plane that morning and I found Claude and called your daddy over at Rayette's house and told him."

I couldn't believe what I was hearing. "But you told me the bullets were from Rayette's gun."

"My God, Daisy, I was half drunk that night and your daddy put me up to telling you that story so he could go on seeing Rayette without you having a fit over it. I never thought you believed it."

I said, "Of course I believed it."

Then he started to cry and kept repeating how sorry he was, that that stupid story was just a joke. I felt like someone had kicked me in the stomach. I don't want to see either one of them again.

August 1, 1959

I have been living at the YWCA and eating at Morrison's Cafeteria. After work yesterday, when I walked into the lobby, there sat Jimmy Snow. He grabbed me by the arm and said, "Come on, we are going home."

I said, "Who are you?" and walked right by him.

He said, "You are too going home with me even if I have to drag you out of here."

I went over to Miss Prisim, who is the switchboard operator, and informed her that the man who looked somewhat like an albino was a total stranger to me and to please call the police. Jimmy kept making a commotion and Miss Prisim got so rattled that when she did get the number, she said, "Hello, this is the police," and hung up.

Finally, Jimmy said, "All right, I didn't want to tell you this, but your daddy has had a heart attack and is not expected to live and we have to go now."

We ran out and got in the truck. Jimmy said they had him over at the bar because he had been in too bad a shape to move.

It was the longest ride in my life. I kept thinking I would never forgive myself if Daddy died before I had a chance to tell him I loved him. When we pulled up to the bar, I jumped out and ran in, but it was pitch-dark. I yelled, "Daddy! where are you?" And all of a sudden the lights came on and about twenty people screamed, "Surprise!!" and Daddy was standing right in the middle of them and there wasn't a thing the matter with him. I was so glad to see him alive and so shocked I started to cry.

Everybody was there. Mr. Cecil and the Cecilettes, Tootie, Helen, Dolores, Paris Knights, and J.R., Professor Teasley and his mother, and they all started singing "For she's a jolly good fellow." On the wall was a big sign that read "Miss Mississippi Pageant or Bust." After they made me sit down, Mr. Cecil went behind the curtains in the back room. Daddy turned on a spotlight he had borrowed and Mr. Cecil came back out in a red sequined jacket and bow tie with a huge book that had "Daisy Fay Harper" written on it and said, "Settle down, Daisy Fay Harper, because THIS IS YOUR LIFE," and everyone applauded.

"Do you remember this person? You haven't seen her since you were twelve years old."

A woman's voice came from the back room. "Daisy, the last time we met was in Shell Beach in 1953." I couldn't think who it could be. Then J.R. put on a record of Jane Froman singing "I'll Walk Alone" and I knew who it was—Betty Caldwell, the crippled girl I had healed. She came in and grabbed me and she looked great.

Mr. Cecil escorted her to a chair and announced, *"Now a special person you have never met . . .* Daisy Fay, say hello to Daisy Fay the second. . . ." Then this little girl ran out and kissed me and handed me an envelope. She was Betty's little girl who they had named after me. Inside the envelope was a note that said, "This entitles Miss Daisy Fay Harper the First to have two chipped teeth fixed free of charge." Betty had married a dentist and had arranged for a friend of his to do it.

The next voice was a man's. "Daisy, are you still eating all those hot fudge sundaes and bananas splits?" J.R. put on the theme music from *Gang Busters . . .* It was Mr. Kilgore, the man from the FBI who had been with Opal Bates the day they had picked me up from school! He gave me a check for $50 signed by the FBI for services rendered, and wished me good luck.

Then Mr. Cecil said, "The next two guests need no introduction," and all of a sudden I heard two women scream "BINGO!!!" I knew who it was, it was Grandma Pettibone and Aunt Bess. I was so happy to see them I started to cry again. Grandma brought me underwear and Aunt Bess had frozen some black-eyed peas and collard greens from her restaurant. Grandma whispered that she was still mad at Bess over the birth control pills but was speaking to her this week in my honor.

After they sat down, the theme music from *The King and I* came on and this deep booming voice said, "Roses are red, violets are blue, boy, do I have a wig for you! Et cetera et cetera et cetera." It was Vernon Mooseburger with a wig and he even had false eyebrows. He kissed me and presented me with a certificate for ten free lessons with Dale Carnegie, where he is now an executive.

After he went over and sat down, the music started, this time with the "Blue Danube Waltz." A very familiar voice said, "Remember, Daisy, nothing succeeds more than personal charm." It was Mrs. Dot!!! She came running in and I grabbed her and started crying again. She has been out of the hospital for three years and is teaching drama at a girls' school in Gulfport, Mississippi, and looks just the same. Her gift was a complete set of Shakespeare's works bound in leather.

J.R. did a drumroll and Mr. Cecil said, "Now, last but not least, a special mystery guest, all the way from Birmingham, Alabama, who wouldn't be here tonight if it hadn't been for you. Mystery guest, sign in please!!!" This pretty girl walked in and started writing her name on a blackboard they had set up. The minute I saw her ears I knew it was Angel Pistal, all grown up! Her mother and daddy were with her, and they gave me a check for $100.

J.R. played "Happy Days Are Here Again" on the record player while Mr. Cecil closed by announcing, "A party in your honor will be held in this room after the show for you and your guests, catered by Tommy and Jim, two of the Cecilettes. Daisy Fay Harper, this is your life!!!"

After that they rolled out a big table with all kinds of presents on it. Mr. Cecil and the Cecilettes bought me a whole new traveling outfit with shoes and hat and purse, and as a joke, Mr. Cecil had made up an ankle bracelet to match. Tootie and Helen and Dolores bought me a bathing suit which the Cecilettes had been up all night covering with white sequins. It's got to be the most fantastic bathing suit in the world. Jimmy Snow gave me $75, and Professor Teasley and his mother gave me 100. Paris Knights bought me a beautiful Samsonite traveling bag with a matching cosmetic case.

But they saved the biggest package till the end. It was a huge pink box and when I opened it, I almost died. Inside was the most beautiful white evening gown I've ever seen. It must have cost a fortune. I couldn't imagine who could have afforded it. I asked who it was from, but nobody knew. J.R. said, "Look at the card."

I'd been in such a hurry I hadn't seen it. It read "Good luck to a friend. Best, Mr. E. Gamble." J.R. was grinning from ear to ear. Mrs. Underwood and her sixth graders sent me a good-luck note, and Peachy Wigham and Ula Sour made me coat hangers with cloth on them and wrote a sweet letter.

At the party afterwards Betty Caldwell told me she had read in the paper that Billy Bundy was in jail again. He'd been trying to heal people over the radio in Humboldt, Tennessee, when some woman had put her hands on the radio while her hands were wet and got knocked clear across the room.

We stayed up until three o'clock in the morning and had a ball. Angel told me all about herself and she is as sweet as ever and Mr. Cecil and Aunt Bess hit it off great. They danced almost every dance together. And I must say that Dale Carnegie course certainly must have paid off for Vernon Mooseburger because he went home with Paris Knights. I just hope his wig stayed on. Helen got so drunk at the end she was sitting there talking to one of those stuffed blowfish Daddy has on a wall. That party is the nicest thing that has ever happened to me in my whole life.

This morning Jimmy flew Grandma and Aunt Bess home in his plane and I went to the dentist and he fixed my teeth in an hour. You would never even know they had been chipped. I am all packed. I left my gown in the box and tied it on top of Jimmy's truck so it won't get mashed. Daddy and Jimmy and I leave for Tupelo the first thing in the morning. I love everybody in the world!

August 3, 1959

We arrived at the Dinkler Tutwiler Hotel in Tupelo at four-thirty this afternoon. As we were unpacking the truck, guess who drove up in a brand-new Cadillac? Kay Bob Benson and her mother! I thought I was rid of her forever, but somebody up there hates me.

I've never seen so many pretty girls. They are from all over the state.

The Dinkler Tutwiler Hotel is beautiful. The lobby is marble with real antique furniture, live palm trees and ferns everywhere. Signs were all over the walls saying, "Welcome, Miss Mississippi Hopefuls." The woman at the registration desk told me that, because 138 girls were entered this year, the Dinkler Tutwiler was all booked and I would have to find another place to stay. So after I learned what time I had to be there tomorrow, Daddy and Jimmy Snow and I went out to look for a new hotel.

The only vacancy we found was the Hotel Dixie on the other side of town. It is pretty seedy, but it will be all right for a week.

Daddy went down in the lobby and made a phone call. After he came back, he gave me the number of the Veterans' Cab Company. When I have to go over to the Dinkler Tutwiler, I am to call that number and ask for Cab No. 22, whose driver is an old drinking buddy of his and will take good care of me. I hoped his old buddy wasn't still drinking because I didn't feel like being killed after I had come this far. Daddy and Jimmy said good-bye and wished me luck and headed on back to Hattiesburg.

I sure hope I do well tomorrow. We finished off Aunt Bess's black-eyed peas and collard greens on the way up here. I don't feel so hot right now.

Kay Bob Benson! Do you believe it?

August 4, 1959

This morning I called the number Daddy gave me and Cab No. 22 arrived in about five minutes. The driver, whose name was Mr. Smith, was pretty old and didn't talk much. From the way the cab smelled, Daddy was dead wrong about him quitting drinking, but he was a safe driver and very courteous and called me "miss." When I got to the Dinkler Tutwiler, I had on the new suit the Cecilettes had given me, and I was glad. All the girls were wearing nice clothes.

The first day is called "Get Acquainted Day." We were handed name tags and heard a speech in this big banquet room by Mrs. Lulie Harde McClay, the woman in charge, who had started the Miss Mississippi pageant in 1929. She spoke to us about how important it was to behave like southern ladies during the coming week, and how Miss Mississippi represented the image of southern womanhood. We were to remember there was only one winner and lots of losers, but losers shouldn't feel bad because it was an honor even to be in the pageant. Then she introduced us to the chaperones and judges. There are six judges: Mrs. Peggy Buchanan, president of the Junior League of Mississippi; Mr. Harrison Swanley, a famous Mississippi painter; last year's Miss Mississippi, Audrey Jones Sommers; Madame Rosa Albergotti, opera teacher and ex-opera star; Mr. Oliver Henry, the vice-president of the Jaycees, who sponsored the pageant; and Dr. Daniel A. Deady, preacher of the Mount Holy Oak Baptist Church in Tupelo. All the new girls in the contest are to come tomorrow morning, prepared to do their talent numbers.

As we were getting ready to leave, Kay Bob Benson walked over and said at the top of her voice, "Daisy Fay Harper, I just knew it was you that got out of that old pickup truck yesterday."

I replied, "Yes, it was, and wasn't that you getting off a broom?"

A big, fat girl standing there heard the whole thing and

started to laugh. She said, "Hey kid, where are you going?"

I told her I had to get back to the truck stop.

She laughed, "Come on up to our room. We're having a little party." I didn't have anything else to do, so I went.

A sign on the door said, "Miss Mississippi Veterans of Foreign Wars, Chaperones Stay Out." Inside I met three other girls. They had all rented the suite together and had been in the pageant for three years in a row. This was the last year they could enter. The fat girl, Darcy Lewis, said the only reason they were there was to get scholarships to college. They asked if I wanted a drink. I said, "Sure," so they locked the door, Darcy went into the bathroom and got a bottle of Old Granddad out of the back of the toilet, and another girl named Mary Cudsworth pulled a bottle of scotch out of a Kotex box. They had a whole bar set up.

Darcy Lewis is in college at Stephens, majoring in speech, and her talent number is a scene from *Joan of Arc* that she has done for the past three years. Mary said Darcy is just too lazy to work on something new. Mary is a musician majoring in music at the University of Mississippi, and Penny Raymond is a singer. She's about six feet tall, piles her hair up on her head and wears drop earrings. Jo Ellen Feely, the fourth girl, is majoring in political science at a college called Goucher. All she wanted to talk about was socialism. Whenever she tried to, the other girls screamed at her to shut up.

They asked me all about myself and if I wanted to be Miss Mississippi. I said, "No, I want to win the scholarship to the American Academy of Dramatic Art in New York." They seemed pleased. None of them were competing for that one. They told me the contest was fixed and this girl named Margaret Poole was going to win. Mrs. Lulie Harde McClay always picks the winner and this time she promised it to the Poole girl, who she's been grooming to be Miss Mississippi for two years. According to them, Margaret Poole is the biggest hypocrite going. She smokes and drinks and screws boys all over town, but when she is around Mrs. McClay, butter wouldn't melt in her mouth. Mrs. Lulie Harde McClay's whole life has been devoted to getting a Miss Mississippi to be Miss America. They also told me anybody who did not come from a good family and was not a Protestant didn't have a chance in hell. It was a good thing I didn't want to win, because where it said religion, I put down "Pagan."

They asked me about my talent number. Because I did comedy, they all agreed I had a good chance to make the finals if I was any good. Most of the girls are interpretive dancers and they like to have a variety of different talent numbers for the big pageant at the State Theater on the ninth.

We sat there most of the night, and I drank all those girls under the table. They must have liked me because before I left, they invited me to come back tomorrow. They also made me promise to vote for Darcy for Miss Congeniality. She's won for three years and is collecting Miss Congeniality statuettes as a hobby. Every year she goes around and tells all the other girls that she is going to vote for them. Then they vote for her and she votes for herself, so she's a shoo-in. The judges got suspicious last year when the vote was unanimou:

August 5, 1959

My cab picked me up early this morning, and I went up to Darcy's room, where they were giving drinks right and left to this poor country girl named Dorothy Clem Kenyard. They told her she needed them to loosen up to do her talent number. Then we all went down and watched while she tried to sing the "Laughing Song" from some opera. All she did was stand there and laugh, she didn't sing at all. You should have seen the looks on the judges' faces. I found out later that Dorothy Clem was trying for the same scholarship as Penny.

You wouldn't believe some of those talent numbers. One girl played the grand piano while standing in authentic Mississippi mud. Another was a dress designer and modeled a dress she'd made out of old menus; and this skinny girl blew up balloons that were supposed to be different animals, but they all looked the same to me.

When I finally did my talent number, it went over good. By that time the judges must have been glad to have some comedy. They had already seen forty-eight interpretive dancers and eighteen girls doing a scene from *Joan of Arc*.

August 6, 1959

Today was my interview with the judges. Darcy and Mary told me what to say to make sure the judges liked me. When they asked who I admired the most in the world, I was to answer my mother or Joan Crawford, either one was surefire. When they asked what I wanted out of life, it was to be a good American, and a wife and a Christian mother. And when they asked me what my hobbies were, I was supposed to say teaching Sunday school and working with poor children. And if they asked me if I wanted to be Miss Mississippi, the answer was "I am sure that there are many other girls more qualified than I am, but if by some chance I do win, it will be the proudest moment of my life." I reminded Darcy I didn't want to be Miss Mississippi, I just wanted a scholarship. She said it didn't matter. You had to make them think you wanted it. When I asked if I shouldn't answer the questions truthfully, she said, "Hell, no, nobody ever tells the truth." The four of them had taken a poll and this is how all the former Miss Mississippis answered the questions. If I spoke the truth, I would never get a scholarship.

When it was their turns to do their talent numbers, I went and watched. Mary, who had played the violin last year, got up in a long black dress and said, "This year, after some deliberation, I feel that my talent lies in the piano." Then she walked over to the piano, opened the lid, took out a musical saw and played "Whispering." I nearly died laughing. Darcy recited her scene from *Joan of Arc*. It was terrible. Her costume was a pair of Chinese pajamas and a colander on her head. I finally found out what a colander was! Jo Ellen, who was half drunk, had on a feather bonnet and did the Lord's Prayer in Indian sign language. I don't know how she kept a straight face. I nearly fell off my chair laughing, but the judge who is a preacher really loved it.

Afterwards we went back up to the room. Jo Ellen told me what she had been doing wasn't Indian sign language at all. She'd just made it up. It didn't matter how bad their talent numbers were. They would get their scholarships anyway because Mrs. McClay was dying for them to finish college so she could brag about how the Miss Mississippi pageant had provided them with a complete college education.

I was glad I listened to the girls. Sure enough, in my question-and-answer period, the questions were exactly what they said they would be. The reverend asked me about being a pagan, and I told him that it was a mistake, my answer was supposed to be a Presbyterian. He would have been happier if I'd answered Baptist, but Presbyterian was the only one I could think of that stated with a *P*. When they wanted to know what my father did, I told them he ran an eating establishment, which wasn't too much of a lie. Daddy does serve hard-boiled eggs. Mrs. Buchanan asked me about the scholarship to the American Academy in New York City and I told her I wanted to go there. When she wondered whether I had a second choice, I answered, "Brooklyn." They said, "Thank you very much."

The pageant rules don't allow any girls' mothers in the hotel, but Kay Bob Benson's mother hides behind the potted plants and every time Kay Bob goes by, she sticks her head through and yells at her to fix her hair or smile. Everyone can see her through the palm tree. I don't know who she thinks she is fooling.

August 7, 1959

Today was bathing suit competition and Darcy warned me to be very careful where I sat. Last year a girl had lost a lot of points when she made the mistake of sitting in a wicker chair right before the bathing suit competition. I stood up and waited for my turn. That girl Margaret Poole, who is going to be Miss Mississippi, has a great figure. So does Kay Bob Benson, although I hate to admit it.

You wouldn't believe what Darcy and Mary did. Darcy modeled her bathing suit and when she turned around, she had a big sign on her behind, "SEE ROCK CITY." If that wasn't enough, here came Mary, sopping wet with fins and a swimming mask, carrying a spear. Everybody cracked up!

Daddy was right about my cabdriver. He takes good care of me. I don't even have to call him when I'm through. I go out in front of the hotel and there he is. He always asks me how it went and I tell him everything. I think he gets a kick out of it. He reminds me of some actor, but I can't think who.

They announced the names of the girls who made the finals this afternoon. Kay Bob was one; and when they called Margaret Poole's name, Mary and Darcy and Jo Ellen and Penny said together, "What a surprise!" Mrs. McClay looked like she could have killed them. They called my name and was I glad. I couldn't wait to tell my cabdriver, so I only had one drink with the girls to celebrate. When I came downstairs, I had to walk through all the contestants who hadn't made the finals and were checking out. I hadn't thought about them. They acted like it didn't matter, but you could tell they were feeling terrible. Some of those girls have to be as talented and pretty as the ones who were chosen. It's just a stupid beauty contest and it's fixed, to boot. The only reason I was chosen for the finals was they needed a comedy talent number on August 9. I told my cabdriver how I felt, but he didn't say too much.

August 8, 1959

We had to do our talent numbers again today. Penny had such a hangover that she just stood on the stage and mouthed the words while Mary hid behind the curtain and sang for her. The judges never knew the difference. They thought Penny had a cold. I saved "Susie Sweetwater" for the second round. They loved it. We had the afternoon off while they decided who was going to do their talent numbers on the stage at the State Theater and at the Tupelo Country Club tonight. Every year, the night before the pageant, the finalists all go to a special dinner at the Country Club given by the Junior League and the Jaycees. After they are presented to the audience, some perform their talent numbers for the group.

I went upstairs to Darcy's room and knocked. She came to the door but wouldn't let me in because they were rehearsing a number they were doing tonight as a special good-bye performance. So I left and found Cab No. 22 outside of the hotel and went to get something to eat. I asked Mr. Smith if he didn't want to come in the restaurant with me, but he preferred to wait in the cab. I brought him a barbecue and Coca-Cola.

When I got back to the hotel, they took all twenty-eight finalists in the banquet room and read off the names of the girls who were going to perform at the Country Club. I was on the list, and so were Mary, Penny and Jo Ellen. Kay Bob Benson and Margaret Poole were also chosen. Surprise! Surprise! Darcy wasn't picked, but Mrs. McClay said, "I'm sure Darcy won't mind if she doesn't do Saint Joan again. We feel that the audience just couldn't take it another year." When she looked at Darcy and said, "You don't mind, do you, dear?" everyone cracked up. When I told my news to my cabdriver I could see he was happy for me.

Later he picked me up and we drove over to the Tupelo Country Club. It's prettier than the Hattiesburg Country Club, with a rotating dance floor that has colored lights in it. All the girls looked beautiful in their evening gowns. Darcy had some old gut bucket with her, and Mary brought a ukulele. I couldn't wait to see their special number. Mrs. McClay had her hair fixed and was wearing a corsage. She went up to the microphone and said, "Ladies and gentlemen, it gives me great pleasure to present to you the twenty-eight lovely finalists in this year's Miss Mississippi Contest." I felt like I was having a debut. I wish Daddy and Jimmy Snow could have been there.

We all walked out, one by one, while the band played "A Pretty Girl Is Like a Melody." After that, the people ate dinner, and we went in the bathroom and changed into our talent costumes. Margaret Poole, Kay Bob Benson and I were the only ones who had to change. Everyone else was going to perform in their evening gowns. I got into my "Susie Sweetwater" outfit. The judges liked my number about the woman who gets shot, but they felt anything about divorce would not be appropriate for a Miss Mississippi contestant.

Margaret Poole was standing in the bathroom smoking a cigarette when Mrs. McClay flew in the door looking for us. Before I knew what had happened, Margaret Poole shoved that cigarette in my hand and said, "I'm ready, Mrs. McClay." Mrs. McClay looked over and saw me and had a hissy fit.

She said, "Frances Harper, what are you doing with that cigarette? You are in a public rest room." Then she jerked the cigarette out of my hand, ran over and flushed it down the toilet before I could even open my mouth. She said, "How dare you disgrace the Miss Mississippi pageant. Don't you come out of this bathroom tonight. I'll deal with you later, Miss!"

I was so surprised I just stood there. As they were leaving, I heard Margaret Poole say, "I told her she shouldn't be smoking, Mrs. McClay." Kay Bob Benson, who had seen the whole thing, laughed her head off and marched out the door with her baton. Not knowing what else to do, I came out of the bathroom and stood there watching everybody perform. When it was my turn, Mrs. McClay went right on to the next name and skipped me altogether.

After everyone had finished, Mrs. McClay said into the microphone, "Ladies and gentlemen, I am sorry to announce we will be losing four of our favorite contestants this year and we will surely miss these four young ladies who have enhanced the pageant with their sweet personalities and outstanding talent for so long. However, the girls tell me they would like to do a special number for us tonight as a little going-away gesture. I'm sure we'll all enjoy it." She read from a card Darcy had given her and said, "So, ladies and gentlemen, it now gives me great pleasure to present to you the Warehouse Quartette." Mary came out with the ukulele, and Darcy had the gut bucket. Mary said, "One, two, three," and this is the song they sang to the tune of "Turkey in the Straw":

> *Oh, she pooted, and she farted and she shit on the floor*
> *She wiped her ass on the knob of the door*
> *The moon shone bright, on the nipple of her tit*
> *She brushed her teeth with blueberry shit*
> *Peeking through the keyhole, to see what she could see*
> *Squatting on the floor, on her bended knee*
> *Her dress was up and her panties were down*
> *She's got the cutest ass we've seen around*
> *Sung by the Whorehouse Quartette!*

Mary and Penny had spent the last two days making up the dirtiest song they could think of. They finished, took a big bow and ran off.

The audience sat there stunned. As Darcy and Mary ran by whooping and hollering, they grabbed me and said, "Come on, kid." We raced out the door and jumped into my cab and all went back to the hotel to have a drink. They said they'd been waiting three years to do that.

August 9, 1959

This morning all the staff and contestants were called to an emergency meeting. Mrs. McClay looked like death warmed over. She must not have gone to bed because she was wearing her half-dead corsage on the same dress from the night before and her hair was as messy as a rat's nest. She announced that due to unfortunate circumstances, Miss Darcy Lewis, Miss Jo Ellen Feely, Miss Mary Cudsworth and Miss Penny Raymond would not be performing at the State Theater. They were to remain backstage and only come out to receive their scholarships.

Then she said, in tears, "I want to wish you all good luck tonight," and blew her nose. "One more thing, a word to the wise. The winner, whoever she may be"—and she looked right at Margaret Poole—"don't crush your roses, they're velvet." After that we all went down to the State Theater and rehearsed. I was still scheduled to perform. After what Darcy and the others had done, she must have figured smoking a cigarette was nothing.

After rehearsal, we were told to be back at six-thirty and ready to go at seven-thirty. I gave my cabdriver a ticket. When he picked me up, he was dressed in a suit and tie, and I was glad I was going to have someone there I knew. That night when we were all backstage, about three old stagehands came by just before the show and wished me luck.

I didn't think I would be so nervous, but the theater held 2,000 people and the place was packed. A million-dollar Hammond organ began playing, and the emcee started calling our names. The girls walked out, one by one. My heart was pounding so hard I was sure I was going to have a heart attack. When my name was announced, the girl behind me had to push me to get me going. As soon as I was onstage, a spotlight hit me right in the face and I was blinded, but I managed to smile and was happy my teeth were fixed. The audience applauded real loud and seemed to like me. I was surprised, but I didn't have too much time to think about it before I had to run and change for the bathing suit competition. You should have heard the audience scream and yell when the spotlight hit my sequined bathing suit. They really loved it. Thank you, Mr. Cecil and the Cecilettes.

The spotlight was so bright and my contact lenses were hurting so that I almost walked off the runway. The audience kept on hollering, and I couldn't get over how much they liked my swimsuit. When I got offstage, I was blind as a bat, but thank goodness Darcy was there and led me to my dressing room. My knees were still shaking.

I changed into my "Susie Sweetwater" outfit in about two minutes and raced downstairs to the stage entrance as fast as I could. As it turned out, I had plenty of time. The emcee had just introduced the first talent number: Betty Lee Hansome, who played "Tiko, Tiko" on the electric organ. She went and sat down and smiled big at the audience and hit her first chord, but the organ didn't make a sound. She tried again, and still nothing happened. She looked panicked and turned around and screamed at a stagehand that something was the matter. He came over and saw she was playing up a storm but no sound was coming out. He finally found the plug and plugged it in, but there must have been a short since all you could hear was every other note and it sounded awful. After her number, Betty Lee ran off screaming she was going to kill somebody. I got out of her way, and so did the stagehands.

The next number was Tappie Lou Norris, doing an interpretive dance to the poem "Trees." Tappie Lou leaped out on the stage, but the spotlight worker missed half her leaps so all the audience saw was an occasional arm or leg. I knew how the spotlight worker must have felt. I had done the same thing once, but on top of that, the spotlight was so dim you could hardly see her at all. I figured it must be mood lighting, or else the whole electrical system was off. Then I began to sweat thinking about my number. It would be impossible to do comedy in the dark. Tappie Lou finally finished and the minute she was done, she grabbed me and said, "Was I all right?" Then she grabbed everybody else she saw and said, "Was I all right?" Everyone said, "Yes, you were great." Nobody had the heart to tell her the audience didn't see her.

The next number was Robbie Sue Spears, with an original monologue about a dead baby. She was doing fine until the mike started going on and off. By this time Margaret Poole, who was performing next, was standing by me, waiting to get the neck mike from Robbie Sue. Her number was a scene from *Gone with the Wind*. When she heard the way the mike was working, she started having a fit. Poor Robbie Sue came off, and Margaret nearly choked her to death trying to get that mike from her.

The stagehands put her prop box of dirt in the middle of the stage, and the emcee announced her. She finally got the mike on and as she started to make her entrance, she turned to the stagehand and said, "You better get this fucking mike to working." Well, evidently someone had gotten the f——ing mike to working because the whole audience heard what she said. As a matter of fact, the volume on that mike was so loud all during her number that the only thing you could hear was all the rocks rattling in that box of dirt she was digging around in. When she got to the part where she says, "I swear, I'll never go hungry again," she about blew the audience away. People sat there with their fingers in their ears. I was getting more and more nervous because I was on next and I had to use the same mike.

She was so upset by the time she finished that she went off the other side of the stage and forgot to give me the mike. They were already setting up my table and chair, and now it was my turn to panic. I started to run around to the other side, but thank goodness the stagehand found another mike and got it on me just in time. Somebody had fixed the spotlight and when I went out, it came on as bright as everything. I did my number and it went over great! After I finished with my last line, "Protect your heart as you would your other vital organs. Bye bye," they clapped and clapped until I had to take a second bow. I'm sure it wasn't me. It was just the first talent number they could see and hear.

I came off, and Darcy and Mary and Jo Ellen and Penny all grabbed me and hugged me and nearly squeezed me to death. Linda Horton was next, and her number went off without a hitch. They had finally got everything fixed. She played "Love Is Where You Find It" on the marimba. I couldn't see all of it because I had to run and change back into my evening gown for the awarding of the scholarships.

When I returned, Darcy said I had missed the funniest number yet. Willima Sue Sockwell, the ventriloquist, started doing her routine, but the mouth of her dummy became stuck and all that moved were the eyes. The audience hated her. Janice Bell, the girl who jumped rope and tap-danced, had been fine but hadn't got nearly as much applause as I had. Jeannie Prior was onstage at the moment, showing her paintings and telling a story about them. Only thing wrong was that two of the paintings were upside down.

Kay Bob Benson was standing in the wings waiting to twirl to "The Stars and Stripes Forever," and looking cool as a cucumber. An American flag would come down at the finish as she twirled her batons around her neck and behind her back. The audience would love it.

Those stagehands had been hanging around her all day at rehearsal. They were crazy about her on account of that skimpy costume, and two or three ran up to her before she went on and shook her hand and wished her luck. She always was popular with the men. You should have heard the audience applaud when she strutted out in her Uncle Sam outfit. The music began and she flashed the audience one of her phony smiles and started twirling. But all of a sudden those batons flew right out of her hands. She couldn't seem to hold onto them for nothing. She kept slinging them everywhere and running after them and picking them up. She wasn't able to hold on long enough even to light her fire batons. I didn't believe it. One finally flew out of her hand into the audience and hit some boy. He picked it up and threw it right back at her. She was frantic. The flag dropped down on cue as the music ended, and she hadn't twirled a baton yet. The curtain fell and the stage manager ran over and told us to get in line on the stage for the awarding of the scholarships.

We were all in our places when the curtain went back up. Some woman who was head of the Scholarship Committee was introduced and said how pleased she was to be there, passing out the awards. They had given almost all of them away when finally the woman announced the winner of the scholarship to the American Academy of Dramatic Arts, Robbie Sue Spears, the girl who did the original monologue about the dead baby. The curtain dropped and I hadn't won anything.

I was very hurt. I thought my talent number was pretty good, and Darcy and the rest of them were mad as hell. They claimed Mrs. McClay had just done it for spite because she knew that I was their friend. I told them not to worry about it, she was mad at me for something else. When I thought about letting down all the people who had worked so hard to get me to the pageant, I wanted to crawl under a rock. While I was considering not going back to Hattiesburg, just disappearing off the face of the earth, we were all pushed back onstage to get ready for the winners to be announced. By this time I wanted to leave, but I had to stay for the end of the show to sing "There Goes Miss Mississippi" like we rehearsed. I was in no mood to sing to Margaret Poole, I'll tell you that.

This was the point in the pageant when the judges go into the manager's office and sit for ten minutes or so and pretend they are picking out the winner. Darcy said all they did was go in there and drink. We waited and waited, and pretty soon half an hour had gone by. Finally, the stage manager came out and said we could sit down. The audience was getting restless and started to stomp their feet and yell. After another twenty minutes, we got a signal to stand up and take our positions on the stage so we would look like the outline of the state of Mississippi.

The curtain rose and the audience was sure glad to see us. The emcee brought out last year's Miss Mississippi, who spoke about how wonderful her reign had been, how she would never forget her year in the pageant and how the most wonderful part of the pageant for her had not been the money or the crown but the wonderful girls she met and how she would treasure their friendship forever. Darcy had told me she was so stuck up she wouldn't speak to anybody. When she was through with her dumb speech, she turned around and faced us and we all had to curtsy to her. Puke! Then she made her "farewell walk" around the runway. I looked backstage and Darcy and Mary were giving her the finger.

Next the emcee introduced the judges to the audience, and he introduced Mrs. McClay, too, but she wasn't there. Instead, Mr. Henry came up onstage and said a few words about how difficult it had been to judge this year because all the girls had been so pretty. He gave the emcee the envelope with the names of the five finalists in it, and the emcee called a drum roll and said, "Ladies and gentlemen, this is the moment you have all been waiting for" . . . drum roll . . . "The names of the five finalists in the Miss Mississippi Pageant are" . . . drum roll . . "Miss Kay Bob Benson" . . . applause, applause . . . I don't know how she had the nerve to show her face after throwing those batons all over the stage like that, but she prissed down there like the Queen of Sheba . . . drum roll . . . "Miss Janice Bell" . . . applause, applause . . . She was the one who jumped rope and tap-danced . . . drum roll . . . "Miss Linda Horton" . . . applause, applause . . . She played "Love Is Where You Find It" on the marimba . . . I was surprised she got in the finals because she is cross-eyed . . . drum roll . . . "Miss Daisy Fay Harper" . . . applause, applause . . . Miss Daisy Fay Harper?! I nearly dropped dead. They had called my name. I just stood there and Darcy yelled from the wings, "Move your ass!" I moved. The audience was yelling and screaming. The emcee

had to wait forever to announce the name of the fifth finalist
. . . drum roll . . . "Miss Margaret Poole" . . . mild applause.
I couldn't believe I had made the finals. There was a slipup
somewhere, that's for sure. I was thrilled because the fourth
runner-up gets $500, and that would be plenty of money to get
me to New York. Yeaaa!

Then the emcee said, "And now, ladies and gentlemen, comes
the question-and-answer period and it is at this time that our
judges will be judging for personality and poise. Remember, one
of these lovely girls will be going to Atlantic City and will be
representing the state of Mississippi in the eyes of the nation.
Kay Bob, your question is this: If you had a fairy godmother and
she could grant you one wish, and one wish only, what would
it be?"

Kay Bob stood there and thought for a while looking real
sincere, then leaned over in the mike and said, "If I had one
wish, I would wish that everybody all over the world would
learn to love each other, and that there would never be another
war, so no more mothers would lose their sons in battle, and
there would be peace on earth forever." I thought she was going
to pull out her American flag next, but I had to admit it was a
good answer worth second runner-up at least.

Then the emcee brought Linda Horton up and said, "Linda,
who is the woman you admire most in the world and why?"
She said, "Mamie Eisenhower." He said, "Why?" And she
thought hard and said, "Because she married a great man." She
blew it. That audience was full of Democrats.

Janice Bell was next. He said, "Janice, your question is: If
you could fulfill your fondest ambitions, what would they be?"

She said, "It would be to become a good wife and mother,
because that is the highest thing a woman can strive for." The
audience liked that. She must be a Rainbow Girl.

I didn't have too much time to think before my name was
called. I went over and he said, "Daisy, I understand that you
want to be an actress." I told him yes. I was hoping that was my
question, but he kept on going. He said, "If you could play
any part in any play, what part would you choose?" I didn't even

have to think about that one, remembering my experience in *Cat on a Hot Tin Roof*. I said, "A Big One!" The audience roared. I heard Darcy and them laughing backstage.

Margaret Poole came next. He said, "Margaret, who do you consider the most important man in the world today and why?" She just jumped right in with the answer before he even finished "I think that Billy Graham is the most important man in the world today because he's spreading the gospel all over the United States, Canada and the world, and that is the most important thing a person can ever do in this life." You can't tell me she didn't know what he was going to ask her. The audience applauded, but they always applaud when you say Billy Graham.

The emcee said, "Thank you, Margaret. Well, there you have it, ladies and gentlemen, the question-and-answer period. Let's have a big hand for our five lovely finalists." Applause, applause. "And now while the judges are busy making their final decisions as to who will be the next Miss Mississippi, we will award one of the most coveted awards of the pageant . . . Miss Congeniality. . . . This is the award that the girls vote on themselves, who they feel has been the friendliest and most helpful contestant throughout pageant week. And to present this Miss Congeniality Award, may I introduce Mr. Frank Self, the acting past president of the Jaycees."

Frank Self came out and gave a long-winded speech about how happy the Jaycees were to sponsor such a fine pageant, and so on and so forth. While this was going on, I looked down in the judges' box. They were fighting like crazy over a piece of paper. Mrs. Buchanan grabbed it out of Mr. Swanley's hand and ripped it in half. Then Reverend Deady grabbed the other half. You should have heard the noise they were making. When Mr. Self announced the winner . . . it was Darcy. Now she had her collection of four Miss Congeniality statuettes. Four is a record!

After that was over, the emcee looked towards the judges and said, "Have the judges reached a decision please?" But they weren't even listening. He had to repeat the question. Finally, Mrs. Buchanan looked up and screamed, "NO!" and went back to arguing. The emcee had to sing a song to kill time, and we stood there and waited while the judges fought it out. I heard one of them say, "You go to hell, you bitch." Finally, Mr. Henry, who had his boutonniere ripped right off him, ran up onstage and threw a piece of paper at the emcee.

The emcee said, "Thank you judges! Ladies and gentlemen, the judges have reached a final decision, and this is the moment we have all been waiting for, a moment when—" but he didn't get to finish his speech because some man in the audience yelled out, "Get on with it!" So he did. "Ladies and gentlemen, the fourth runner-up in the Miss Mississippi Pageant, and the winner of a five-hundred-dollar cash award scholarship and an Elgin seventeen-jewel ladies' wristwatch, supplied by Couch's Jewelry Store, is" . . . drum roll . . . "Miss Janice Bell." Applause, applause. I knew she had blown it with Mamie Eisenhower and I was sorry for her, but then I realized that I had a chance to win $1,000. This was getting exciting!

"Ladies and gentlemen, the third runner-up in the Miss Mississippi Contest and the recipient of a one-thousand-dollar cash scholarship award plus" . . . drum roll . . . "a portrait from Robert Boutwell's photographic studio, valued at five hundred dollars" . . . another drum roll . . . I was holding my breath, hoping to get my $1,000, when he said, "Miss Kay Bob Benson." Applause, applause. You could have knocked me over with a toothpick. Then it dawned on me that I was going to win more money.

The audience was going crazy by this time and so was I. I couldn't believe I was still in it. Then he said, "Ladies and gentlemen, the second runner-up to Miss Mississippi and the winner of the most coveted award in the pageant, an all-expense paid scholarship to the famous Pasadena Playhouse in Hollywood, California, and" . . . drum roll . . . "a guarantee of a part in the network television show *Death Valley Days*" . . . drum roll . . . "Linda Horton" . . . applause . . . I was amazed. I thought why in the world would they send a marimba player to the Pasadena Playhouse? But I stopped thinking because I looked around and there were just two of us left on the stage, Margaret Poole and me, and she grabbed the hand I had Momma's ring on and squeezed it so hard all I could think about was pain. The audience was getting wild.

The emcee said in a hushed voice, "The next award is that of the first runner-up and it is the most important award, second only to that of Miss Mississippi, because at any time during the coming year, if Miss Mississippi cannot fulfill her duties, the first runner-up will take over the title and reign as Queen. Ladies and gentlemen, the first runner-up and the winner of a fifteen-hundred-dollar cash award" . . . drum roll . . . "plus a brand new twenty-six-inch official Miss America television console, and a complete wardrobe from Banlon and" . . . drum roll . . . "an all-expense paid trip to New York City for a Broadway audition" . . . when I heard that I almost died, I was going to New York after all . . . "Miss Margaret Poole." The audience went insane. They were so happy for her they stood up and yelled and cheered and started jumping up and down. And then it hit me. They weren't screaming for Margaret Poole. They were screaming for me.

SHIT . . . I WAS MISS MISSISSIPPI!!

Everybody was going crazy. All of a sudden they grabbed hold of me and somebody handed me a dozen roses and threw a red cape around me, and the ex-Miss Mississippi slammed a crown on my head and pushed me out on the runway, but I just stood there stunned. I couldn't move a step. People were screaming and they were singing "There Goes Miss Mississippi." From backstage I heard Darcy: "Don't just stand there, move, you asshole!"

I don't remember much after that. I was in such a state of shock that I forgot and mashed hell out of those velvet roses. I had to stay there for about two hours while they took my picture for the paper and the television. When it was all over, this man from the Jaycees told me I had an official Miss Mississippi car waiting outside to take me back to my hotel. But I remembered to run out in the alley and there stood Mr. Smith, my cabdriver, with his hat in his hands waiting on me. He'd been there for two hours. He was as happy for me as anybody. I went back in and told those Jaycees I had come in a cab and I was going home in a cab.

I called Daddy and Jimmy Snow to tell them and they were

beside themselves. They had already heard it on the television news, where there was a picture of me and everything. The pageant has arranged to fly me home. I still can't believe it. I am going to Atlantic City in September and be in the Miss America Contest!

August 11, 1959

I flew home today; all day yesterday was spent having my picture taken and making arrangements with the Jaycees about getting to Atlantic City in September. When we finished, a group of them took me to the airport this morning and as I walked in, I saw my cabdriver, Mr. Smith, hiding in a corner by the baggage. I went over to him and he said he was waiting for a fare, but I knew he had just come out there to see me off. He seemed embarrassed and wished me luck. I hadn't been in the air five minutes when it dawned on me who Mr. Smith had reminded me of. That man's name wasn't Mr. Smith at all. He was my Granddaddy Pettibone, who everyone had thought was dead!

At first Daddy lied to me, but finally, he admitted I was right. They thought I wouldn't remember because I hadn't seen him for so many years. I wanted to call him right away, but Daddy said it would be much better if I never let him realize I knew who he was, he was so ashamed of himself for drinking so much and disappearing like that. That's why he had pretended to be dead all these years. Daddy had always known where he was. Although Grandpa hated Daddy, he trusted him not to tell. He said that Grandpa used to call him about once every six months to see how I was doing and he had all my school pictures from the time I was six. Imagine all these years he was just up the road in Tupelo.

August 17, 1959

Mr. Curl, who is the manager of the State Theater in Tupelo where the pageant took place and who knows Daddy, called to tell him what really happened the night of the pageant.

My other granddaddy, who still isn't speaking to Daddy, is president of the stagehands' union, and the men like him a lot. When they found out Blondie Harper's granddaughter was one of the finalists, they decided to do him a favor, so they went out and got three extra spotlights for the booth, and every time I came out onstage, they hit me with four spotlights! A reporter put in the paper that "Her smile lit up the whole audience." No wonder! They had screwed up the mikes, glued Willima Sue's dummy's mouth shut and unplugged Betty Lee Hansome's organ and everything.

The reason Kay Bob Benson hadn't been able to hold onto her batons was because two of the stagehands had put axle grease on their hands and made it a point to go up and shake hands with her right before she did her number. And I thought they liked her!

I tell you, I can never say anything unkind about organized labor as long as I live.

We also found out when the judges went in the manager's office to pretend to vote, the owner of the theater had gone in and told them if they didn't let me win, the audience was going to rip his theater apart, and it would be the last year they could hold the pageant there. Mrs. McClay got in a huff and said she didn't care if they ripped his theater apart. The Miss Mississippi title was not going to white trash whose daddy ran a bar as long as she was in charge, and I would be Miss Mississippi over her dead body. Then Madame Albergotti said, "I don't see how we could possibly give the title to a girl who screamed FUCK into the microphone." Mrs. McClay got mad and told her to shut up, Margaret Poole had not screamed FUCK in the microphone. The mike had been broken. It just sounded like she had said it, that's all. Mrs. McClay yelled it was her pageant and if they dared give me the title, they would have to kill her first.

She must have scared them, because she was winning her point. Just then Darcy went around to the side of the theater and delivered the judges a note:

Dear Mrs. McClay and Judges,

Please don't make me Miss Mississippi, because I am secretly married to a Negro and I am pregnant. I feel that it might be an embarrassment to the pageant.

Regrets,
Margaret Poole

They say Mrs. McClay screamed and hollered it was a lie and she was being sabotaged. But the other judges said their reputations were on the line. They all had good names in the community to protect and couldn't afford to take a chance on it being true. Mrs. Buchanan was the only one who held out for Margaret Poole. When they finally had to go back out to the judges' box, they left Mrs. McClay on the couch prostrate with grief and a cold rag on her head. The last thing she did was to raise up and say to Mrs. Buchanan, "Don't let them do this to me, Peggy." Then she fell back in a dead faint.

So that's what the big fight had been about. The judges were so upset they got everything screwed up. Linda Horton, the marimba player, wasn't even supposed to be in the top five finalists, much less go to the Pasadena Playhouse and be on *Death*

Valley Days. Anyway, Mrs. McClay quit the Miss Mississippi pageant forever, saying she was betrayed by a nest of adders and she wouldn't go to Atlantic City with that piece of white trash, meaning me, for anything. I feel kind of sorry for her. I didn't win fair and square, but Jimmy Snow said for me to forget it, that I owed it to myself to just get the hell out of Mississippi.

Here I thought I didn't have any family, but all these people were out there pulling for me. I have so many people to thank I just have to make good.

Since I've been back I've been interviewed on the television station where I got fired, and received letters and telegrams from people all over the state. The governor sent me a letter of congratulations and a couple of senators wrote. I've heard from everyone, including the International Order of Rainbow Girls, who sent me a telegram saying how proud they were that one of their girls was Miss Mississippi. I guess they forgot I had been thrown out. I wrote and thanked them for their good wishes, anyway. Pickle and Mustard wrote. She has another baby. I even heard from Billy Bundy who's in some prison in Tennessee.

But the letter I got today means more to me than any of them. It said:

Dear Miss Harper,
    I enjoyed meeting you. You are a nice girl.

Your driver,
Cab No. 22

I go to Atlantic City in fifteen days!

Jimmy Snow has renamed his plane *The Miss Mississippi* and is going to dust crops all next week in my honor. Daddy painted a big sign over the door of the bar that says, "Official Headquarters of Miss Mississippi." Mrs. McClay would die if she could see that. The other day I went down to Gamble's Department Store and had my official "Miss Mississippi" portrait made. They wanted to photograph me in my white evening gown, but Mr. Cecil said I should wear something other than a white gown because that's what all the other girls would do. So I had my picture taken in a brown suede jacket. You know Mr. Cecil. He is going with me to Atlantic City and all the Cecilettes are coming on the same train. We should have a ball. You'd be surprised how people treat me now. I was even invited to the Hattiesburg Country Club on the twenty-sixth for a dinner in my honor by the Junior League. I am going to take Daddy and Jimmy Snow. I have to go downtown with Mr. Cecil tomorrow and help him pick out his Atlantic City wardrobe. I swear you'd think that he was the one who was Miss Mississippi.

August 25, 1959

The hospital called Thursday. Jimmy Snow died at 5:47 that morning of a broken neck. His plane crashed in Madison County on Wednesday. Daddy and I went down to get him and bring him home. We buried him this afternoon. Nobody was at the funeral except for Mr. Cecil and a few men from the bar who had come to be pallbearers. Daddy has taken it pretty hard. When they put Jimmy in the ground, he stood there and cried like a baby. Jimmy was the best friend he ever had. I think he was the best friend I ever had, too. I don't know what it's going to be like without him. I thought he would always be around. It was sad he had no family at his funeral. I asked Daddy why he thought Jimmy had never married and had children. He looked at me real strange and said, "You're the only person he ever really loved. Didn't you know that?"

No, I didn't know that. I didn't know that at all.

September 3, 1959

I'm all packed. I leave for Atlantic City in the morning. I don't know what's going to happen to me, or if I will ever come back, but I do know I owe a lot of people a lot of things and I promise I won't come back until I'm somebody.

And I won't.